THE MISADVENTURES OF Grumpy Cat® (And Pokey!)

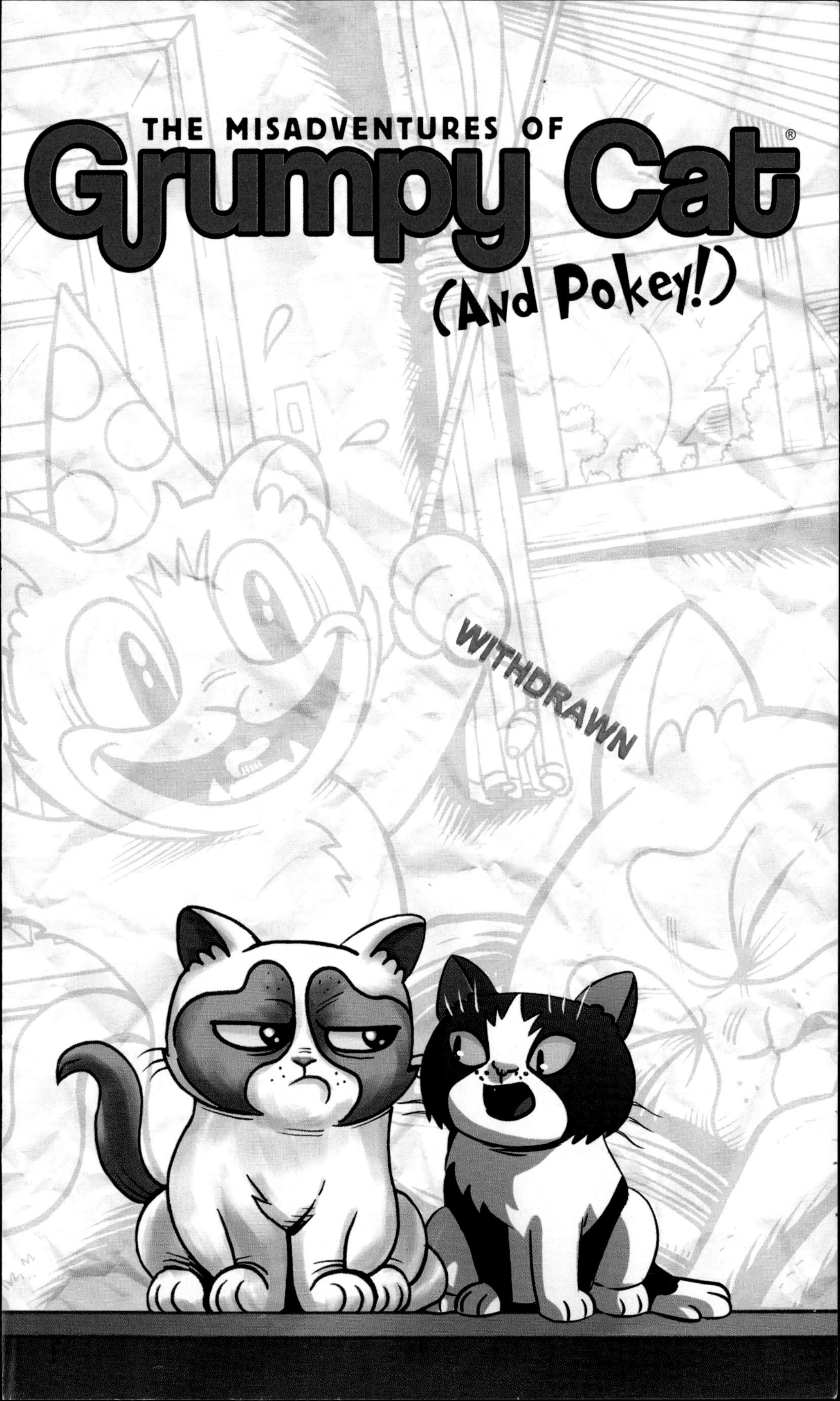

THE MISADVENTURES OF
Grumpy Cat ®
(And Pokey!)

TREASURE MAP
Written by: **Ben McCool** Art/Colors by: **Steve Uy**
Letters by: **Bill Tortolini**

GRUMPY IN HD
Written by: **Ben Fisher** Art/Colors by: **Michelle Nguyen**
Letters by: **Bill Tortolini**

PAWS OF JUSTICE
Written by: **Royal McGraw** Art by: **Ken Haeser**
Colors by: **Mohan** Letters by: **Bill Tortolini**

GRUMPY CAT GOES TO COMIC-CON
Written by: **Elliott Serrano** Art/Colors/Letters by: **Steve Uy**

CELL PHONE
Written by: **Ben McCool** Art/Colors by: **Steve Uy**
Letters by: **Bill Tortolini**

VINCENT VAN GRUMP
Written by: **Ben Fisher** Art/Colors by: **Michelle Nguyen**
Letters by: **Bill Tortolini**

GRUMPY BIRTHDAY TO YOU
Written by: **Elliott Serrano** Art by: **Ken Haeser**
Colors by: **Mohan** Letters by: **Bill Tortolini**

DETECTIVE CATS

Written by: **Ben McCool** Art/Colors by: **Steve Uy**
Letters by: Bill Tortolini

A GRUMP IN TIME

Written by: **Ben Fisher** Art/Colors by: **Michelle Nguyen**
Letters by: **Bill Tortolini**

CLOSE ENCOUNTERS OF THE GRUMPY KIND

Written by: **Elliott Serrano** Art by: **Ken Haeser**
Colors by: **Mohan** Letters by: **Bill Tortolini**

I KNOW WHAT YOU DID LAST SUMMER ...I JUST DON'T CARE (Groupees Exclusive Story)

Written by: **Ben Fisher** Art/Colors by: **Steve Uy**
Letters by: **Bill Tortolini**

Series edited by: **Rich Young**

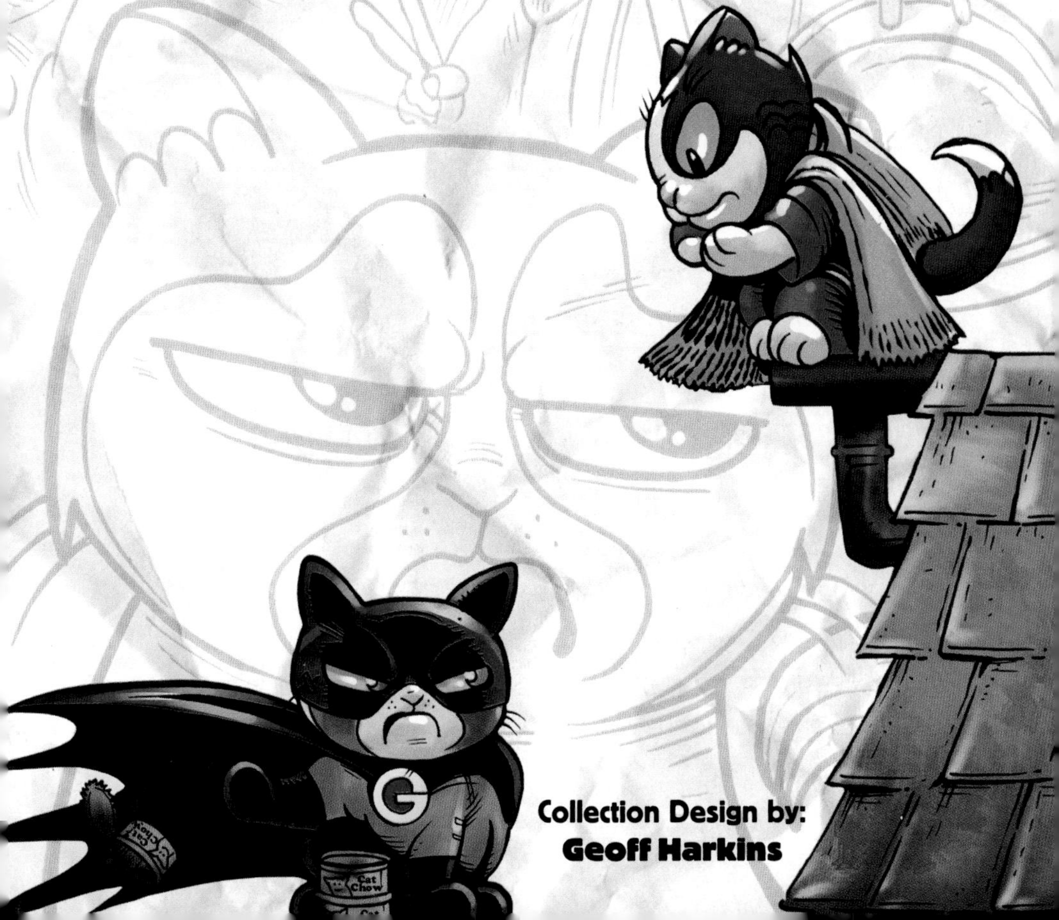

Cat Chow

Collection Design by:
Geoff Harkins

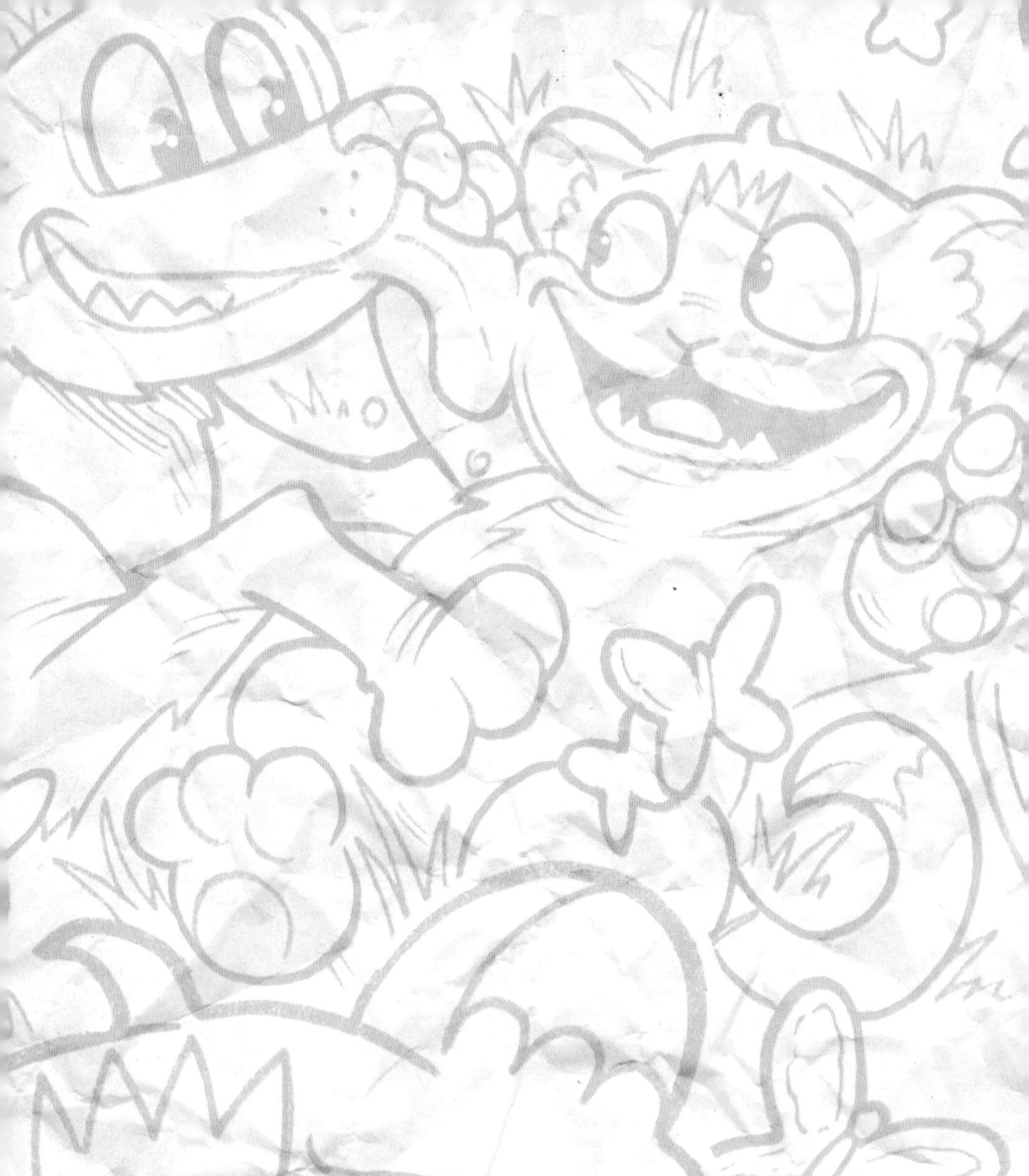

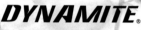

DYNAMITE®

Nick Barrucci, CEO / Publisher
Juan Collado, President / COO

Joe Rybandt, Executive Editor
Matt Idelson, Senior Editor
Rachel Pinnelas, Associate Editor
Anthony Marques, Assistant Editor
Kevin Ketner, Editorial Assistant

Jason Ullmeyer, Art Director
Geoff Harkins, Senior Graphic Designer
Alexis Persson, Production Artist

Chris Caniano, Digital Associate
Rachel Kilbury, Digital Assistant

Brandon Dante Primavera, V.P. of IT/Operations
Rich Young, Director of Business Development

Alan Payne, V.P. of Sales and Marketing
Keith Davidsen, Marketing Manager
Pat O'Connell, Sales Manager

Visit us online at **www.DYNAMITE.com**
Follow us on Instagram **/Dynamitecomics**
Follow us on Twitter **@dynamitecomics**
Like us on Facebook **/Dynamitecomics**
Watch us on YouTube **/Dynamitecomics**
On Tumblr **dynamitecomics.tumblr.com**

Second Printing
HARDCOVER ISBN-10: 1-60690-796-4
ISBN-13: 978-1-60690-796-2
10 9 8 7 6 5 4 3 2

Second Printing
SOFTCOVER ISBN-10: 1-60690-909-6
ISBN-13: 978-1-60690-909-6
10 9 8 7 6 5 4 3 2

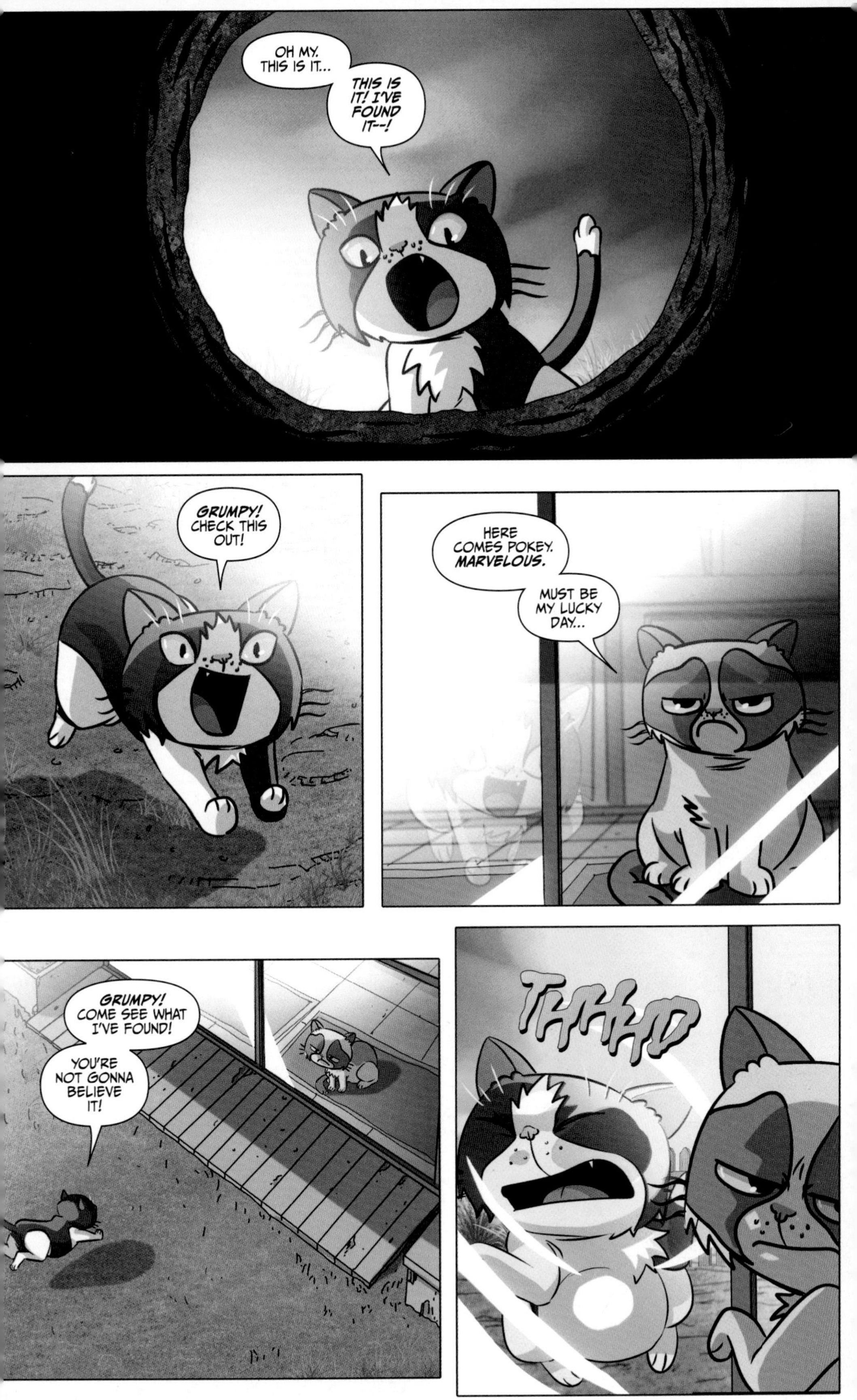
OH MY. THIS IS IT...
THIS IS IT! I'VE FOUND IT--!
GRUMPY! CHECK THIS OUT!
HERE COMES POKEY. MARVELOUS.
MUST BE MY LUCKY DAY...
GRUMPY! COME SEE WHAT I'VE FOUND!
YOU'RE NOT GONNA BELIEVE IT!
THHUD

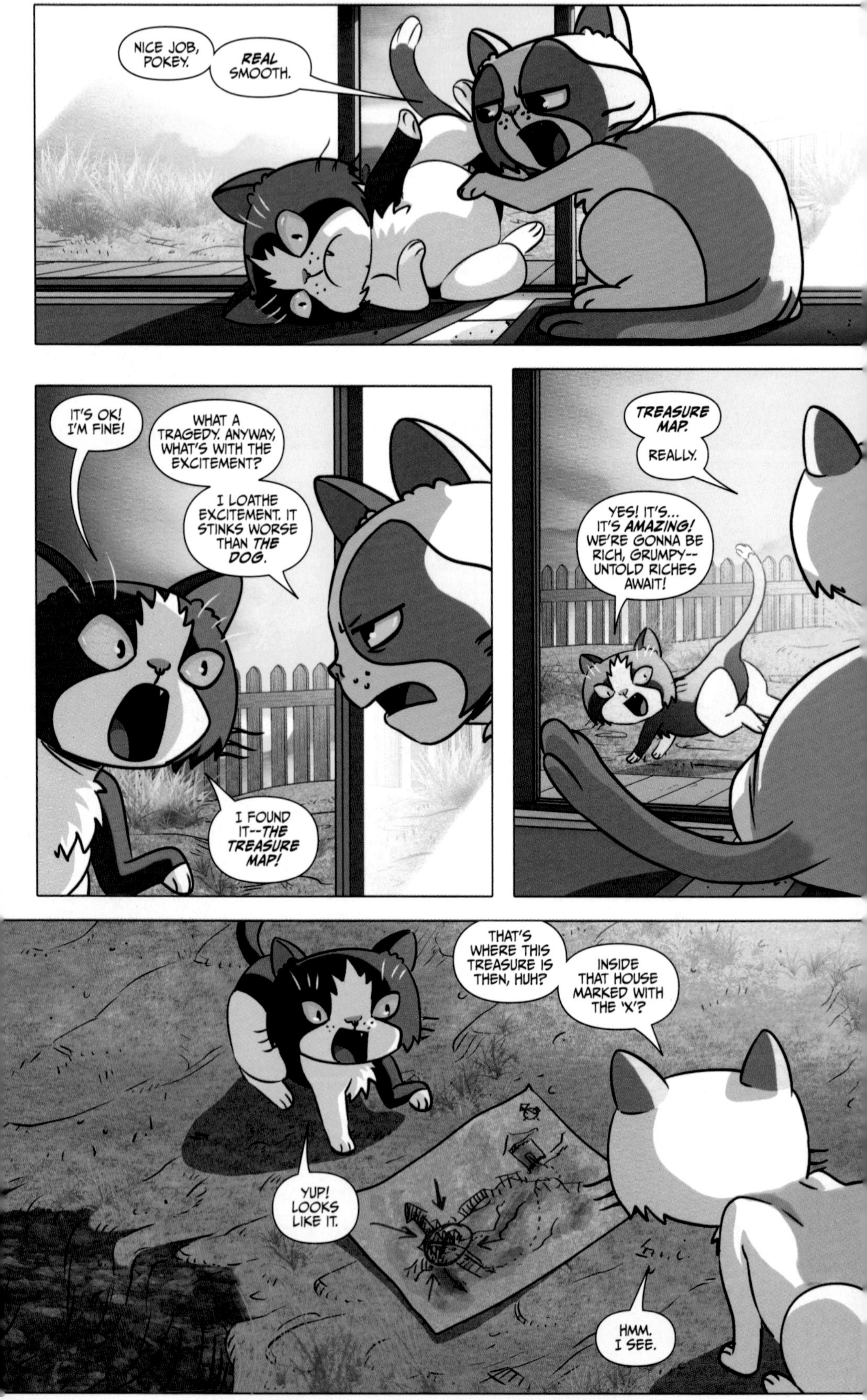
NICE JOB, POKEY.
REAL SMOOTH.
IT'S OK! I'M FINE!
WHAT A TRAGEDY. ANYWAY, WHAT'S WITH THE EXCITEMENT?
I LOATHE EXCITEMENT. IT STINKS WORSE THAN THE DOG.
I FOUND IT--THE TREASURE MAP!
TREASURE MAP.
REALLY.
YES! IT'S... IT'S AMAZING! WE'RE GONNA BE RICH, GRUMPY--UNTOLD RICHES AWAIT!
THAT'S WHERE THIS TREASURE IS THEN, HUH?
INSIDE THAT HOUSE MARKED WITH THE 'X'?
YUP! LOOKS LIKE IT.
HMM. I SEE.

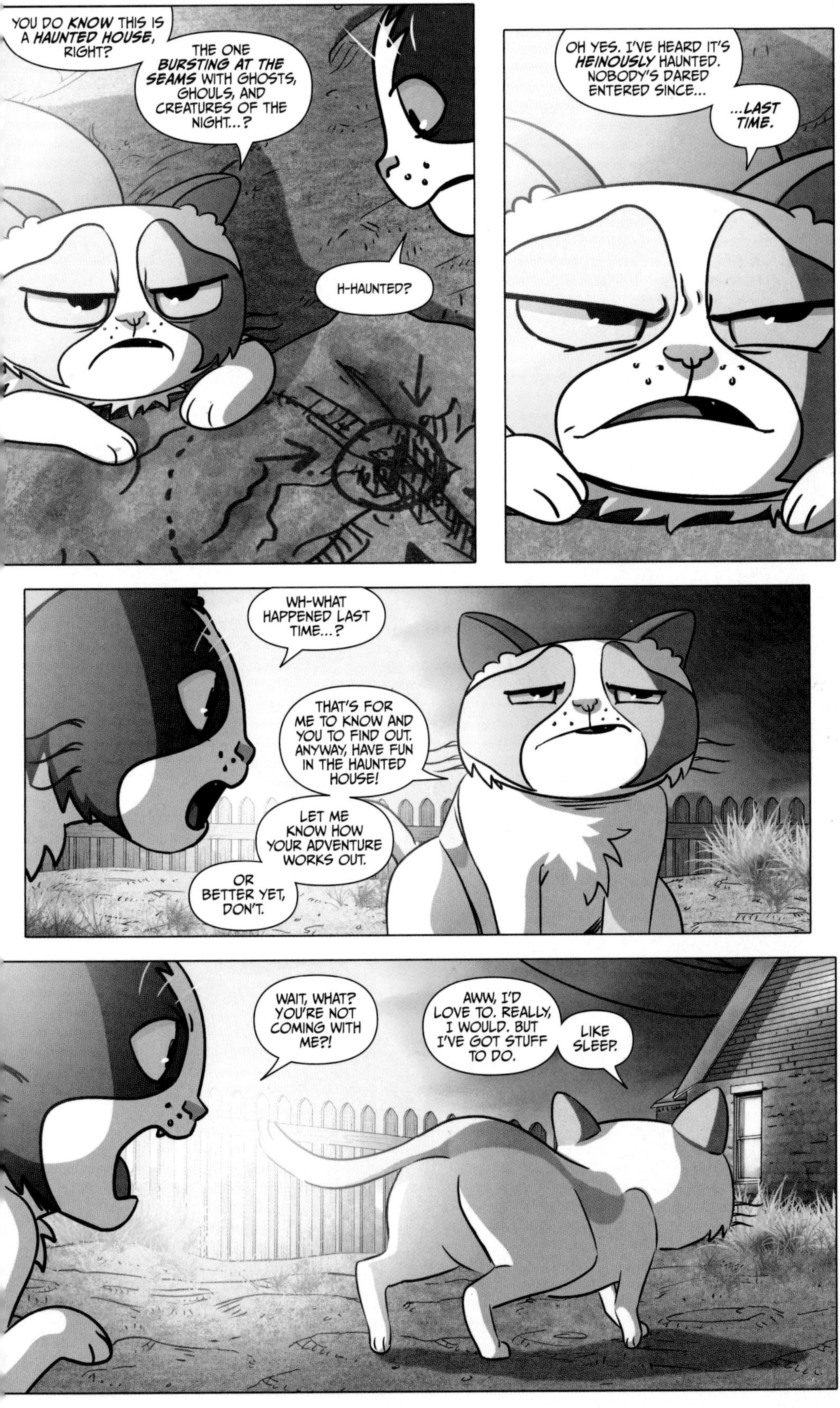
YOU DO KNOW THIS IS A HAUNTED HOUSE, RIGHT?
THE ONE BURSTING AT THE SEAMS WITH GHOSTS, GHOULS, AND CREATURES OF THE NIGHT...?
H-HAUNTED?
OH YES. I'VE HEARD IT'S HEINOUSLY HAUNTED. NOBODY'S DARED ENTERED SINCE...
...LAST TIME.
WH-WHAT HAPPENED LAST TIME...?
THAT'S FOR ME TO KNOW AND YOU TO FIND OUT. ANYWAY, HAVE FUN IN THE HAUNTED HOUSE!
LET ME KNOW HOW YOUR ADVENTURE WORKS OUT.
OR BETTER YET, DON'T.
WAIT, WHAT? YOU'RE NOT COMING WITH ME?!
AWW, I'D LOVE TO. REALLY, I WOULD. BUT I'VE GOT STUFF TO DO.
LIKE SLEEP.

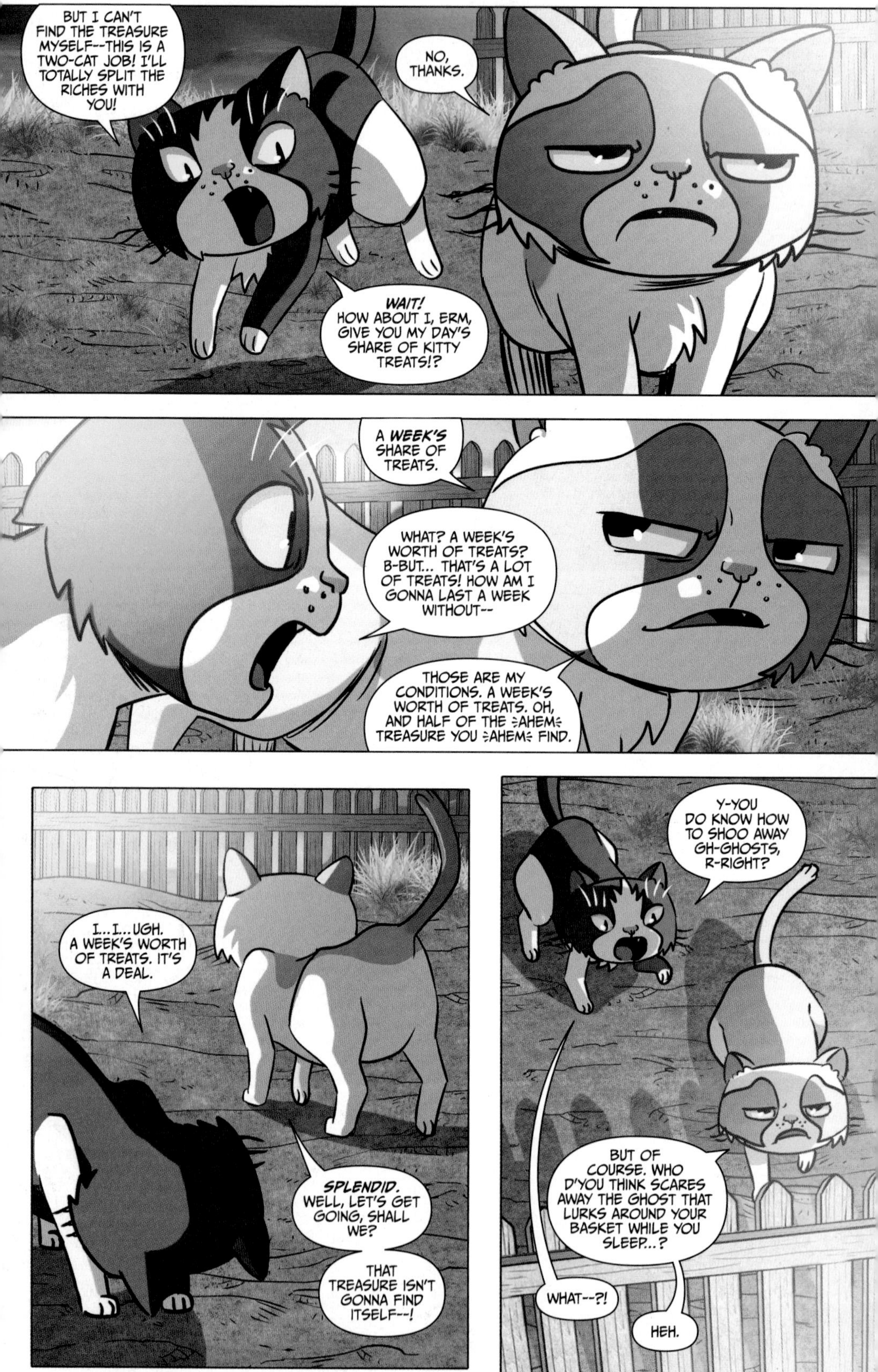
BUT I CAN'T FIND THE TREASURE MYSELF--THIS IS A TWO-CAT JOB! I'LL TOTALLY SPLIT THE RICHES WITH YOU!
NO, THANKS.
WAIT! HOW ABOUT I, ERM, GIVE YOU MY DAY'S SHARE OF KITTY TREATS!?
A WEEK'S SHARE OF TREATS.
WHAT? A WEEK'S WORTH OF TREATS? B-BUT... THAT'S A LOT OF TREATS! HOW AM I GONNA LAST A WEEK WITHOUT--
THOSE ARE MY CONDITIONS. A WEEK'S WORTH OF TREATS. OH, AND HALF OF THE *AHEM* TREASURE YOU *AHEM* FIND.
I...I...UGH. A WEEK'S WORTH OF TREATS. IT'S A DEAL.
SPLENDID. WELL, LET'S GET GOING, SHALL WE?
THAT TREASURE ISN'T GONNA FIND ITSELF--!
Y-YOU DO KNOW HOW TO SHOO AWAY GH-GHOSTS, R-RIGHT?
BUT OF COURSE. WHO D'YOU THINK SCARES AWAY THE GHOST THAT LURKS AROUND YOUR BASKET WHILE YOU SLEEP...?
WHAT--?!
HEH.

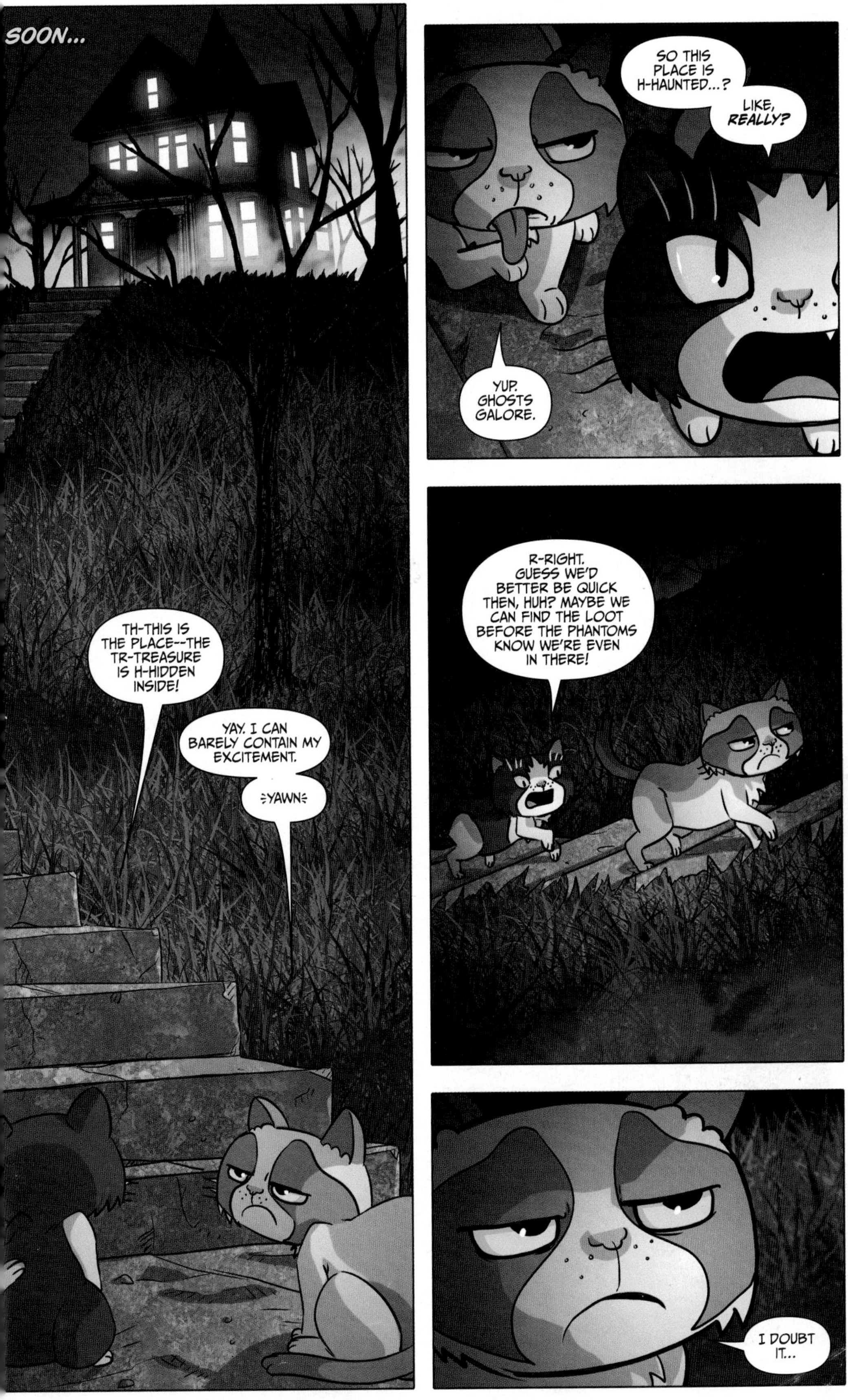
SOON...
TH-THIS IS THE PLACE--THE TR-TREASURE IS H-HIDDEN INSIDE!
YAY. I CAN BARELY CONTAIN MY EXCITEMENT.
=YAWN=
SO THIS PLACE IS H-HAUNTED...?
LIKE, REALLY?
YUP. GHOSTS GALORE.
R-RIGHT. GUESS WE'D BETTER BE QUICK THEN, HUH? MAYBE WE CAN FIND THE LOOT BEFORE THE PHANTOMS KNOW WE'RE EVEN IN THERE!
I DOUBT IT...

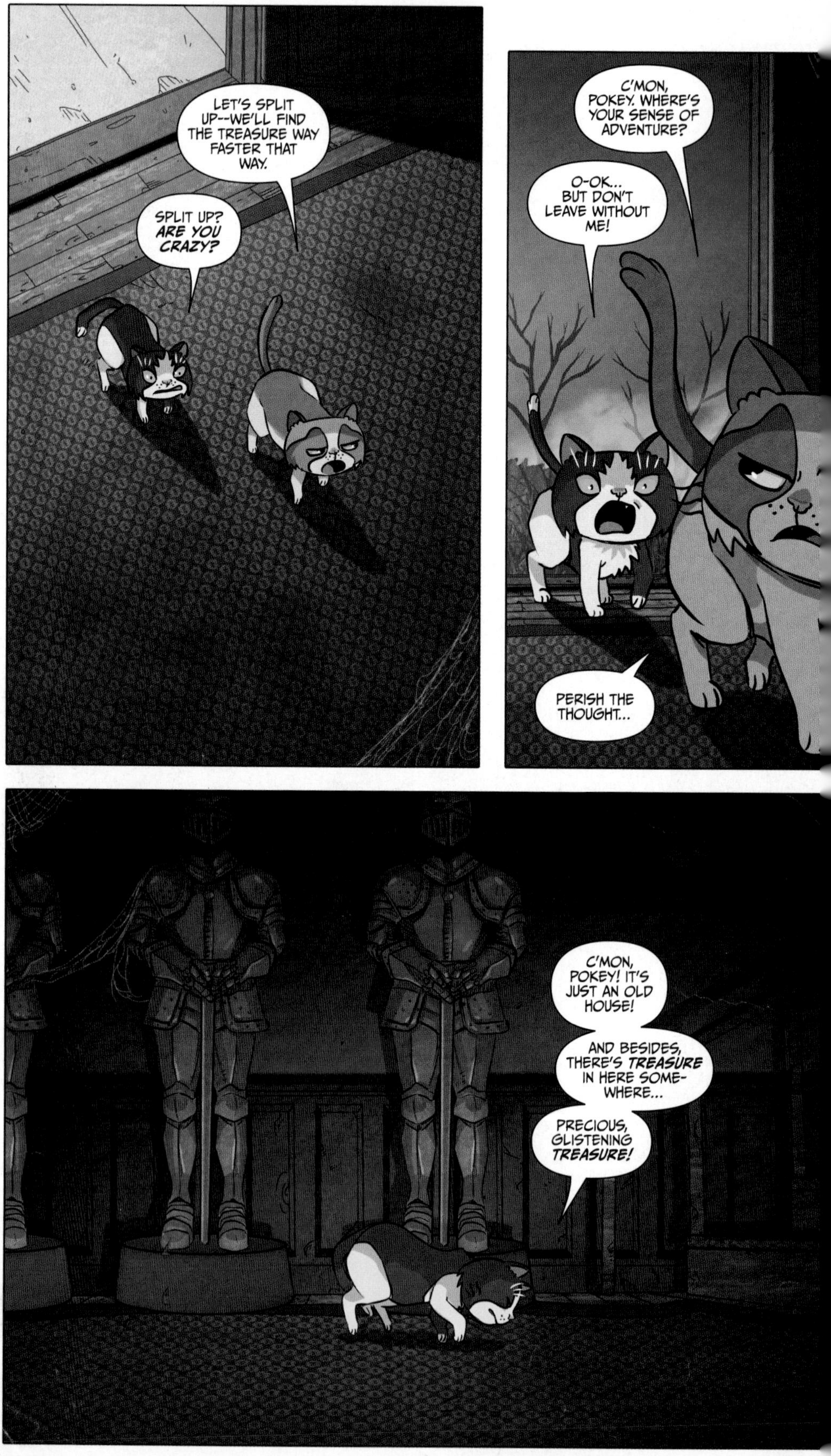
LET'S SPLIT UP--WE'LL FIND THE TREASURE WAY FASTER THAT WAY.
SPLIT UP? *ARE YOU CRAZY?*
C'MON, POKEY. WHERE'S YOUR SENSE OF ADVENTURE?
O-OK... BUT DON'T LEAVE WITHOUT ME!
PERISH THE THOUGHT...
C'MON, POKEY! IT'S JUST AN OLD HOUSE!
AND BESIDES, THERE'S *TREASURE* IN HERE SOME-WHERE...
PRECIOUS, GLISTENING *TREASURE!*

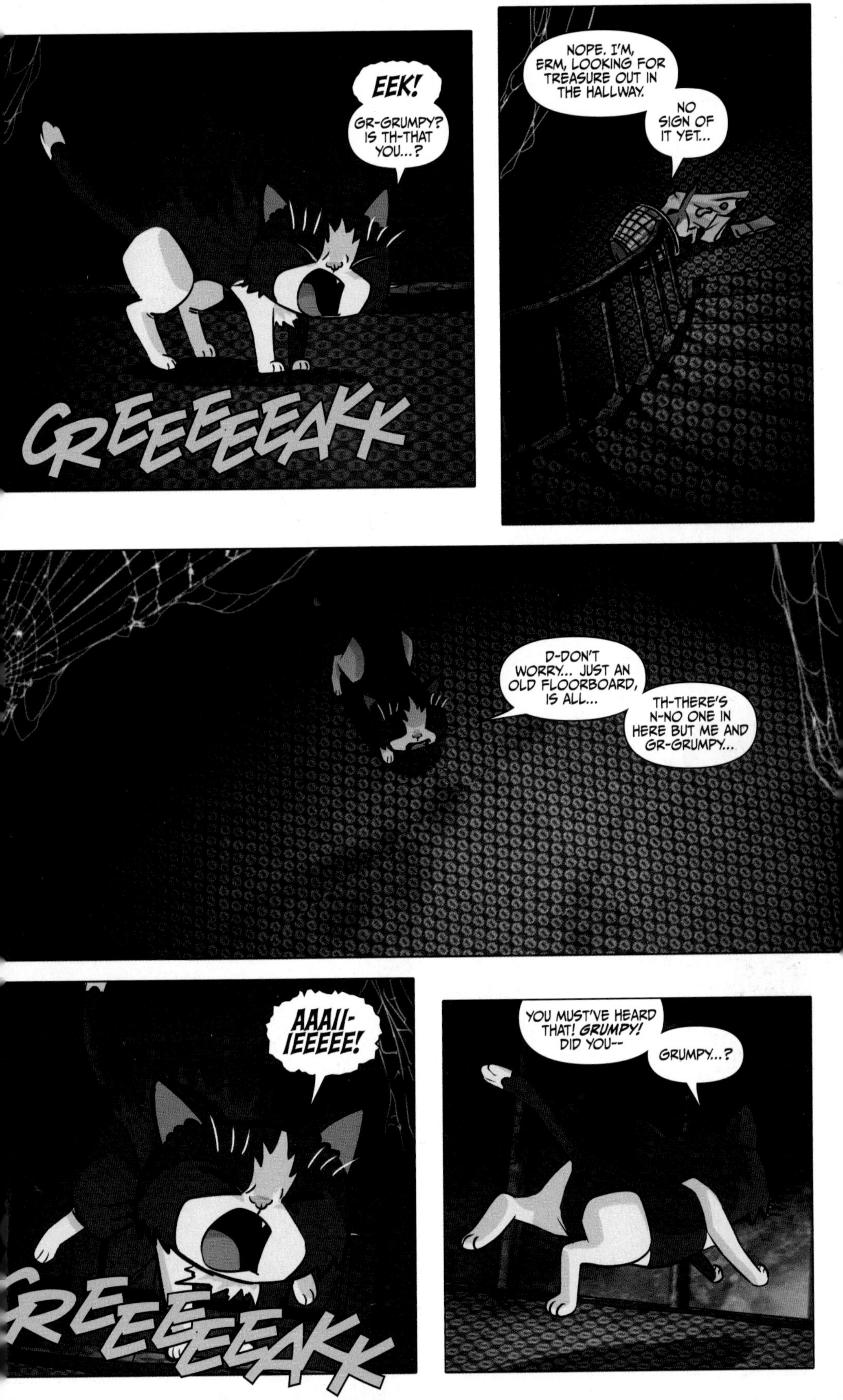
EEK!
GR-GRUMPY? IS TH-THAT YOU...?
GREEEEEAKK
NOPE. I'M, ERM, LOOKING FOR TREASURE OUT IN THE HALLWAY.
NO SIGN OF IT YET...
D-DON'T WORRY... JUST AN OLD FLOORBOARD, IS ALL...
TH-THERE'S N-NO ONE IN HERE BUT ME AND GR-GRUMPY...
AAAII-IEEEEE!
REEEEEAKK
YOU MUST'VE HEARD THAT! GRUMPY! DID YOU--
GRUMPY...?

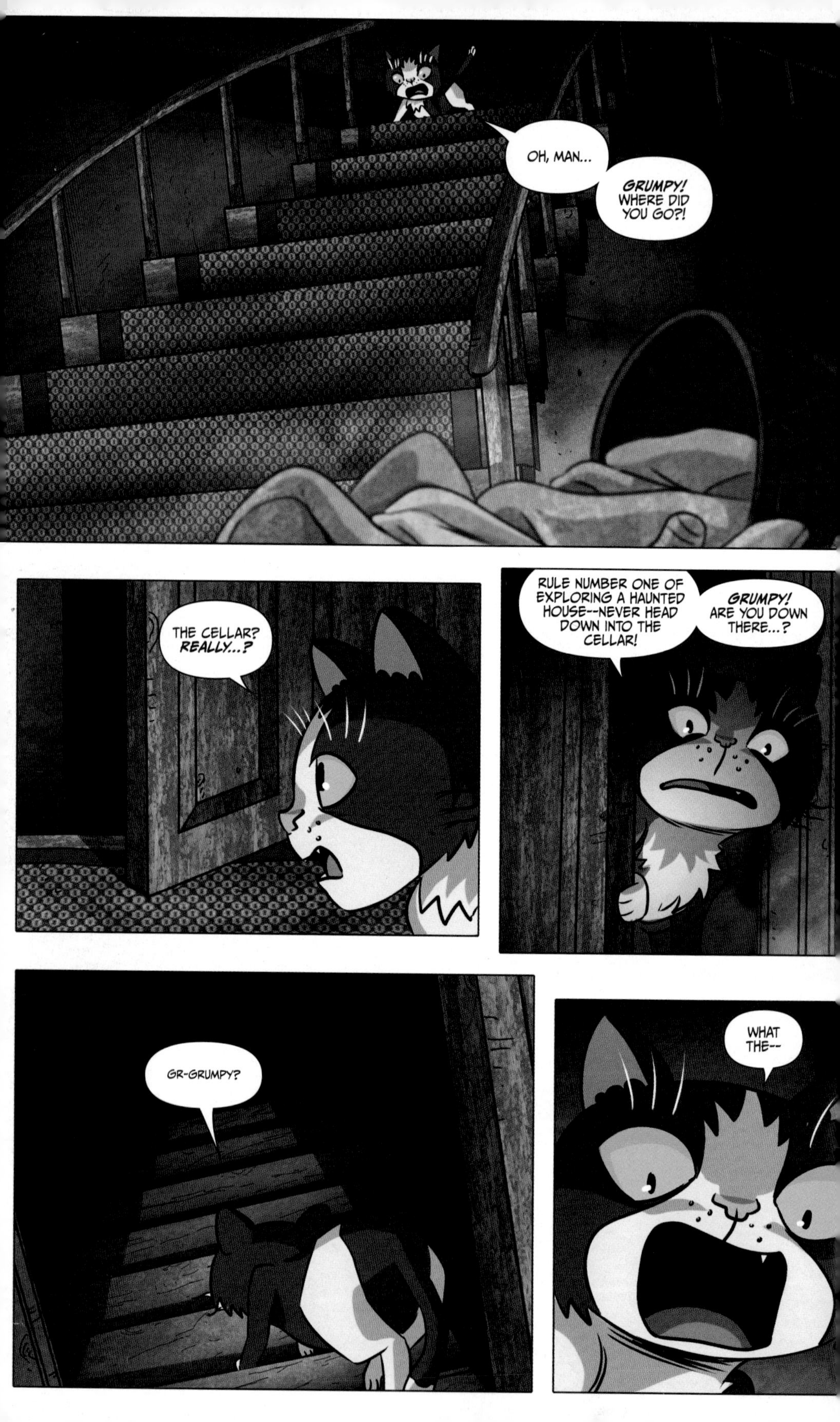
OH, MAN...
GRUMPY! WHERE DID YOU GO?!
THE CELLAR? *REALLY...?*
RULE NUMBER ONE OF EXPLORING A HAUNTED HOUSE--NEVER HEAD DOWN INTO THE CELLAR!
GRUMPY! ARE YOU DOWN THERE...?
GR-GRUMPY?
WHAT THE--

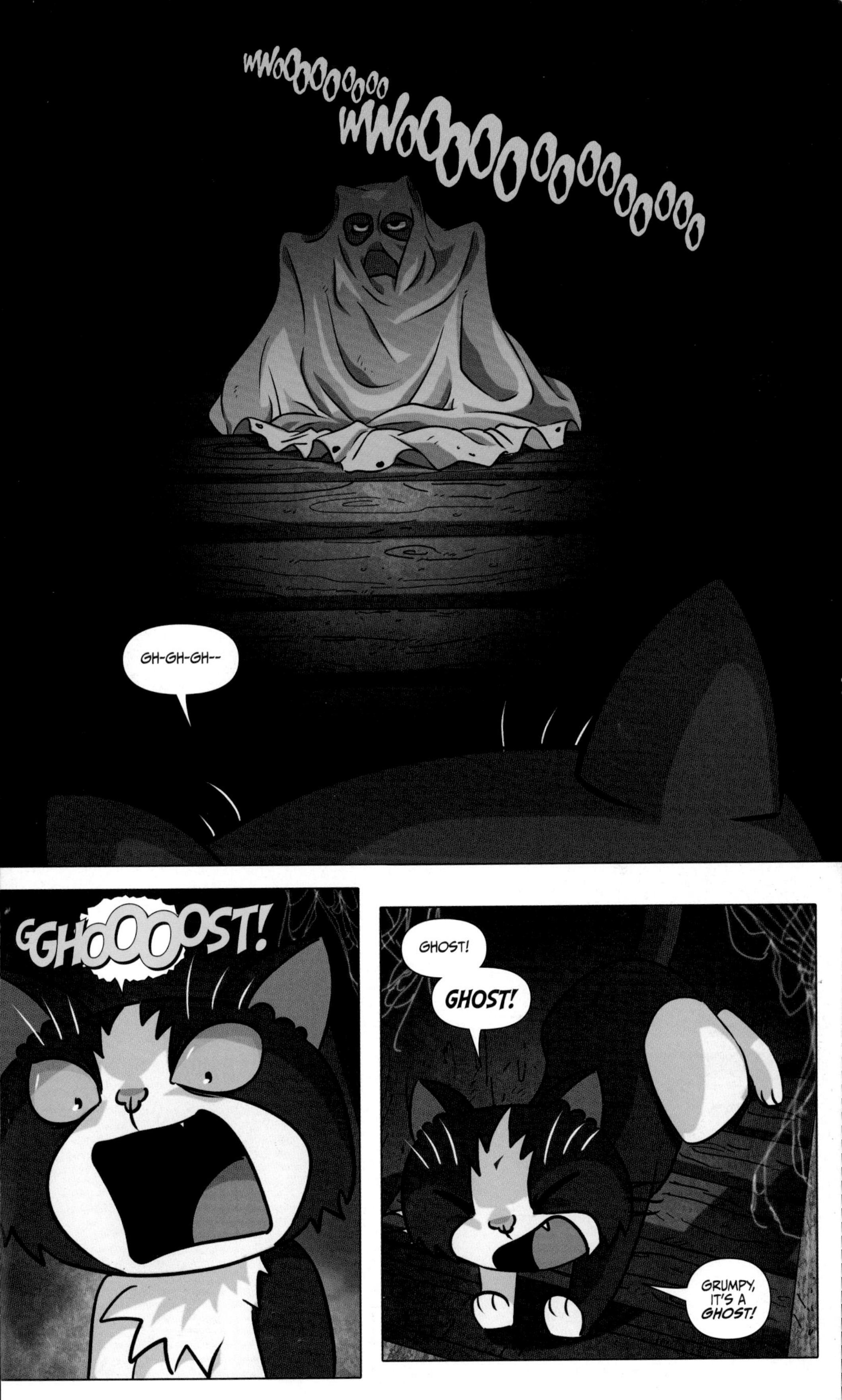

WWOOOOOOOO
WWOOOOOOOOOOOOOO
GH-GH-GH--
GGHOOOOOST!
GHOST!
GHOST!
GRUMPY, IT'S A GHOST!

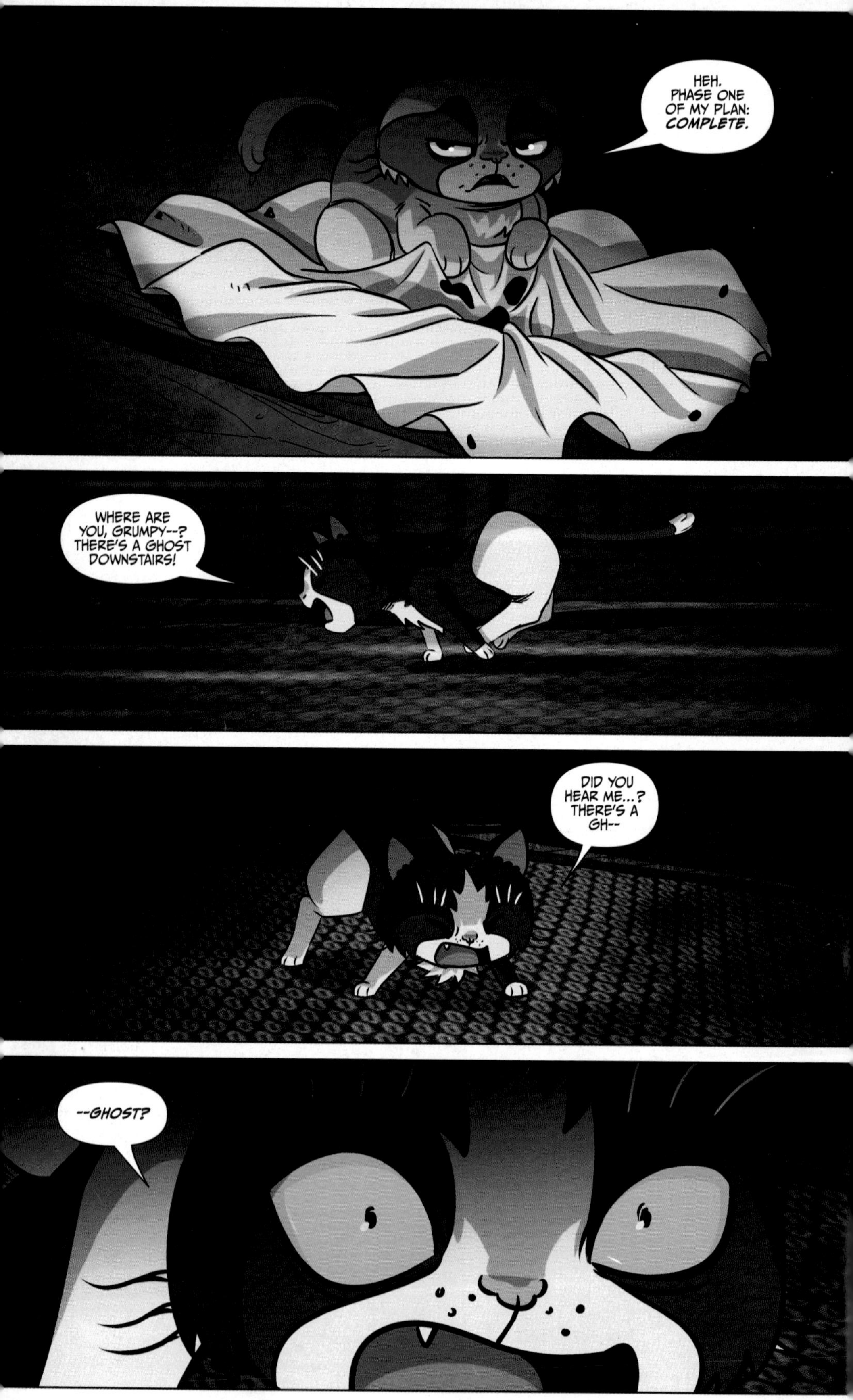
HEH. PHASE ONE OF MY PLAN: *COMPLETE.*
WHERE ARE YOU, GRUMPY--? THERE'S A GHOST DOWNSTAIRS!
DID YOU HEAR ME...? THERE'S A GH--
--GHOST?

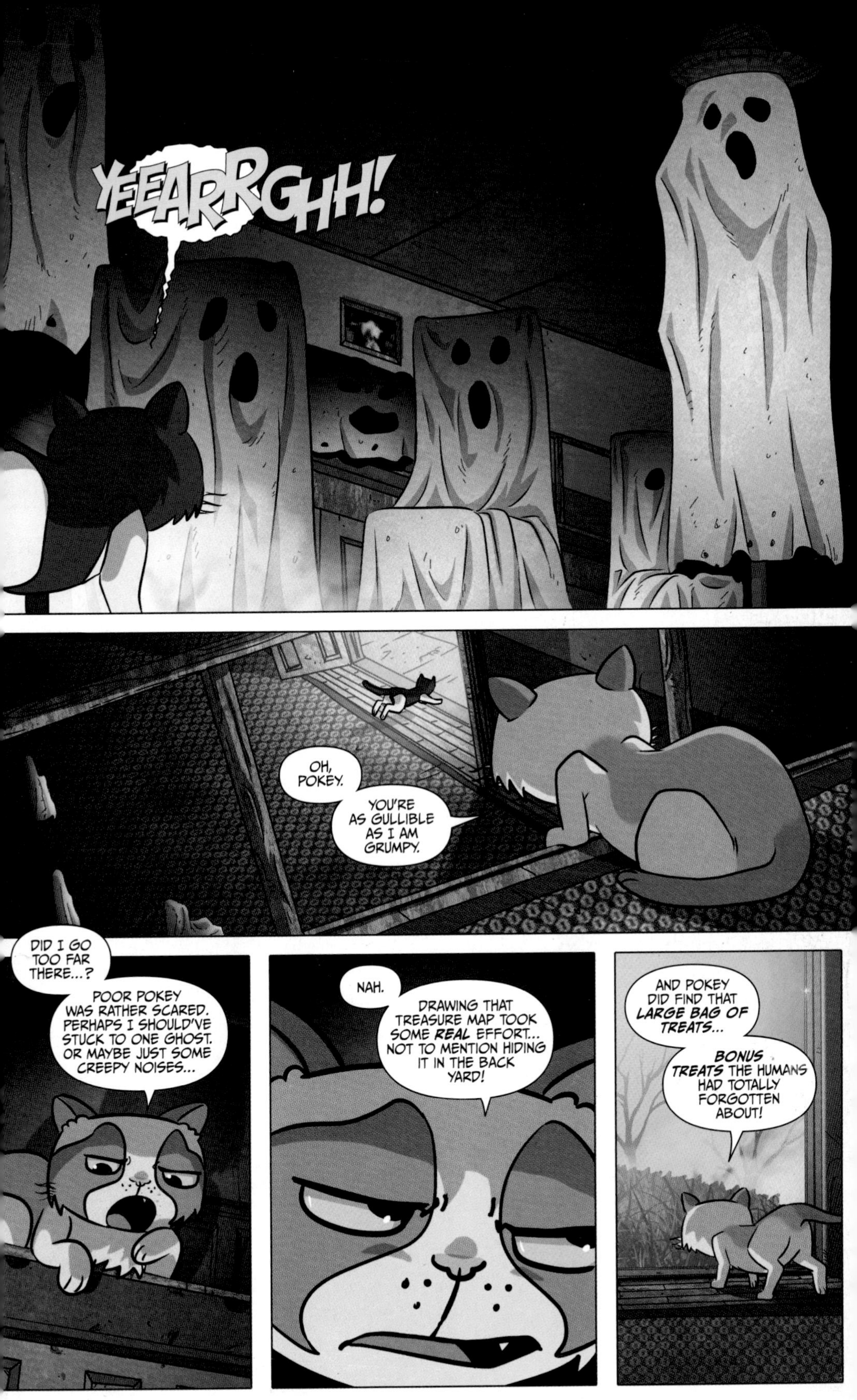
YEEARRGHH!
OH, POKEY.
YOU'RE AS GULLIBLE AS I AM GRUMPY.
DID I GO TOO FAR THERE...?
POOR POKEY WAS RATHER SCARED. PERHAPS I SHOULD'VE STUCK TO ONE GHOST. OR MAYBE JUST SOME CREEPY NOISES...
NAH.
DRAWING THAT TREASURE MAP TOOK SOME *REAL* EFFORT... NOT TO MENTION HIDING IT IN THE BACK YARD!
AND POKEY DID FIND THAT ***LARGE BAG OF TREATS...***
BONUS TREATS THE HUMANS HAD TOTALLY FORGOTTEN ABOUT!

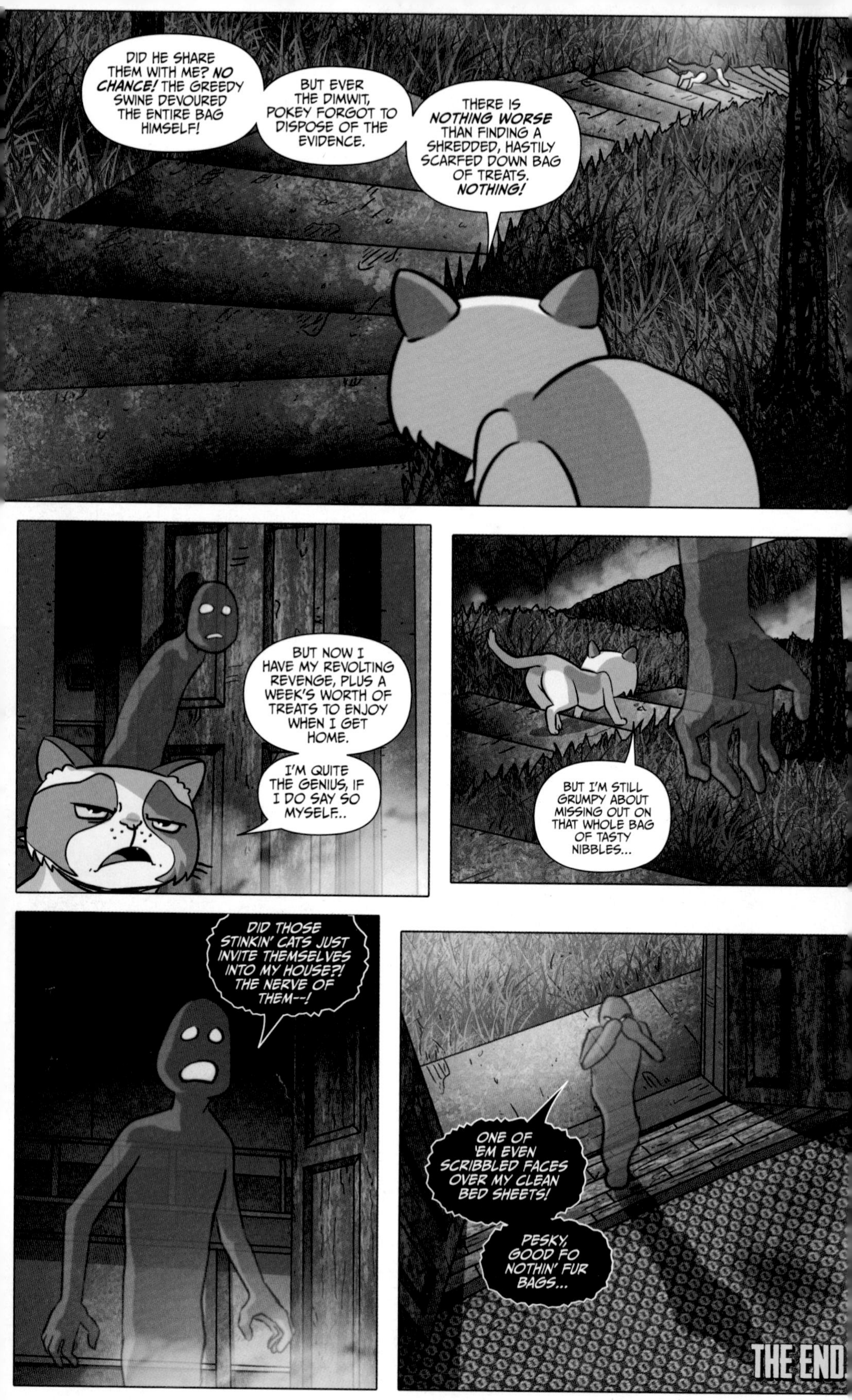

DID HE SHARE THEM WITH ME? NO CHANCE! THE GREEDY SWINE DEVOURED THE ENTIRE BAG HIMSELF!
BUT EVER THE DIMWIT, POKEY FORGOT TO DISPOSE OF THE EVIDENCE.
THERE IS NOTHING WORSE THAN FINDING A SHREDDED, HASTILY SCARFED DOWN BAG OF TREATS. NOTHING!
BUT NOW I HAVE MY REVOLTING REVENGE, PLUS A WEEK'S WORTH OF TREATS TO ENJOY WHEN I GET HOME.
I'M QUITE THE GENIUS, IF I DO SAY SO MYSELF...
BUT I'M STILL GRUMPY ABOUT MISSING OUT ON THAT WHOLE BAG OF TASTY NIBBLES...
DID THOSE STINKIN' CATS JUST INVITE THEMSELVES INTO MY HOUSE?! THE NERVE OF THEM--!
ONE OF 'EM EVEN SCRIBBLED FACES OVER MY CLEAN BED SHEETS!
PESKY, GOOD FO NOTHIN' FUR BAGS...
THE END

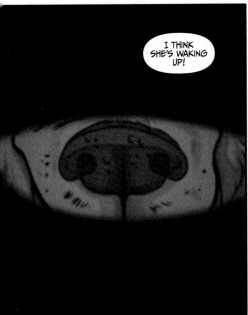

I THINK SHE'S WAKING UP!

GOOD MORNING!!

I NEED COFFEE.

IT NEEDS TO BE STRONG.

AND VERY, VERY HOT.

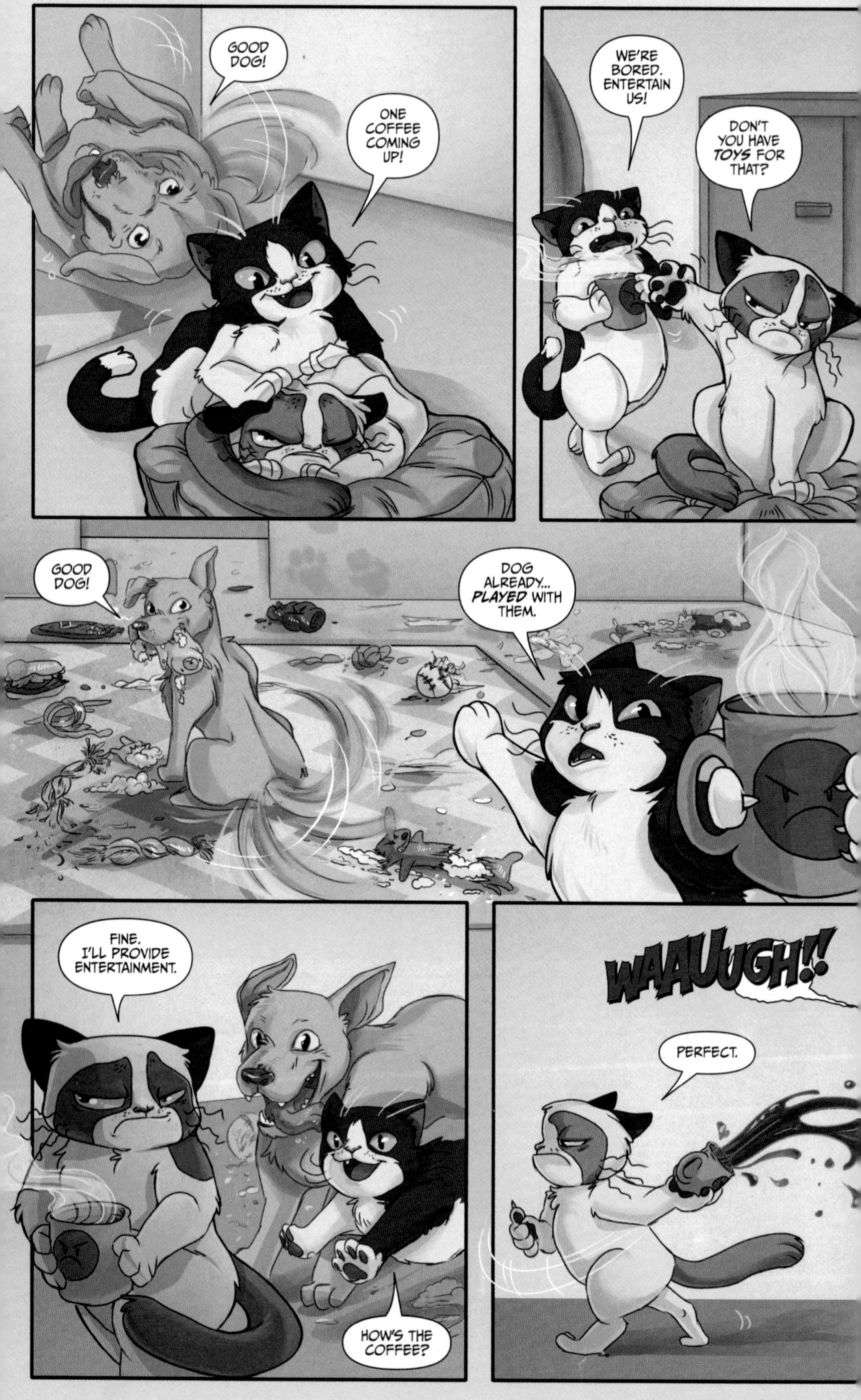
GOOD DOG!
ONE COFFEE COMING UP!
WE'RE BORED. ENTERTAIN US!
DON'T YOU HAVE *TOYS* FOR THAT?
GOOD DOG!
DOG ALREADY... *PLAYED* WITH THEM.
FINE. I'LL PROVIDE ENTERTAINMENT.
HOW'S THE COFFEE?
WAAUUGH!!
PERFECT.

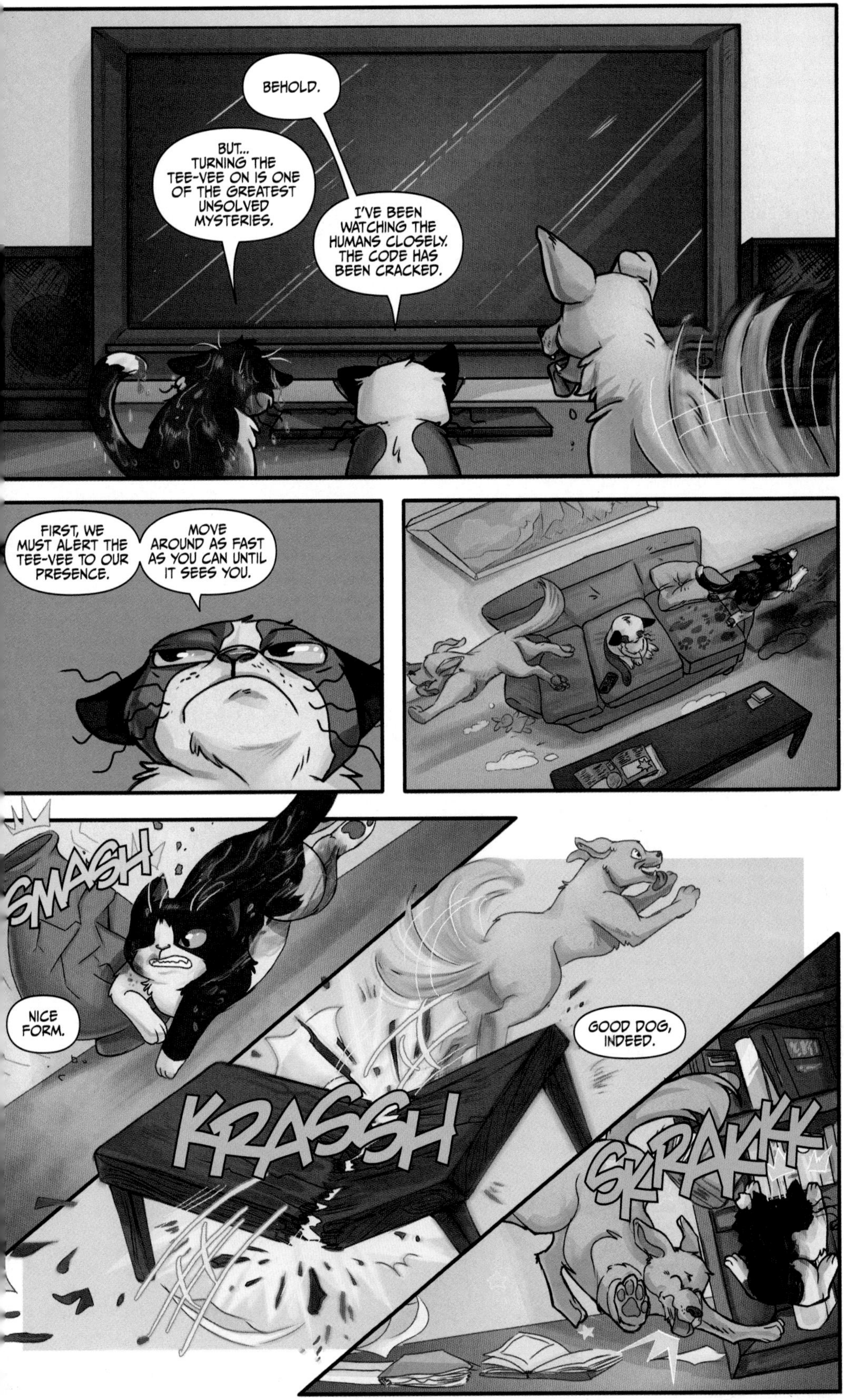
BEHOLD.
BUT... TURNING THE TEE-VEE ON IS ONE OF THE GREATEST UNSOLVED MYSTERIES.
I'VE BEEN WATCHING THE HUMANS CLOSELY. THE CODE HAS BEEN CRACKED.
FIRST, WE MUST ALERT THE TEE-VEE TO OUR PRESENCE.
MOVE AROUND AS FAST AS YOU CAN UNTIL IT SEES YOU.
SMASH
NICE FORM.
KRASSH
GOOD DOG, INDEED.
SKRAKKK

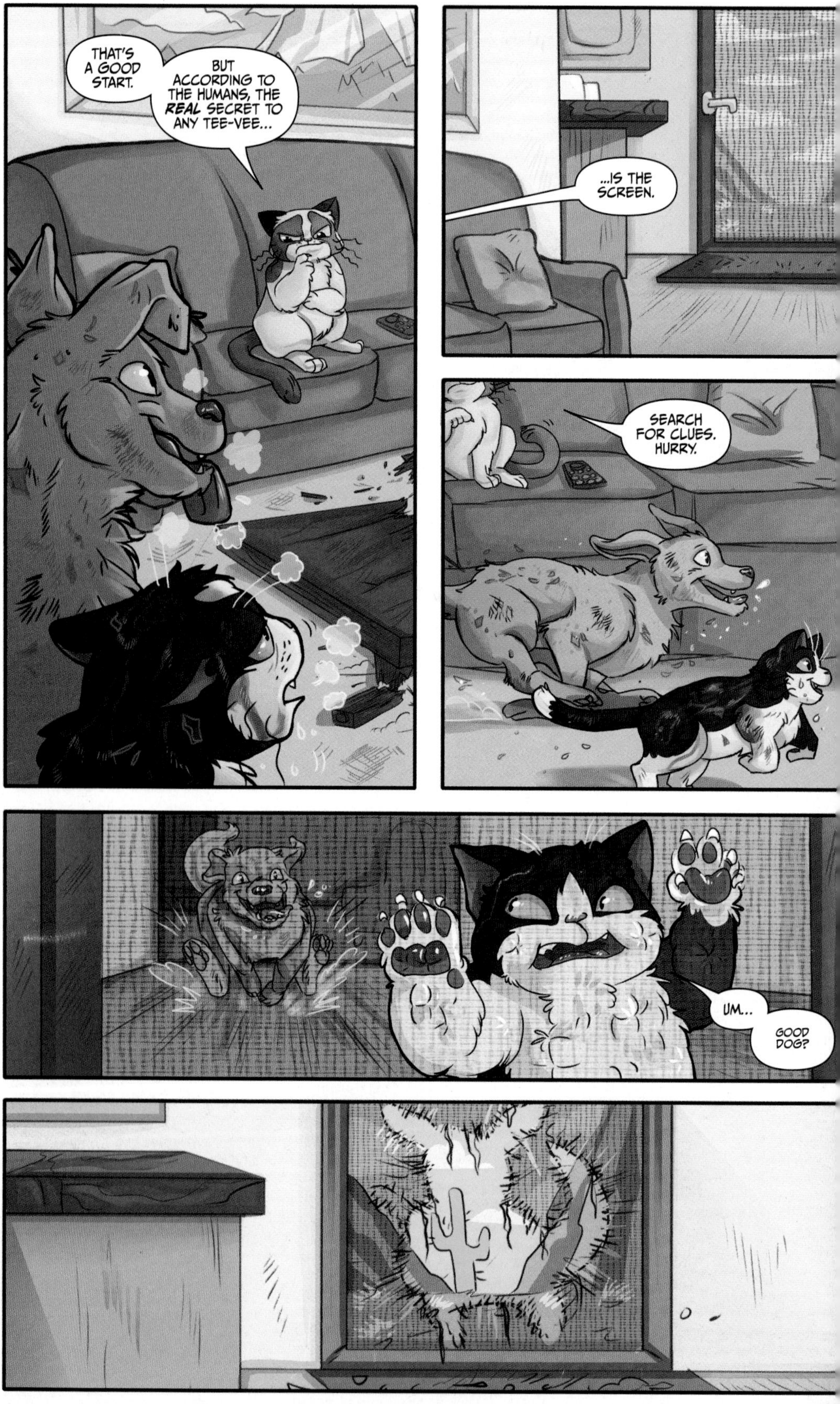
THAT'S A GOOD START.
BUT ACCORDING TO THE HUMANS, THE *REAL* SECRET TO ANY TEE-VEE...
...IS THE SCREEN.
SEARCH FOR CLUES. HURRY.
UM...
GOOD DOG?

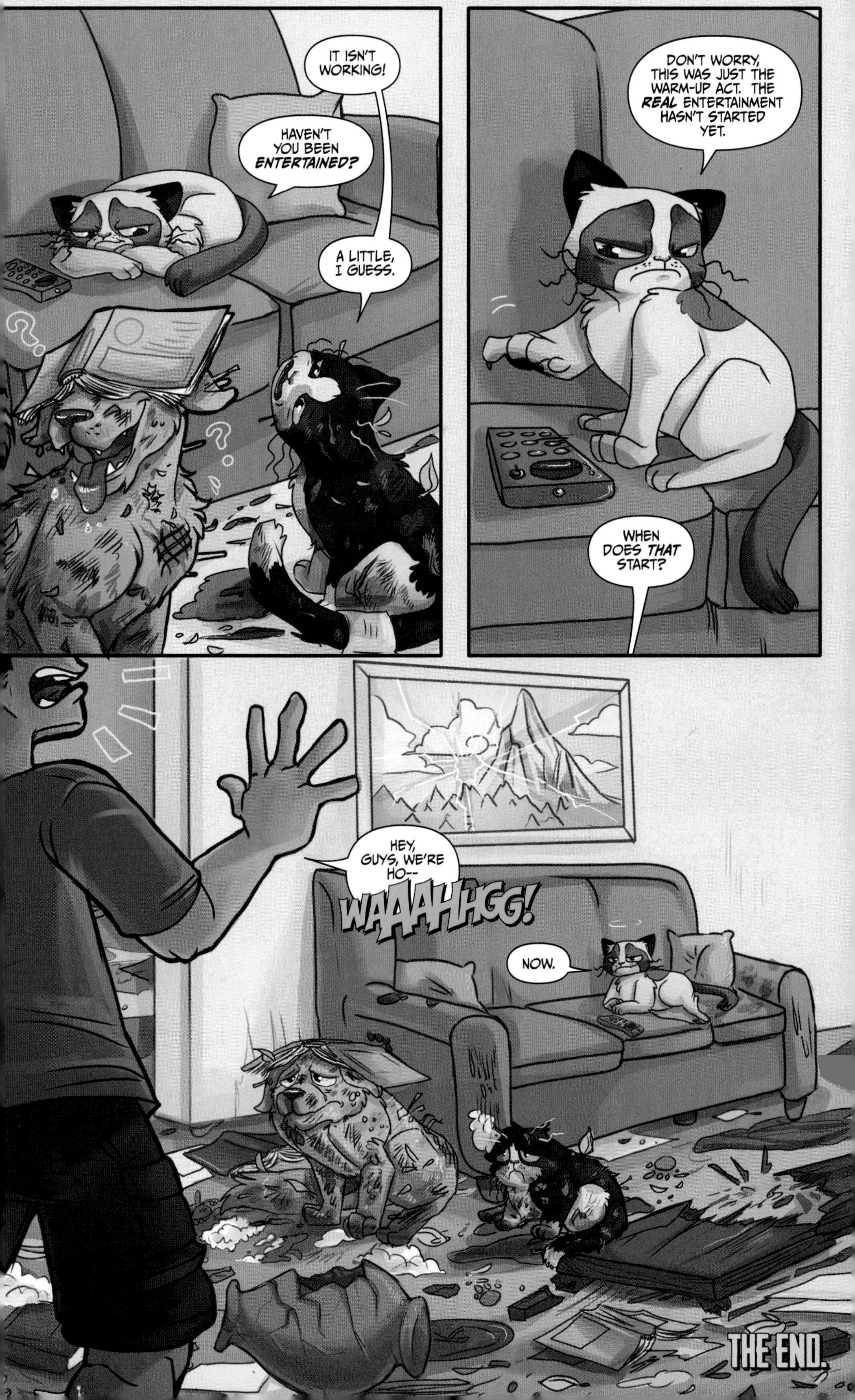
IT ISN'T WORKING!
HAVEN'T YOU BEEN *ENTERTAINED?*
A LITTLE, I GUESS.
DON'T WORRY, THIS WAS JUST THE WARM-UP ACT. THE *REAL* ENTERTAINMENT HASN'T STARTED YET.
WHEN DOES *THAT* START?
HEY, GUYS, WE'RE HO--
WAAAHHGG!
NOW.
THE END.

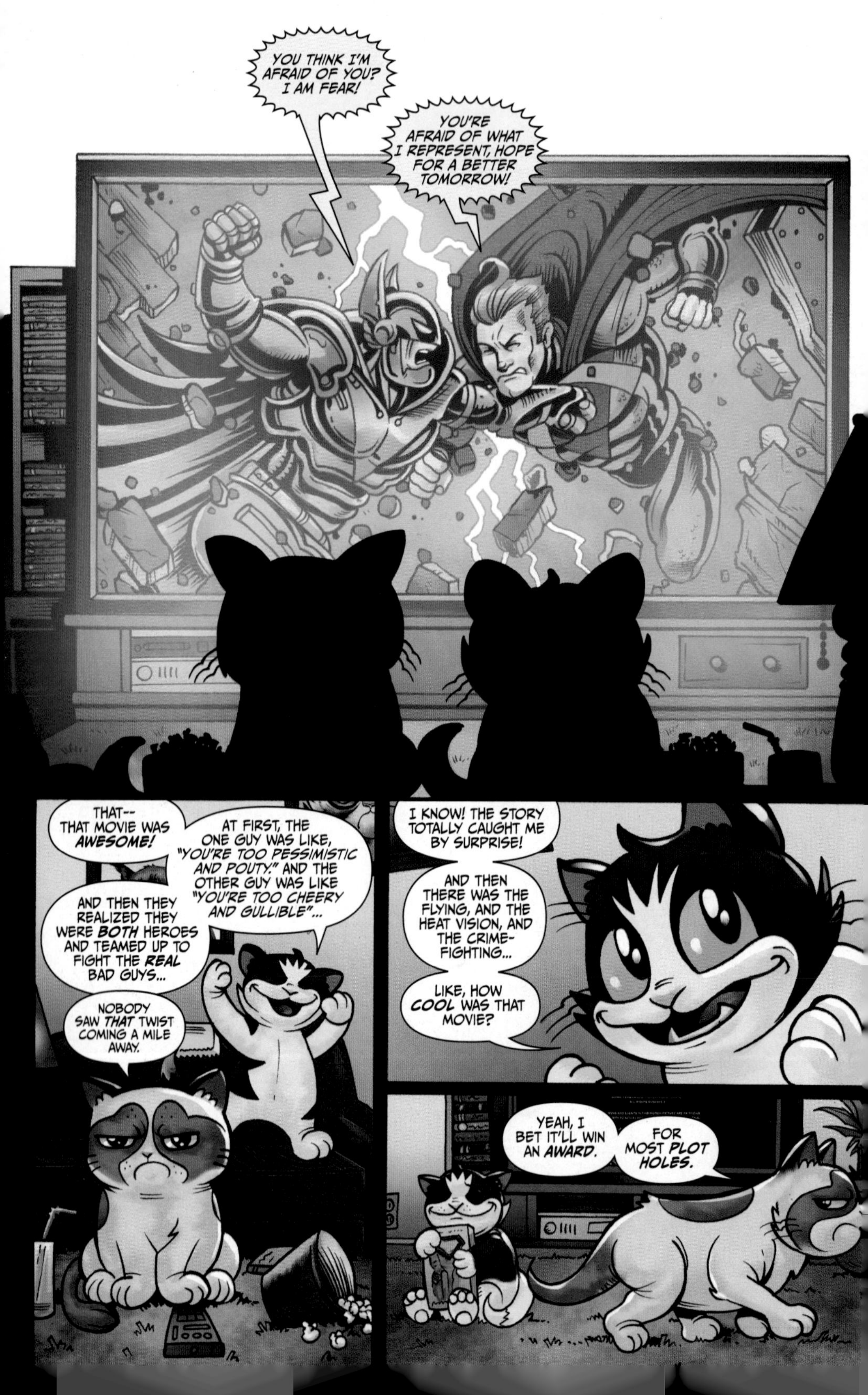

YOU THINK I'M AFRAID OF YOU? I AM FEAR!
YOU'RE AFRAID OF WHAT I REPRESENT, HOPE FOR A BETTER TOMORROW!
THAT-- THAT MOVIE WAS AWESOME!
AT FIRST, THE ONE GUY WAS LIKE, "YOU'RE TOO PESSIMISTIC AND POUTY." AND THE OTHER GUY WAS LIKE "YOU'RE TOO CHEERY AND GULLIBLE"...
AND THEN THEY REALIZED THEY WERE BOTH HEROES AND TEAMED UP TO FIGHT THE REAL BAD GUYS...
NOBODY SAW THAT TWIST COMING A MILE AWAY.
I KNOW! THE STORY TOTALLY CAUGHT ME BY SURPRISE!
AND THEN THERE WAS THE FLYING, AND THE HEAT VISION, AND THE CRIME-FIGHTING...
LIKE, HOW COOL WAS THAT MOVIE?
YEAH, I BET IT'LL WIN AN AWARD.
FOR MOST PLOT HOLES.

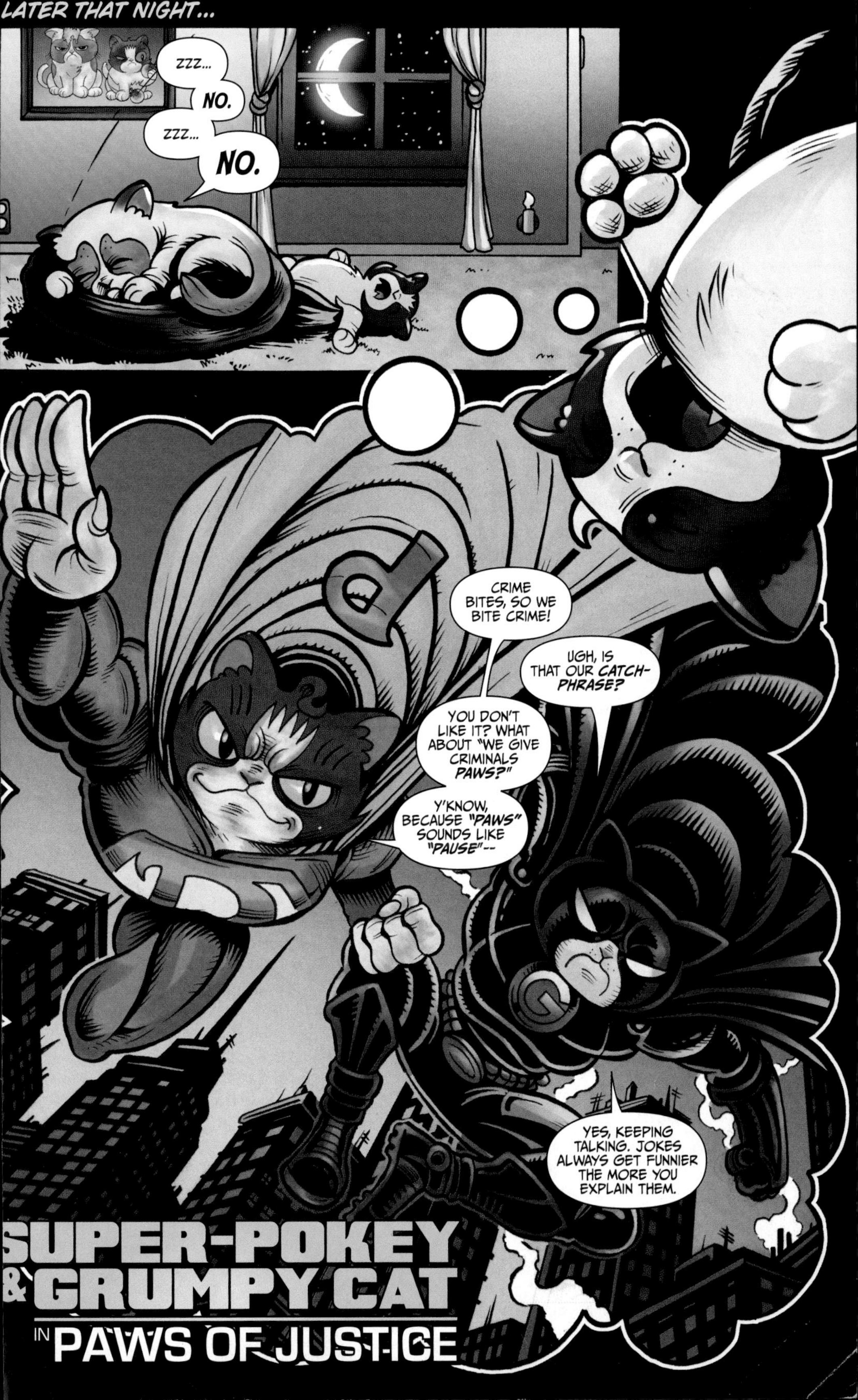

LATER THAT NIGHT...
ZZZ...
NO.
ZZZ...
NO.
CRIME BITES, SO WE BITE CRIME!
UGH, IS THAT OUR CATCH-PHRASE?
YOU DON'T LIKE IT? WHAT ABOUT "WE GIVE CRIMINALS PAWS?"
Y'KNOW, BECAUSE "PAWS" SOUNDS LIKE "PAUSE"--
YES, KEEPING TALKING. JOKES ALWAYS GET FUNNIER THE MORE YOU EXPLAIN THEM.
SUPER-POKEY & GRUMPY CAT
IN PAWS OF JUSTICE

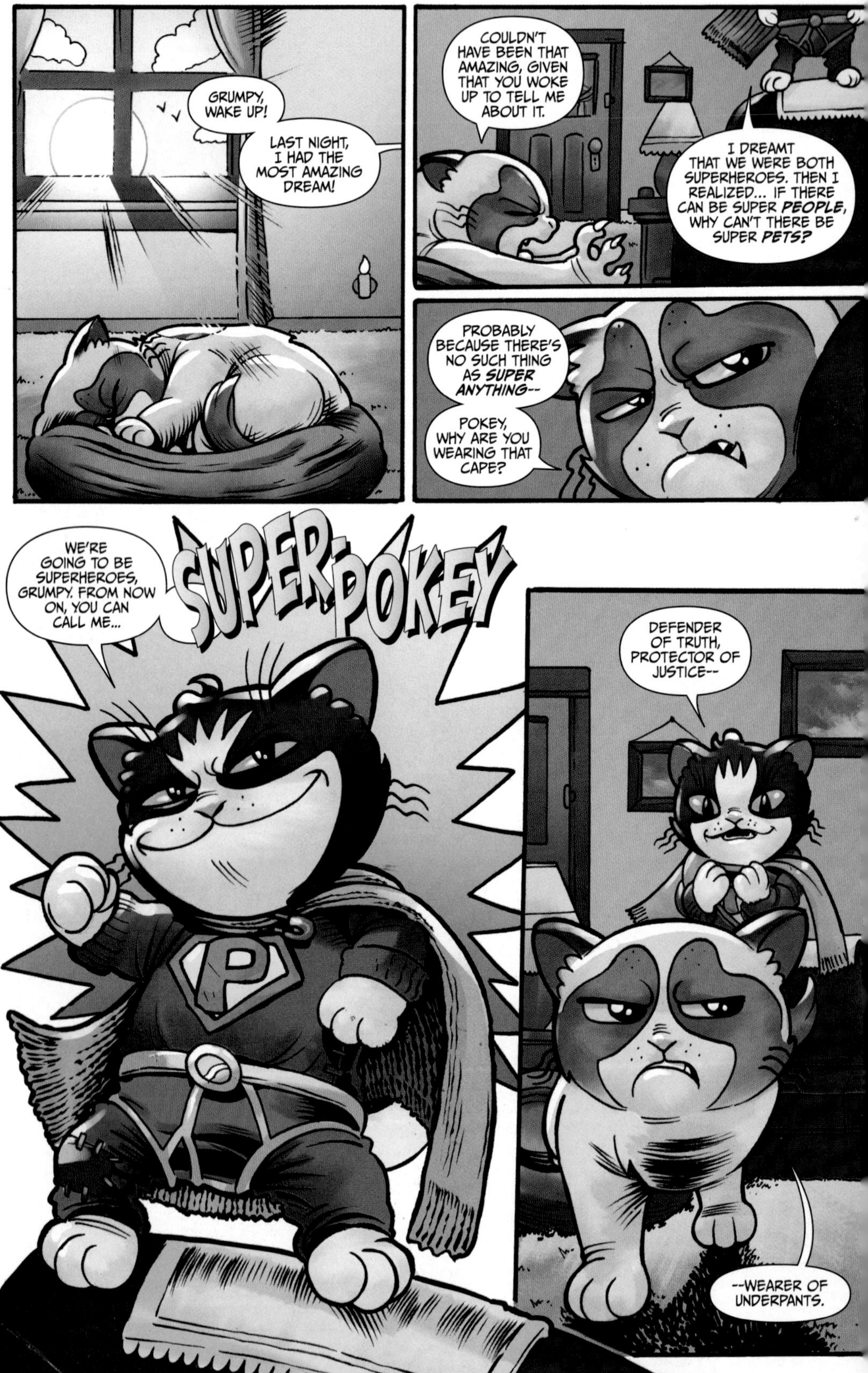
GRUMPY, WAKE UP!
LAST NIGHT, I HAD THE MOST AMAZING DREAM!
COULDN'T HAVE BEEN THAT AMAZING, GIVEN THAT YOU WOKE UP TO TELL ME ABOUT IT.
I DREAMT THAT WE WERE BOTH SUPERHEROES. THEN I REALIZED... IF THERE CAN BE SUPER *PEOPLE*, WHY CAN'T THERE BE SUPER *PETS?*
PROBABLY BECAUSE THERE'S NO SUCH THING AS *SUPER ANYTHING*--
POKEY, WHY ARE YOU WEARING THAT CAPE?
WE'RE GOING TO BE SUPERHEROES, GRUMPY. FROM NOW ON, YOU CAN CALL ME...
SUPER-POKEY
DEFENDER OF TRUTH, PROTECTOR OF JUSTICE--
--WEARER OF UNDERPANTS.

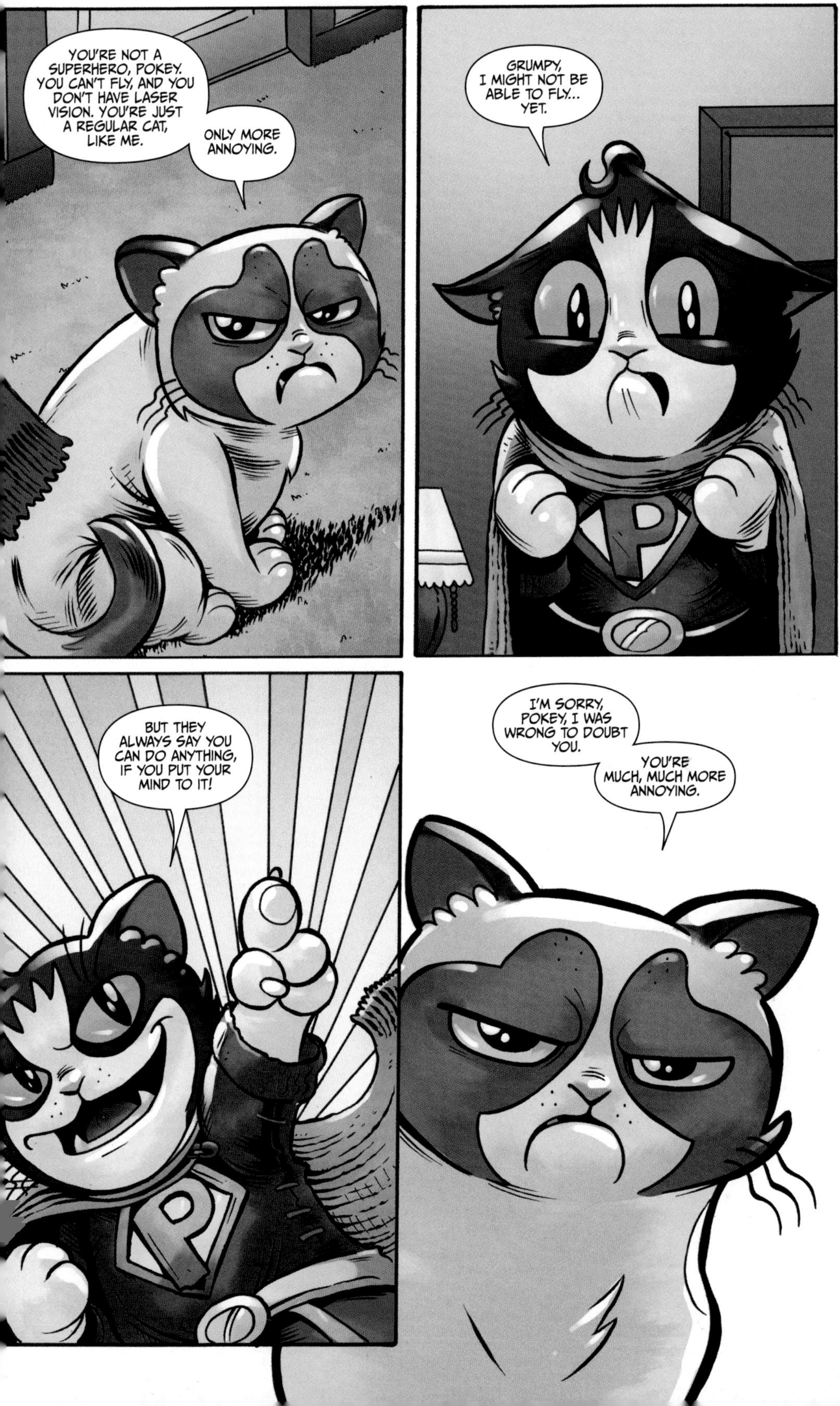
YOU'RE NOT A SUPERHERO, POKEY. YOU CAN'T FLY, AND YOU DON'T HAVE LASER VISION. YOU'RE JUST A REGULAR CAT, LIKE ME.
ONLY MORE ANNOYING.
GRUMPY, I MIGHT NOT BE ABLE TO FLY... YET.
BUT THEY ALWAYS SAY YOU CAN DO ANYTHING, IF YOU PUT YOUR MIND TO IT!
I'M SORRY, POKEY, I WAS WRONG TO DOUBT YOU.
YOU'RE MUCH, MUCH MORE ANNOYING.

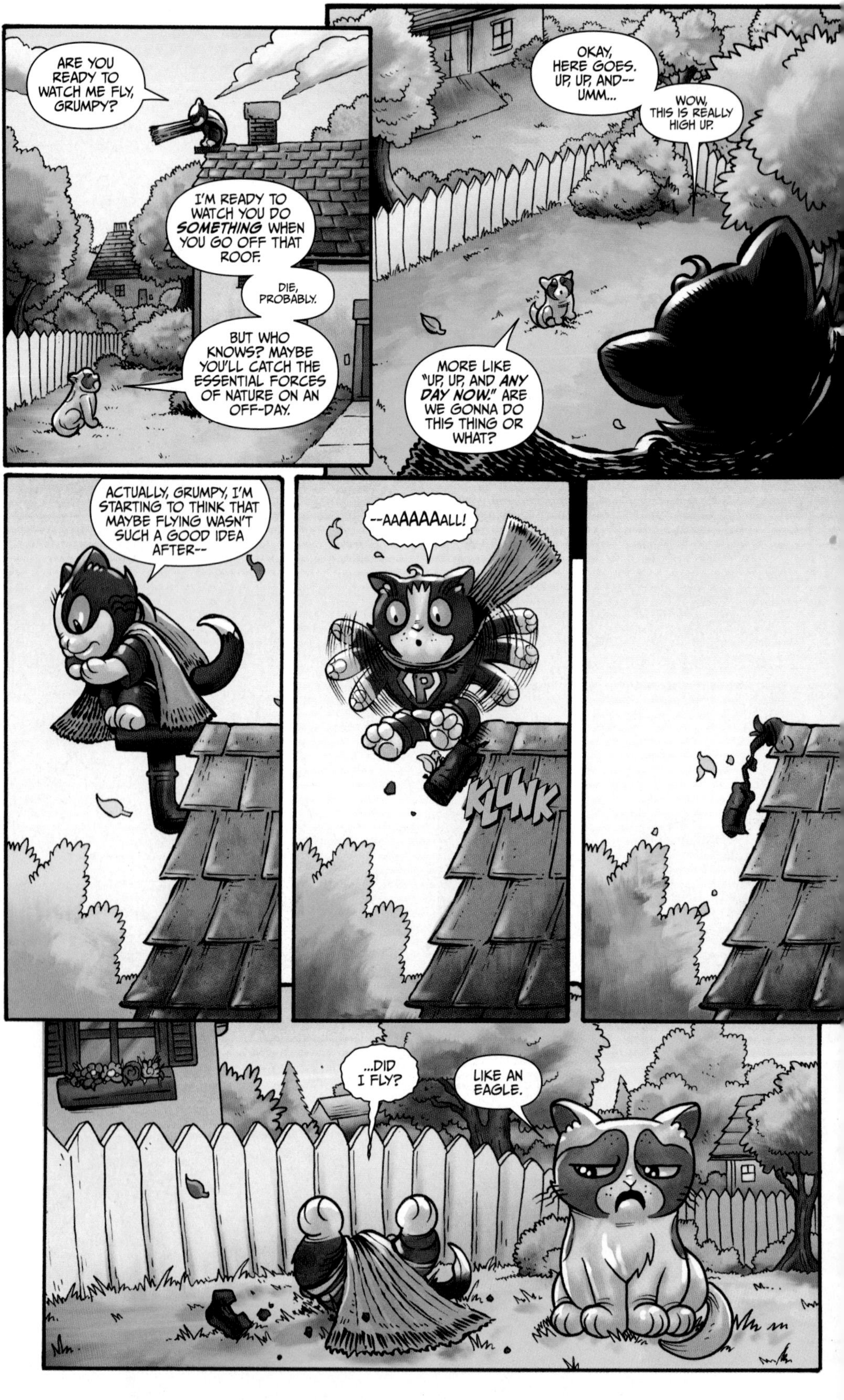
ARE YOU READY TO WATCH ME FLY, GRUMPY?
I'M READY TO WATCH YOU DO SOMETHING WHEN YOU GO OFF THAT ROOF.
DIE, PROBABLY.
BUT WHO KNOWS? MAYBE YOU'LL CATCH THE ESSENTIAL FORCES OF NATURE ON AN OFF-DAY.
OKAY, HERE GOES. UP, UP, AND-- UMM...
WOW, THIS IS REALLY HIGH UP.
MORE LIKE "UP, UP, AND ANY DAY NOW." ARE WE GONNA DO THIS THING OR WHAT?
ACTUALLY, GRUMPY, I'M STARTING TO THINK THAT MAYBE FLYING WASN'T SUCH A GOOD IDEA AFTER--
--AAAAAAALL!
KLUNK
...DID I FLY?
LIKE AN EAGLE.

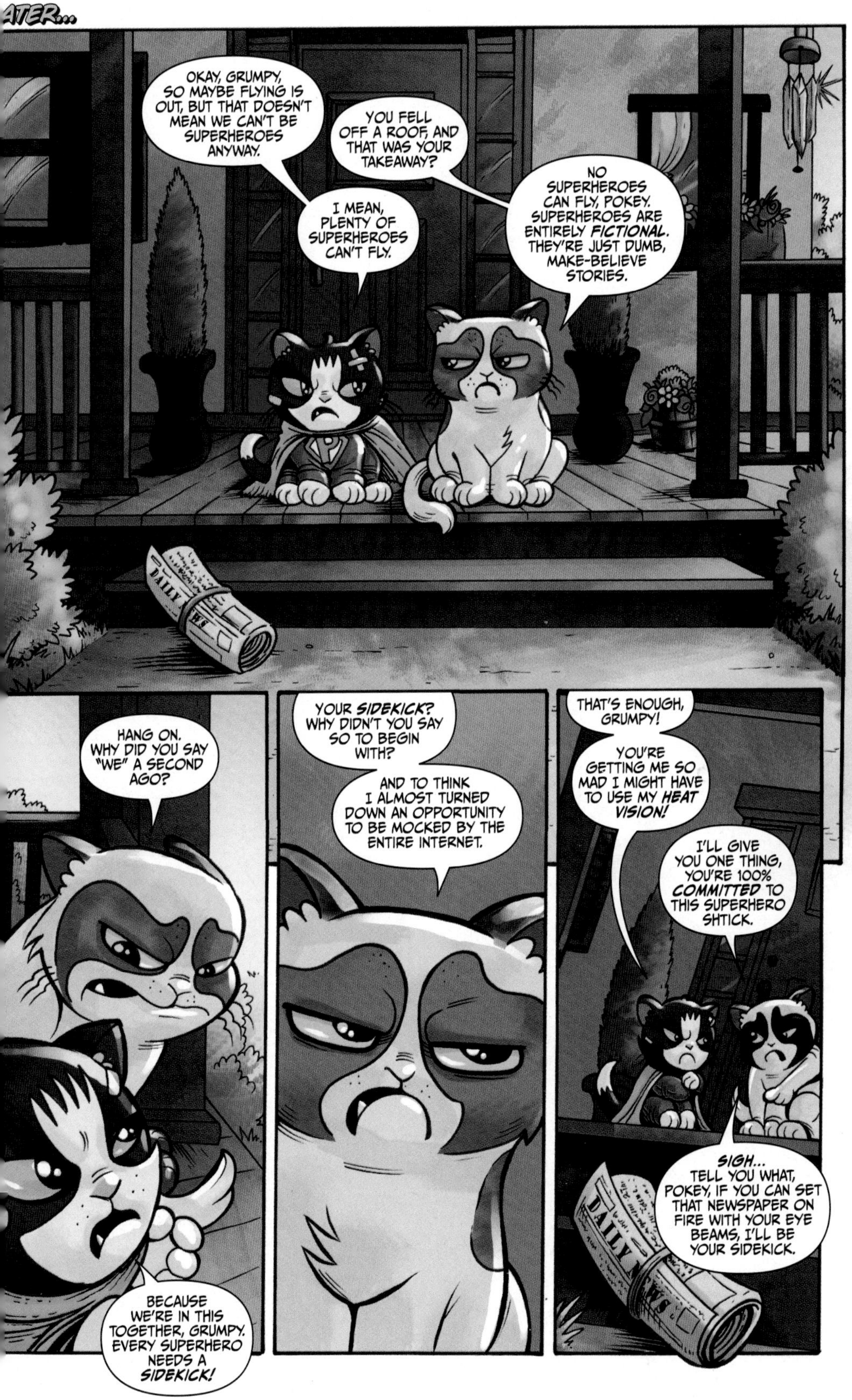
...LATER...
OKAY, GRUMPY, SO MAYBE FLYING IS OUT, BUT THAT DOESN'T MEAN WE CAN'T BE SUPERHEROES ANYWAY.
YOU FELL OFF A ROOF, AND THAT WAS YOUR TAKEAWAY?
I MEAN, PLENTY OF SUPERHEROES CAN'T FLY.
NO SUPERHEROES CAN FLY, POKEY. SUPERHEROES ARE ENTIRELY *FICTIONAL*. THEY'RE JUST DUMB, MAKE-BELIEVE STORIES.
DAILY NEWS
HANG ON. WHY DID YOU SAY "WE" A SECOND AGO?
BECAUSE WE'RE IN THIS TOGETHER, GRUMPY. EVERY SUPERHERO NEEDS A *SIDEKICK!*
YOUR *SIDEKICK?* WHY DIDN'T YOU SAY SO TO BEGIN WITH?
AND TO THINK I ALMOST TURNED DOWN AN OPPORTUNITY TO BE MOCKED BY THE ENTIRE INTERNET.
THAT'S ENOUGH, GRUMPY!
YOU'RE GETTING ME SO MAD I MIGHT HAVE TO USE MY *HEAT VISION!*
I'LL GIVE YOU ONE THING, YOU'RE 100% *COMMITTED* TO THIS SUPERHERO SHTICK.
SIGH... TELL YOU WHAT, POKEY, IF YOU CAN SET THAT NEWSPAPER ON FIRE WITH YOUR EYE BEAMS, I'LL BE YOUR SIDEKICK.
DAILY NEWS

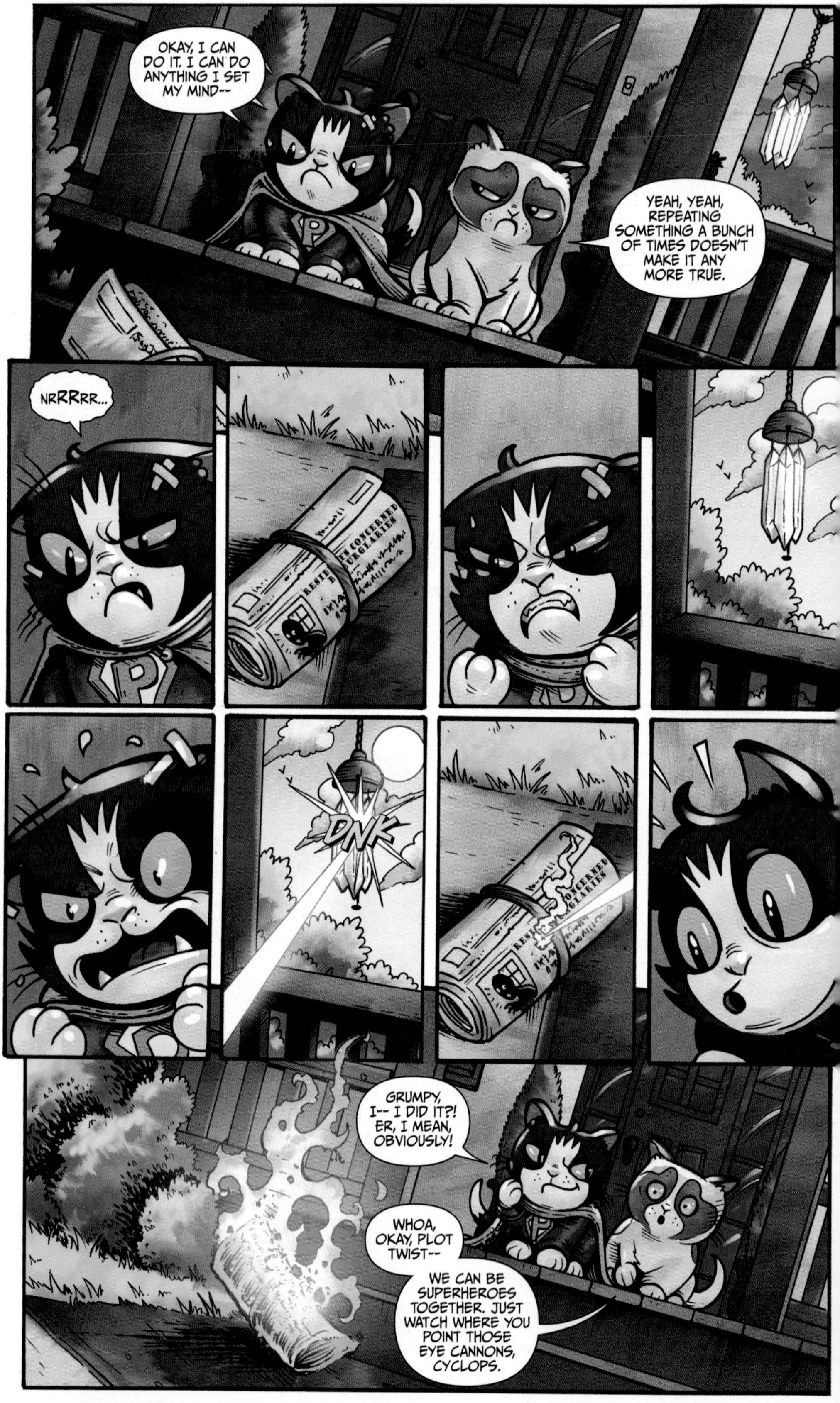
OKAY, I CAN DO IT. I CAN DO ANYTHING I SET MY MIND--
YEAH, YEAH, REPEATING SOMETHING A BUNCH OF TIMES DOESN'T MAKE IT ANY MORE TRUE.
NRRRRR...
DNK
GRUMPY, I-- I DID IT?! ER, I MEAN, OBVIOUSLY!
WHOA, OKAY, PLOT TWIST--
WE CAN BE SUPERHEROES TOGETHER. JUST WATCH WHERE YOU POINT THOSE EYE CANNONS, CYCLOPS.

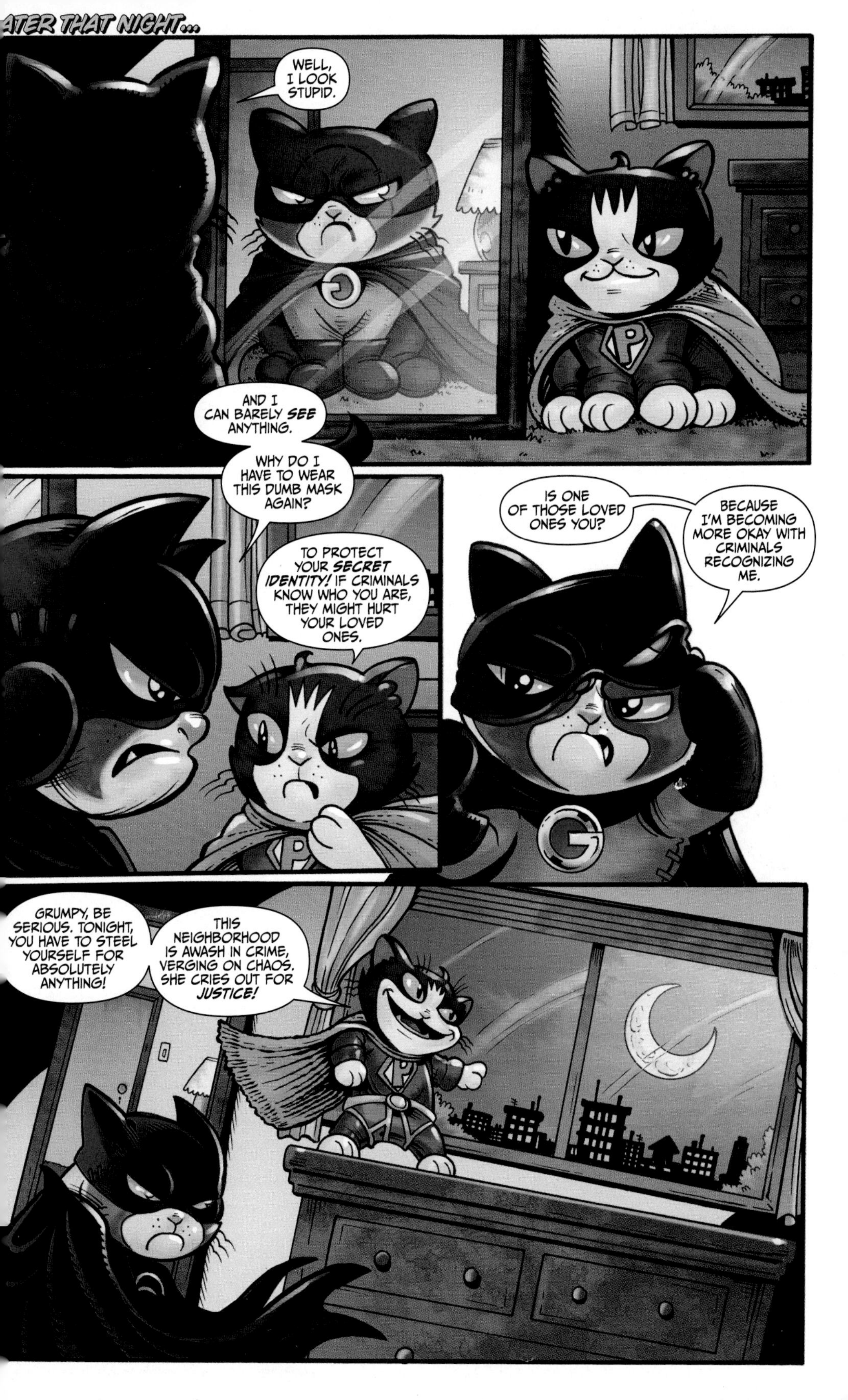
LATER THAT NIGHT...
WELL, I LOOK STUPID.
AND I CAN BARELY SEE ANYTHING.
WHY DO I HAVE TO WEAR THIS DUMB MASK AGAIN?
TO PROTECT YOUR SECRET IDENTITY! IF CRIMINALS KNOW WHO YOU ARE, THEY MIGHT HURT YOUR LOVED ONES.
IS ONE OF THOSE LOVED ONES YOU?
BECAUSE I'M BECOMING MORE OKAY WITH CRIMINALS RECOGNIZING ME.
GRUMPY, BE SERIOUS. TONIGHT, YOU HAVE TO STEEL YOURSELF FOR ABSOLUTELY ANYTHING!
THIS NEIGHBORHOOD IS AWASH IN CRIME, VERGING ON CHAOS. SHE CRIES OUT FOR JUSTICE!

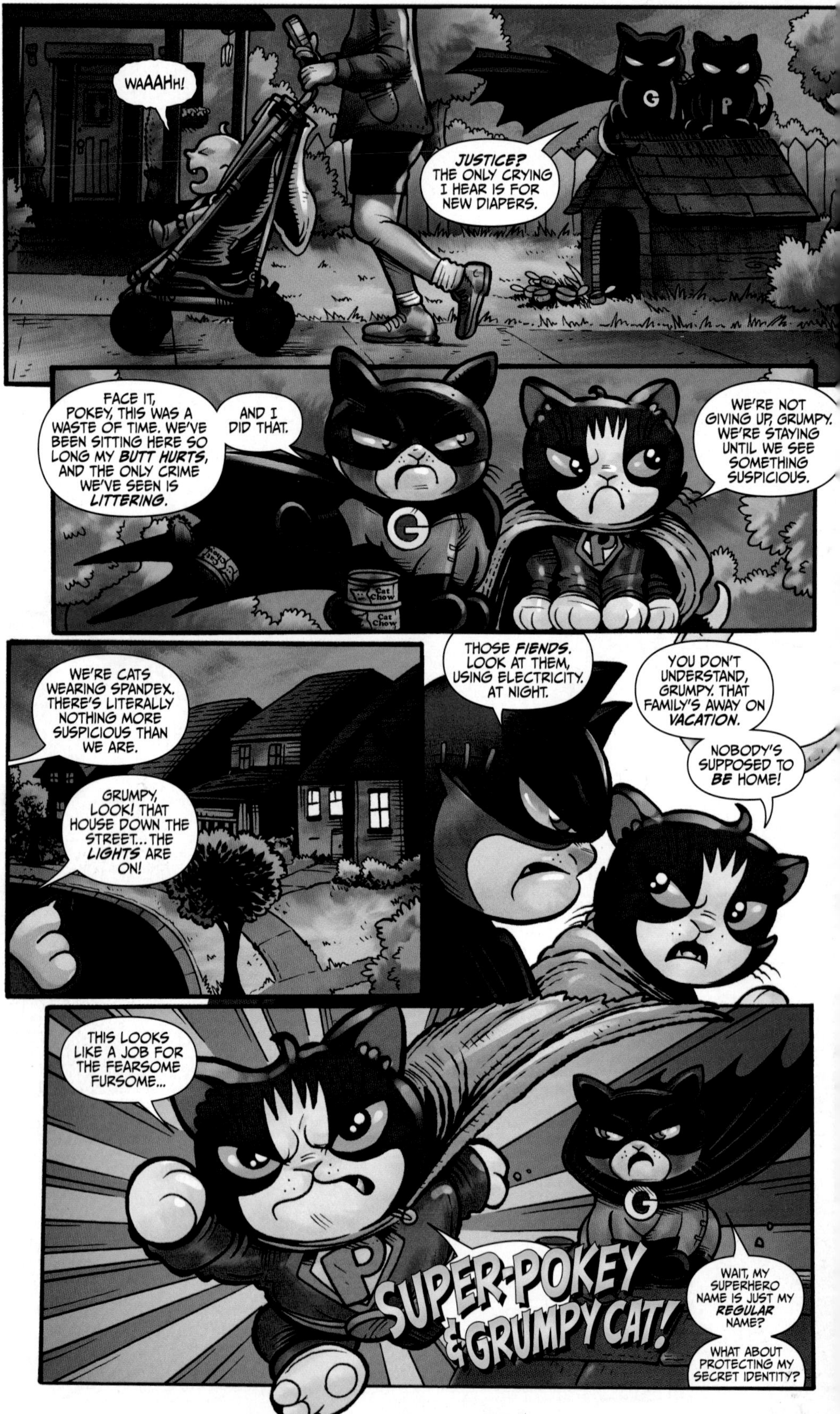

WAAAHH!
JUSTICE? THE ONLY CRYING I HEAR IS FOR NEW DIAPERS.
FACE IT, POKEY, THIS WAS A WASTE OF TIME. WE'VE BEEN SITTING HERE SO LONG MY BUTT HURTS, AND THE ONLY CRIME WE'VE SEEN IS LITTERING.
AND I DID THAT.
WE'RE NOT GIVING UP, GRUMPY. WE'RE STAYING UNTIL WE SEE SOMETHING SUSPICIOUS.
Cat Chow
Cat Chow
WE'RE CATS WEARING SPANDEX. THERE'S LITERALLY NOTHING MORE SUSPICIOUS THAN WE ARE.
GRUMPY, LOOK! THAT HOUSE DOWN THE STREET... THE LIGHTS ARE ON!
THOSE FIENDS. LOOK AT THEM, USING ELECTRICITY. AT NIGHT.
YOU DON'T UNDERSTAND, GRUMPY. THAT FAMILY'S AWAY ON VACATION.
NOBODY'S SUPPOSED TO BE HOME!
THIS LOOKS LIKE A JOB FOR THE FEARSOME FURSOME...
SUPER-POKEY & GRUMPY CAT!
WAIT, MY SUPERHERO NAME IS JUST MY REGULAR NAME?
WHAT ABOUT PROTECTING MY SECRET IDENTITY?

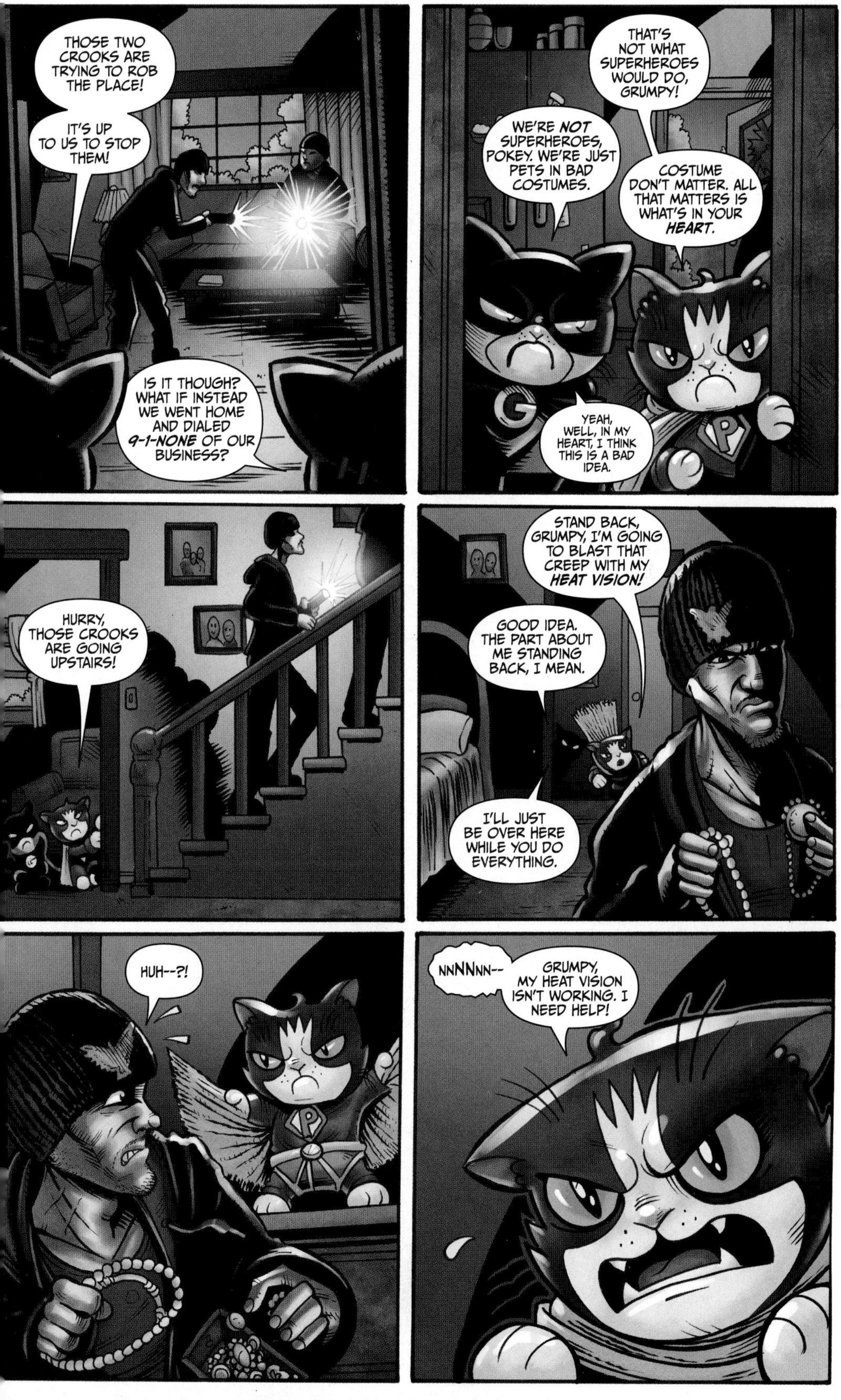
THOSE TWO CROOKS ARE TRYING TO ROB THE PLACE!
IT'S UP TO US TO STOP THEM!
IS IT THOUGH? WHAT IF INSTEAD WE WENT HOME AND DIALED 9-1-NONE OF OUR BUSINESS?
THAT'S NOT WHAT SUPERHEROES WOULD DO, GRUMPY!
WE'RE NOT SUPERHEROES, POKEY. WE'RE JUST PETS IN BAD COSTUMES.
COSTUME DON'T MATTER. ALL THAT MATTERS IS WHAT'S IN YOUR HEART.
YEAH, WELL, IN MY HEART, I THINK THIS IS A BAD IDEA.
HURRY, THOSE CROOKS ARE GOING UPSTAIRS!
STAND BACK, GRUMPY, I'M GOING TO BLAST THAT CREEP WITH MY HEAT VISION!
GOOD IDEA. THE PART ABOUT ME STANDING BACK, I MEAN.
I'LL JUST BE OVER HERE WHILE YOU DO EVERYTHING.
HUH--?!
NNNNNN--
GRUMPY, MY HEAT VISION ISN'T WORKING. I NEED HELP!

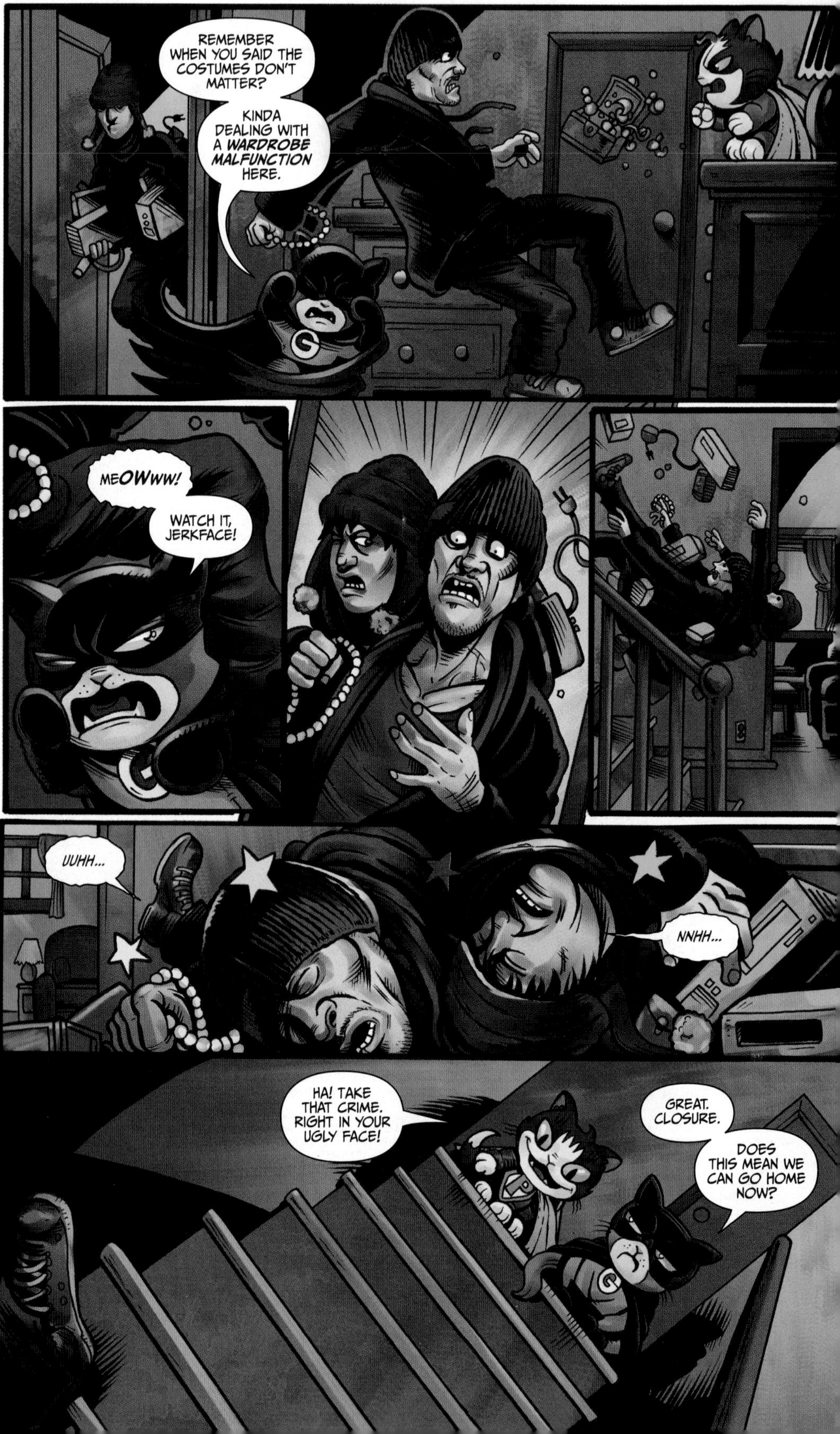
REMEMBER WHEN YOU SAID THE COSTUMES DON'T MATTER?
KINDA DEALING WITH A *WARDROBE MALFUNCTION* HERE.
MEOWWW!
WATCH IT, JERKFACE!
UUHH...
NNHH...
HA! TAKE THAT CRIME. RIGHT IN YOUR UGLY FACE!
GREAT. CLOSURE.
DOES THIS MEAN WE CAN GO HOME NOW?

WE WOULDA GOTTEN AWAY WITH IT TOO. IF IT WEREN'T FOR THOSE PESKY PETS--

SHUT UP, PETE.

WE DID IT, GRUMPY. WE STOPPED A CRIME. WE WERE REAL-LIFE SUPERHEROES TONIGHT.

MEH, I PREFER MY SECRET IDENTITY. LESS EFFORT.

YEAH, IT TURNS OUT CRIME-FIGHTING IS PRETTY SCARY.

WE'LL PUT AWAY THE COSTUMES FOR NOW...

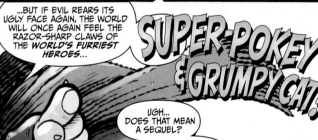

...BUT IF EVIL REARS ITS UGLY FACE AGAIN, THE WORLD WILL ONCE AGAIN FEEL THE RAZOR-SHARP CLAWS OF THE WORLD'S FURRIEST HEROES...

SUPER-POKEY & GRUMPY CAT!

UGH... DOES THAT MEAN A SEQUEL?

OR WORSE, SOME KIND OF SHARED CINEMATIC UNIVERSE?

JUST TERRIBLE.

THE END....?!

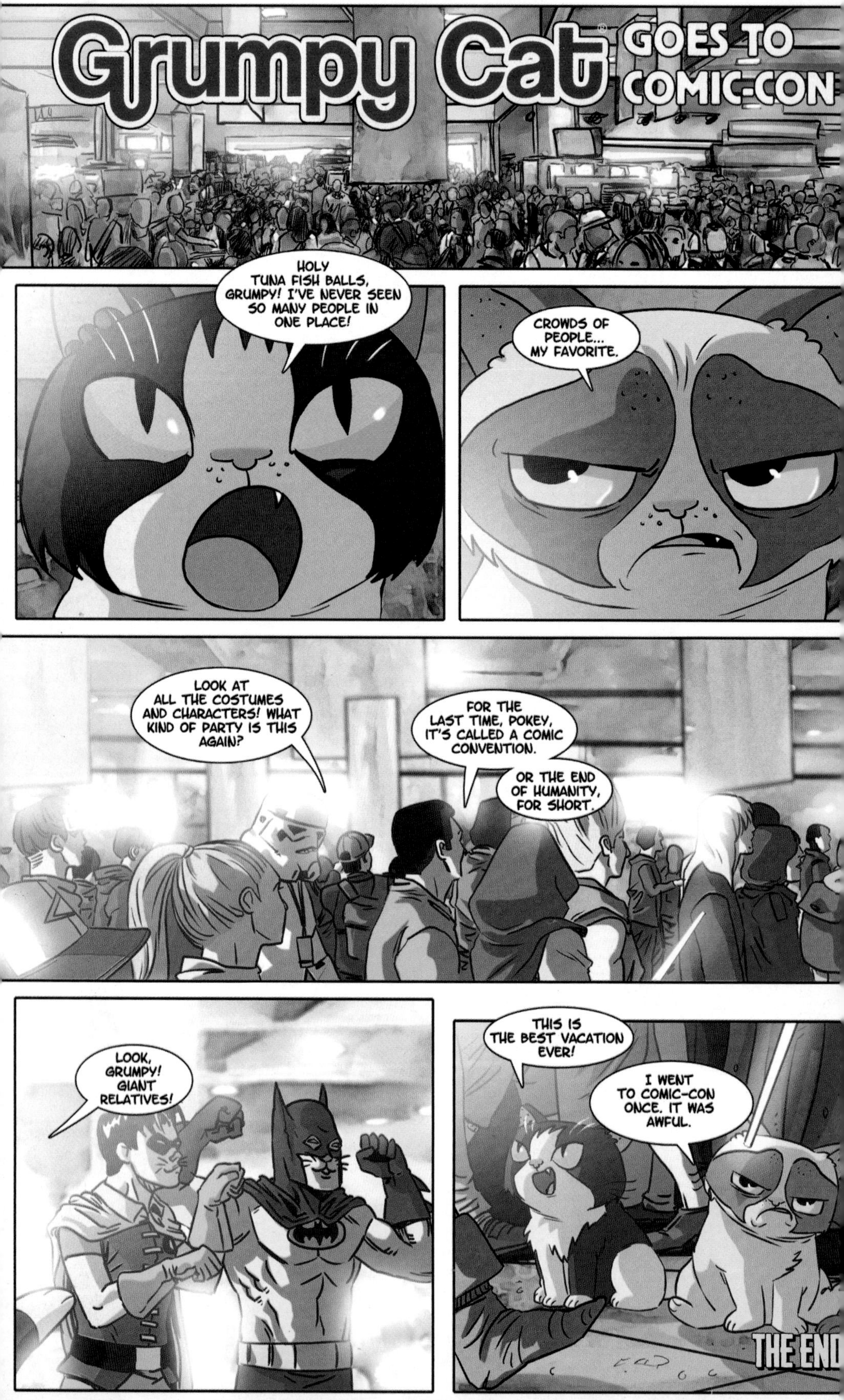
Grumpy Cat® GOES TO COMIC-CON
HOLY TUNA FISH BALLS, GRUMPY! I'VE NEVER SEEN SO MANY PEOPLE IN ONE PLACE!
CROWDS OF PEOPLE... MY FAVORITE.
LOOK AT ALL THE COSTUMES AND CHARACTERS! WHAT KIND OF PARTY IS THIS AGAIN?
FOR THE LAST TIME, POKEY, IT'S CALLED A COMIC CONVENTION.
OR THE END OF HUMANITY, FOR SHORT.
LOOK, GRUMPY! GIANT RELATIVES!
THIS IS THE BEST VACATION EVER!
I WENT TO COMIC-CON ONCE. IT WAS AWFUL.
THE END

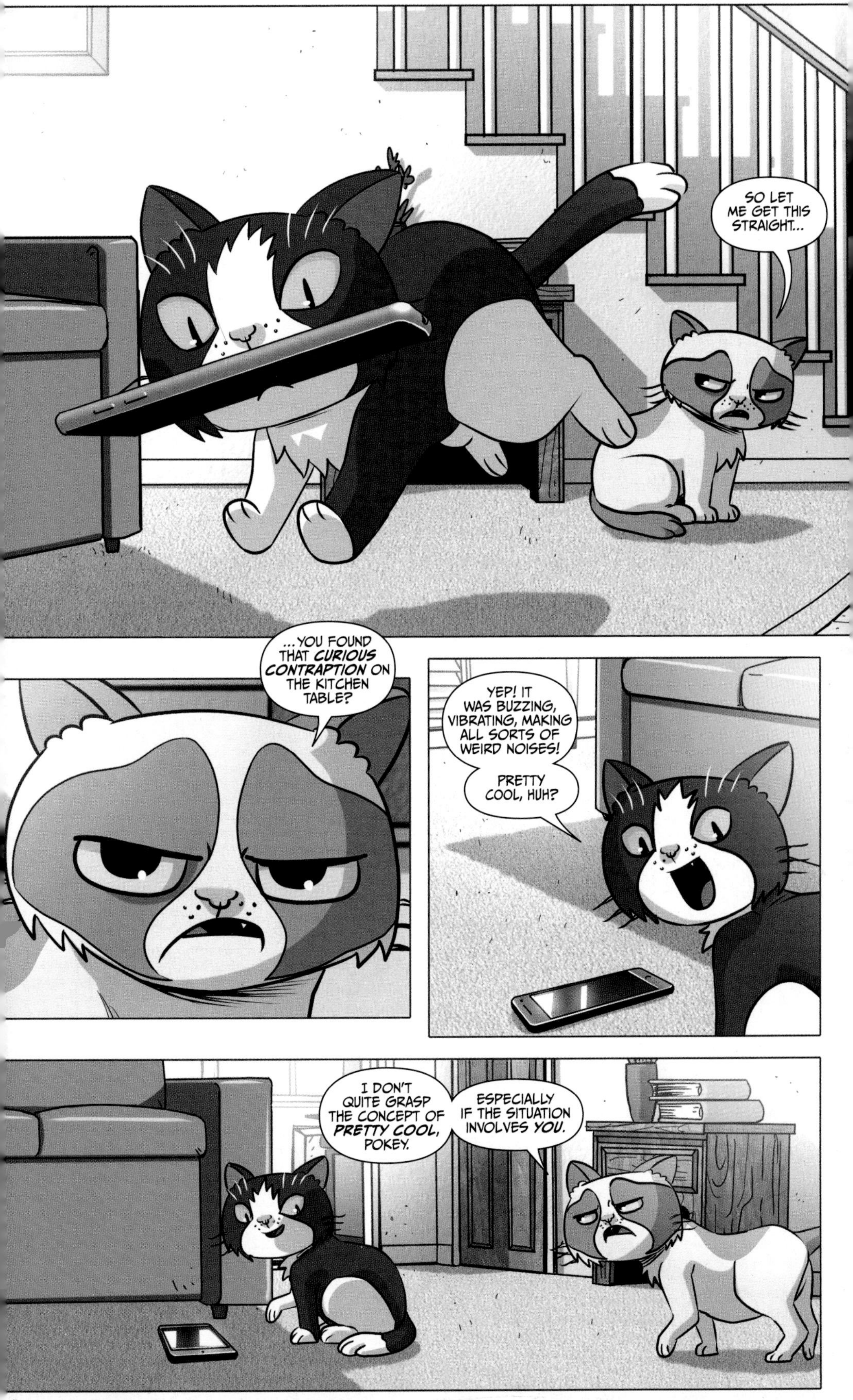

SO LET ME GET THIS STRAIGHT...
...YOU FOUND THAT *CURIOUS CONTRAPTION* ON THE KITCHEN TABLE?
YEP! IT WAS BUZZING, VIBRATING, MAKING ALL SORTS OF WEIRD NOISES!
PRETTY COOL, HUH?
I DON'T QUITE GRASP THE CONCEPT OF *PRETTY COOL*, POKEY.
ESPECIALLY IF THE SITUATION INVOLVES *YOU*.

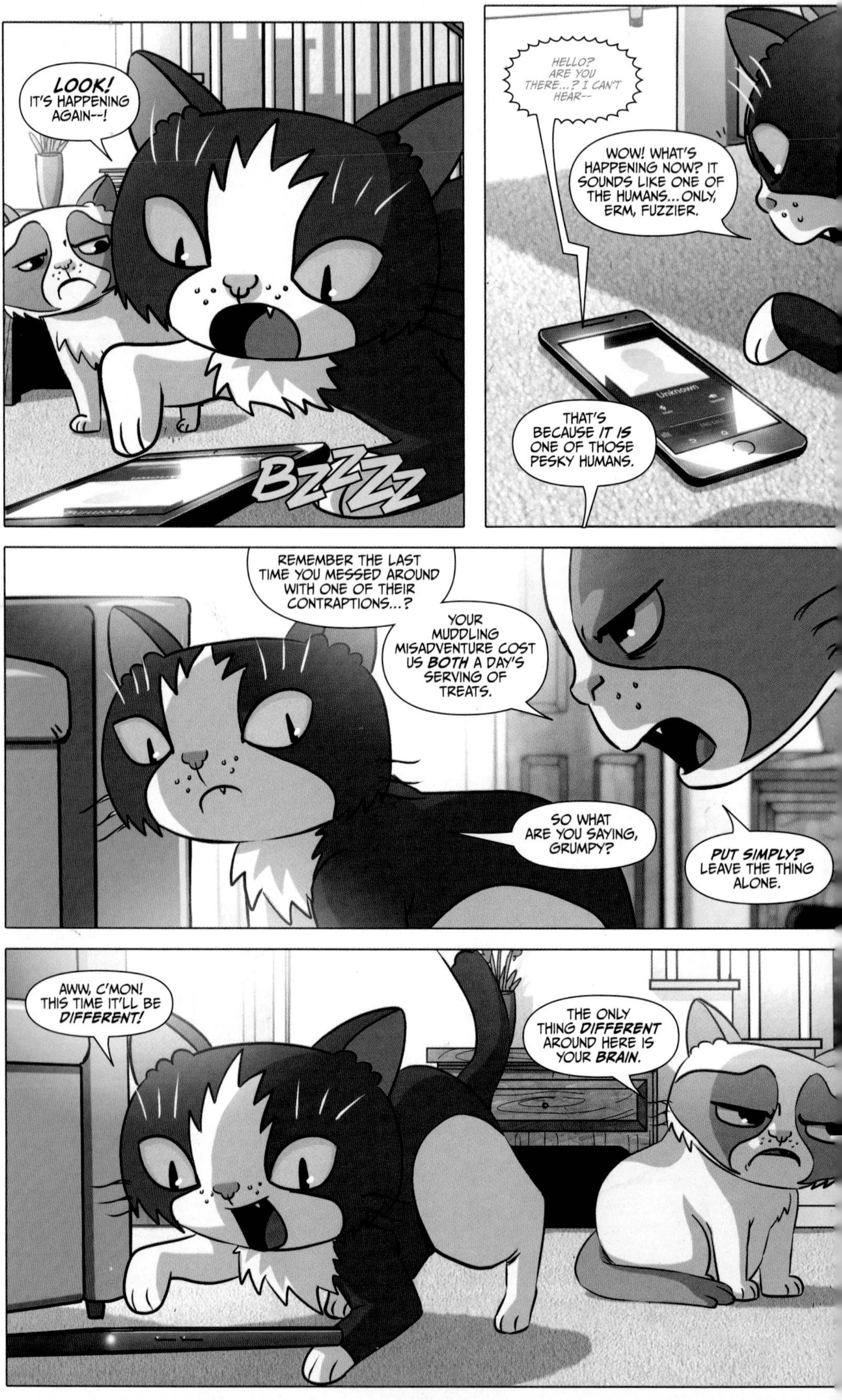

LOOK! IT'S HAPPENING AGAIN--!
BZZZZZ
HELLO? ARE YOU THERE...? I CAN'T HEAR--
WOW! WHAT'S HAPPENING NOW? IT SOUNDS LIKE ONE OF THE HUMANS...ONLY, ERM, FUZZIER.
Unknown
THAT'S BECAUSE IT IS ONE OF THOSE PESKY HUMANS.
REMEMBER THE LAST TIME YOU MESSED AROUND WITH ONE OF THEIR CONTRAPTIONS...?
YOUR MUDDLING MISADVENTURE COST US BOTH A DAY'S SERVING OF TREATS.
SO WHAT ARE YOU SAYING, GRUMPY?
PUT SIMPLY? LEAVE THE THING ALONE.
AWW, C'MON! THIS TIME IT'LL BE DIFFERENT!
THE ONLY THING DIFFERENT AROUND HERE IS YOUR BRAIN.

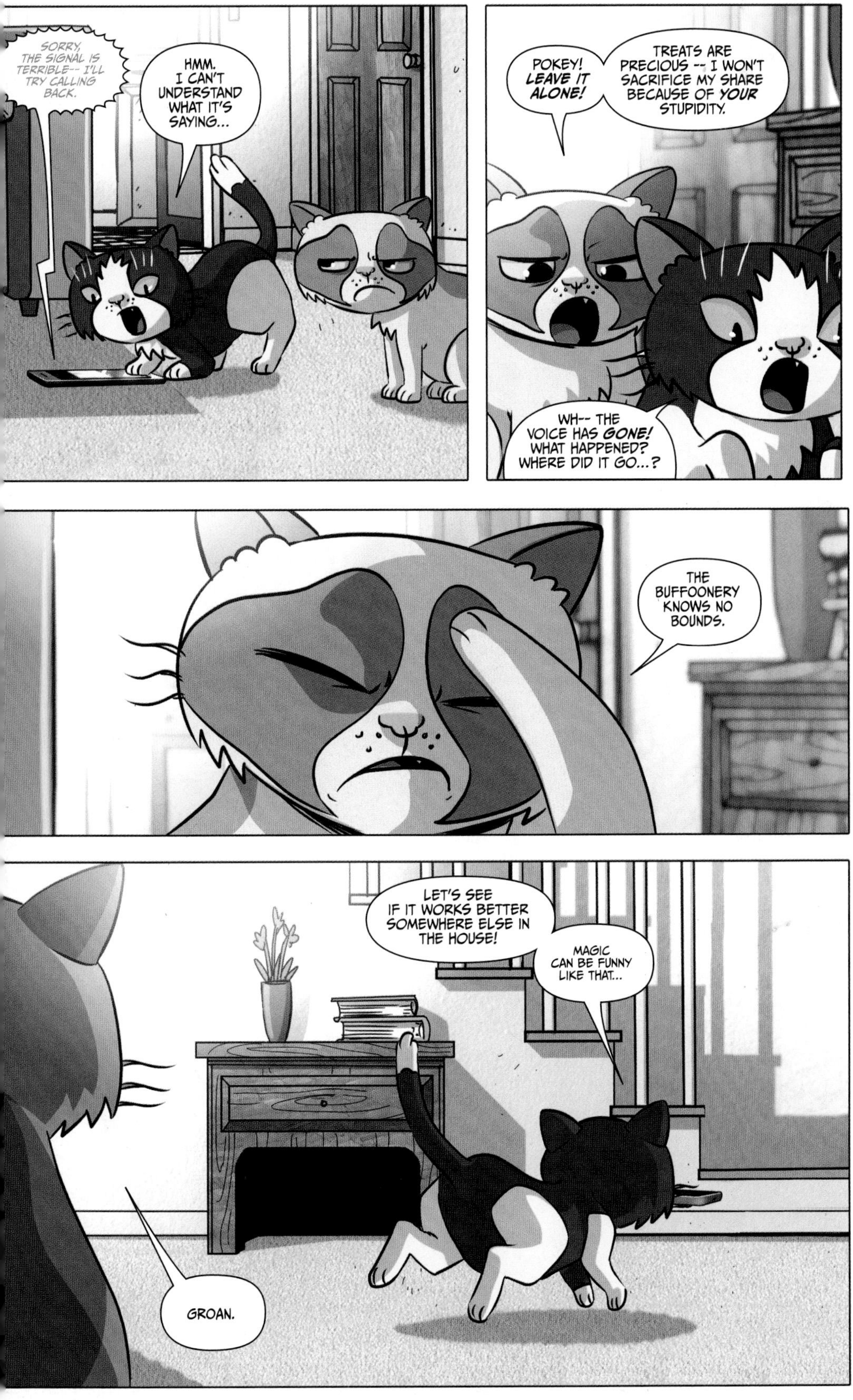
SORRY, THE SIGNAL IS TERRIBLE-- I'LL TRY CALLING BACK.
HMM. I CAN'T UNDERSTAND WHAT IT'S SAYING...
POKEY! LEAVE IT ALONE!
TREATS ARE PRECIOUS -- I WON'T SACRIFICE MY SHARE BECAUSE OF YOUR STUPIDITY.
WH-- THE VOICE HAS GONE! WHAT HAPPENED? WHERE DID IT GO...?
THE BUFFOONERY KNOWS NO BOUNDS.
LET'S SEE IF IT WORKS BETTER SOMEWHERE ELSE IN THE HOUSE!
MAGIC CAN BE FUNNY LIKE THAT...
GROAN.

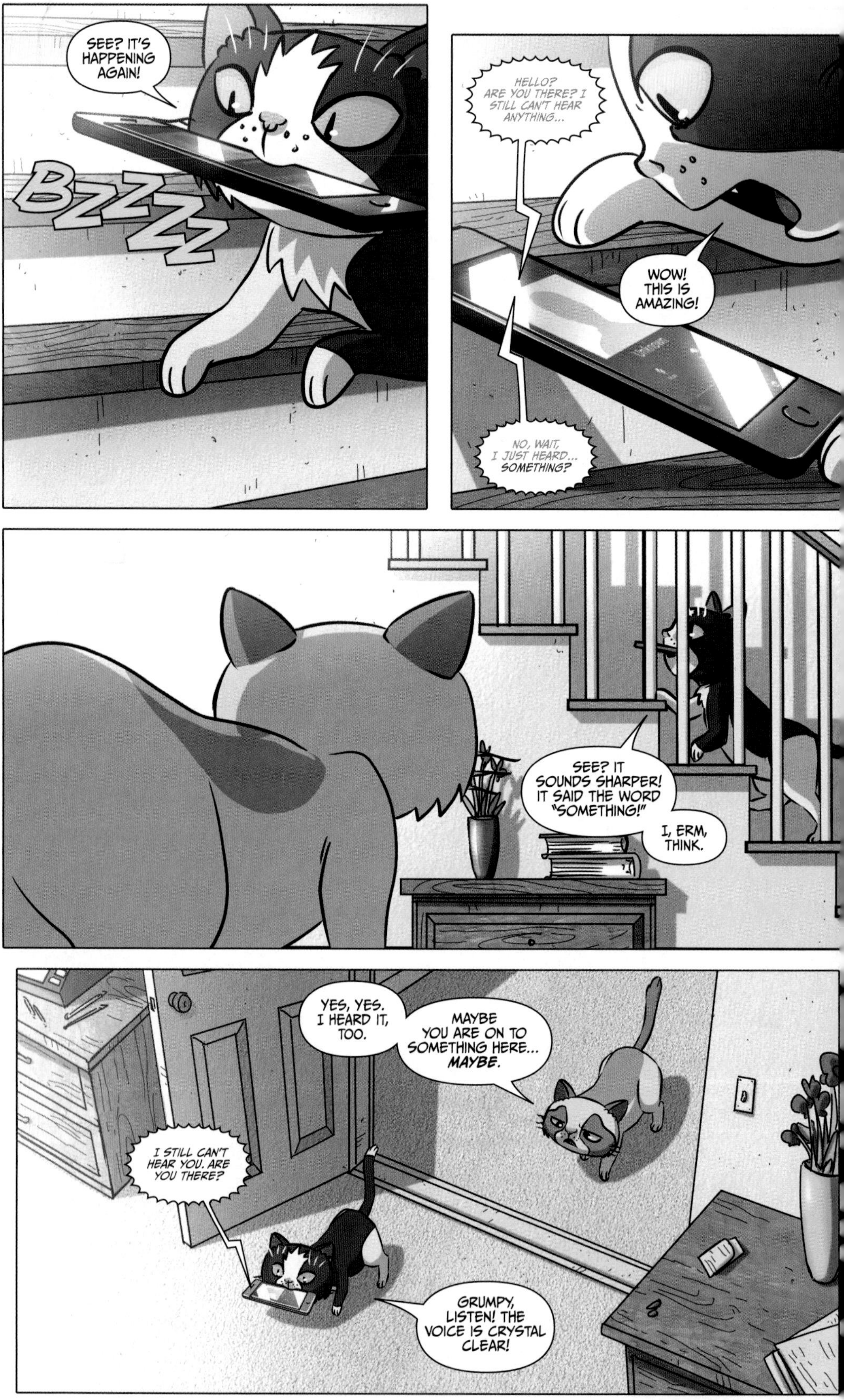
SEE? IT'S HAPPENING AGAIN!
BZZZZ
HELLO? ARE YOU THERE? I STILL CAN'T HEAR ANYTHING...
WOW! THIS IS AMAZING!
NO, WAIT, I JUST HEARD... SOMETHING?
SEE? IT SOUNDS SHARPER! IT SAID THE WORD "SOMETHING!"
I, ERM, THINK.
YES, YES. I HEARD IT, TOO.
MAYBE YOU ARE ON TO SOMETHING HERE... MAYBE.
I STILL CAN'T HEAR YOU. ARE YOU THERE?
GRUMPY, LISTEN! THE VOICE IS CRYSTAL CLEAR!

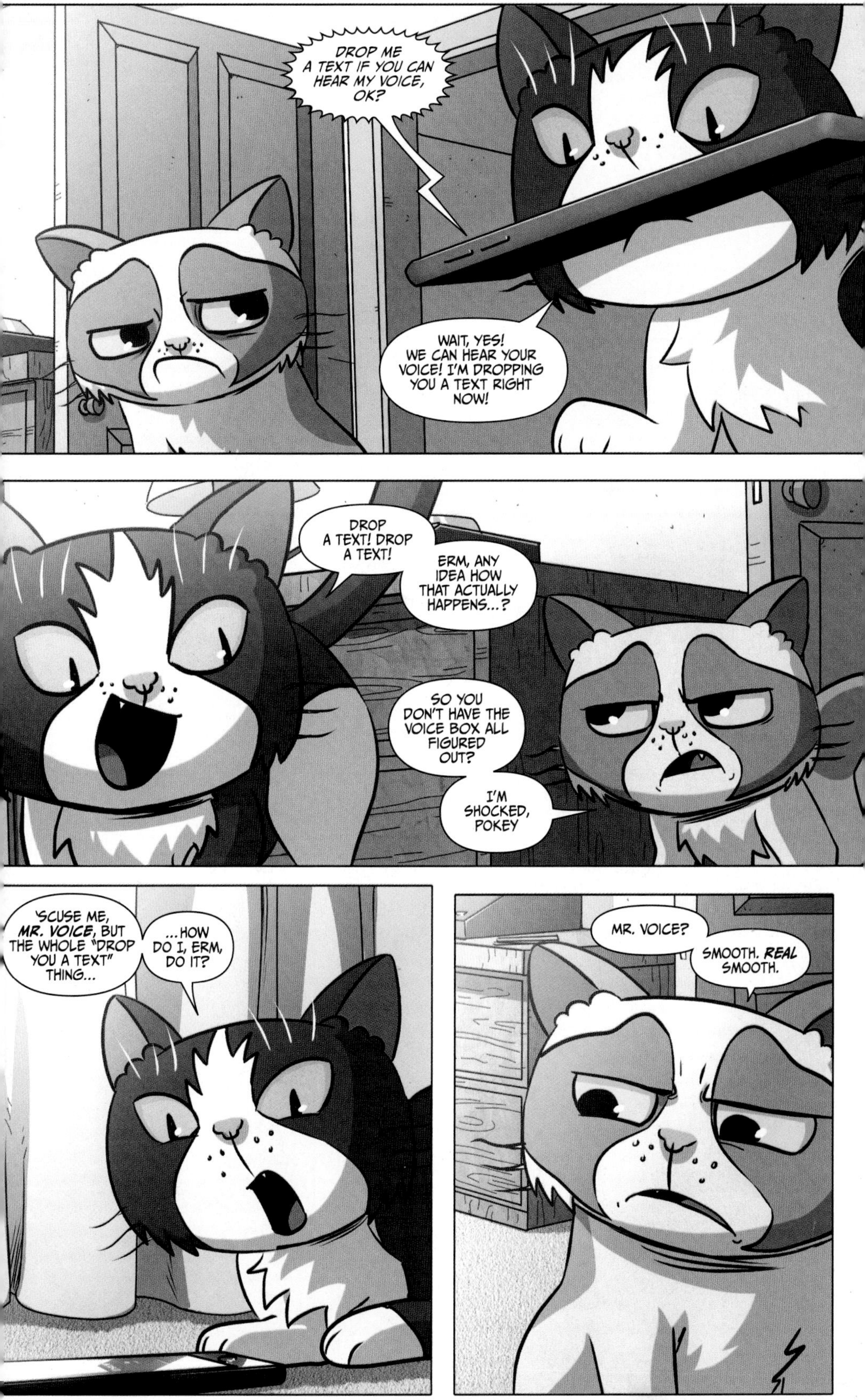
DROP ME A TEXT IF YOU CAN HEAR MY VOICE, OK?
WAIT, YES! WE CAN HEAR YOUR VOICE! I'M DROPPING YOU A TEXT RIGHT NOW!
DROP A TEXT! DROP A TEXT!
ERM, ANY IDEA HOW THAT ACTUALLY HAPPENS...?
SO YOU DON'T HAVE THE VOICE BOX ALL FIGURED OUT?
I'M SHOCKED, POKEY
'SCUSE ME, **MR. VOICE**, BUT THE WHOLE "DROP YOU A TEXT" THING...
...HOW DO I, ERM, DO IT?
MR. VOICE?
SMOOTH. **REAL** SMOOTH.

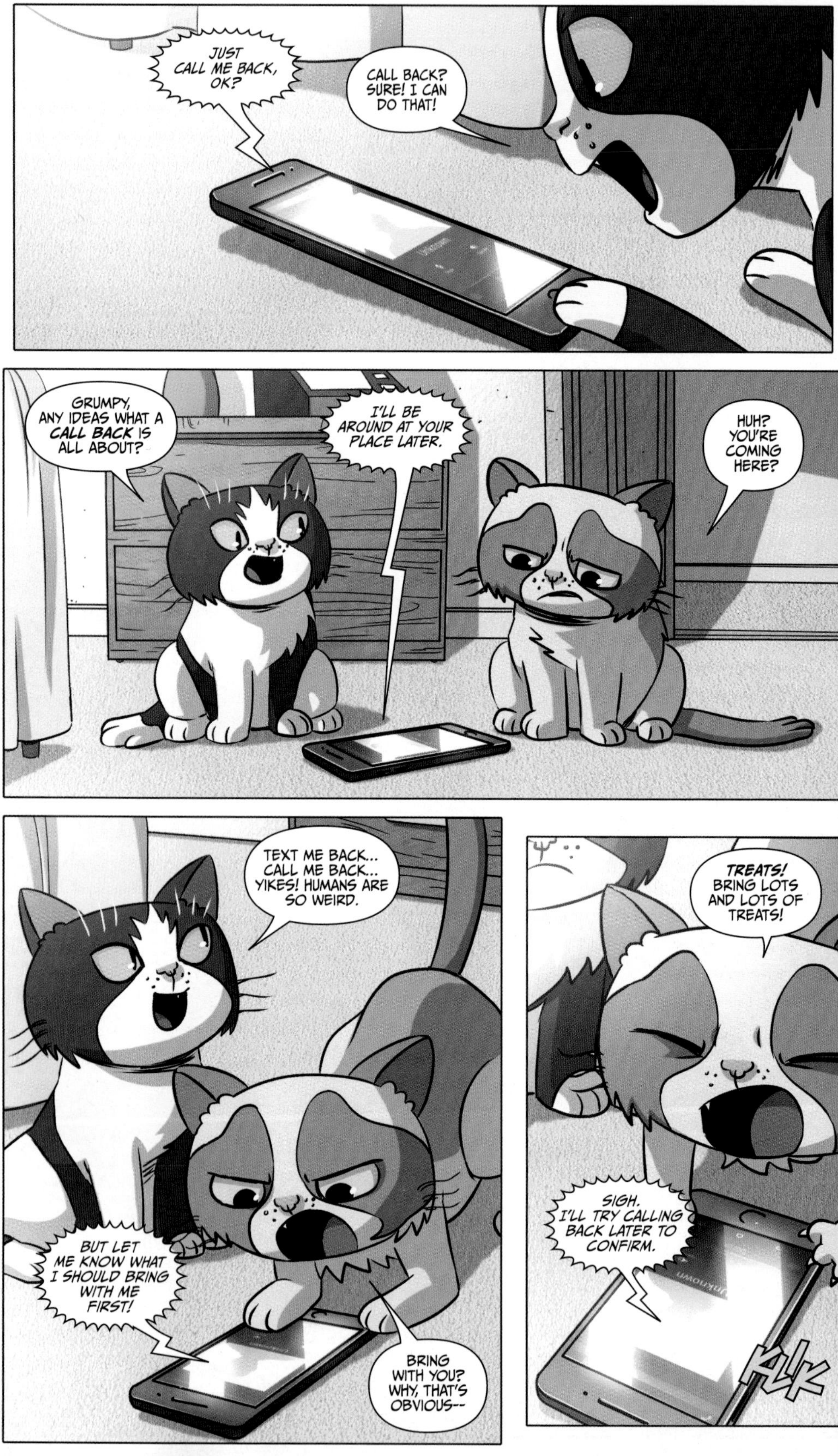
JUST CALL ME BACK, OK?
CALL BACK? SURE! I CAN DO THAT!
GRUMPY, ANY IDEAS WHAT A CALL BACK IS ALL ABOUT?
I'LL BE AROUND AT YOUR PLACE LATER.
HUH? YOU'RE COMING HERE?
TEXT ME BACK... CALL ME BACK... YIKES! HUMANS ARE SO WEIRD.
BUT LET ME KNOW WHAT I SHOULD BRING WITH ME FIRST!
BRING WITH YOU? WHY, THAT'S OBVIOUS--
TREATS! BRING LOTS AND LOTS OF TREATS!
SIGH. I'LL TRY CALLING BACK LATER TO CONFIRM.
KLIK

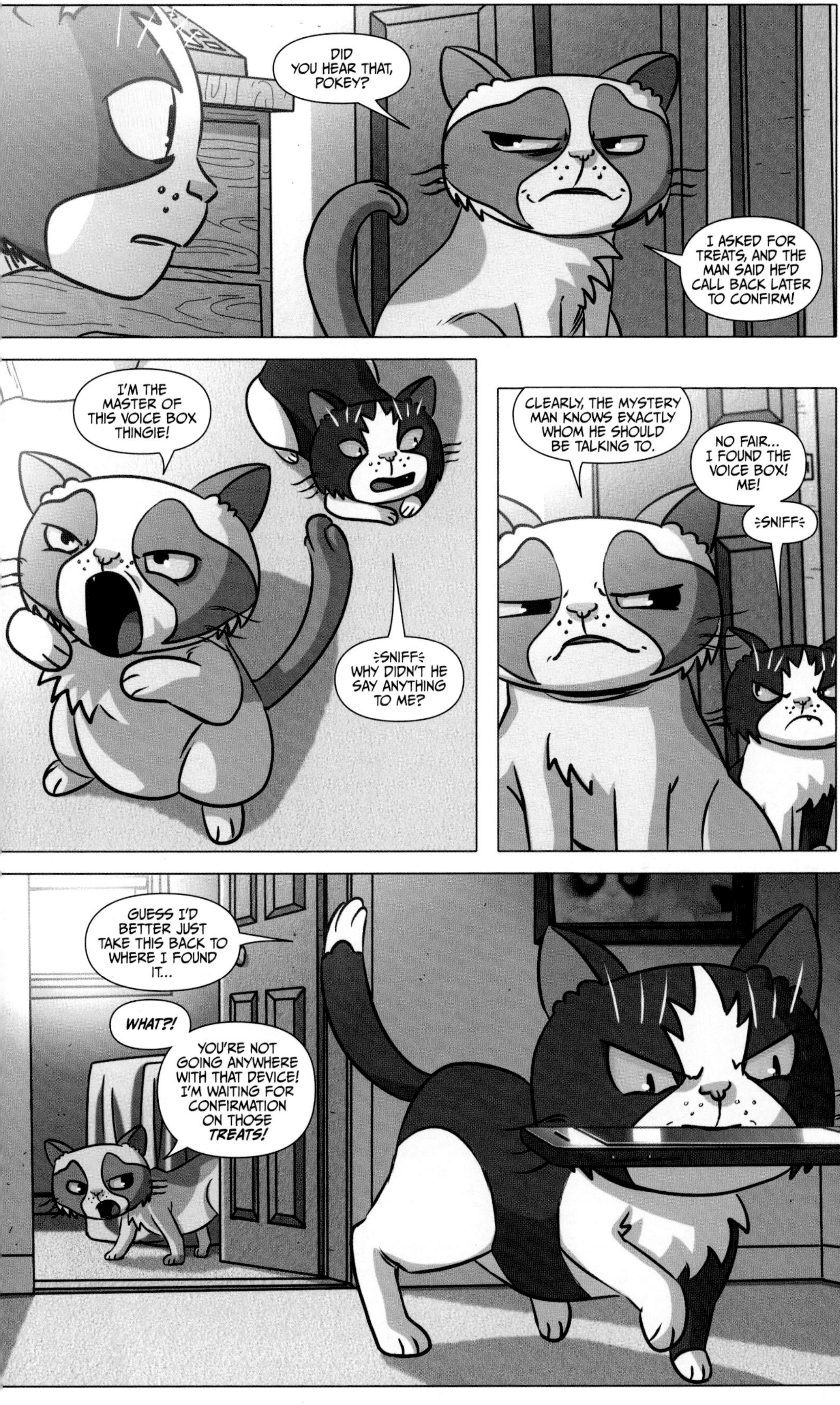
DID YOU HEAR THAT, POKEY?
I ASKED FOR TREATS, AND THE MAN SAID HE'D CALL BACK LATER TO CONFIRM!
I'M THE MASTER OF THIS VOICE BOX THINGIE!
≑SNIFF≑ WHY DIDN'T HE SAY ANYTHING TO ME?
CLEARLY, THE MYSTERY MAN KNOWS EXACTLY WHOM HE SHOULD BE TALKING TO.
NO FAIR... I FOUND THE VOICE BOX! ME!
≑SNIFF≑
GUESS I'D BETTER JUST TAKE THIS BACK TO WHERE I FOUND IT...
WHAT?!
YOU'RE NOT GOING ANYWHERE WITH THAT DEVICE! I'M WAITING FOR CONFIRMATION ON THOSE TREATS!

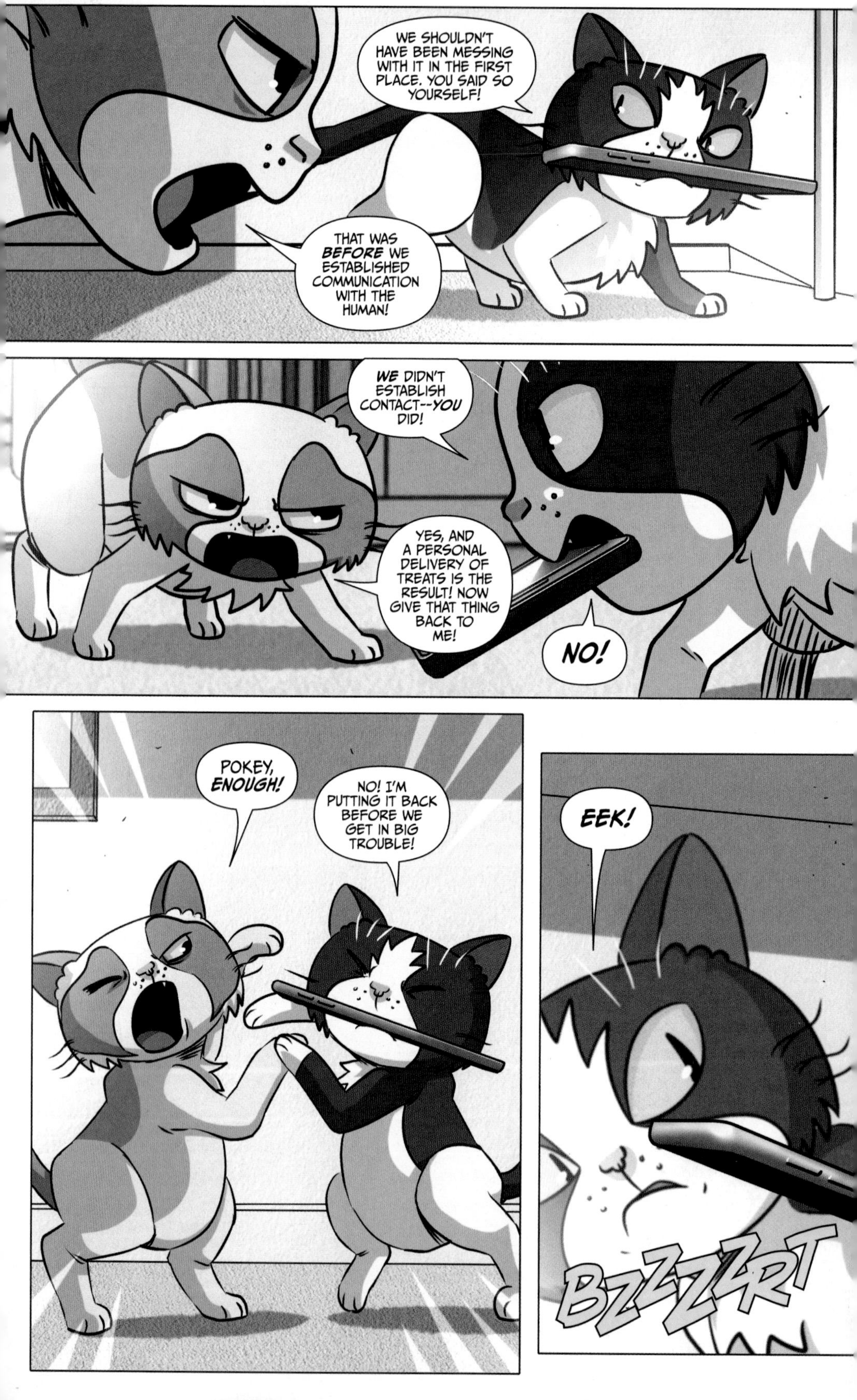
WE SHOULDN'T HAVE BEEN MESSING WITH IT IN THE FIRST PLACE. YOU SAID SO YOURSELF!
THAT WAS *BEFORE* WE ESTABLISHED COMMUNICATION WITH THE HUMAN!
WE DIDN'T ESTABLISH CONTACT--*YOU* DID!
YES, AND A PERSONAL DELIVERY OF TREATS IS THE RESULT! NOW GIVE THAT THING BACK TO ME!
NO!
POKEY, *ENOUGH!*
NO! I'M PUTTING IT BACK BEFORE WE GET IN BIG TROUBLE!
EEK!
BZZZZRT

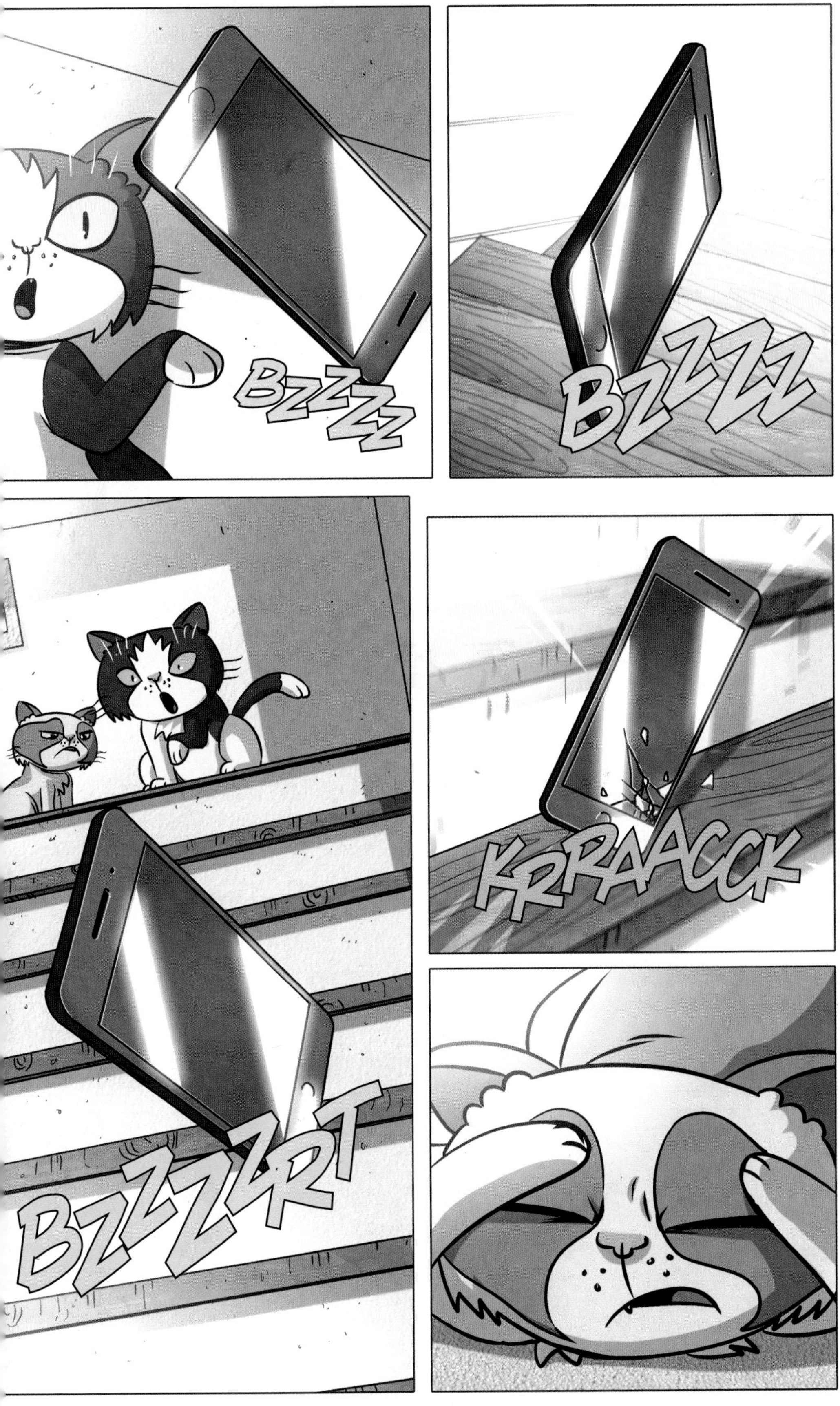
BZZZZ
BZZZZZ
BZZZZRT
KRRAACCK

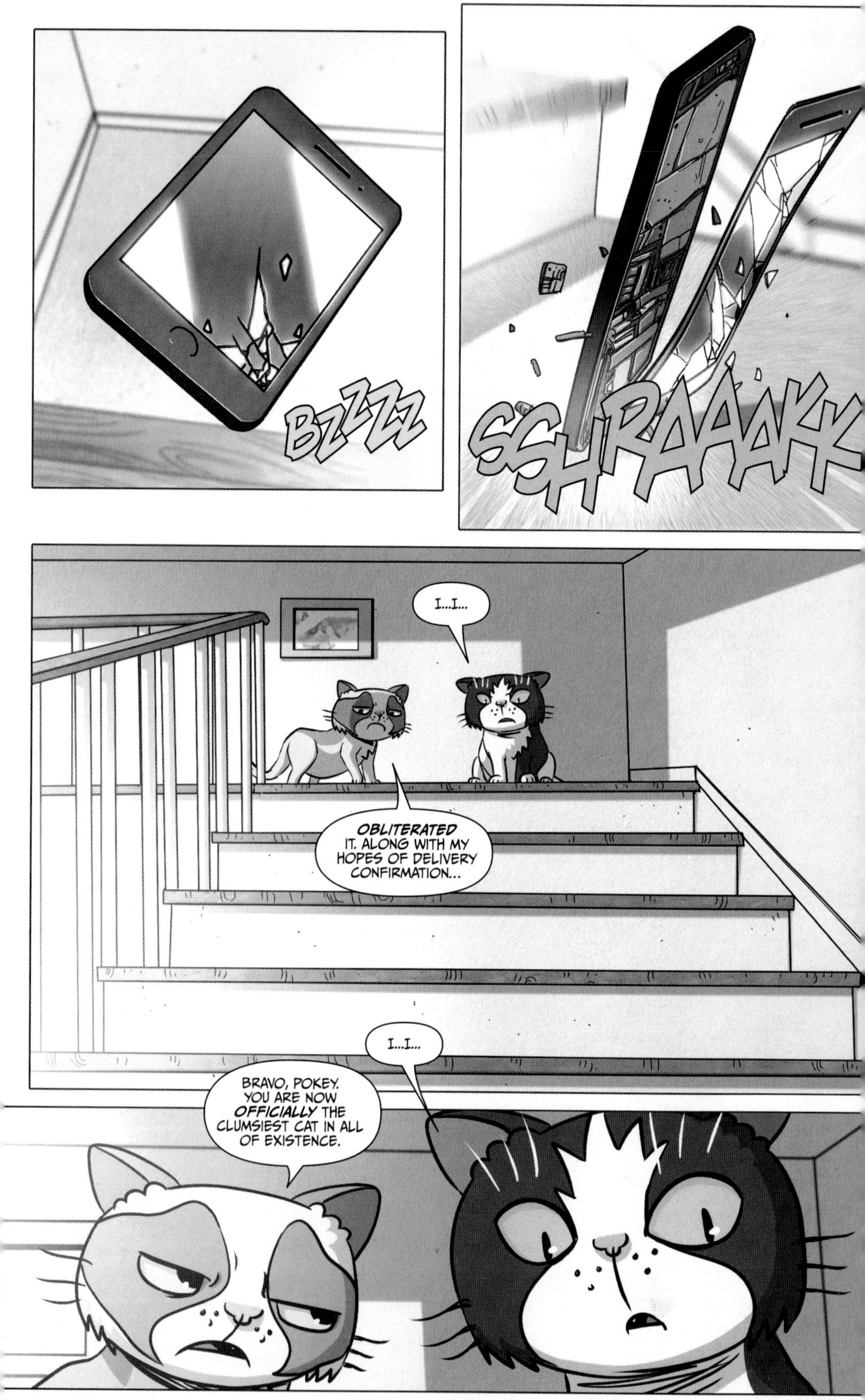
BZZZZ
SSHRAAAKK
I...I...
OBLITERATED IT. ALONG WITH MY HOPES OF DELIVERY CONFIRMATION...
I...I...
BRAVO, POKEY. YOU ARE NOW OFFICIALLY THE CLUMSIEST CAT IN ALL OF EXISTENCE.

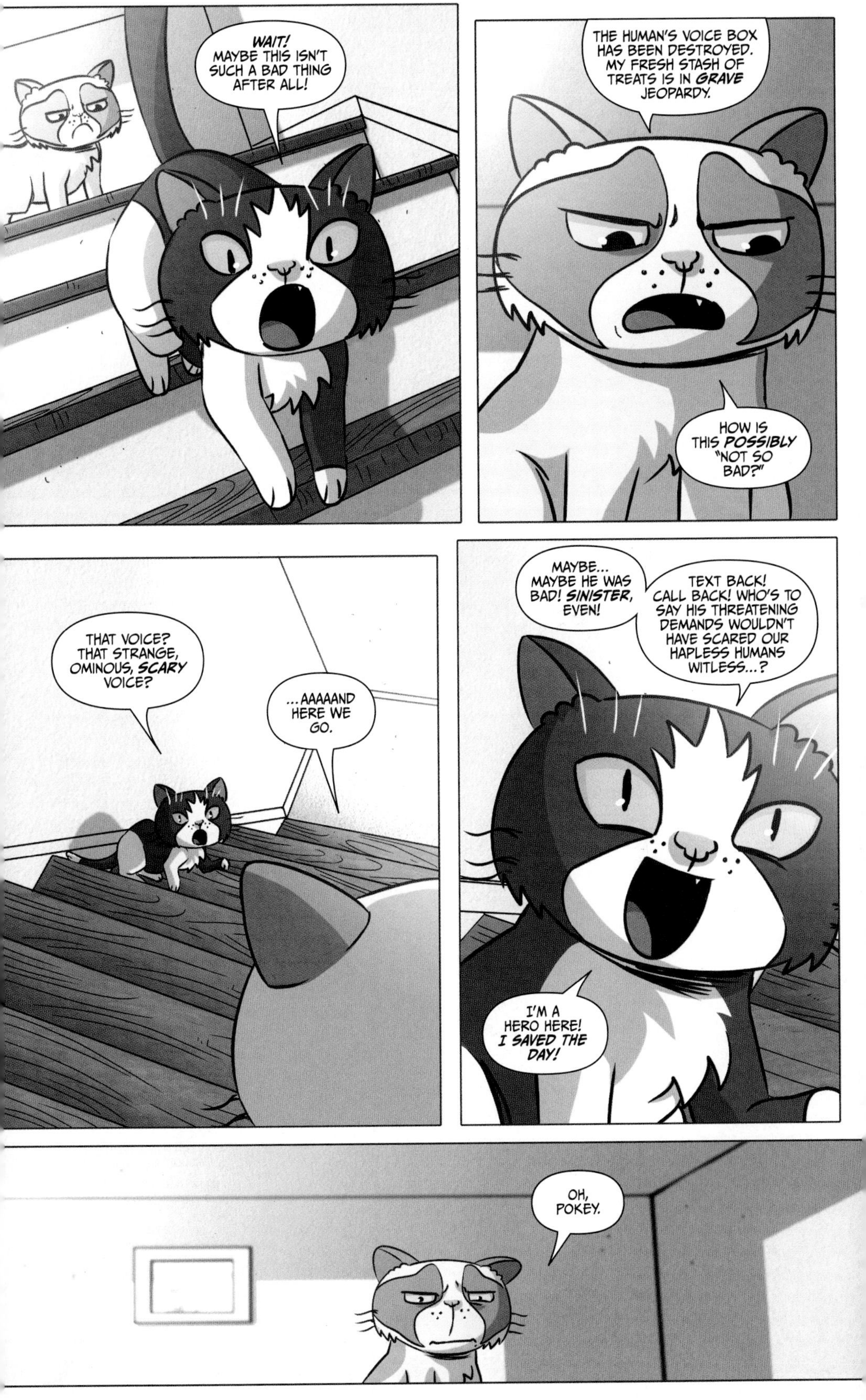

WAIT! MAYBE THIS ISN'T SUCH A BAD THING AFTER ALL!
THE HUMAN'S VOICE BOX HAS BEEN DESTROYED. MY FRESH STASH OF TREATS IS IN *GRAVE* JEOPARDY.
HOW IS THIS *POSSIBLY* "NOT SO BAD?"
THAT VOICE? THAT STRANGE, OMINOUS, *SCARY* VOICE?
...AAAAAND HERE WE GO.
MAYBE... MAYBE HE WAS BAD! *SINISTER*, EVEN!
TEXT BACK! CALL BACK! WHO'S TO SAY HIS THREATENING DEMANDS WOULDN'T HAVE SCARED OUR HAPLESS HUMANS WITLESS...?
I'M A HERO HERE! *I SAVED THE DAY!*
OH, POKEY.

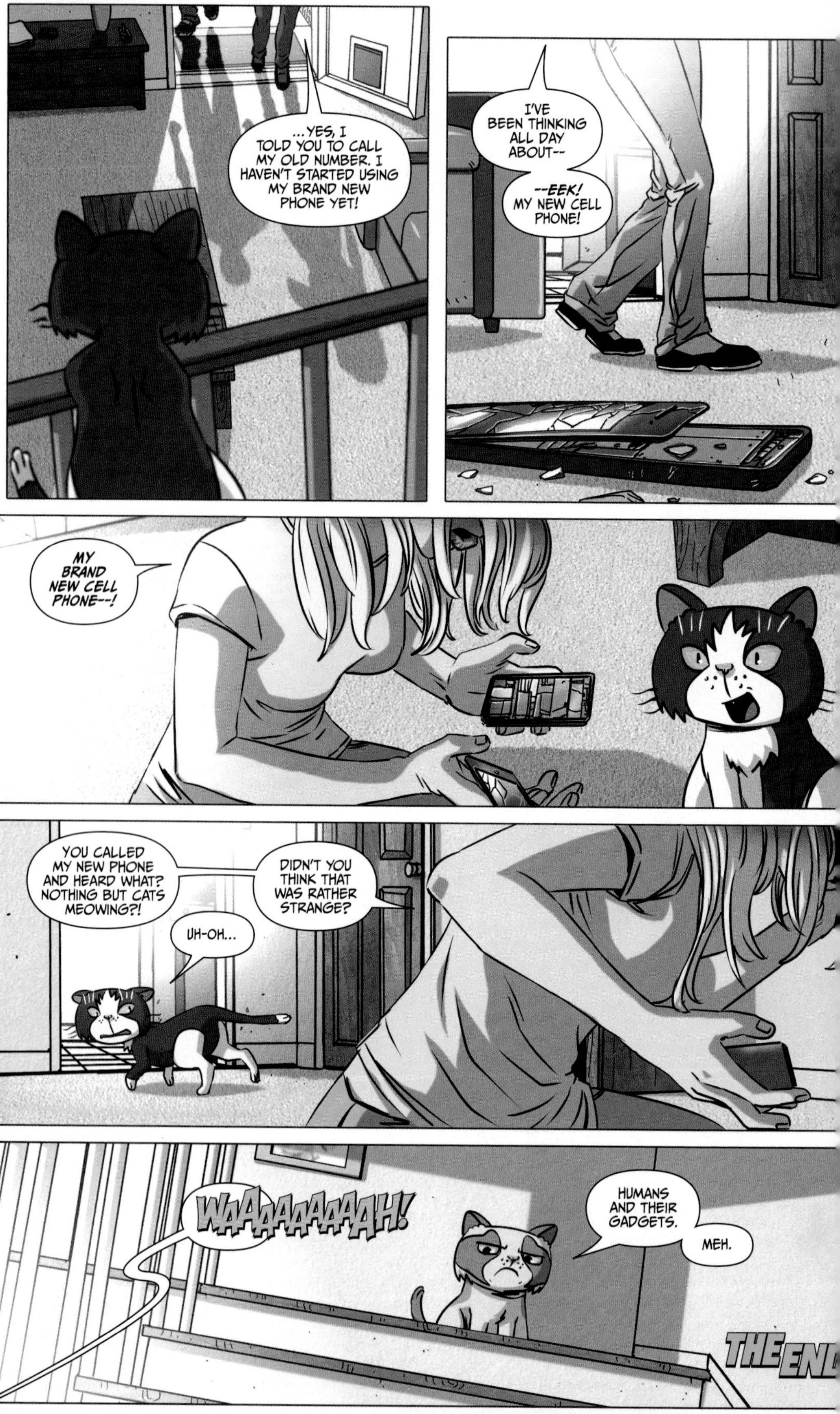
...YES, I TOLD YOU TO CALL MY OLD NUMBER. I HAVEN'T STARTED USING MY BRAND NEW PHONE YET!
I'VE BEEN THINKING ALL DAY ABOUT--
--EEK! MY NEW CELL PHONE!
MY BRAND NEW CELL PHONE--!
YOU CALLED MY NEW PHONE AND HEARD WHAT? NOTHING BUT CATS MEOWING?!
DIDN'T YOU THINK THAT WAS RATHER STRANGE?
UH-OH...
WAAAAAAAAAH!
HUMANS AND THEIR GADGETS.
MEH.
THE END

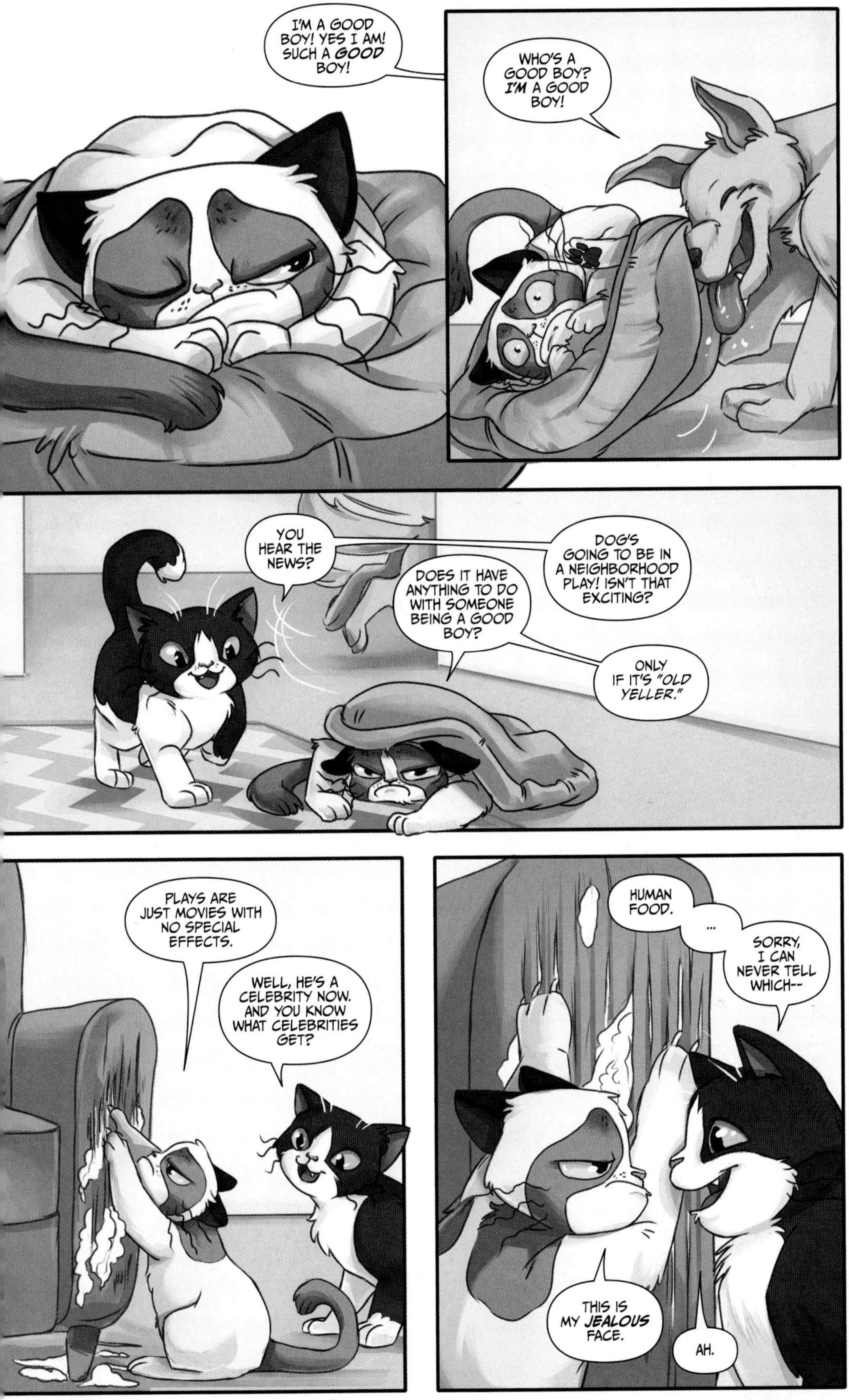
I'M A GOOD BOY! YES I AM! SUCH A GOOD BOY!
WHO'S A GOOD BOY? I'M A GOOD BOY!
YOU HEAR THE NEWS?
DOG'S GOING TO BE IN A NEIGHBORHOOD PLAY! ISN'T THAT EXCITING?
DOES IT HAVE ANYTHING TO DO WITH SOMEONE BEING A GOOD BOY?
ONLY IF IT'S "OLD YELLER."
PLAYS ARE JUST MOVIES WITH NO SPECIAL EFFECTS.
WELL, HE'S A CELEBRITY NOW. AND YOU KNOW WHAT CELEBRITIES GET?
HUMAN FOOD.
...
SORRY, I CAN NEVER TELL WHICH--
THIS IS MY JEALOUS FACE.
AH.

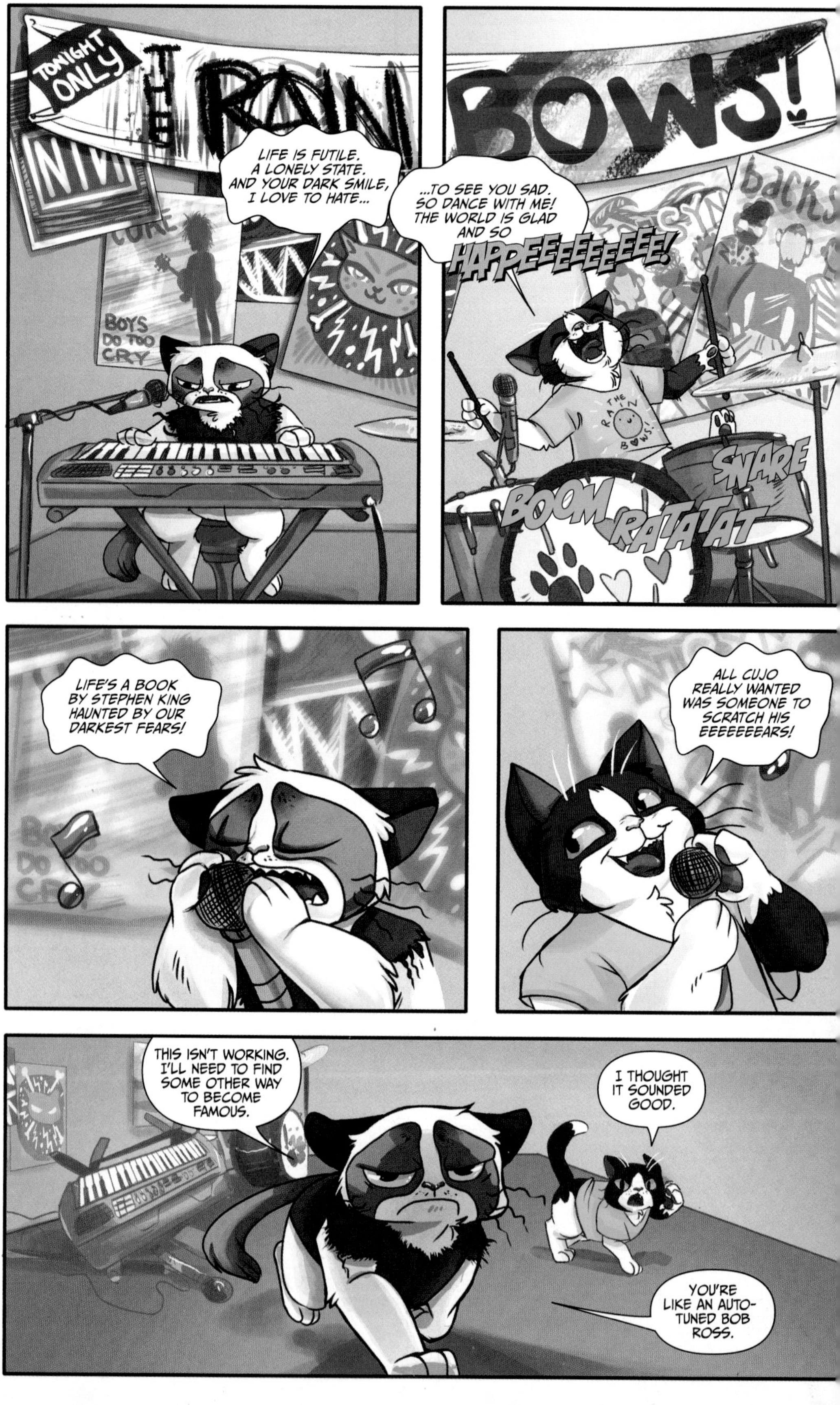
TONIGHT ONLY
THE RAIN
BOWS!
LIFE IS FUTILE. A LONELY STATE. AND YOUR DARK SMILE, I LOVE TO HATE...
...TO SEE YOU SAD. SO DANCE WITH ME! THE WORLD IS GLAD AND SO HAPPEEEEEEEEE!
BOYS DO TOO CRY
SNARE
BOOM
RATATAT
LIFE'S A BOOK BY STEPHEN KING HAUNTED BY OUR DARKEST FEARS!
ALL CUJO REALLY WANTED WAS SOMEONE TO SCRATCH HIS EEEEEEEARS!
THIS ISN'T WORKING. I'LL NEED TO FIND SOME OTHER WAY TO BECOME FAMOUS.
I THOUGHT IT SOUNDED GOOD.
YOU'RE LIKE AN AUTO-TUNED BOB ROSS.

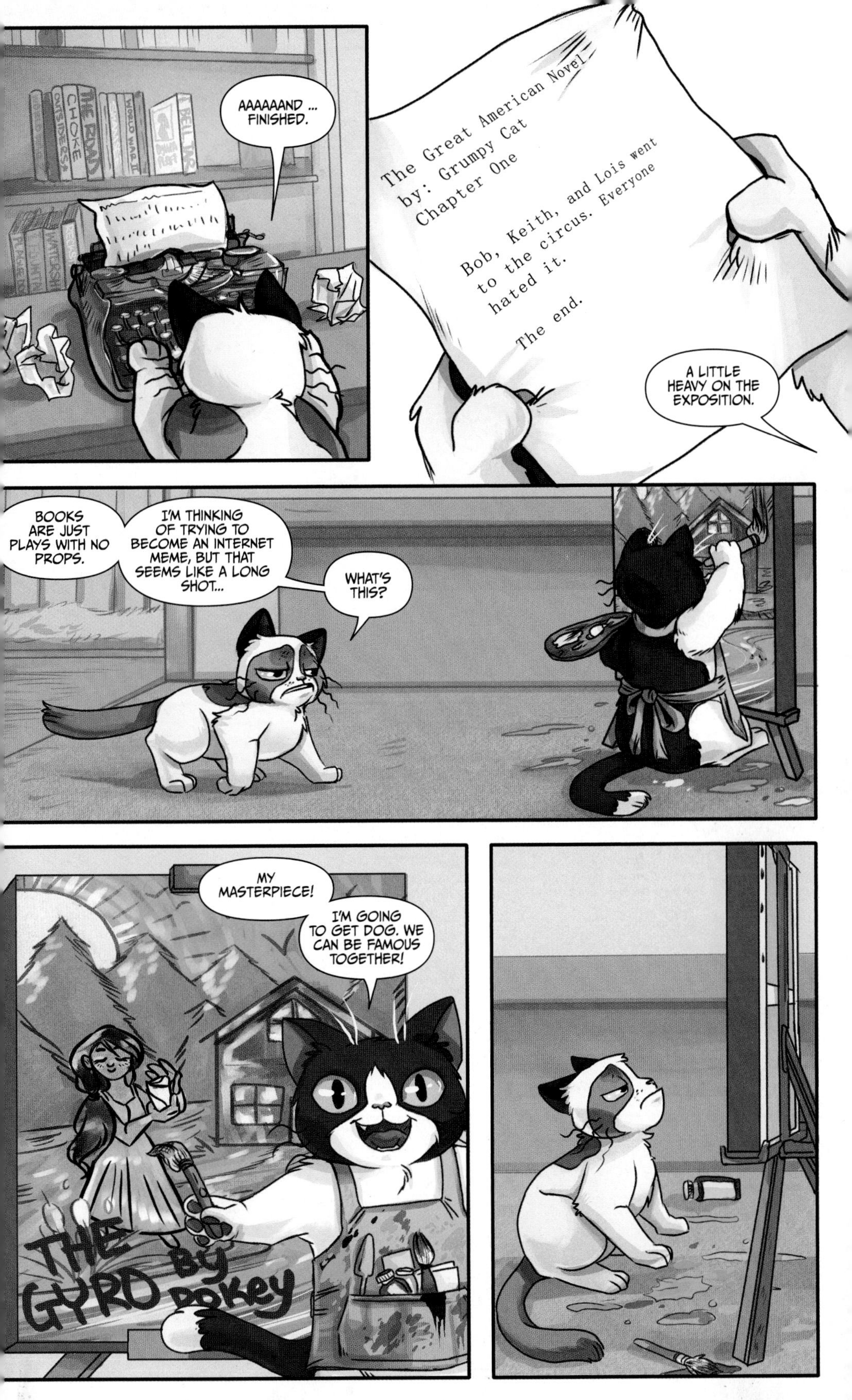

AAAAAAND ... FINISHED.
The Great American Novel
by: Grumpy Cat
Chapter One
Bob, Keith, and Lois went to the circus. Everyone hated it.
The end.
A LITTLE HEAVY ON THE EXPOSITION.
BOOKS ARE JUST PLAYS WITH NO PROPS.
I'M THINKING OF TRYING TO BECOME AN INTERNET MEME, BUT THAT SEEMS LIKE A LONG SHOT...
WHAT'S THIS?
MY MASTERPIECE!
I'M GOING TO GET DOG. WE CAN BE FAMOUS TOGETHER!
THE GYRO By Pokey

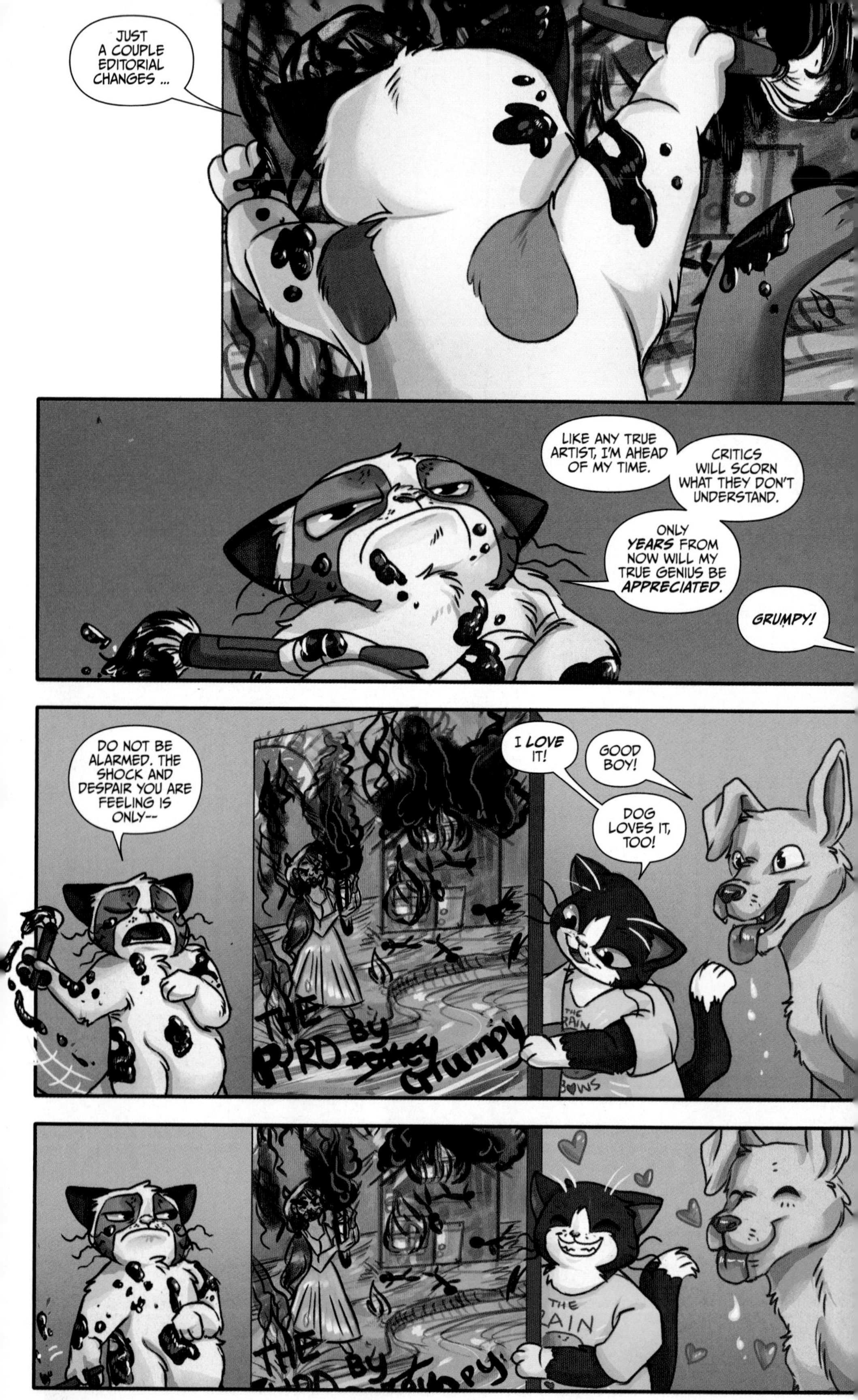

JUST A COUPLE EDITORIAL CHANGES ...
LIKE ANY TRUE ARTIST, I'M AHEAD OF MY TIME.
CRITICS WILL SCORN WHAT THEY DON'T UNDERSTAND.
ONLY *YEARS* FROM NOW WILL MY TRUE GENIUS BE *APPRECIATED*.
GRUMPY!
DO NOT BE ALARMED. THE SHOCK AND DESPAIR YOU ARE FEELING IS ONLY--
I *LOVE* IT!
GOOD BOY!
DOG LOVES IT, TOO!
THE PYRO BY GRUMPY
THE RAIN BOWS
THE RAIN

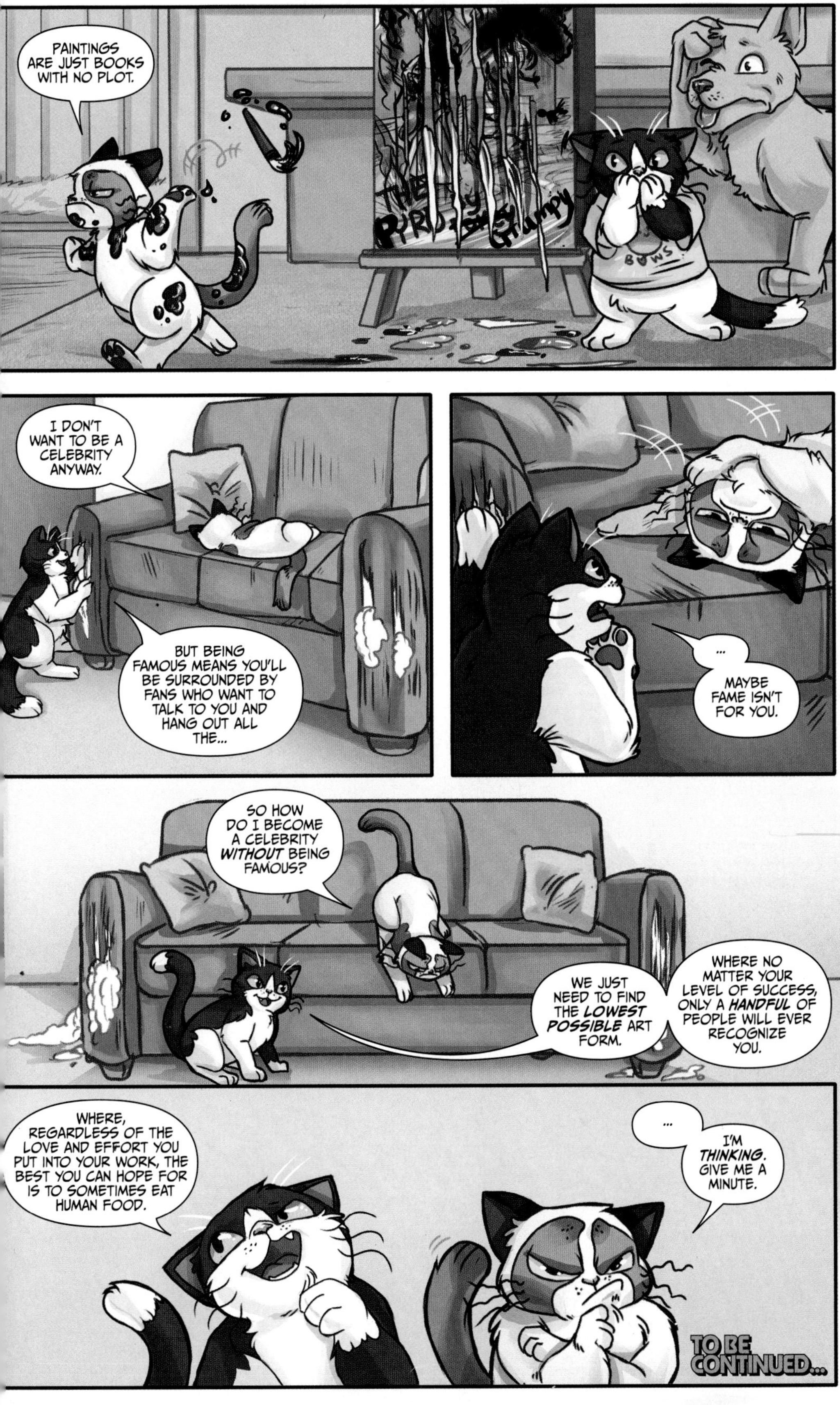

PAINTINGS ARE JUST BOOKS WITH NO PLOT.
BOWS
I DON'T WANT TO BE A CELEBRITY ANYWAY.
BUT BEING FAMOUS MEANS YOU'LL BE SURROUNDED BY FANS WHO WANT TO TALK TO YOU AND HANG OUT ALL THE...
...
MAYBE FAME ISN'T FOR YOU.
SO HOW DO I BECOME A CELEBRITY *WITHOUT* BEING FAMOUS?
WE JUST NEED TO FIND THE ***LOWEST POSSIBLE*** ART FORM.
WHERE NO MATTER YOUR LEVEL OF SUCCESS, ONLY A ***HANDFUL*** OF PEOPLE WILL EVER RECOGNIZE YOU.
WHERE, REGARDLESS OF THE LOVE AND EFFORT YOU PUT INTO YOUR WORK, THE BEST YOU CAN HOPE FOR IS TO SOMETIMES EAT HUMAN FOOD.
...
I'M *THINKING*. GIVE ME A MINUTE.
TO BE CONTINUED...

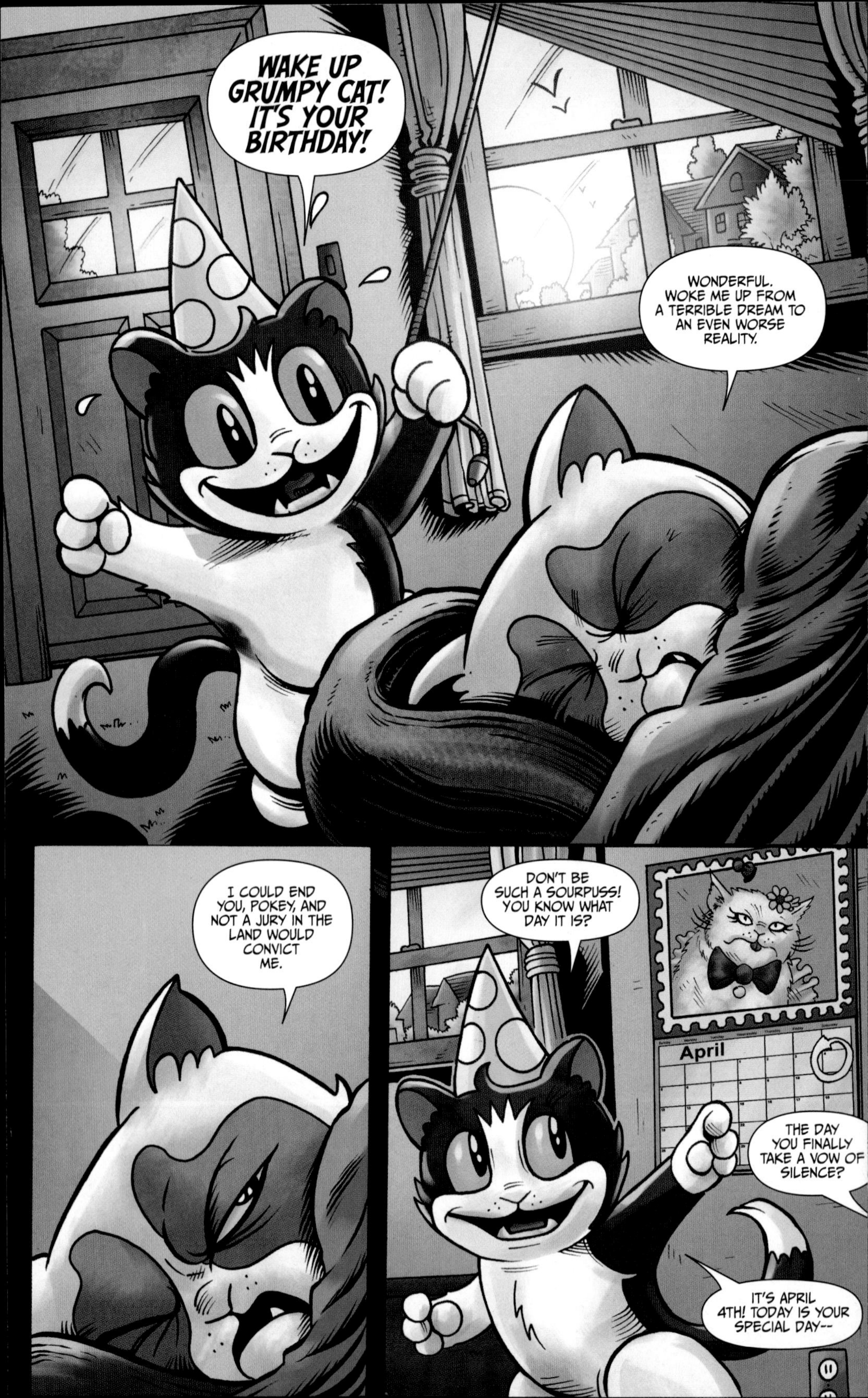
WAKE UP GRUMPY CAT! IT'S YOUR BIRTHDAY!
WONDERFUL. WOKE ME UP FROM A TERRIBLE DREAM TO AN EVEN WORSE REALITY.
I COULD END YOU, POKEY, AND NOT A JURY IN THE LAND WOULD CONVICT ME.
DON'T BE SUCH A SOURPUSS! YOU KNOW WHAT DAY IT IS?
April
THE DAY YOU FINALLY TAKE A VOW OF SILENCE?
IT'S APRIL 4TH! TODAY IS YOUR SPECIAL DAY--

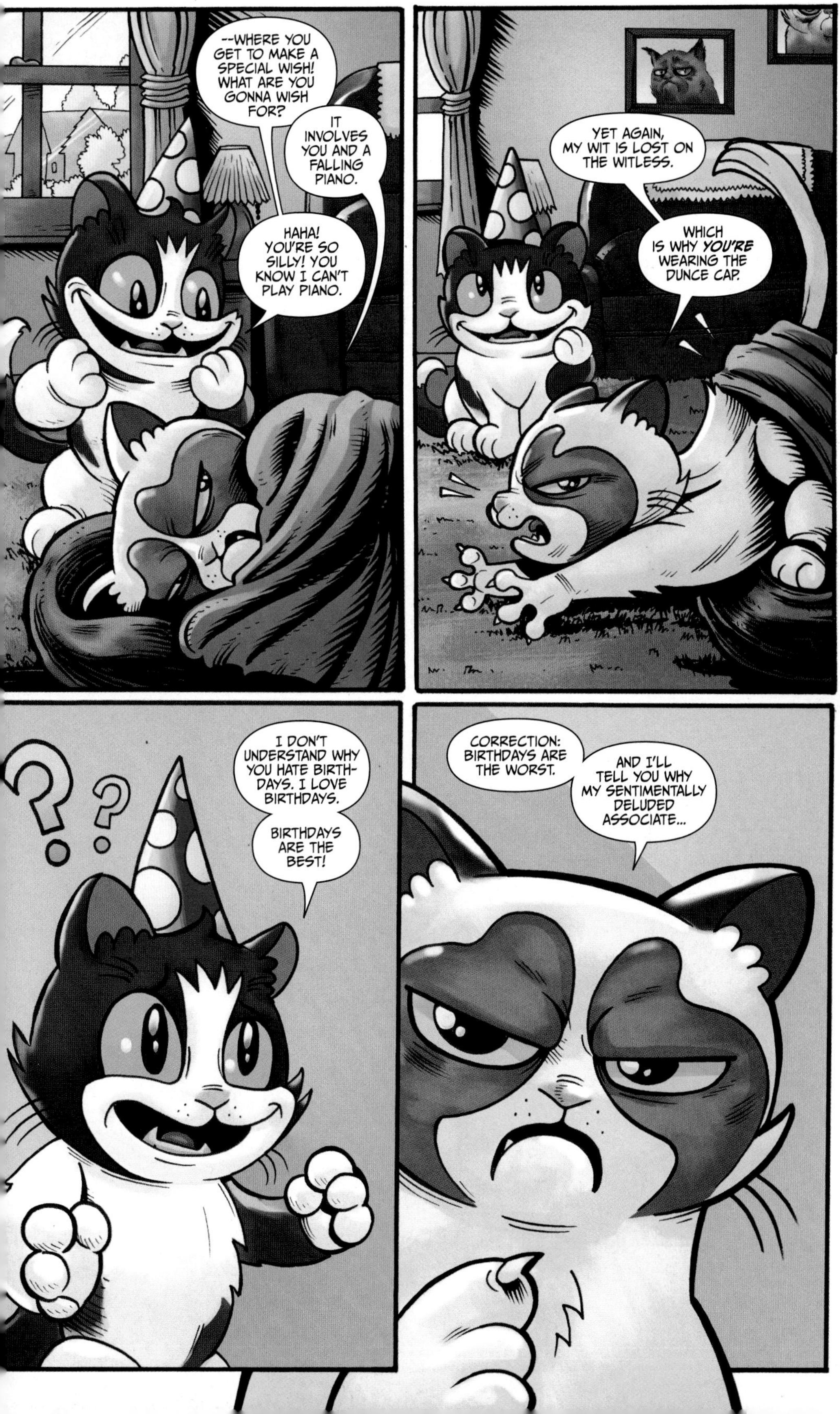
--WHERE YOU GET TO MAKE A SPECIAL WISH! WHAT ARE YOU GONNA WISH FOR?
IT INVOLVES YOU AND A FALLING PIANO.
HAHA! YOU'RE SO SILLY! YOU KNOW I CAN'T PLAY PIANO.
YET AGAIN, MY WIT IS LOST ON THE WITLESS.
WHICH IS WHY *YOU'RE* WEARING THE DUNCE CAP.
I DON'T UNDERSTAND WHY YOU HATE BIRTH-DAYS. I LOVE BIRTHDAYS.
BIRTHDAYS ARE THE BEST!
CORRECTION: BIRTHDAYS ARE THE WORST.
AND I'LL TELL YOU WHY MY SENTIMENTALLY DELUDED ASSOCIATE...

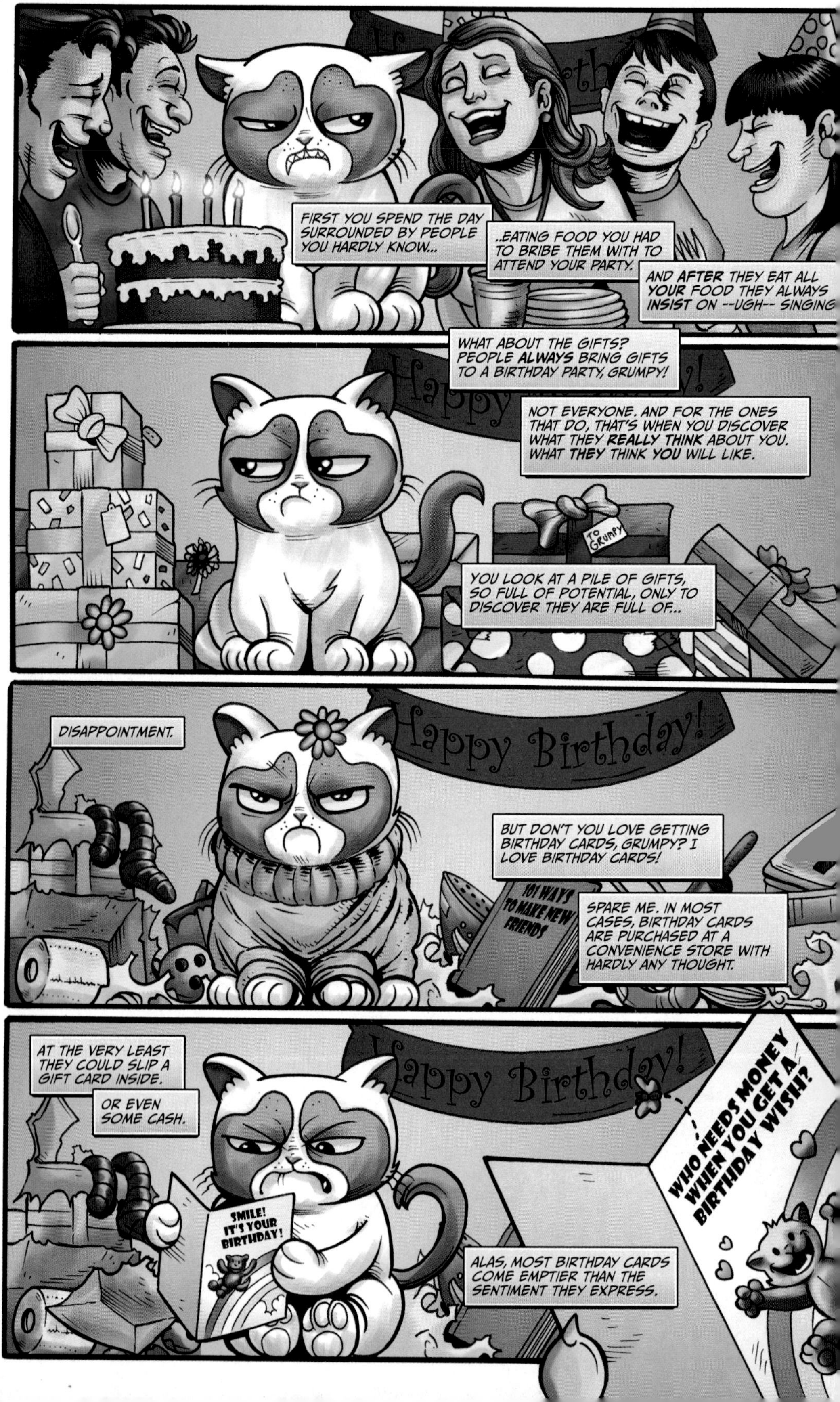
FIRST YOU SPEND THE DAY SURROUNDED BY PEOPLE YOU HARDLY KNOW...
..EATING FOOD YOU HAD TO BRIBE THEM WITH TO ATTEND YOUR PARTY.
AND AFTER THEY EAT ALL YOUR FOOD THEY ALWAYS INSIST ON --UGH-- SINGING
WHAT ABOUT THE GIFTS? PEOPLE ALWAYS BRING GIFTS TO A BIRTHDAY PARTY, GRUMPY!
NOT EVERYONE. AND FOR THE ONES THAT DO, THAT'S WHEN YOU DISCOVER WHAT THEY REALLY THINK ABOUT YOU. WHAT THEY THINK YOU WILL LIKE.
TO GRUMPY
YOU LOOK AT A PILE OF GIFTS, SO FULL OF POTENTIAL, ONLY TO DISCOVER THEY ARE FULL OF...
DISAPPOINTMENT.
Happy Birthday!
BUT DON'T YOU LOVE GETTING BIRTHDAY CARDS, GRUMPY? I LOVE BIRTHDAY CARDS!
101 WAYS TO MAKE NEW FRIENDS
SPARE ME. IN MOST CASES, BIRTHDAY CARDS ARE PURCHASED AT A CONVENIENCE STORE WITH HARDLY ANY THOUGHT.
AT THE VERY LEAST THEY COULD SLIP A GIFT CARD INSIDE.
OR EVEN SOME CASH.
SMILE! IT'S YOUR BIRTHDAY!
WHO NEEDS MONEY WHEN YOU GET A BIRTHDAY WISH?
ALAS, MOST BIRTHDAY CARDS COME EMPTIER THAN THE SENTIMENT THEY EXPRESS.

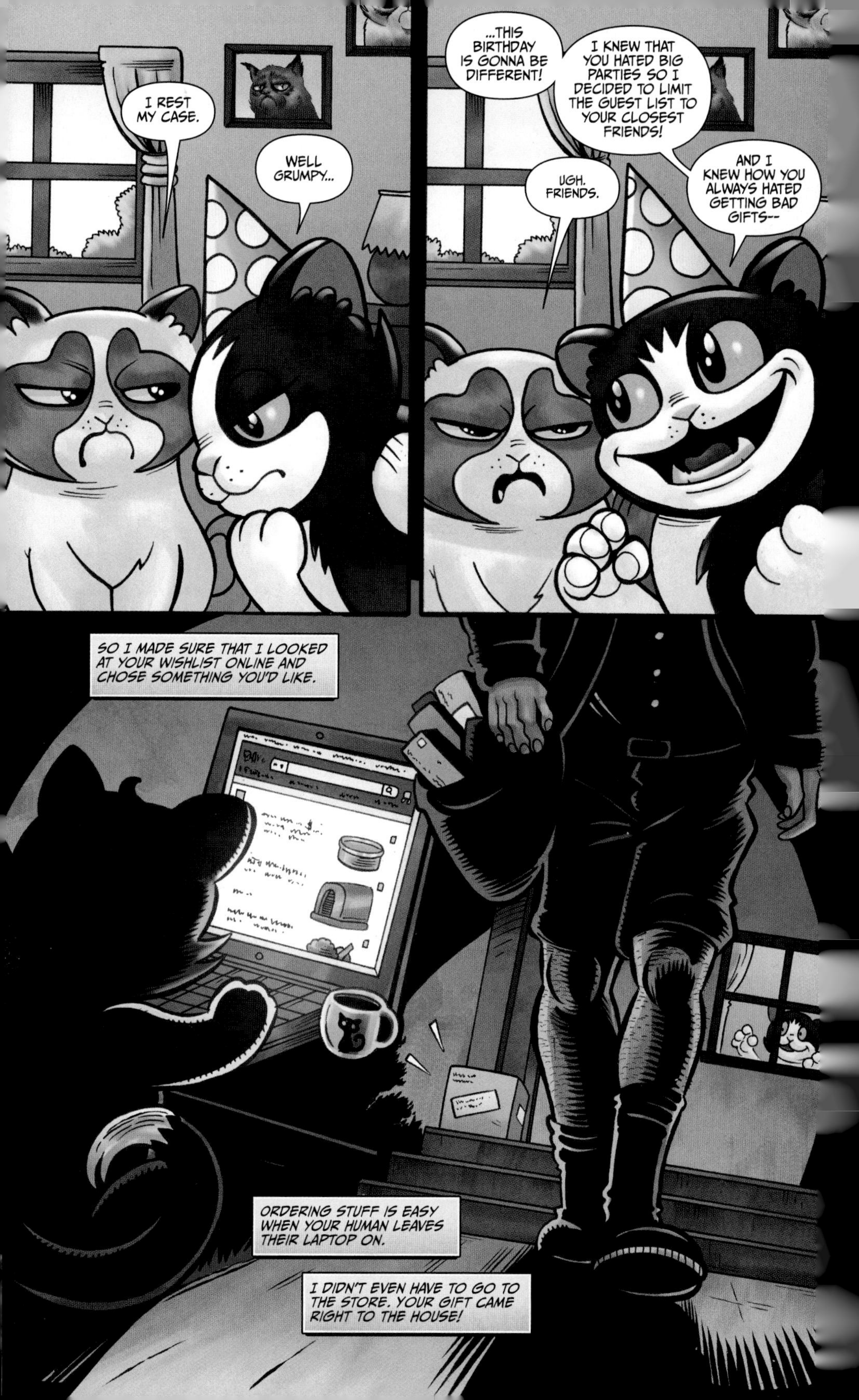
I REST MY CASE.
WELL GRUMPY...
...THIS BIRTHDAY IS GONNA BE DIFFERENT!
I KNEW THAT YOU HATED BIG PARTIES SO I DECIDED TO LIMIT THE GUEST LIST TO YOUR CLOSEST FRIENDS!
UGH. FRIENDS.
AND I KNEW HOW YOU ALWAYS HATED GETTING BAD GIFTS--
SO I MADE SURE THAT I LOOKED AT YOUR WISHLIST ONLINE AND CHOSE SOMETHING YOU'D LIKE.
ORDERING STUFF IS EASY WHEN YOUR HUMAN LEAVES THEIR LAPTOP ON.
I DIDN'T EVEN HAVE TO GO TO THE STORE. YOUR GIFT CAME RIGHT TO THE HOUSE!

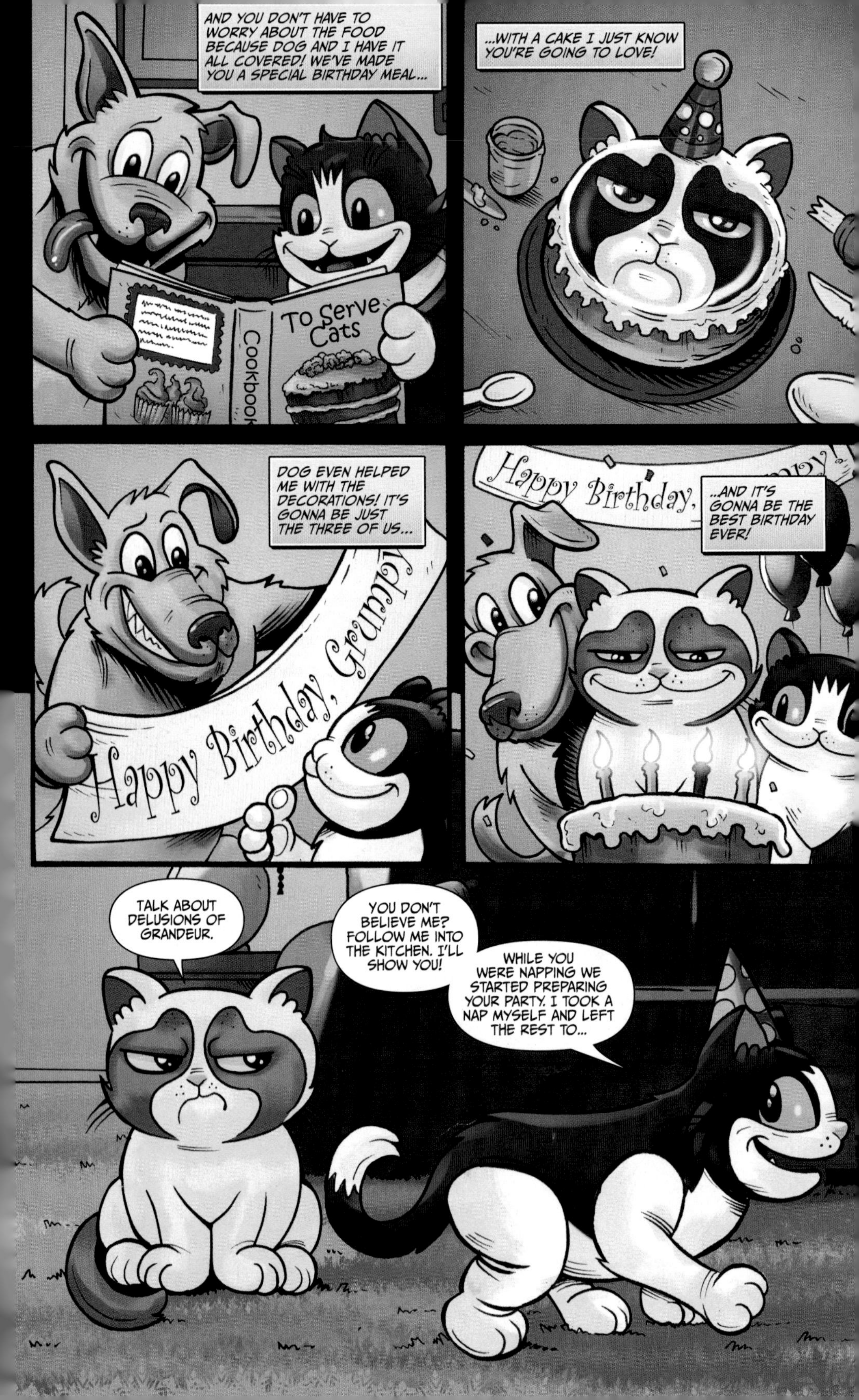
AND YOU DON'T HAVE TO WORRY ABOUT THE FOOD BECAUSE DOG AND I HAVE IT ALL COVERED! WE'VE MADE YOU A SPECIAL BIRTHDAY MEAL...
To Serve Cats
Cookbook
...WITH A CAKE I JUST KNOW YOU'RE GOING TO LOVE!
DOG EVEN HELPED ME WITH THE DECORATIONS! IT'S GONNA BE JUST THE THREE OF US...
Happy Birthday, Grumpy
Happy Birthday,
...AND IT'S GONNA BE THE BEST BIRTHDAY EVER!
TALK ABOUT DELUSIONS OF GRANDEUR.
YOU DON'T BELIEVE ME? FOLLOW ME INTO THE KITCHEN. I'LL SHOW YOU!
WHILE YOU WERE NAPPING WE STARTED PREPARING YOUR PARTY. I TOOK A NAP MYSELF AND LEFT THE REST TO...

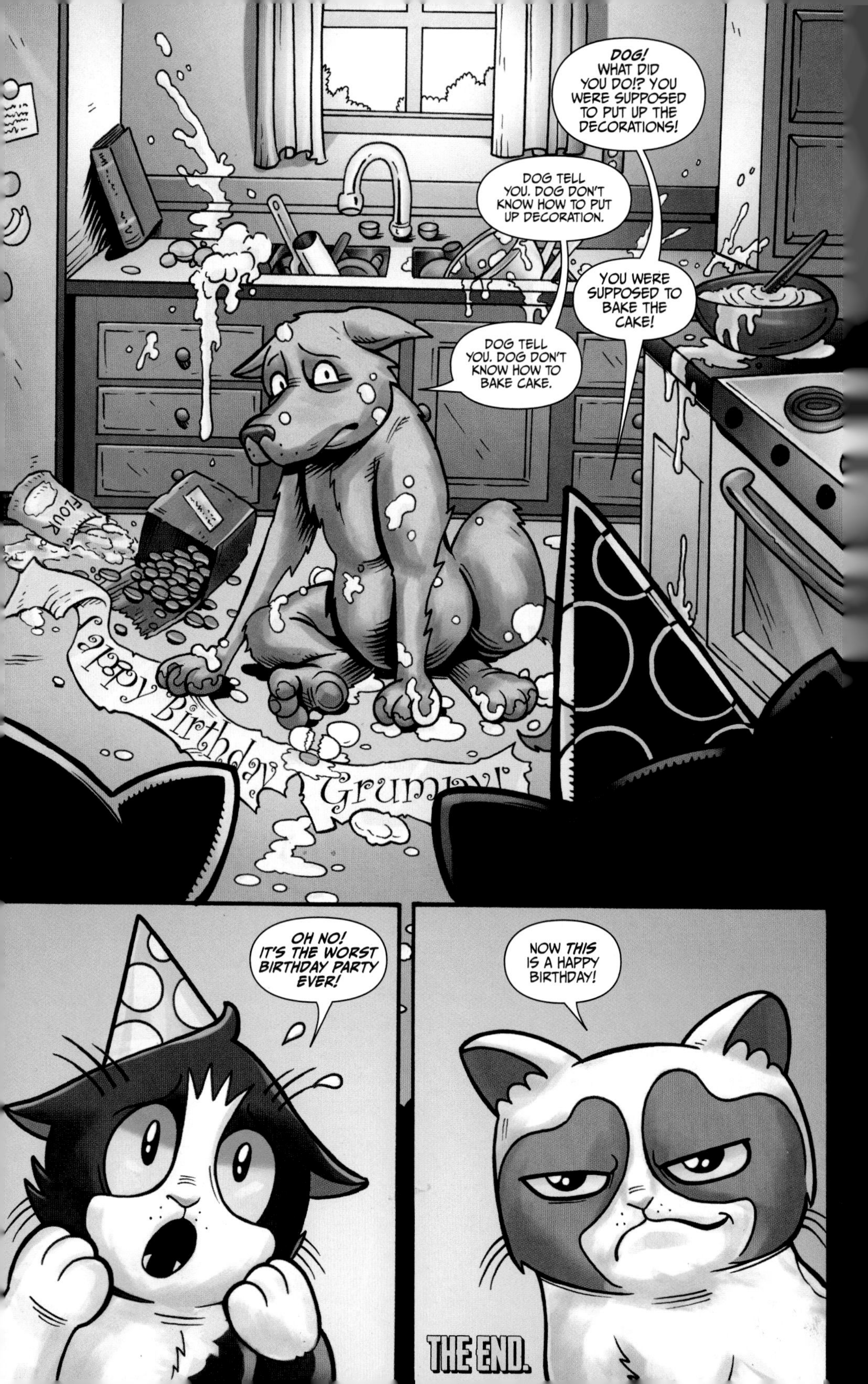
DOG! WHAT DID YOU DO!? YOU WERE SUPPOSED TO PUT UP THE DECORATIONS!
DOG TELL YOU. DOG DON'T KNOW HOW TO PUT UP DECORATION.
YOU WERE SUPPOSED TO BAKE THE CAKE!
DOG TELL YOU. DOG DON'T KNOW HOW TO BAKE CAKE.
FLOUR
Happy Birthday Grumpy!
OH NO! IT'S THE WORST BIRTHDAY PARTY EVER!
NOW THIS IS A HAPPY BIRTHDAY!
THE END.

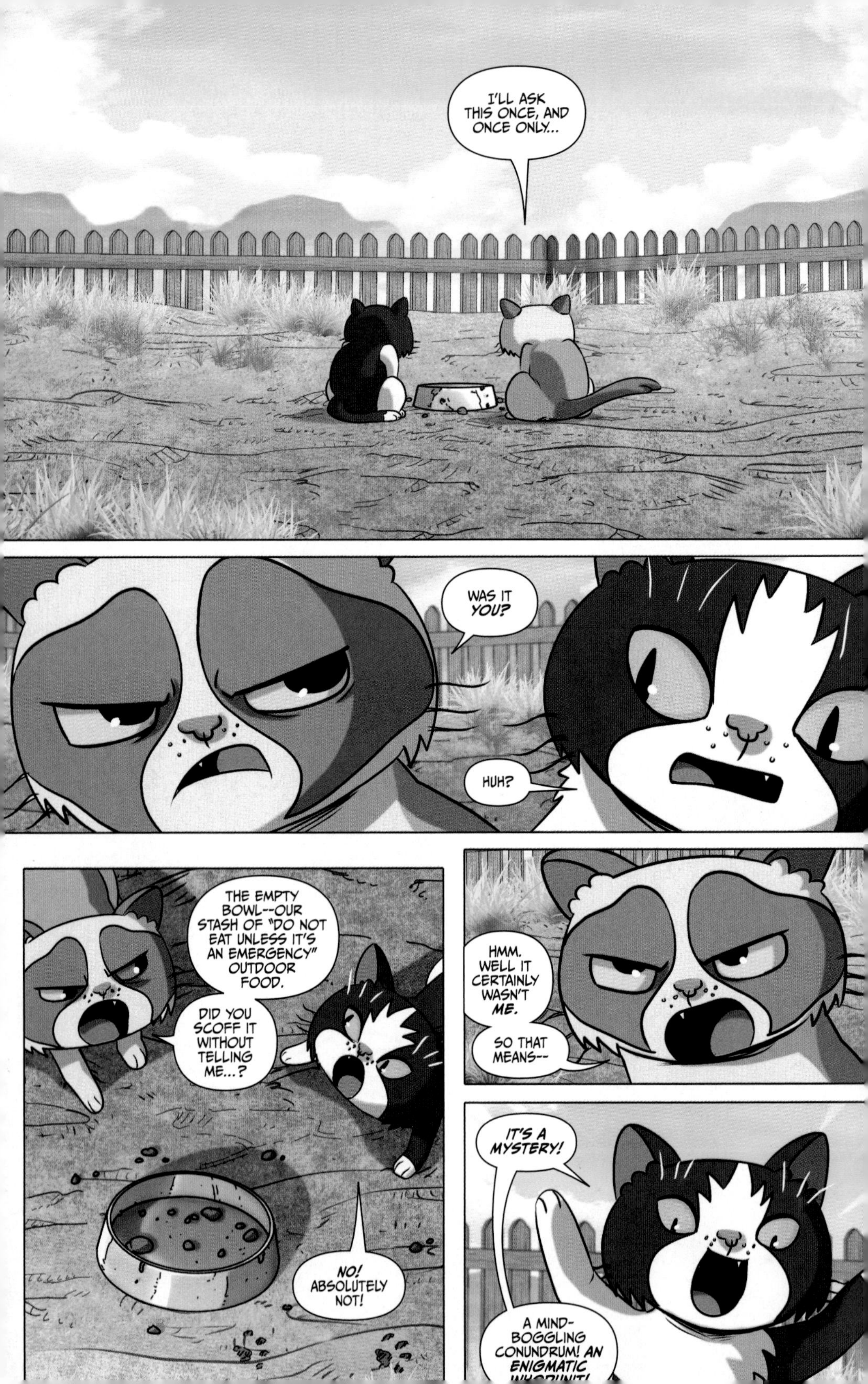
I'LL ASK THIS ONCE, AND ONCE ONLY...
WAS IT *YOU?*
HUH?
THE EMPTY BOWL--OUR STASH OF "DO NOT EAT UNLESS IT'S AN EMERGENCY" OUTDOOR FOOD.
DID YOU SCOFF IT WITHOUT TELLING ME...?
NO! ABSOLUTELY NOT!
HMM. WELL IT CERTAINLY WASN'T *ME.*
SO THAT MEANS--
IT'S A MYSTERY!
A MIND-BOGGLING CONUNDRUM! *AN ENIGMATIC*

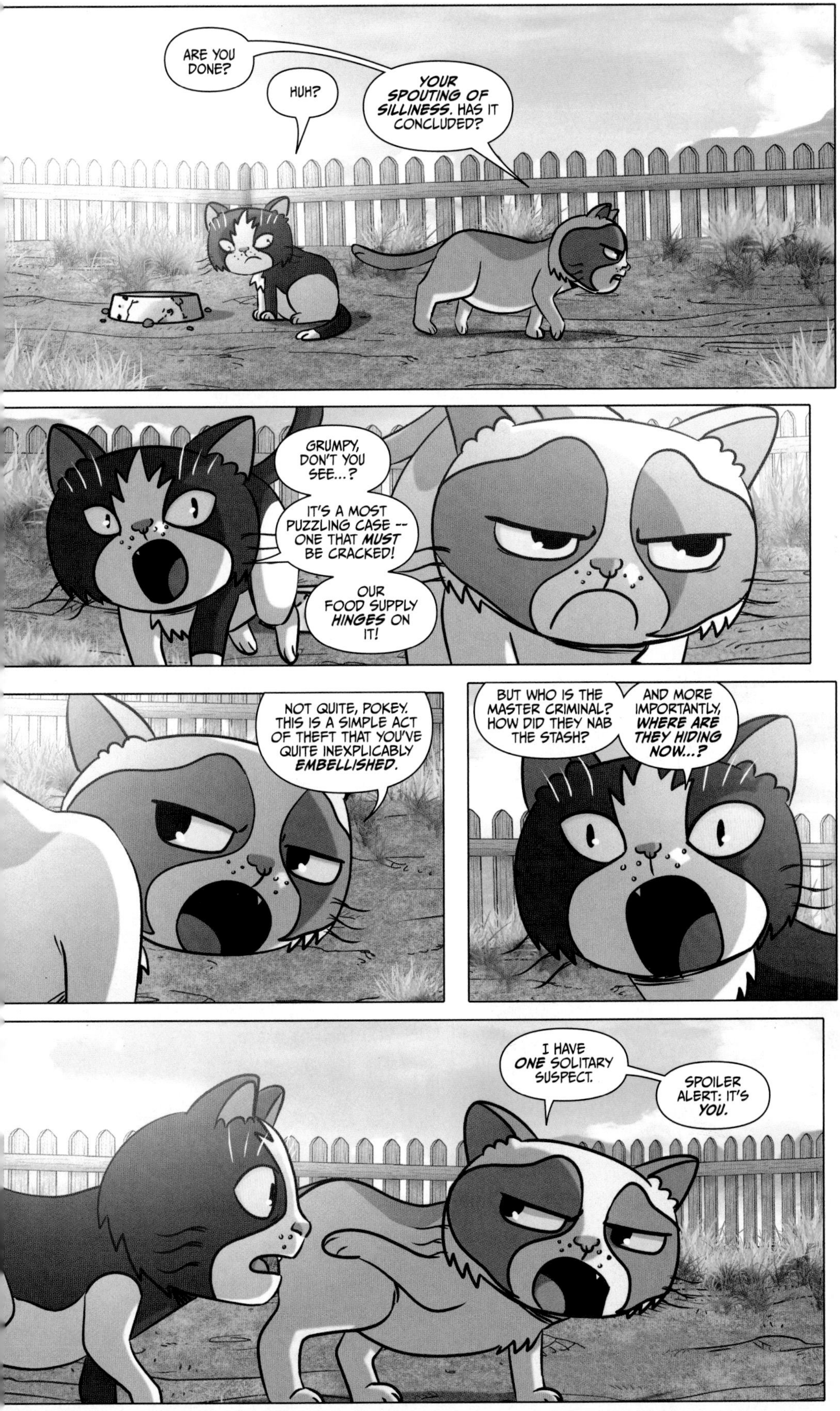

ARE YOU DONE?
HUH?
YOUR SPOUTING OF SILLINESS. HAS IT CONCLUDED?
GRUMPY, DON'T YOU SEE...?
IT'S A MOST PUZZLING CASE -- ONE THAT MUST BE CRACKED!
OUR FOOD SUPPLY HINGES ON IT!
NOT QUITE, POKEY. THIS IS A SIMPLE ACT OF THEFT THAT YOU'VE QUITE INEXPLICABLY EMBELLISHED.
BUT WHO IS THE MASTER CRIMINAL? HOW DID THEY NAB THE STASH?
AND MORE IMPORTANTLY, WHERE ARE THEY HIDING NOW...?
I HAVE ONE SOLITARY SUSPECT.
SPOILER ALERT: IT'S YOU.

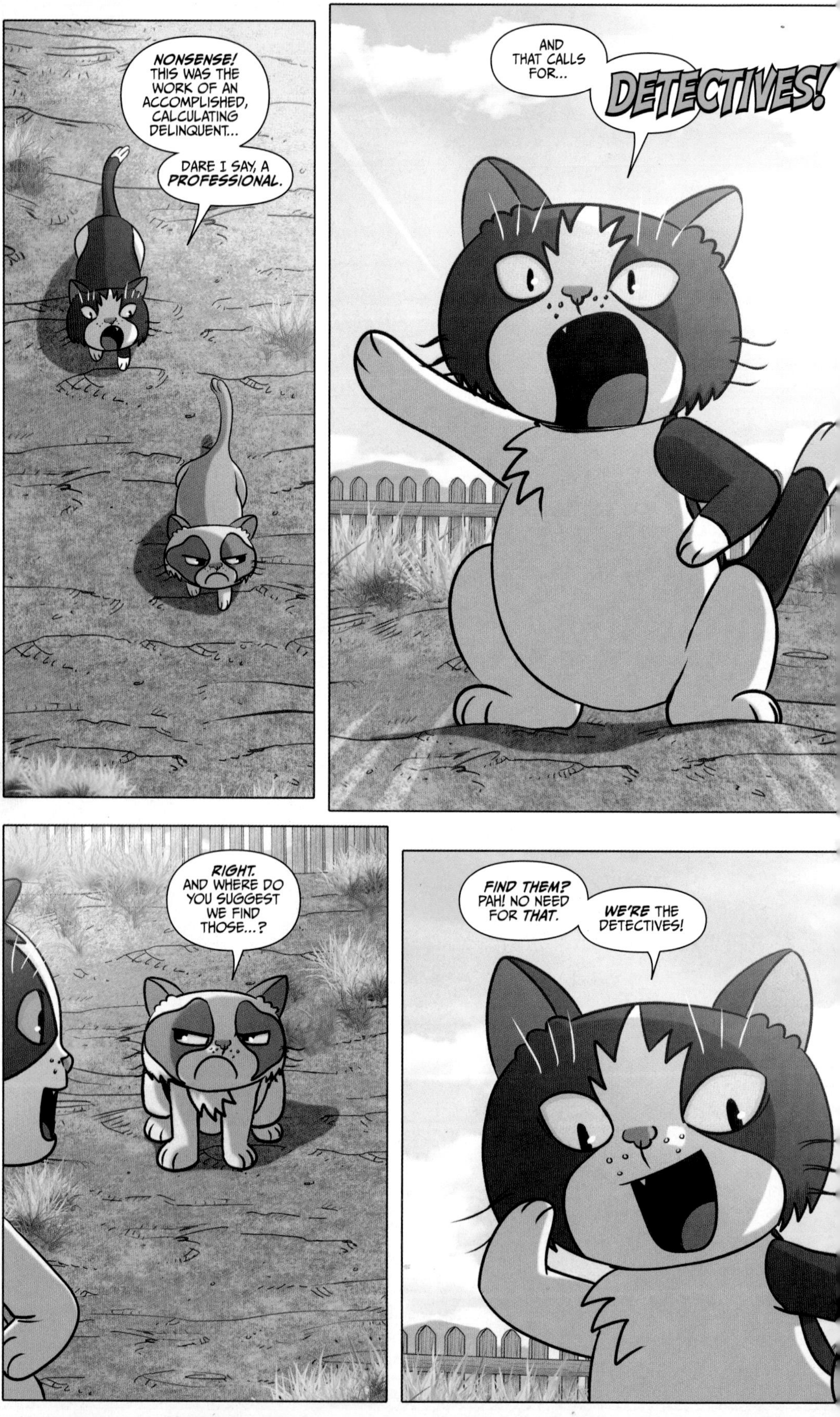
NONSENSE! THIS WAS THE WORK OF AN ACCOMPLISHED, CALCULATING DELINQUENT...
DARE I SAY, A PROFESSIONAL.
AND THAT CALLS FOR...
DETECTIVES!
RIGHT. AND WHERE DO YOU SUGGEST WE FIND THOSE...?
FIND THEM? PAH! NO NEED FOR THAT.
WE'RE THE DETECTIVES!

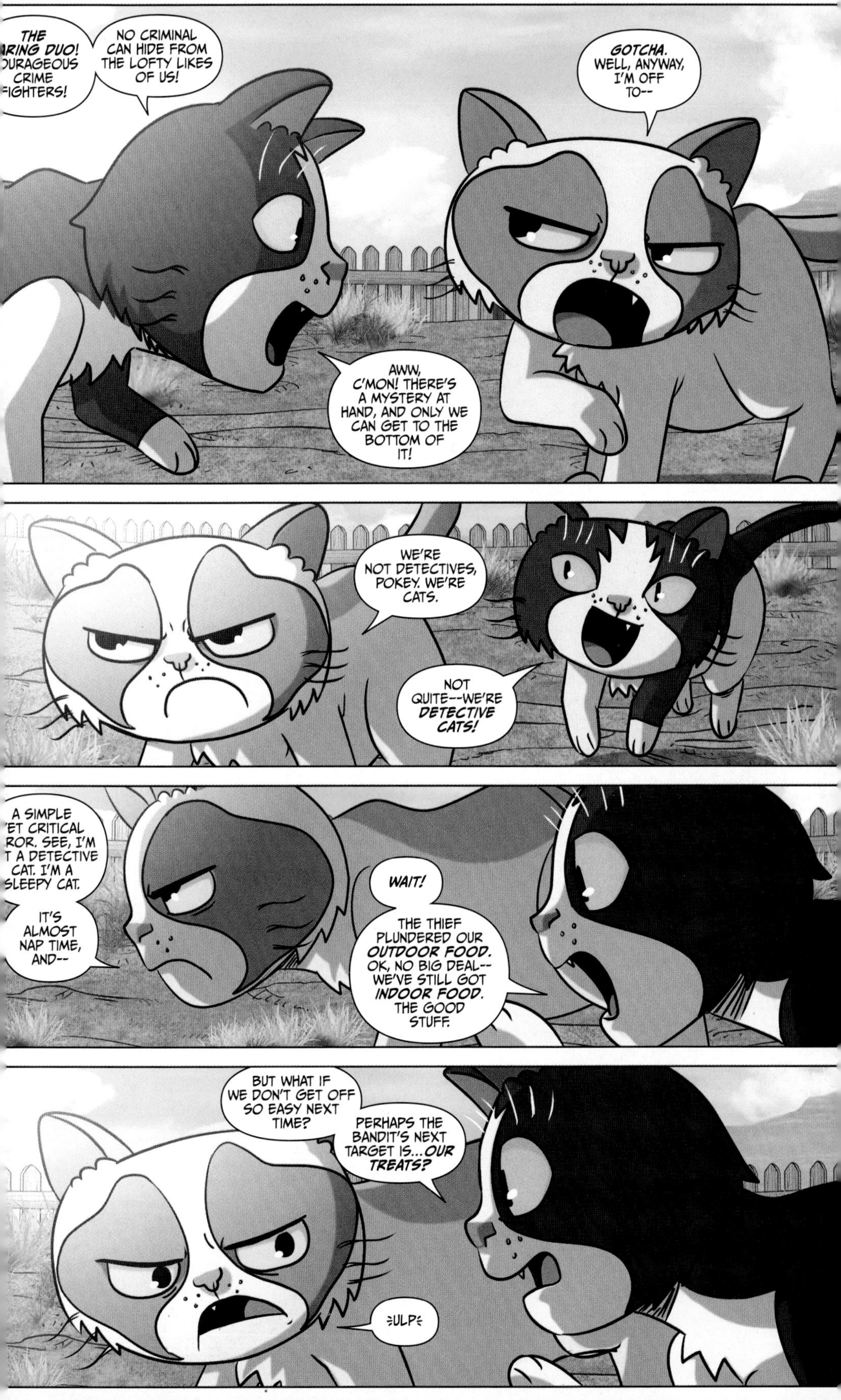
THE ...ARING DUO! ...OURAGEOUS CRIME ...FIGHTERS!
NO CRIMINAL CAN HIDE FROM THE LOFTY LIKES OF US!
GOTCHA. WELL, ANYWAY, I'M OFF TO--
AWW, C'MON! THERE'S A MYSTERY AT HAND, AND ONLY WE CAN GET TO THE BOTTOM OF IT!
WE'RE NOT DETECTIVES, POKEY. WE'RE CATS.
NOT QUITE--WE'RE DETECTIVE CATS!
A SIMPLE ...ET CRITICAL ...ROR. SEE, I'M ...T A DETECTIVE CAT. I'M A ...SLEEPY CAT.
IT'S ALMOST NAP TIME, AND--
WAIT!
THE THIEF PLUNDERED OUR OUTDOOR FOOD. OK, NO BIG DEAL-- WE'VE STILL GOT INDOOR FOOD. THE GOOD STUFF.
BUT WHAT IF WE DON'T GET OFF SO EASY NEXT TIME?
PERHAPS THE BANDIT'S NEXT TARGET IS...OUR TREATS?
ULP

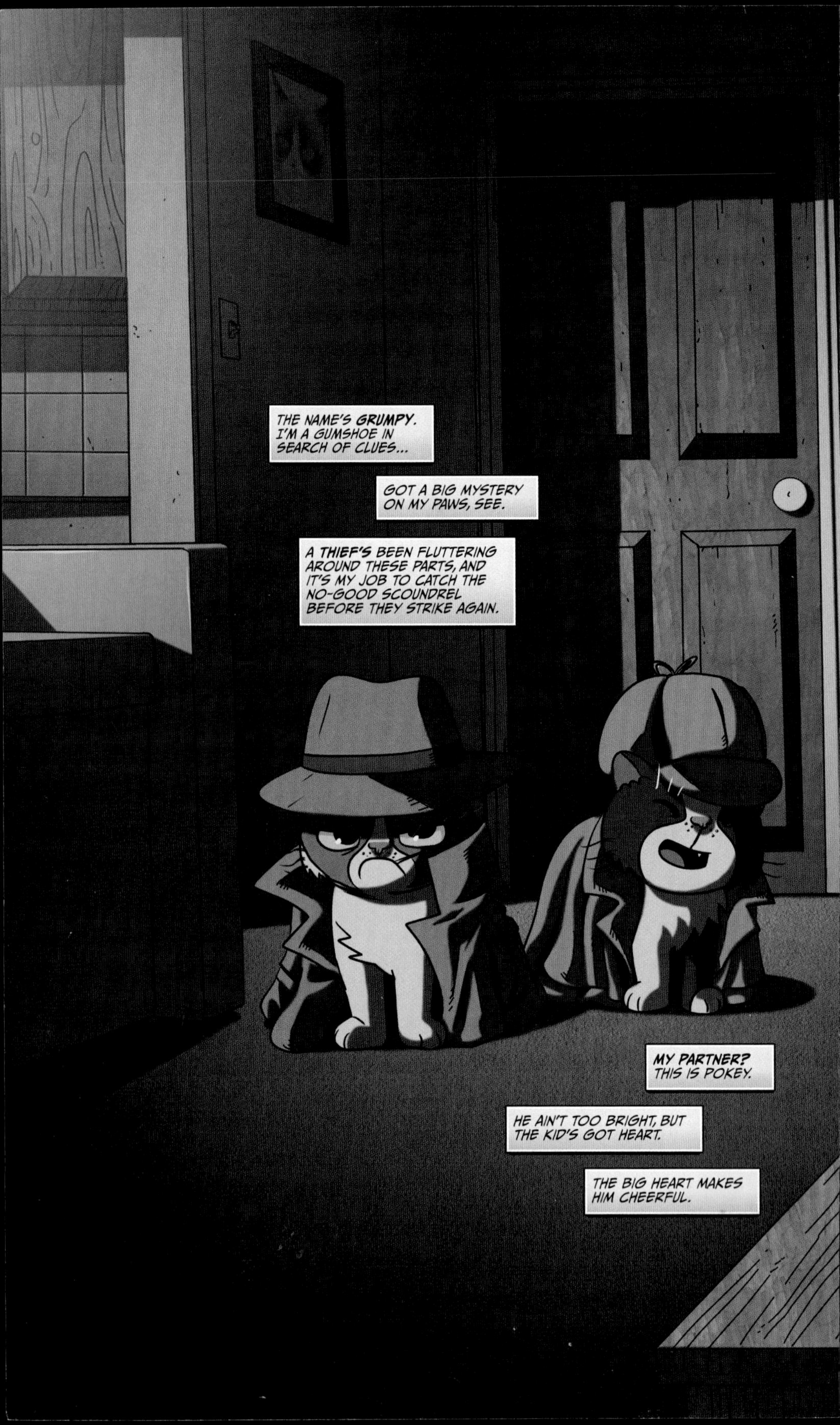
THE NAME'S **GRUMPY**. I'M A GUMSHOE IN SEARCH OF CLUES...
GOT A BIG MYSTERY ON MY PAWS, SEE.
A **THIEF'S** BEEN FLUTTERING AROUND THESE PARTS, AND IT'S MY JOB TO CATCH THE NO-GOOD SCOUNDREL BEFORE THEY STRIKE AGAIN.
MY PARTNER? THIS IS POKEY.
HE AIN'T TOO BRIGHT, BUT THE KID'S GOT HEART.
THE BIG HEART MAKES HIM CHEERFUL.

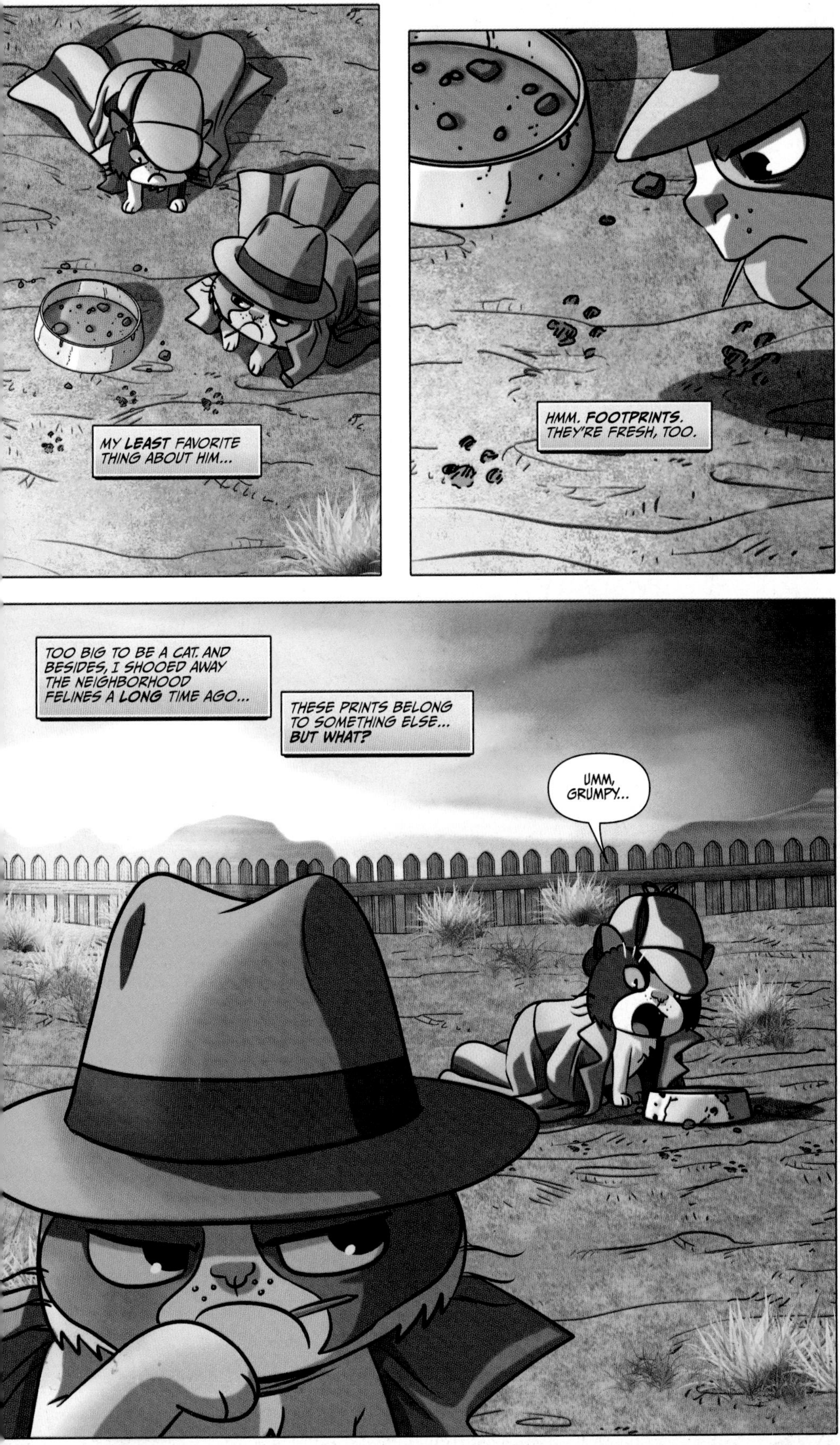
MY LEAST FAVORITE THING ABOUT HIM...
HMM. FOOTPRINTS. THEY'RE FRESH, TOO.
TOO BIG TO BE A CAT. AND BESIDES, I SHOOED AWAY THE NEIGHBORHOOD FELINES A LONG TIME AGO...
THESE PRINTS BELONG TO SOMETHING ELSE... BUT WHAT?
UMM, GRUMPY...

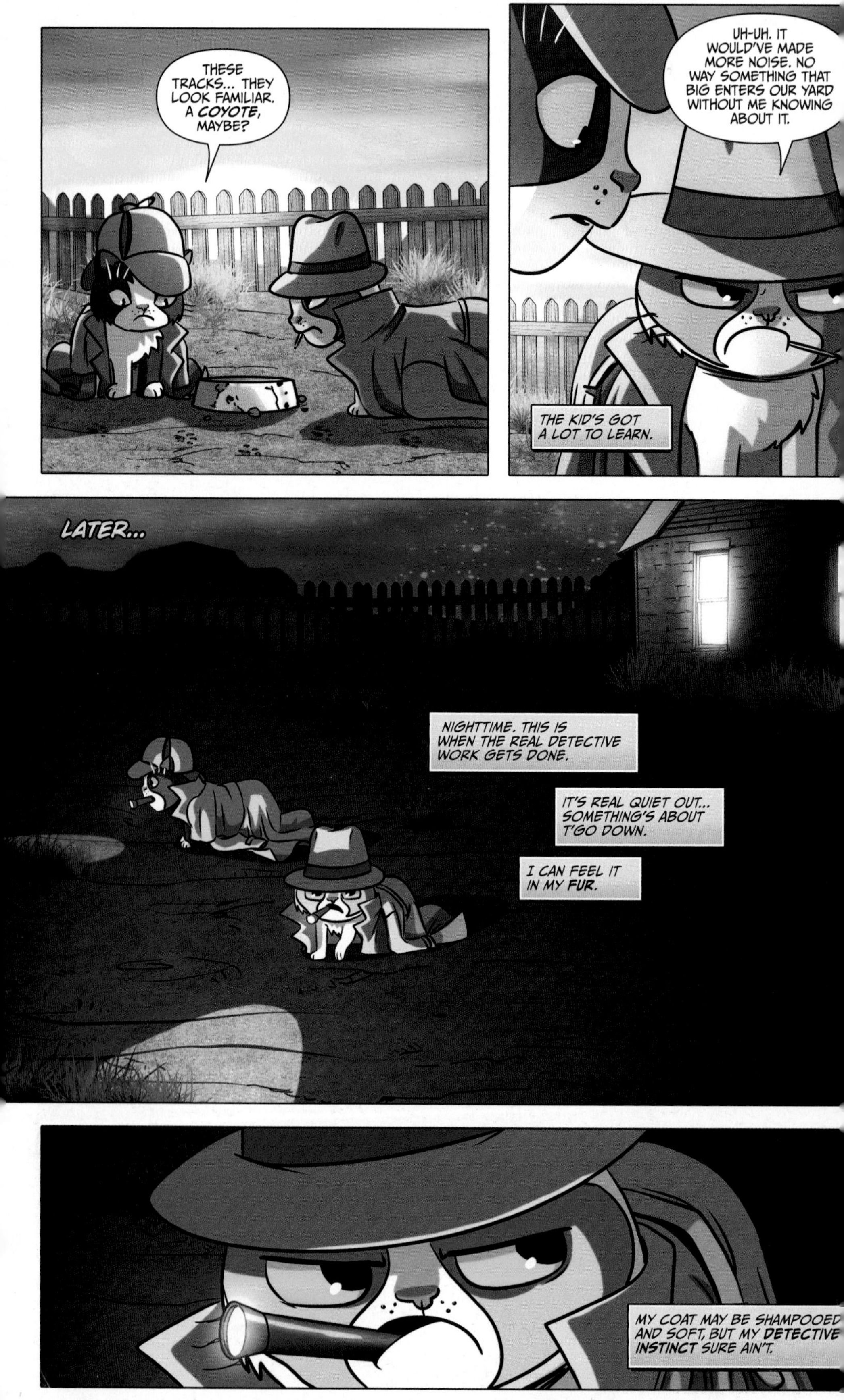
THESE TRACKS... THEY LOOK FAMILIAR. A COYOTE, MAYBE?
UH-UH. IT WOULD'VE MADE MORE NOISE. NO WAY SOMETHING THAT BIG ENTERS OUR YARD WITHOUT ME KNOWING ABOUT IT.
THE KID'S GOT A LOT TO LEARN.
LATER...
NIGHTTIME. THIS IS WHEN THE REAL DETECTIVE WORK GETS DONE.
IT'S REAL QUIET OUT... SOMETHING'S ABOUT T'GO DOWN.
I CAN FEEL IT IN MY FUR.
MY COAT MAY BE SHAMPOOED AND SOFT, BUT MY DETECTIVE INSTINCT SURE AIN'T.

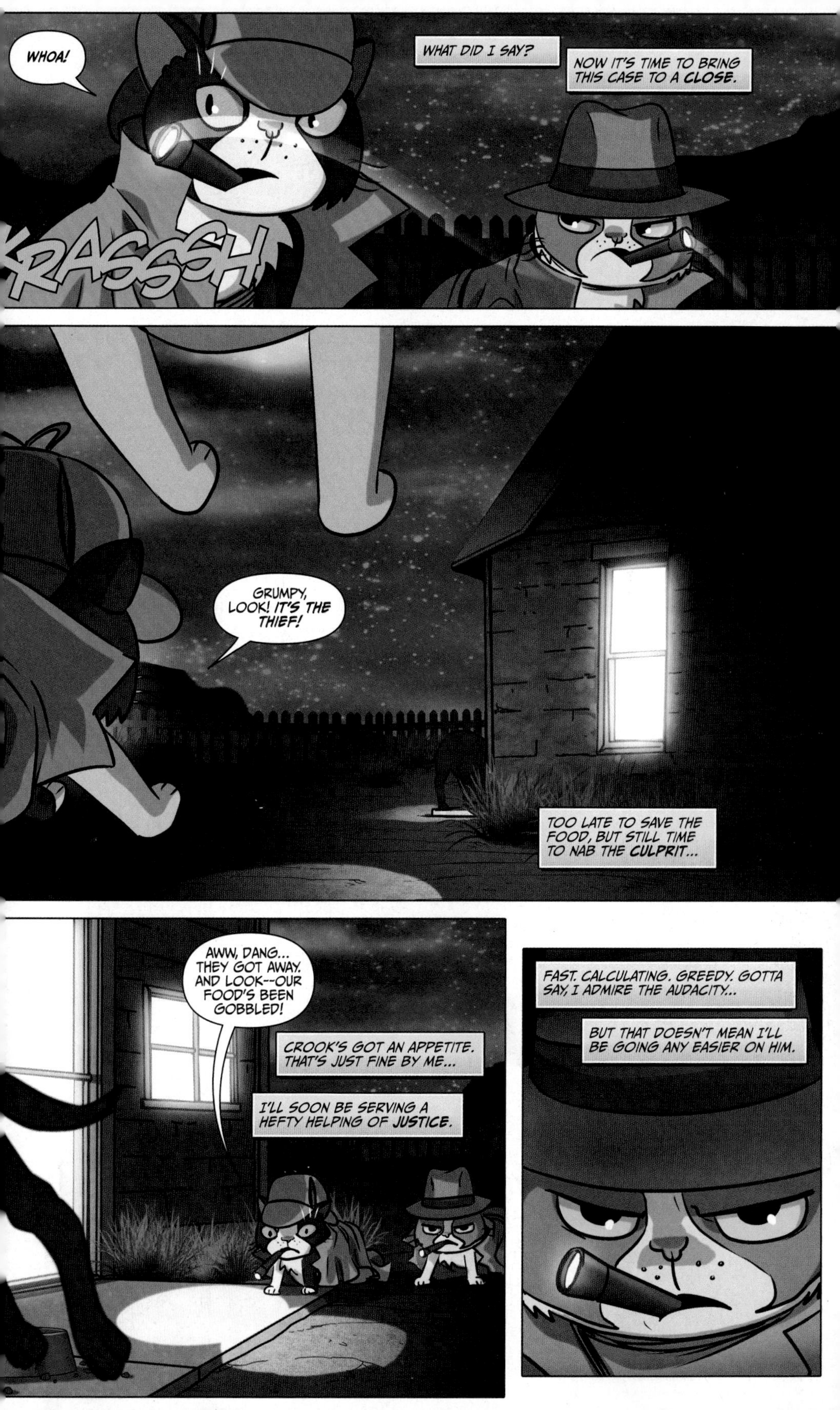

WHOA!
KRASSSH
WHAT DID I SAY?
NOW IT'S TIME TO BRING THIS CASE TO A CLOSE.
GRUMPY, LOOK! IT'S THE THIEF!
TOO LATE TO SAVE THE FOOD, BUT STILL TIME TO NAB THE CULPRIT...
AWW, DANG... THEY GOT AWAY. AND LOOK--OUR FOOD'S BEEN GOBBLED!
CROOK'S GOT AN APPETITE. THAT'S JUST FINE BY ME...
I'LL SOON BE SERVING A HEFTY HELPING OF JUSTICE.
FAST. CALCULATING. GREEDY. GOTTA SAY, I ADMIRE THE AUDACITY...
BUT THAT DOESN'T MEAN I'LL BE GOING ANY EASIER ON HIM.

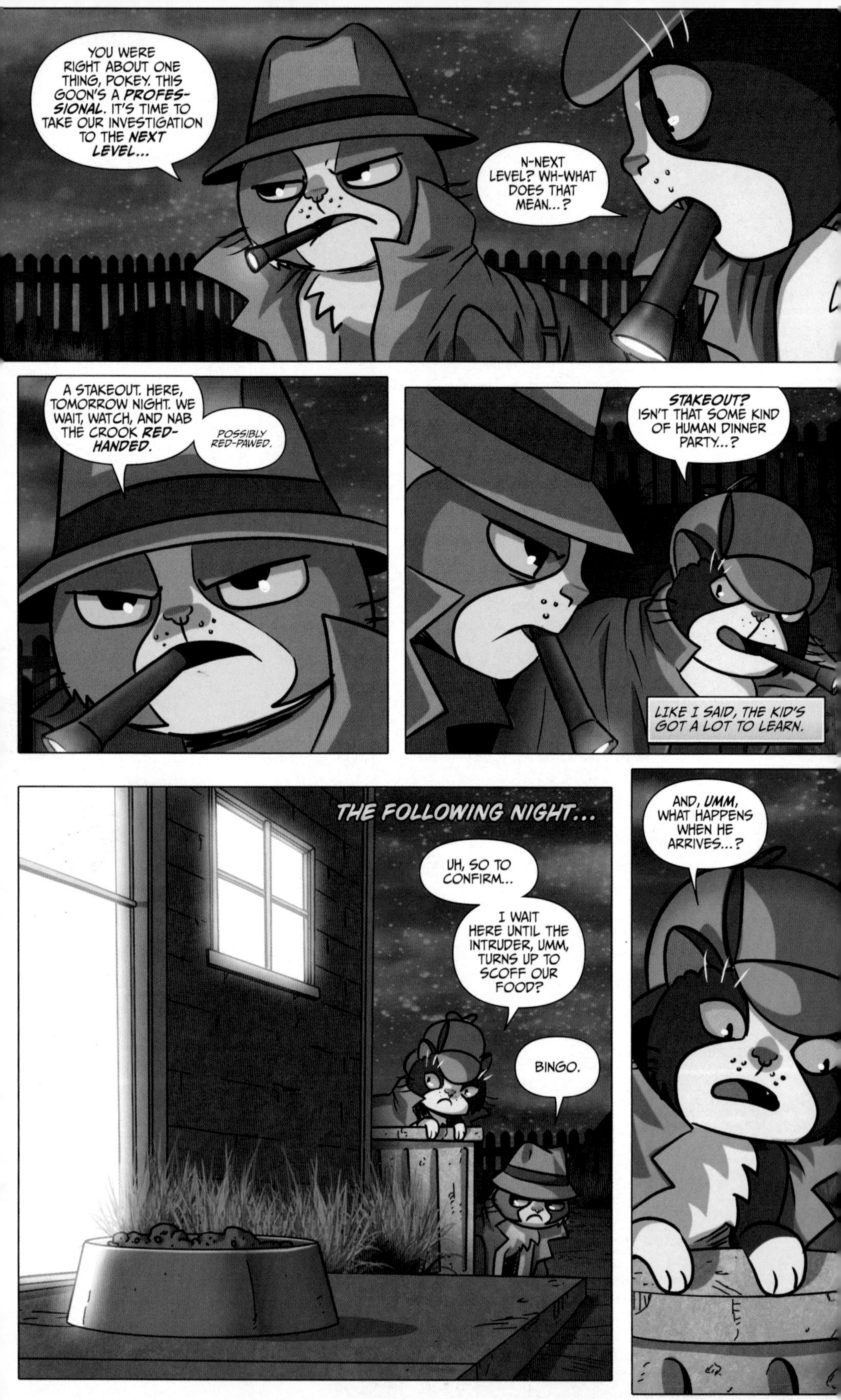
YOU WERE RIGHT ABOUT ONE THING, POKEY. THIS GOON'S A PROFESSIONAL. IT'S TIME TO TAKE OUR INVESTIGATION TO THE NEXT LEVEL...
N-NEXT LEVEL? WH-WHAT DOES THAT MEAN...?
A STAKEOUT. HERE, TOMORROW NIGHT. WE WAIT, WATCH, AND NAB THE CROOK RED-HANDED.
POSSIBLY RED-PAWED.
STAKEOUT? ISN'T THAT SOME KIND OF HUMAN DINNER PARTY...?
LIKE I SAID, THE KID'S GOT A LOT TO LEARN.
THE FOLLOWING NIGHT...
UH, SO TO CONFIRM...
I WAIT HERE UNTIL THE INTRUDER, UMM, TURNS UP TO SCOFF OUR FOOD?
BINGO.
AND, UMM, WHAT HAPPENS WHEN HE ARRIVES...?

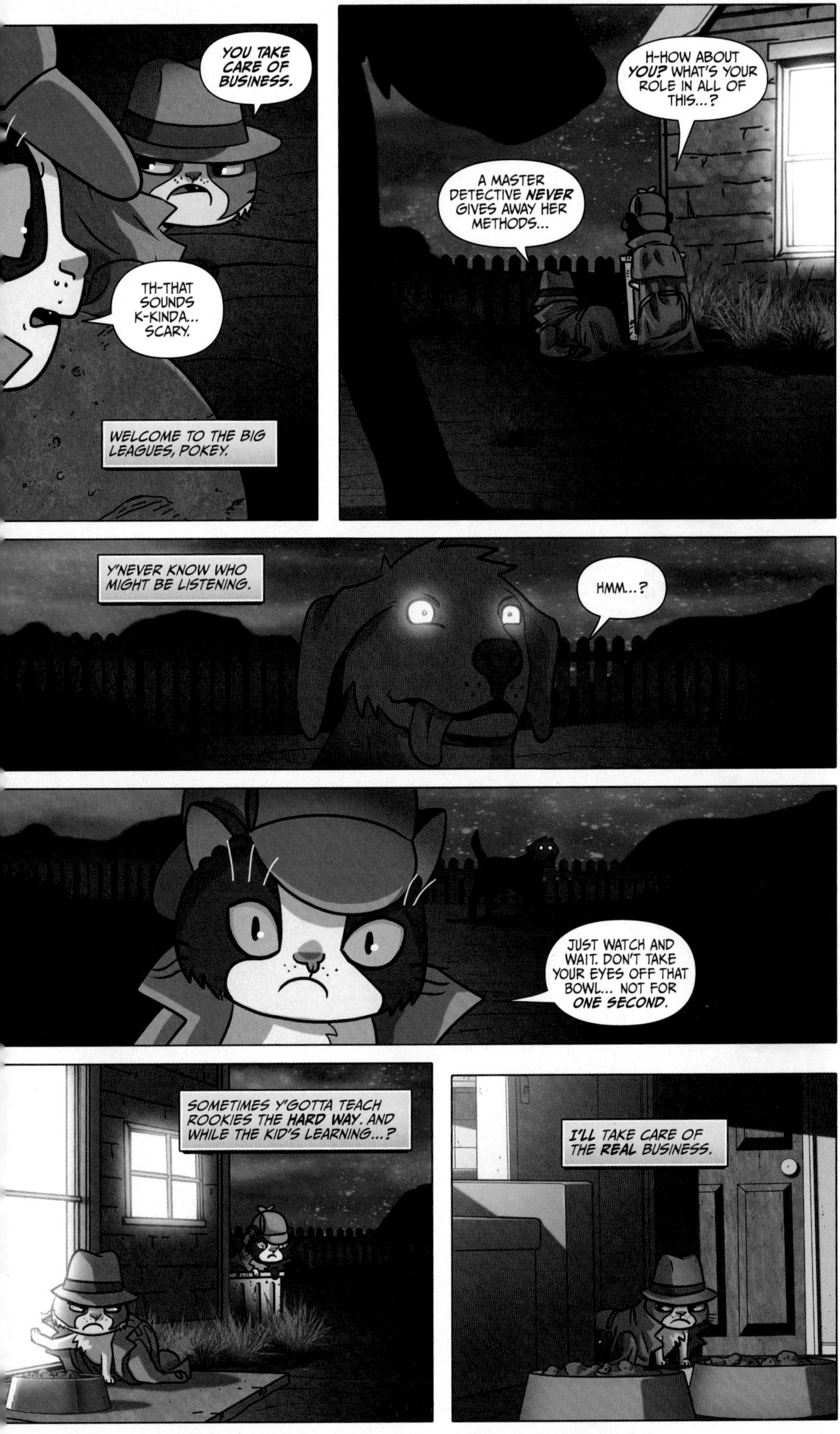
YOU TAKE CARE OF BUSINESS.
TH-THAT SOUNDS K-KINDA... SCARY.
WELCOME TO THE BIG LEAGUES, POKEY.
H-HOW ABOUT YOU? WHAT'S YOUR ROLE IN ALL OF THIS...?
A MASTER DETECTIVE NEVER GIVES AWAY HER METHODS...
Y'NEVER KNOW WHO MIGHT BE LISTENING.
HMM...?
JUST WATCH AND WAIT. DON'T TAKE YOUR EYES OFF THAT BOWL... NOT FOR ONE SECOND.
SOMETIMES Y'GOTTA TEACH ROOKIES THE HARD WAY. AND WHILE THE KID'S LEARNING...?
I'LL TAKE CARE OF THE REAL BUSINESS.

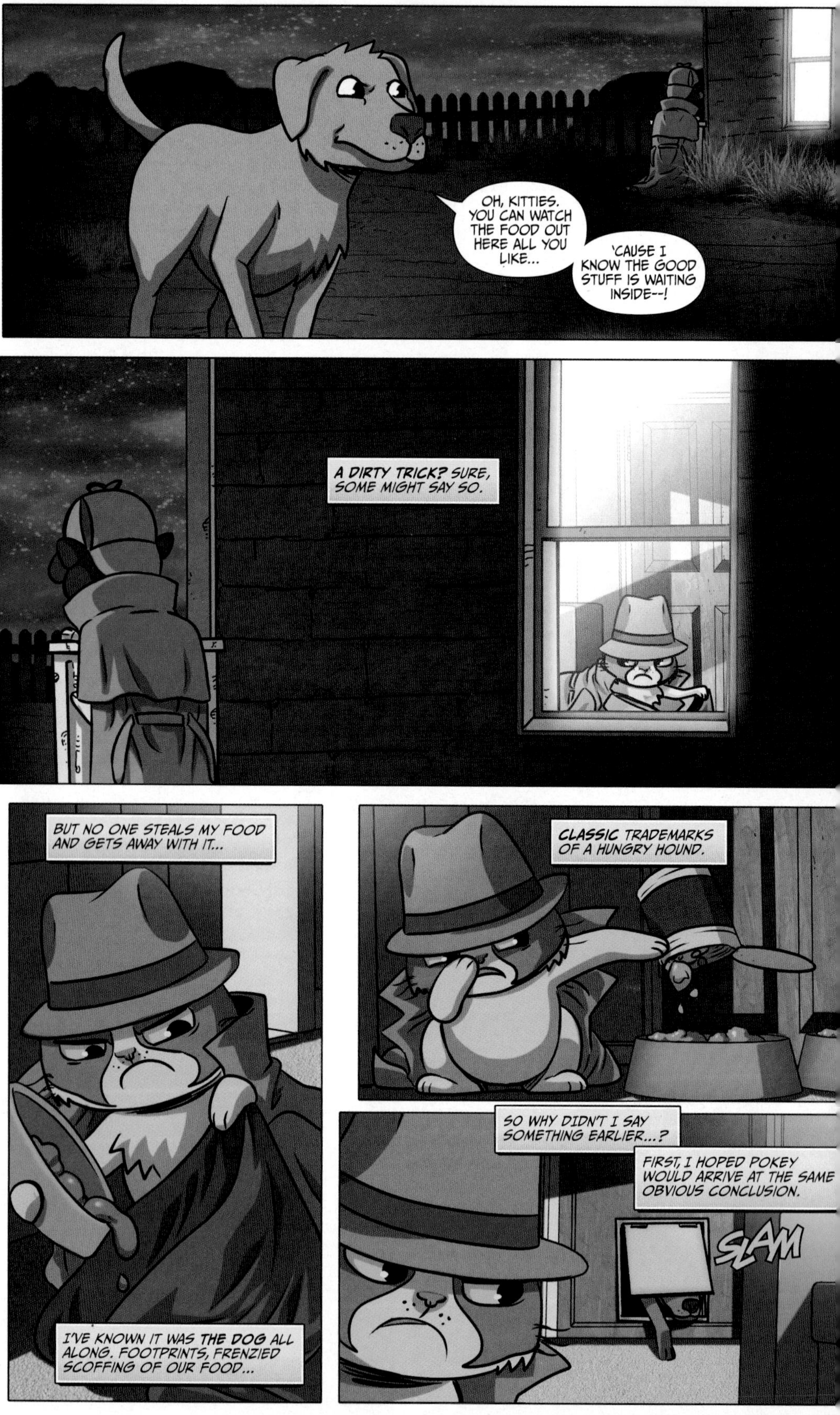

OH, KITTIES. YOU CAN WATCH THE FOOD OUT HERE ALL YOU LIKE...
'CAUSE I KNOW THE GOOD STUFF IS WAITING INSIDE--!
A DIRTY TRICK? SURE, SOME MIGHT SAY SO.
BUT NO ONE STEALS MY FOOD AND GETS AWAY WITH IT...
I'VE KNOWN IT WAS THE DOG ALL ALONG. FOOTPRINTS, FRENZIED SCOFFING OF OUR FOOD...
CLASSIC TRADEMARKS OF A HUNGRY HOUND.
SO WHY DIDN'T I SAY SOMETHING EARLIER...?
FIRST, I HOPED POKEY WOULD ARRIVE AT THE SAME OBVIOUS CONCLUSION.
SLAM

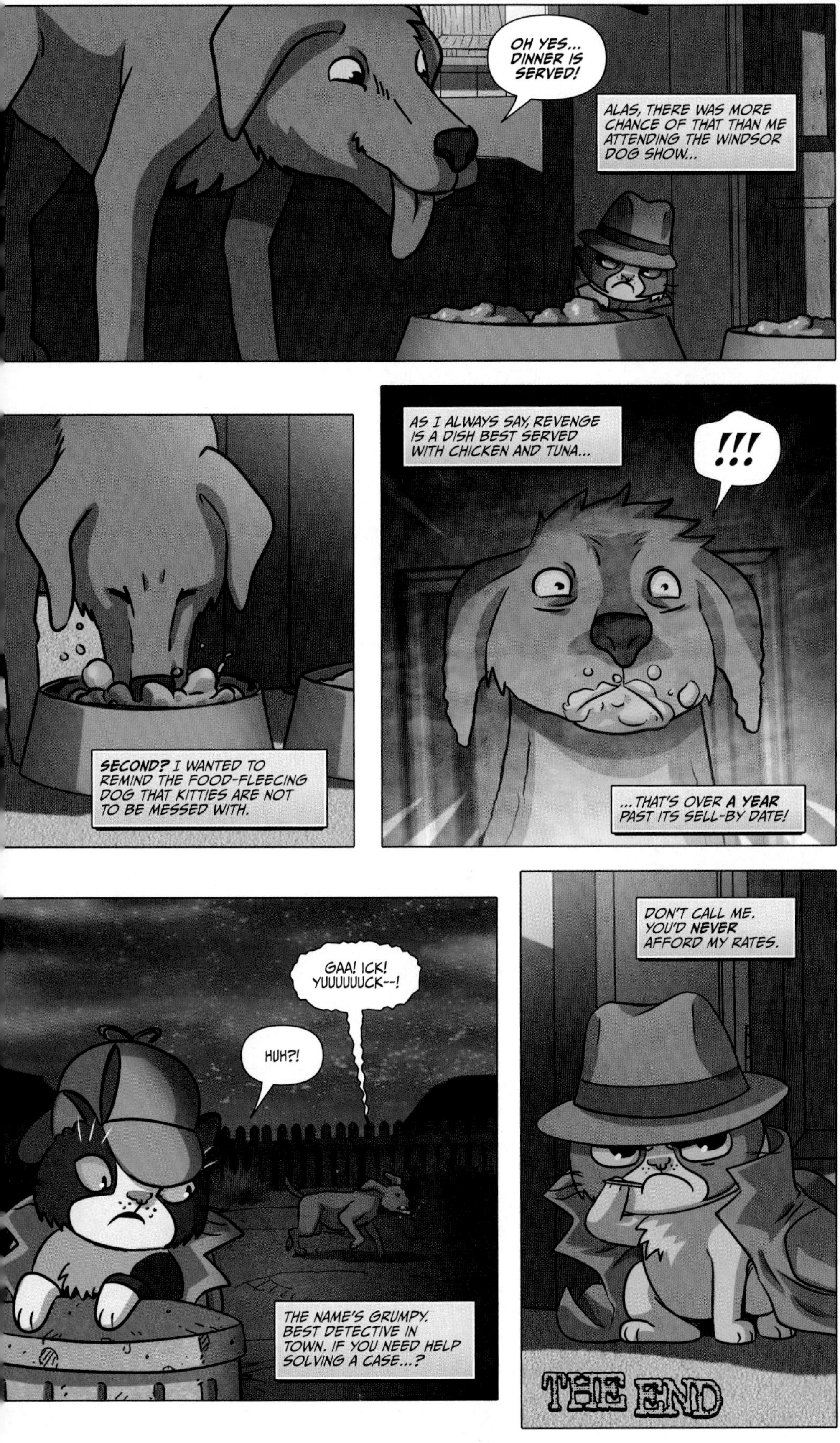
OH YES... DINNER IS SERVED!
ALAS, THERE WAS MORE CHANCE OF THAT THAN ME ATTENDING THE WINDSOR DOG SHOW...
SECOND? I WANTED TO REMIND THE FOOD-FLEECING DOG THAT KITTIES ARE NOT TO BE MESSED WITH.
AS I ALWAYS SAY, REVENGE IS A DISH BEST SERVED WITH CHICKEN AND TUNA...
!!!
...THAT'S OVER A YEAR PAST ITS SELL-BY DATE!
GAA! ICK! YUUUUUUCK--!
HUH?!
THE NAME'S GRUMPY. BEST DETECTIVE IN TOWN. IF YOU NEED HELP SOLVING A CASE...?
DON'T CALL ME. YOU'D NEVER AFFORD MY RATES.
THE END

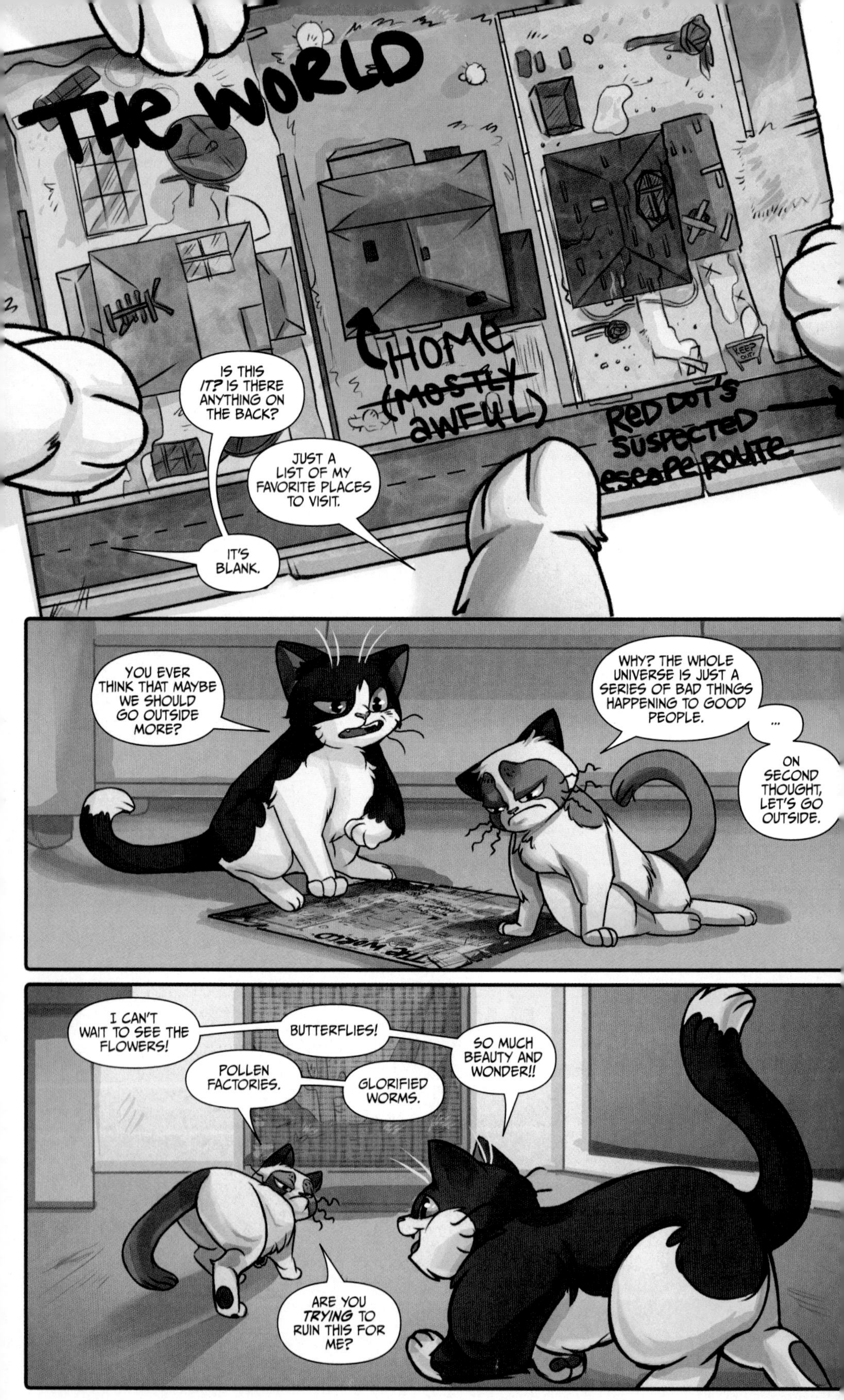
THE WORLD
HOME
(MOSTLY AWFUL)
RED DOT'S SUSPECTED ESCAPE ROUTE
KEEP OUT!
IS THIS *IT?* IS THERE ANYTHING ON THE BACK?
JUST A LIST OF MY FAVORITE PLACES TO VISIT.
IT'S BLANK.
YOU EVER THINK THAT MAYBE WE SHOULD GO OUTSIDE MORE?
WHY? THE WHOLE UNIVERSE IS JUST A SERIES OF BAD THINGS HAPPENING TO GOOD PEOPLE.
...
ON SECOND THOUGHT, LET'S GO OUTSIDE.
I CAN'T WAIT TO SEE THE FLOWERS!
POLLEN FACTORIES.
BUTTERFLIES!
GLORIFIED WORMS.
SO MUCH BEAUTY AND WONDER!!
ARE YOU *TRYING* TO RUIN THIS FOR ME?

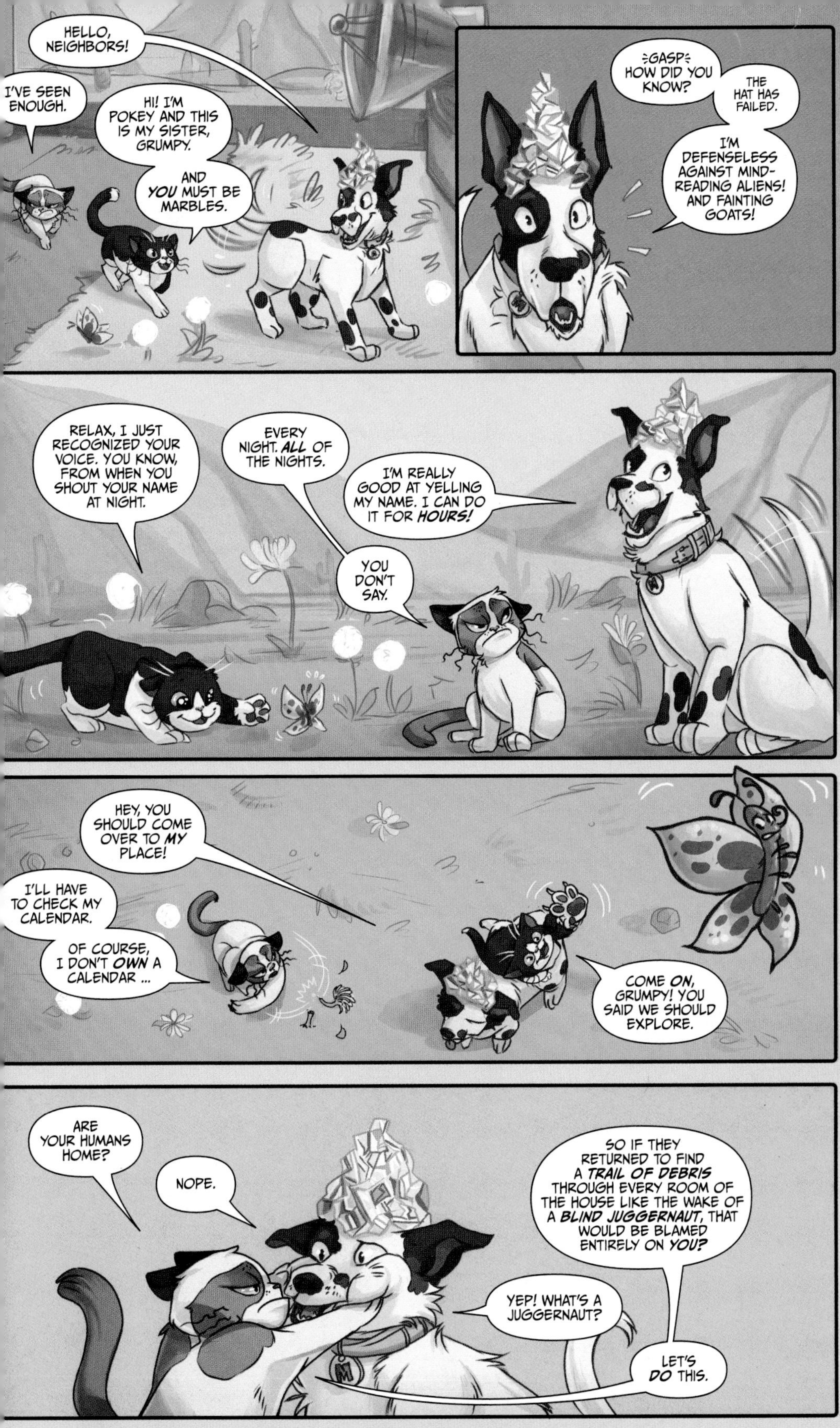

HELLO, NEIGHBORS!
I'VE SEEN ENOUGH.
HI! I'M POKEY AND THIS IS MY SISTER, GRUMPY.
AND *YOU* MUST BE MARBLES.
GASP HOW DID YOU KNOW?
THE HAT HAS FAILED.
I'M DEFENSELESS AGAINST MIND-READING ALIENS! AND FAINTING GOATS!
RELAX, I JUST RECOGNIZED YOUR VOICE. YOU KNOW, FROM WHEN YOU SHOUT YOUR NAME AT NIGHT.
EVERY NIGHT. *ALL* OF THE NIGHTS.
I'M REALLY GOOD AT YELLING MY NAME. I CAN DO IT FOR *HOURS!*
YOU DON'T SAY.
HEY, YOU SHOULD COME OVER TO *MY* PLACE!
I'LL HAVE TO CHECK MY CALENDAR.
OF COURSE, I DON'T *OWN* A CALENDAR ...
COME *ON*, GRUMPY! YOU SAID WE SHOULD EXPLORE.
ARE YOUR HUMANS HOME?
NOPE.
SO IF THEY RETURNED TO FIND A *TRAIL OF DEBRIS* THROUGH EVERY ROOM OF THE HOUSE LIKE THE WAKE OF A *BLIND JUGGERNAUT*, THAT WOULD BE BLAMED ENTIRELY ON *YOU?*
YEP! WHAT'S A JUGGERNAUT?
LET'S *DO* THIS.

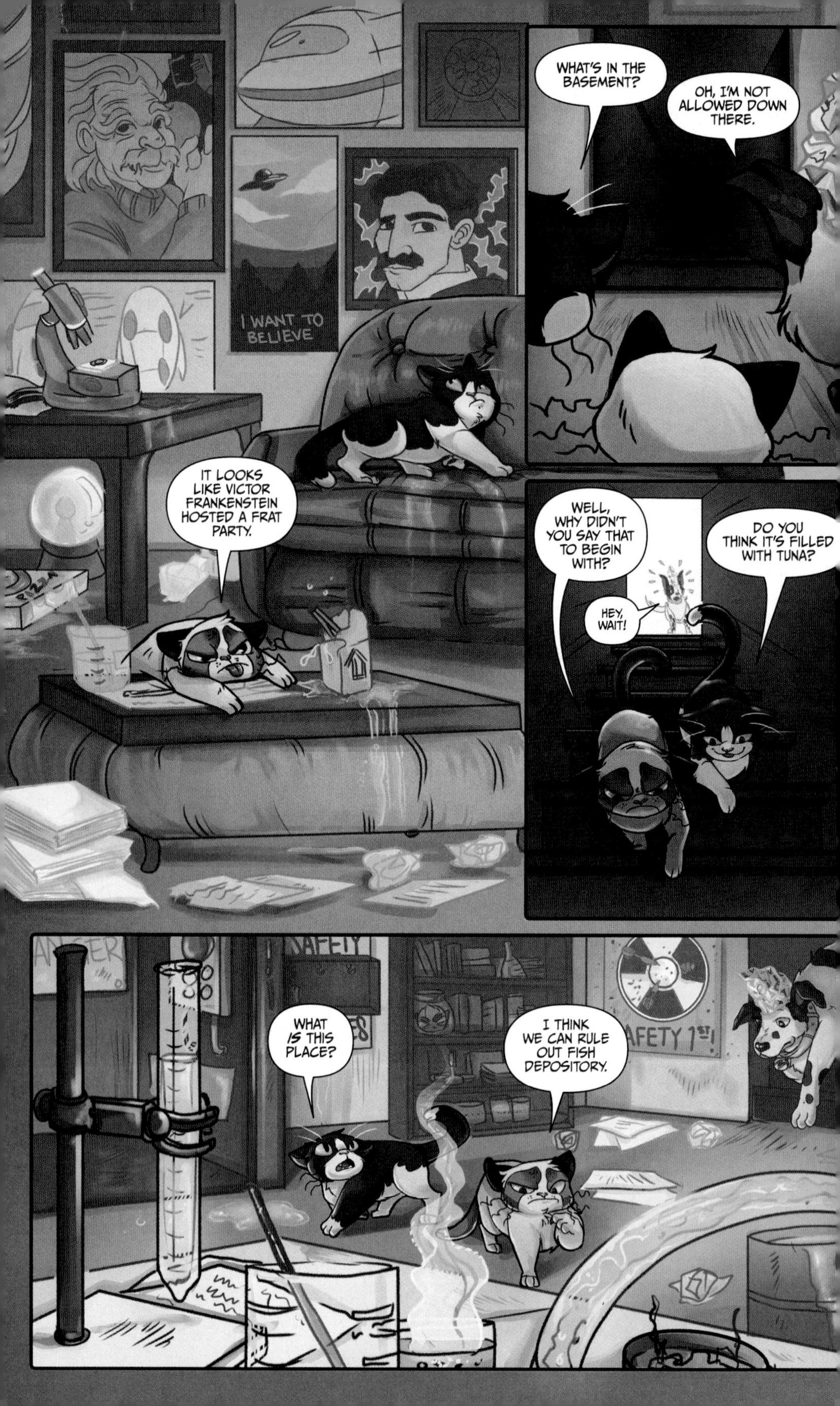
I WANT TO BELIEVE
WHAT'S IN THE BASEMENT?
OH, I'M NOT ALLOWED DOWN THERE.
IT LOOKS LIKE VICTOR FRANKENSTEIN HOSTED A FRAT PARTY.
WELL, WHY DIDN'T YOU SAY THAT TO BEGIN WITH?
DO YOU THINK IT'S FILLED WITH TUNA?
HEY, WAIT!
SAFETY 1ST!
WHAT *IS* THIS PLACE?
I THINK WE CAN RULE OUT FISH DEPOSITORY.

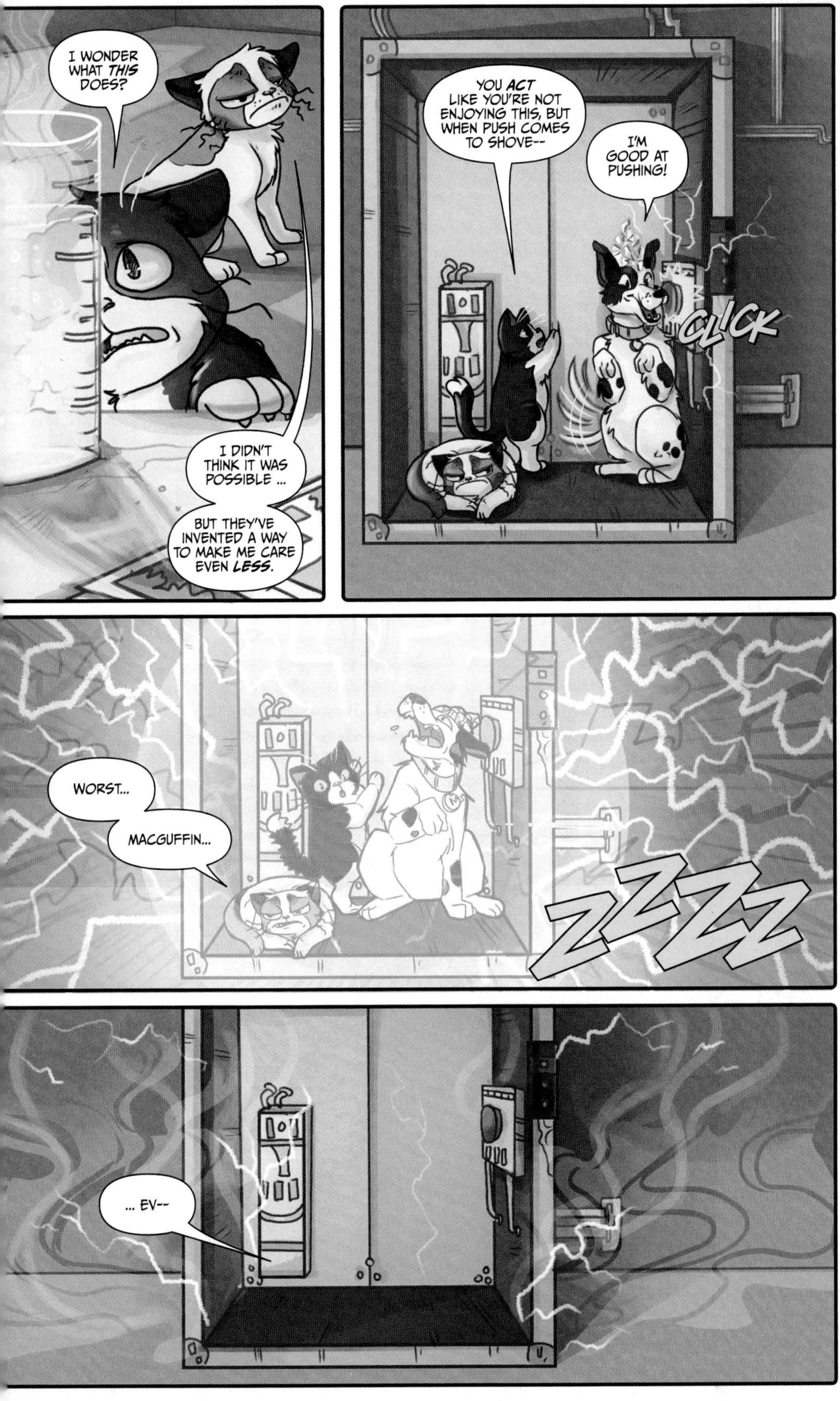

I WONDER WHAT *THIS* DOES?
I DIDN'T THINK IT WAS POSSIBLE ...
BUT THEY'VE INVENTED A WAY TO MAKE ME CARE EVEN *LESS*.
YOU *ACT* LIKE YOU'RE NOT ENJOYING THIS, BUT WHEN PUSH COMES TO SHOVE--
I'M GOOD AT PUSHING!
CLICK
WORST...
MACGUFFIN...
ZZZZZ
... EV--

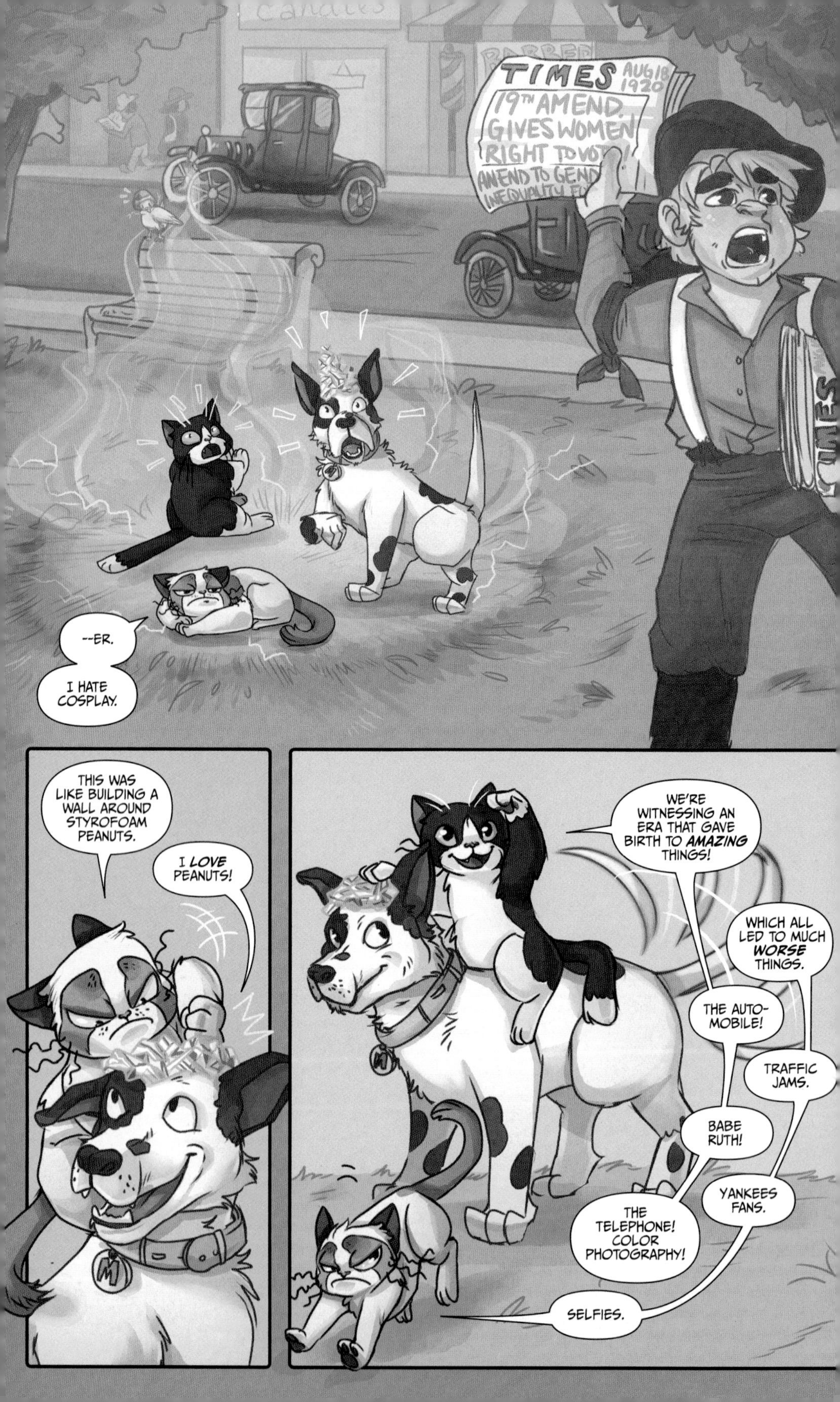
TIMES AUG 18 1920
19TH AMEND. GIVES WOMEN RIGHT TO VOT
--ER.
I HATE COSPLAY.
THIS WAS LIKE BUILDING A WALL AROUND STYROFOAM PEANUTS.
I LOVE PEANUTS!
WE'RE WITNESSING AN ERA THAT GAVE BIRTH TO AMAZING THINGS!
WHICH ALL LED TO MUCH WORSE THINGS.
THE AUTO-MOBILE!
TRAFFIC JAMS.
BABE RUTH!
YANKEES FANS.
THE TELEPHONE! COLOR PHOTOGRAPHY!
SELFIES.

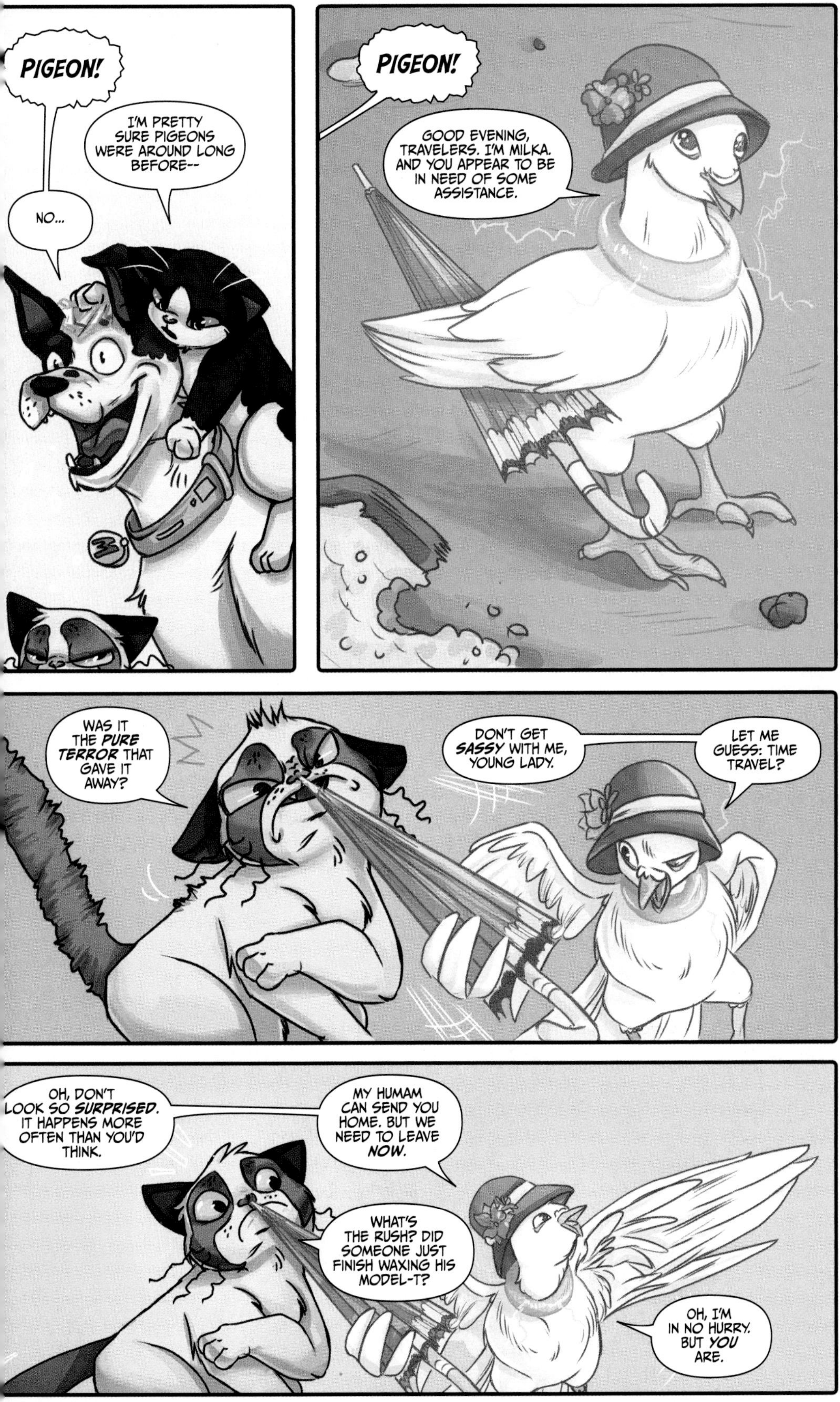
PIGEON!
I'M PRETTY SURE PIGEONS WERE AROUND LONG BEFORE--
NO...
PIGEON!
GOOD EVENING, TRAVELERS. I'M MILKA. AND YOU APPEAR TO BE IN NEED OF SOME ASSISTANCE.
WAS IT THE PURE TERROR THAT GAVE IT AWAY?
DON'T GET SASSY WITH ME, YOUNG LADY.
LET ME GUESS: TIME TRAVEL?
OH, DON'T LOOK SO SURPRISED. IT HAPPENS MORE OFTEN THAN YOU'D THINK.
MY HUMAM CAN SEND YOU HOME. BUT WE NEED TO LEAVE NOW.
WHAT'S THE RUSH? DID SOMEONE JUST FINISH WAXING HIS MODEL-T?
OH, I'M IN NO HURRY. BUT YOU ARE.

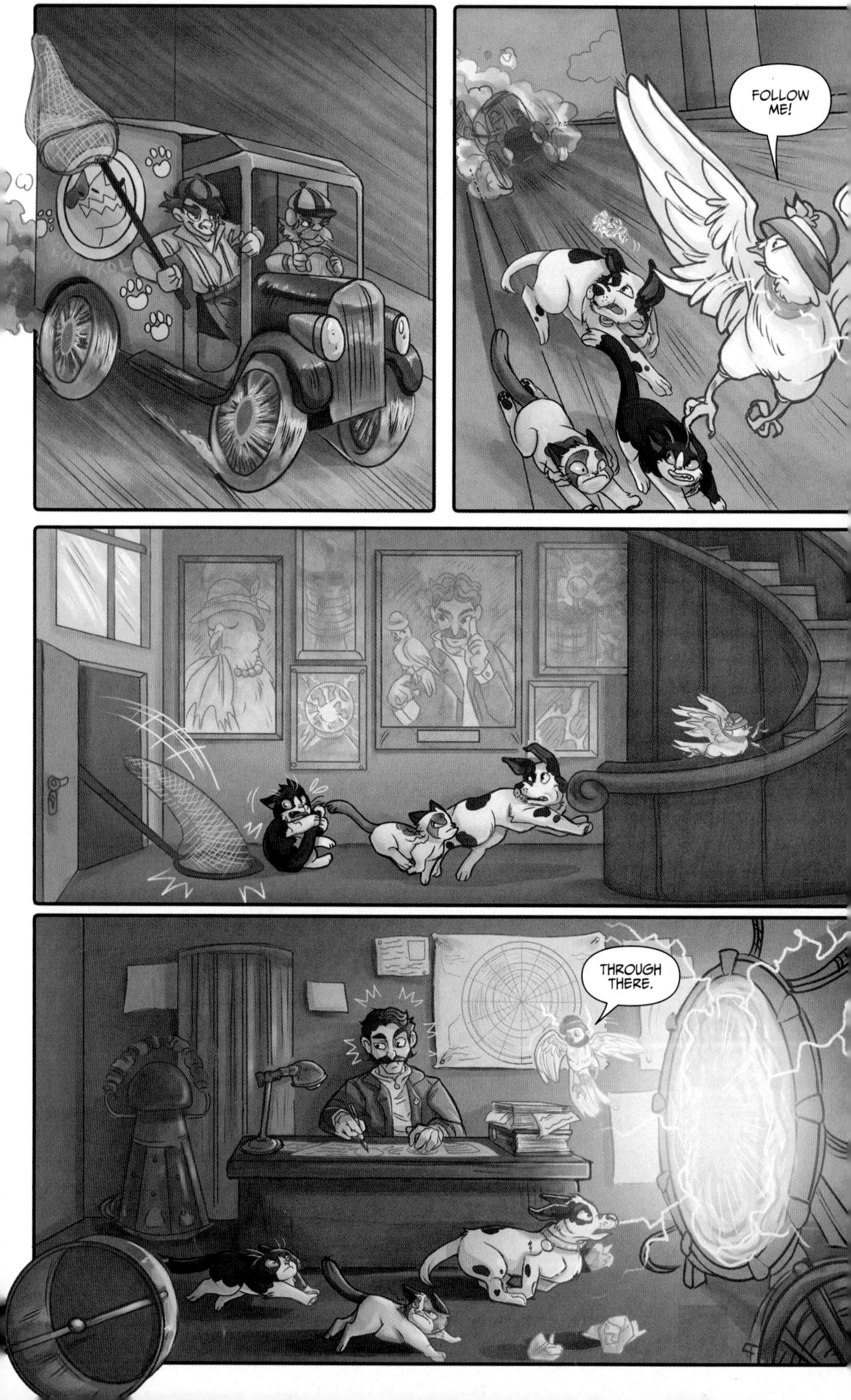
FOLLOW ME!
THROUGH THERE.

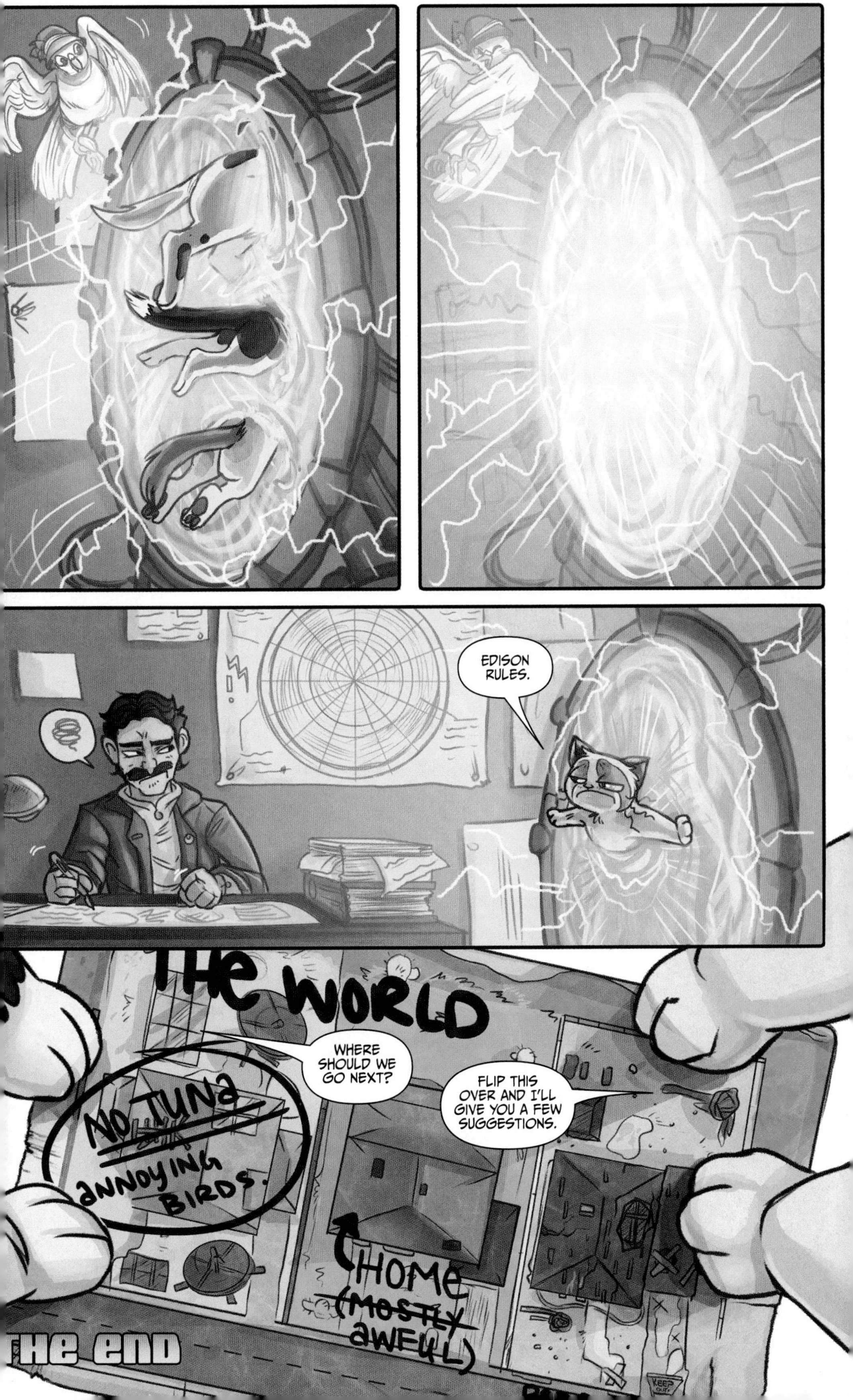
EDISON RULES.
THE WORLD
WHERE SHOULD WE GO NEXT?
FLIP THIS OVER AND I'LL GIVE YOU A FEW SUGGESTIONS.
NO TUNA
ANNOYING BIRDS.
HOME
(MOSTLY
AWFUL)
THE END

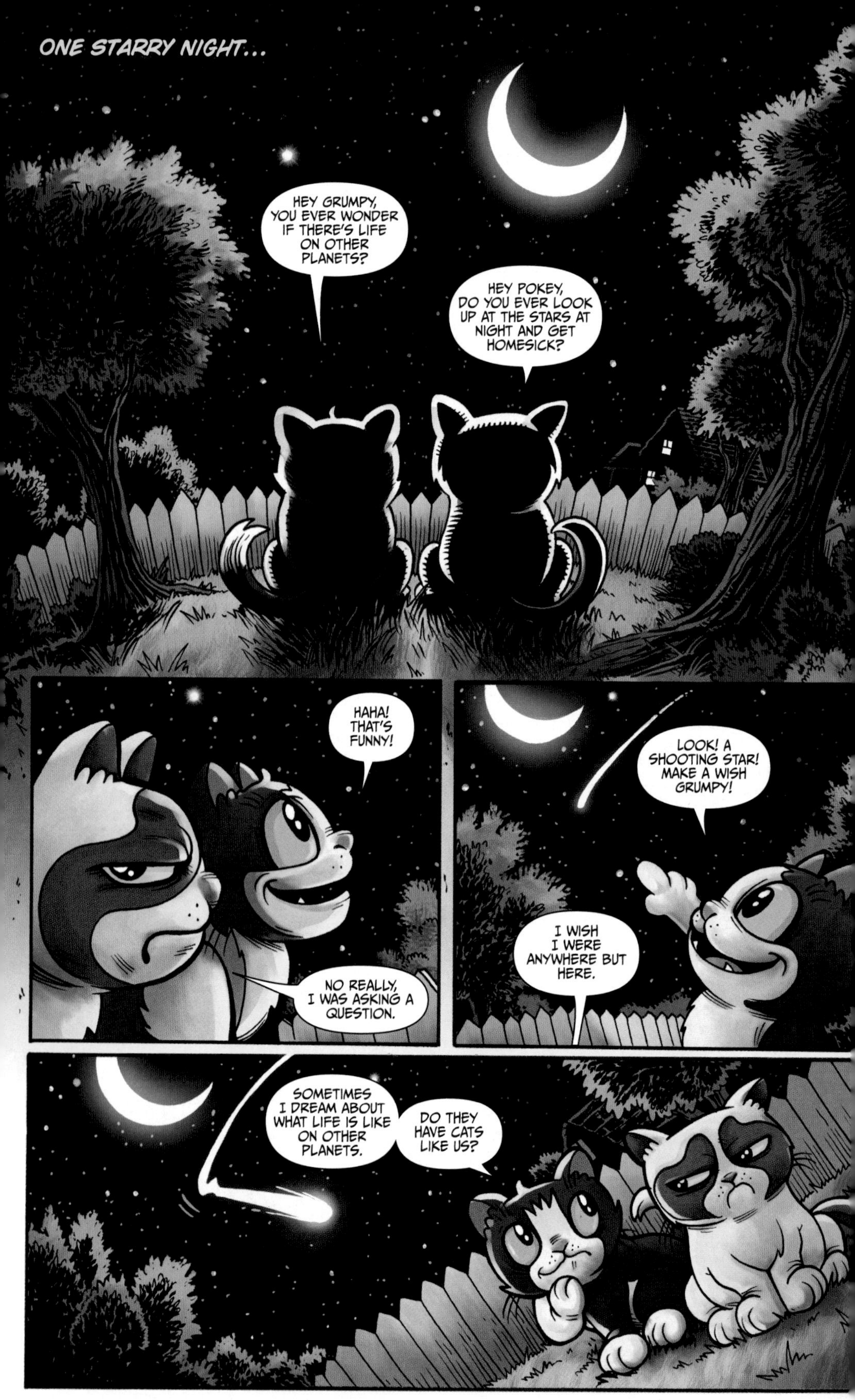
ONE STARRY NIGHT...
HEY GRUMPY, YOU EVER WONDER IF THERE'S LIFE ON OTHER PLANETS?
HEY POKEY, DO YOU EVER LOOK UP AT THE STARS AT NIGHT AND GET HOMESICK?
HAHA! THAT'S FUNNY!
NO REALLY, I WAS ASKING A QUESTION.
LOOK! A SHOOTING STAR! MAKE A WISH GRUMPY!
I WISH I WERE ANYWHERE BUT HERE.
SOMETIMES I DREAM ABOUT WHAT LIFE IS LIKE ON OTHER PLANETS.
DO THEY HAVE CATS LIKE US?

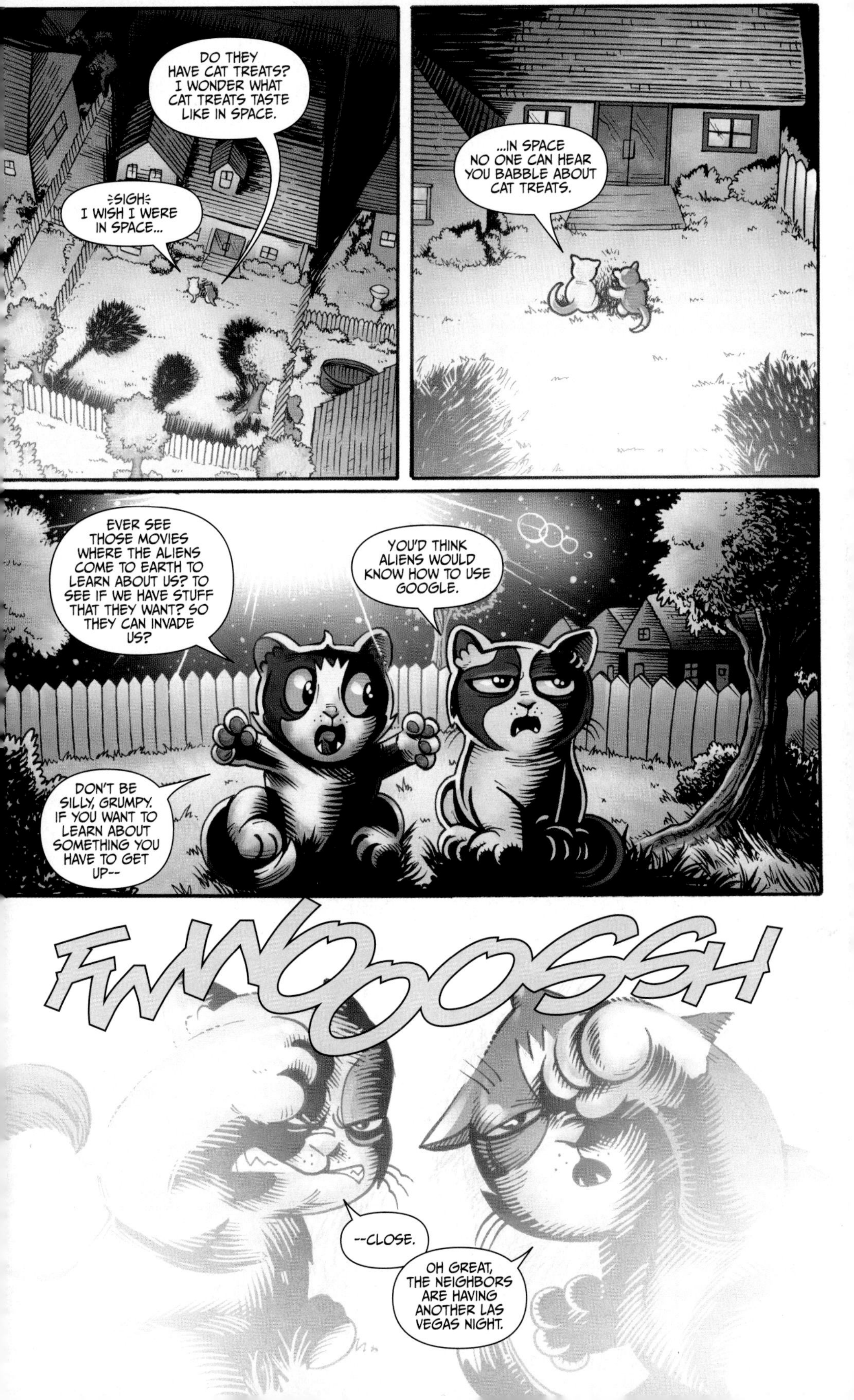
DO THEY HAVE CAT TREATS? I WONDER WHAT CAT TREATS TASTE LIKE IN SPACE.
≈SIGH≈ I WISH I WERE IN SPACE...
...IN SPACE NO ONE CAN HEAR YOU BABBLE ABOUT CAT TREATS.
EVER SEE THOSE MOVIES WHERE THE ALIENS COME TO EARTH TO LEARN ABOUT US? TO SEE IF WE HAVE STUFF THAT THEY WANT? SO THEY CAN INVADE US?
YOU'D THINK ALIENS WOULD KNOW HOW TO USE GOOGLE.
DON'T BE SILLY, GRUMPY. IF YOU WANT TO LEARN ABOUT SOMETHING YOU HAVE TO GET UP--
FWOOOSH
--CLOSE.
OH GREAT, THE NEIGHBORS ARE HAVING ANOTHER LAS VEGAS NIGHT.

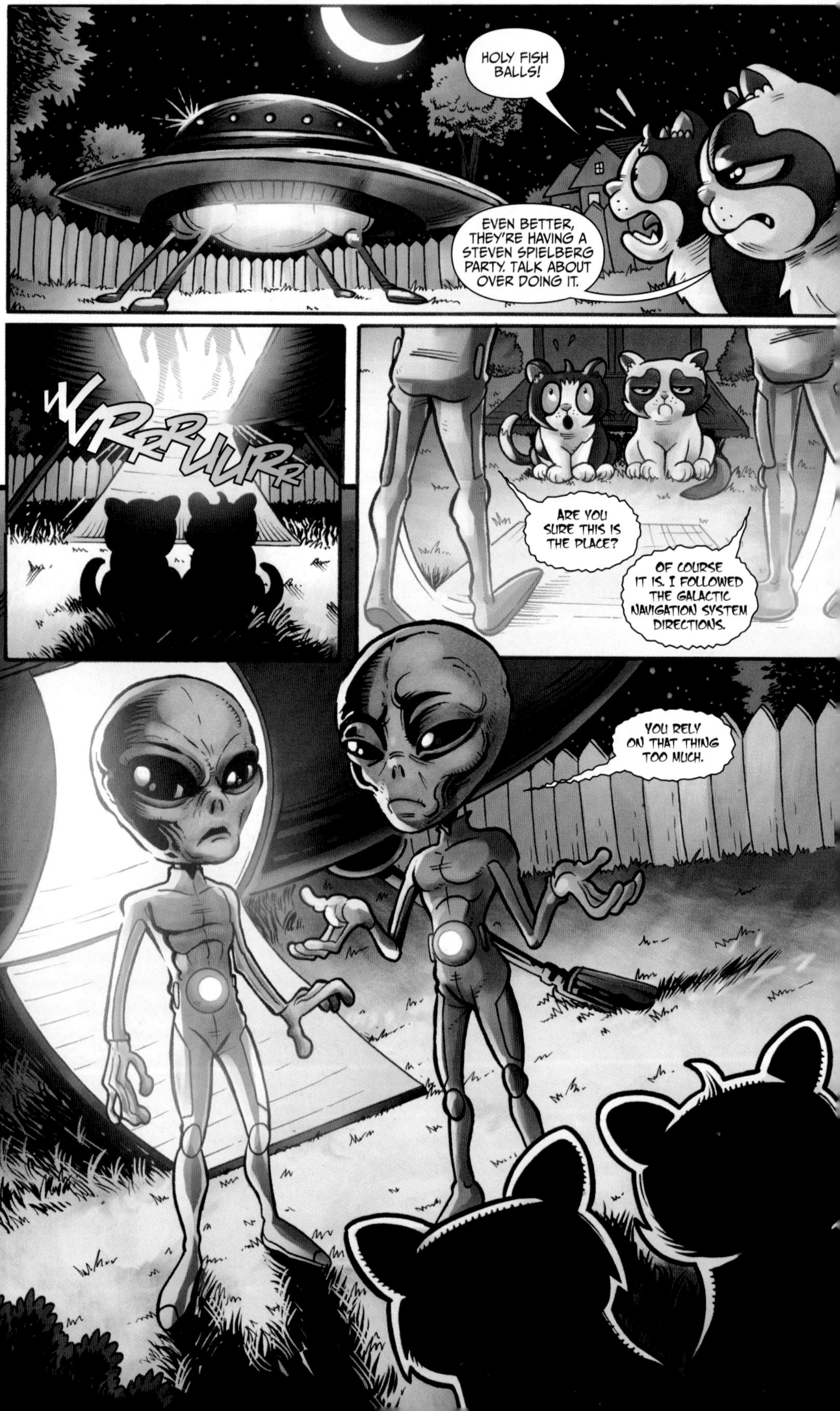
HOLY FISH BALLS!
EVEN BETTER, THEY'RE HAVING A STEVEN SPIELBERG PARTY. TALK ABOUT OVER DOING IT.
WRRRUURR
ARE YOU SURE THIS IS THE PLACE?
OF COURSE IT IS. I FOLLOWED THE GALACTIC NAVIGATION SYSTEM DIRECTIONS.
YOU RELY ON THAT THING TOO MUCH.

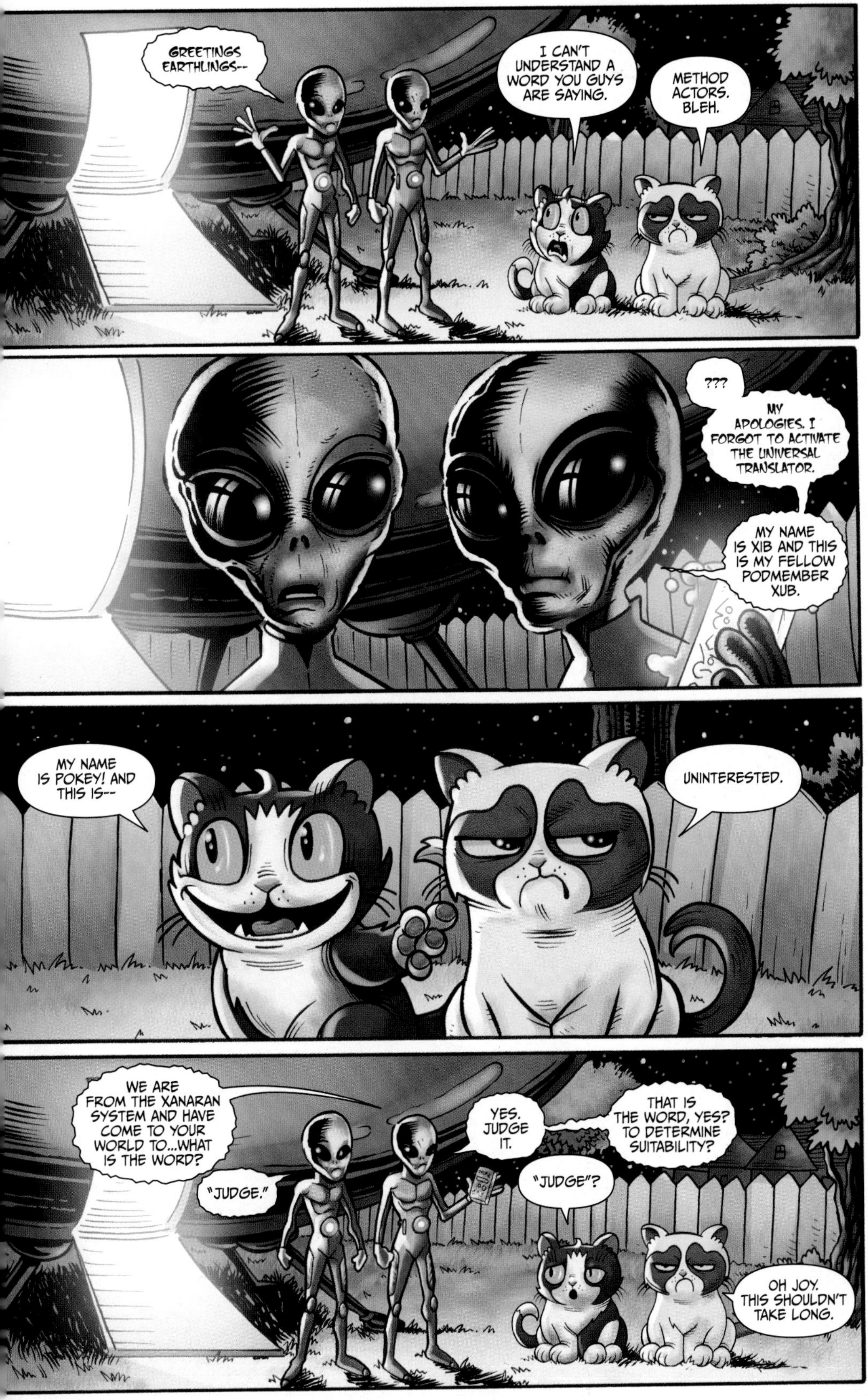
GREETINGS EARTHLINGS--
I CAN'T UNDERSTAND A WORD YOU GUYS ARE SAYING.
METHOD ACTORS. BLEH.
???
MY APOLOGIES. I FORGOT TO ACTIVATE THE UNIVERSAL TRANSLATOR.
MY NAME IS XIB AND THIS IS MY FELLOW PODMEMBER XUB.
MY NAME IS POKEY! AND THIS IS--
UNINTERESTED.
WE ARE FROM THE XANARAN SYSTEM AND HAVE COME TO YOUR WORLD TO...WHAT IS THE WORD?
"JUDGE."
YES. JUDGE IT.
THAT IS THE WORD, YES? TO DETERMINE SUITABILITY?
"JUDGE"?
OH JOY. THIS SHOULDN'T TAKE LONG.

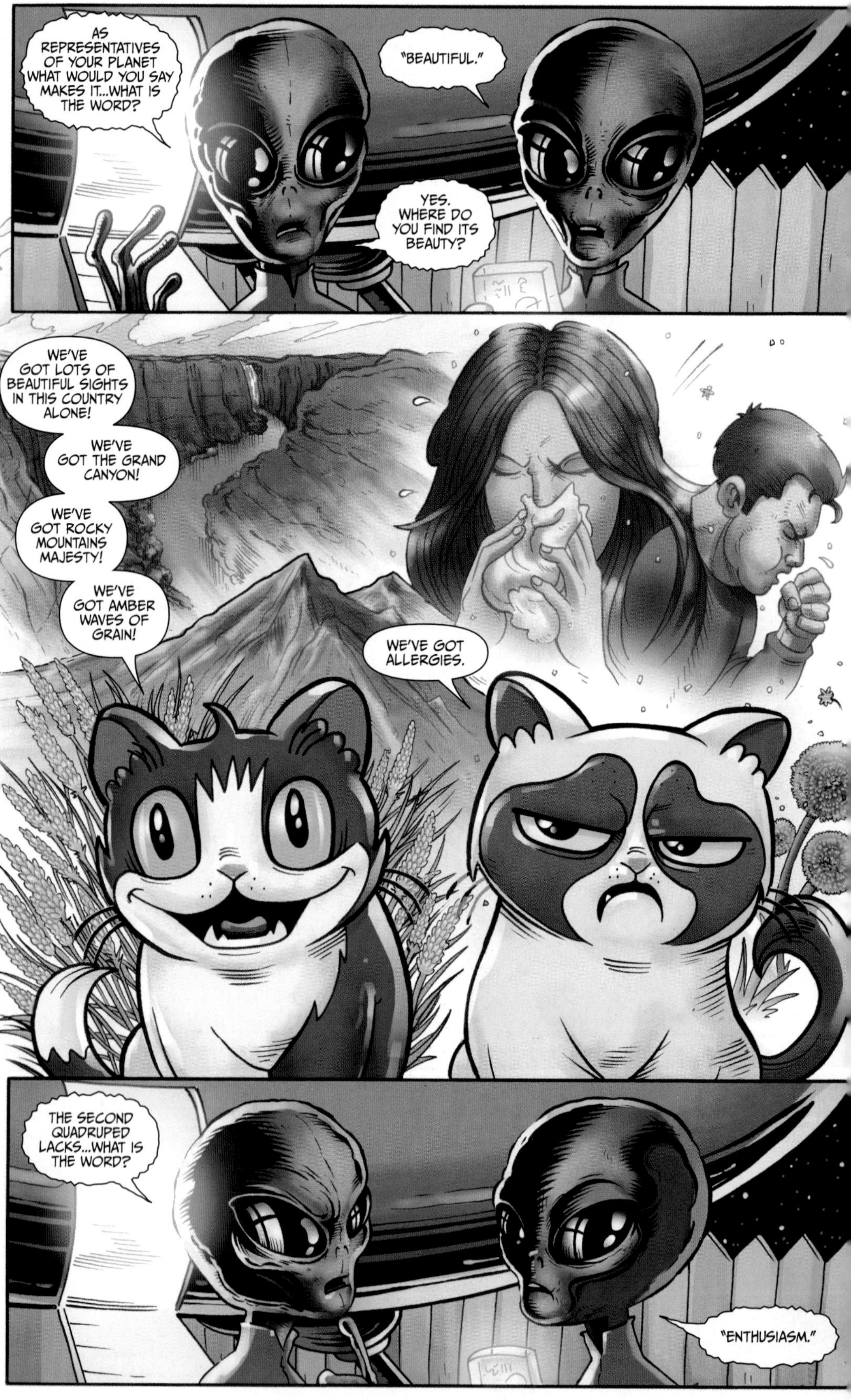

AS REPRESENTATIVES OF YOUR PLANET WHAT WOULD YOU SAY MAKES IT...WHAT IS THE WORD?
"BEAUTIFUL."
YES. WHERE DO YOU FIND ITS BEAUTY?
WE'VE GOT LOTS OF BEAUTIFUL SIGHTS IN THIS COUNTRY ALONE!
WE'VE GOT THE GRAND CANYON!
WE'VE GOT ROCKY MOUNTAINS MAJESTY!
WE'VE GOT AMBER WAVES OF GRAIN!
WE'VE GOT ALLERGIES.
THE SECOND QUADRUPED LACKS...WHAT IS THE WORD?
"ENTHUSIASM."

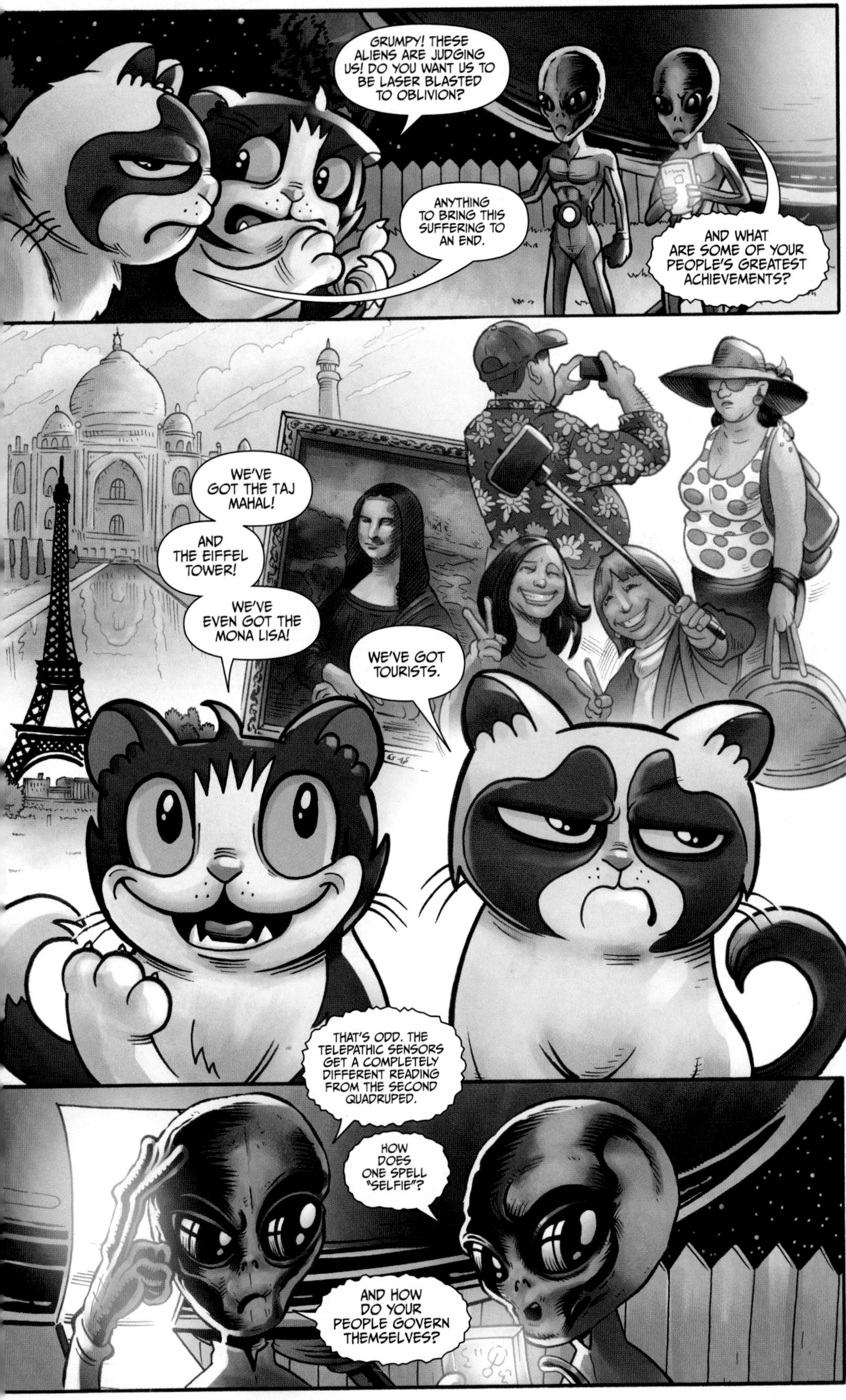
GRUMPY! THESE ALIENS ARE JUDGING US! DO YOU WANT US TO BE LASER BLASTED TO OBLIVION?
ANYTHING TO BRING THIS SUFFERING TO AN END.
AND WHAT ARE SOME OF YOUR PEOPLE'S GREATEST ACHIEVEMENTS?
WE'VE GOT THE TAJ MAHAL!
AND THE EIFFEL TOWER!
WE'VE EVEN GOT THE MONA LISA!
WE'VE GOT TOURISTS.
THAT'S ODD. THE TELEPATHIC SENSORS GET A COMPLETELY DIFFERENT READING FROM THE SECOND QUADRUPED.
HOW DOES ONE SPELL "SELFIE"?
AND HOW DO YOUR PEOPLE GOVERN THEMSELVES?

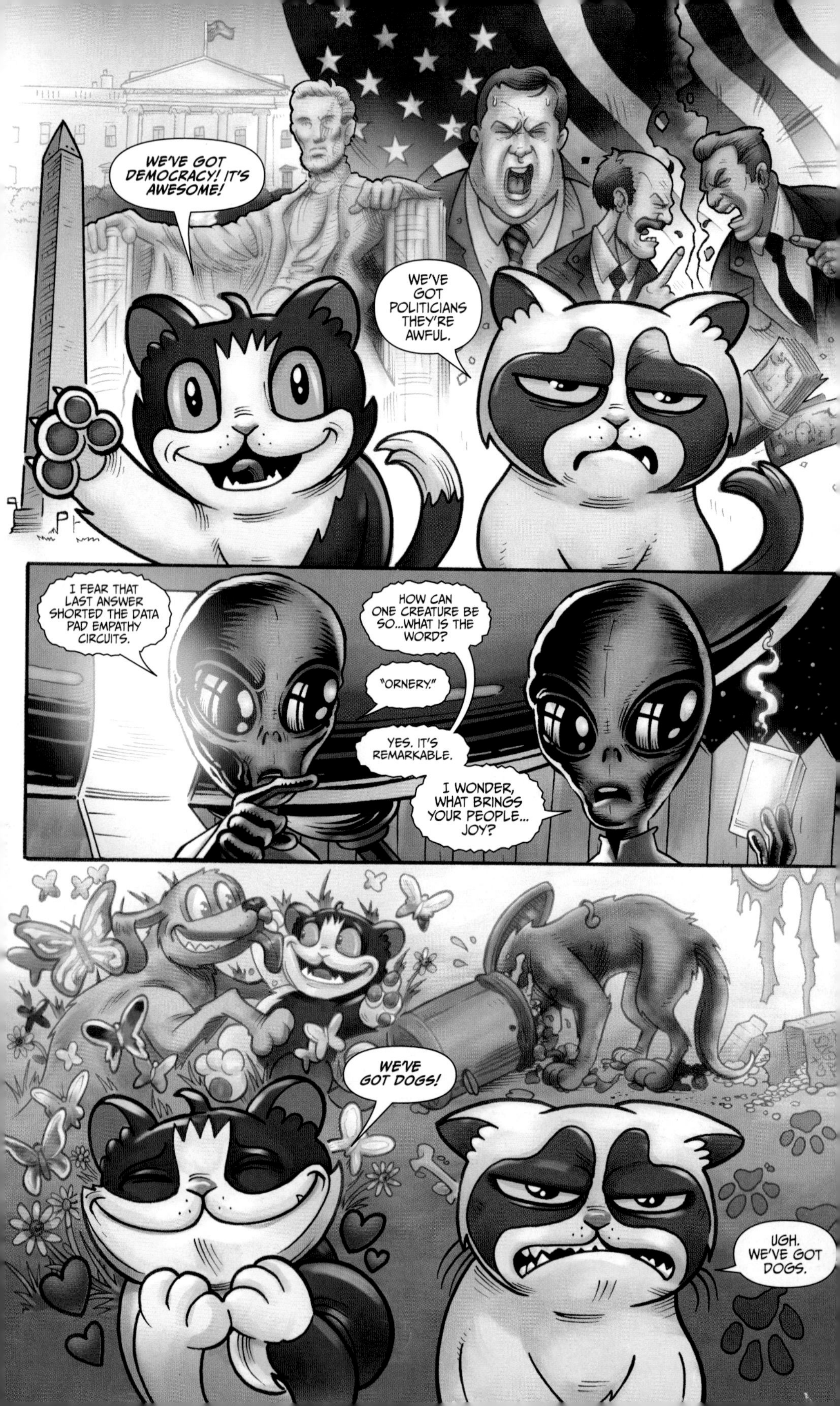
WE'VE GOT DEMOCRACY! IT'S AWESOME!
WE'VE GOT POLITICIANS THEY'RE AWFUL.
I FEAR THAT LAST ANSWER SHORTED THE DATA PAD EMPATHY CIRCUITS.
HOW CAN ONE CREATURE BE SO...WHAT IS THE WORD?
"ORNERY."
YES. IT'S REMARKABLE.
I WONDER, WHAT BRINGS YOUR PEOPLE... JOY?
WE'VE GOT DOGS!
UGH. WE'VE GOT DOGS.

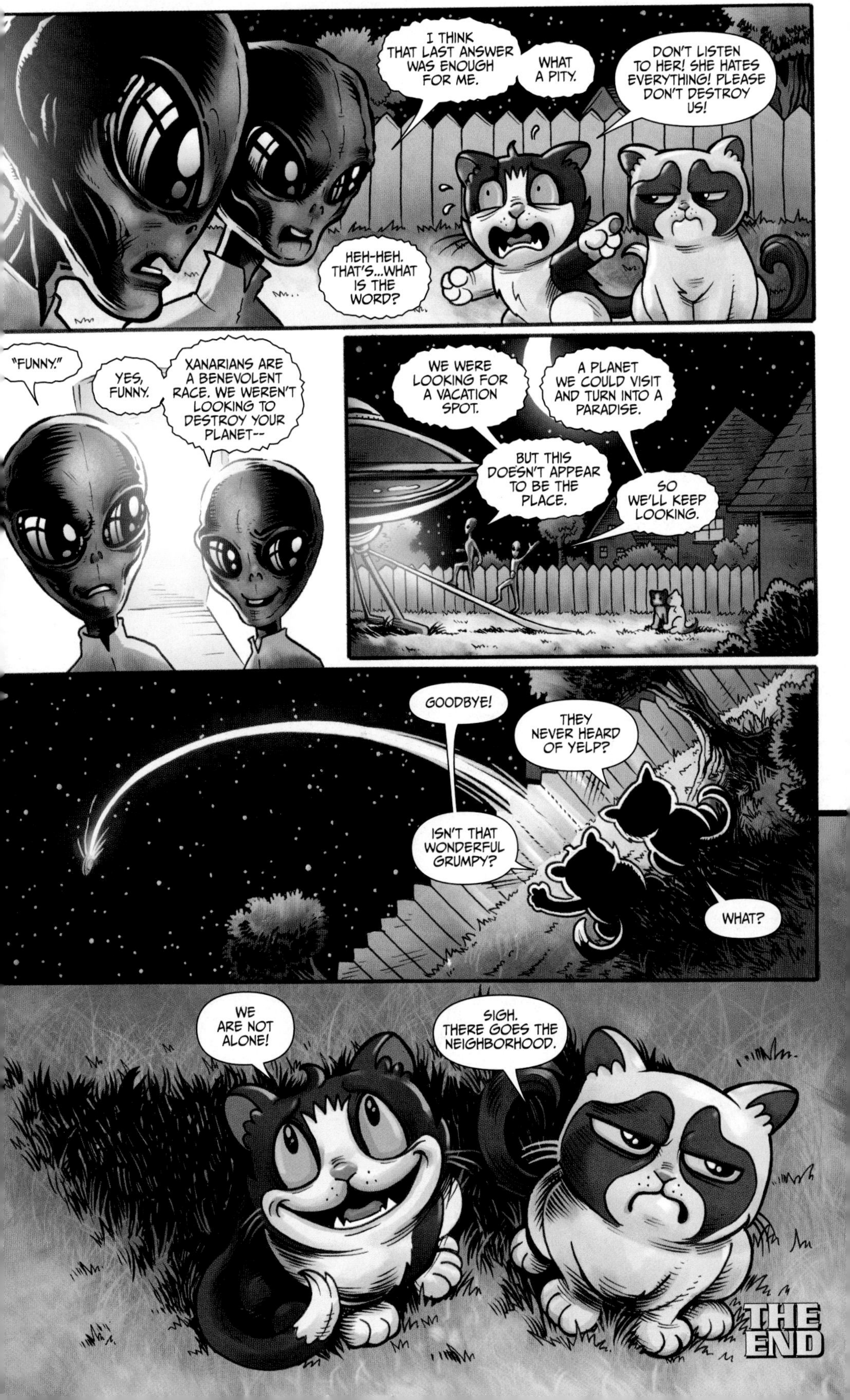
I THINK THAT LAST ANSWER WAS ENOUGH FOR ME.
WHAT A PITY.
DON'T LISTEN TO HER! SHE HATES EVERYTHING! PLEASE DON'T DESTROY US!
HEH-HEH. THAT'S...WHAT IS THE WORD?
"FUNNY."
YES, FUNNY.
XANARIANS ARE A BENEVOLENT RACE. WE WEREN'T LOOKING TO DESTROY YOUR PLANET--
WE WERE LOOKING FOR A VACATION SPOT.
A PLANET WE COULD VISIT AND TURN INTO A PARADISE.
BUT THIS DOESN'T APPEAR TO BE THE PLACE.
SO WE'LL KEEP LOOKING.
GOODBYE!
THEY NEVER HEARD OF YELP?
ISN'T THAT WONDERFUL GRUMPY?
WHAT?
WE ARE NOT ALONE!
SIGH. THERE GOES THE NEIGHBORHOOD.
THE END

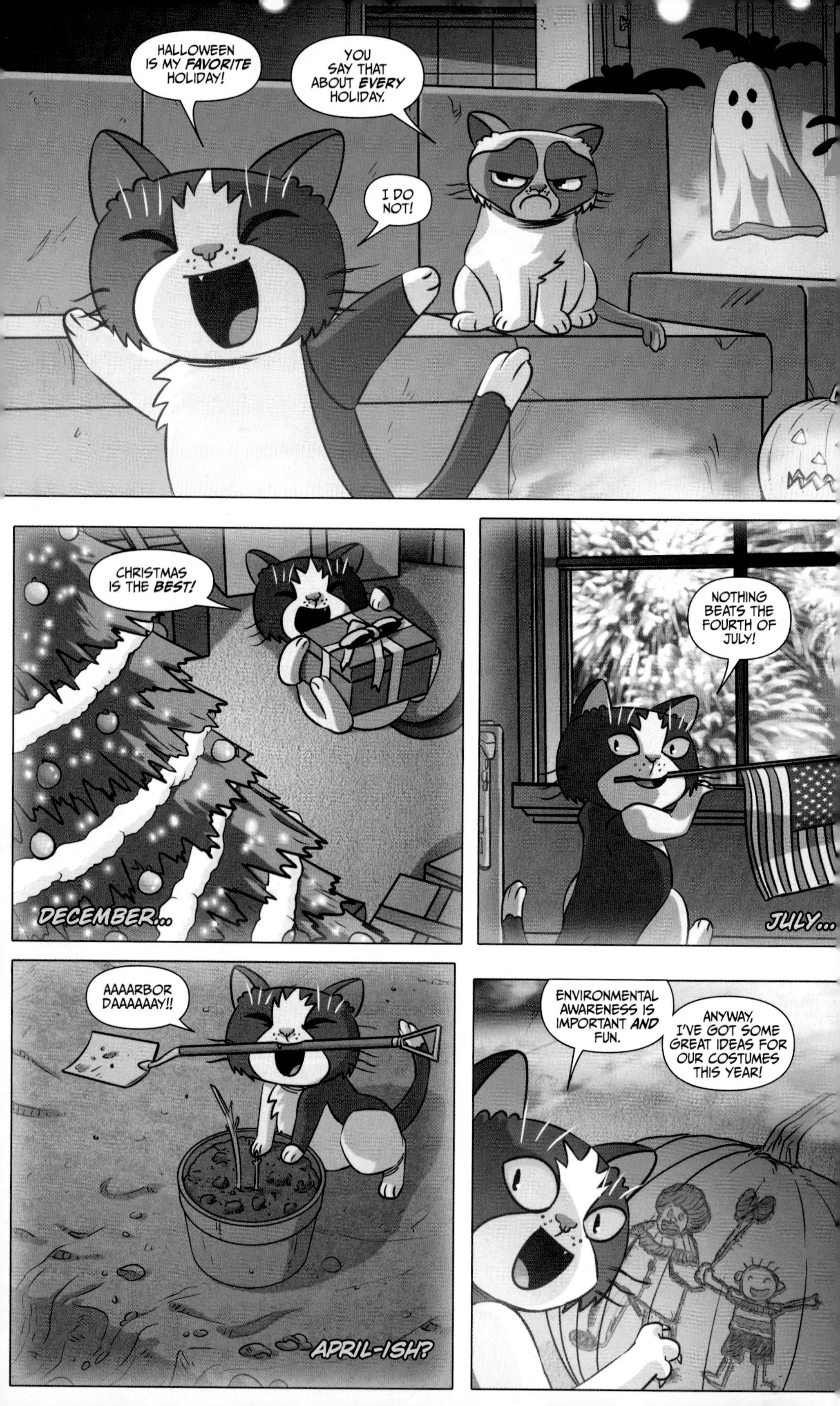

HALLOWEEN IS MY FAVORITE HOLIDAY!
YOU SAY THAT ABOUT EVERY HOLIDAY.
I DO NOT!
CHRISTMAS IS THE BEST!
DECEMBER...
NOTHING BEATS THE FOURTH OF JULY!
JULY...
AAAARBOR DAAAAAAY!!
APRIL-ISH?
ENVIRONMENTAL AWARENESS IS IMPORTANT AND FUN.
ANYWAY, I'VE GOT SOME GREAT IDEAS FOR OUR COSTUMES THIS YEAR!

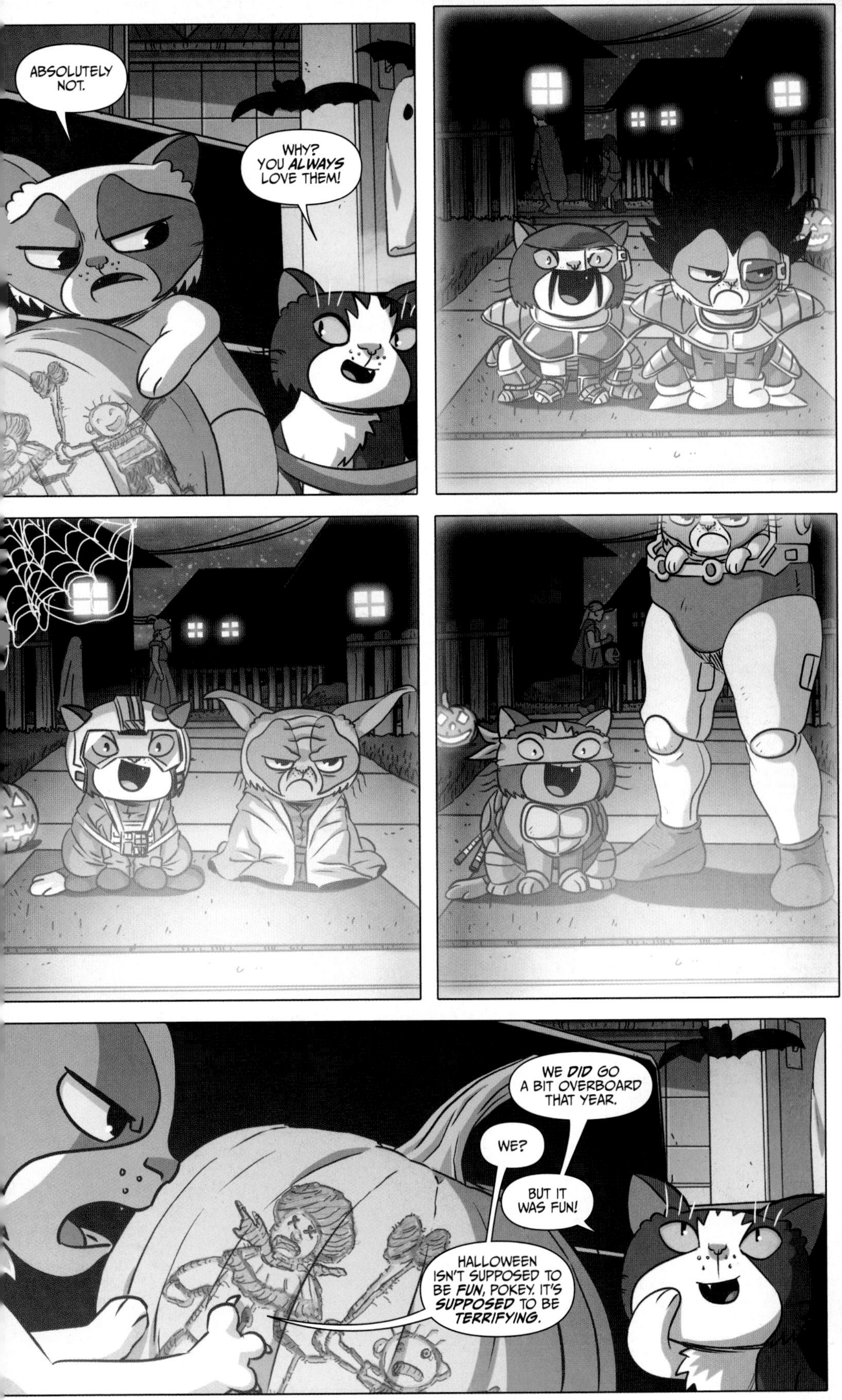
ABSOLUTELY NOT.
WHY? YOU ALWAYS LOVE THEM!
WE DID GO A BIT OVERBOARD THAT YEAR.
WE?
BUT IT WAS FUN!
HALLOWEEN ISN'T SUPPOSED TO BE FUN, POKEY. IT'S SUPPOSED TO BE TERRIFYING.

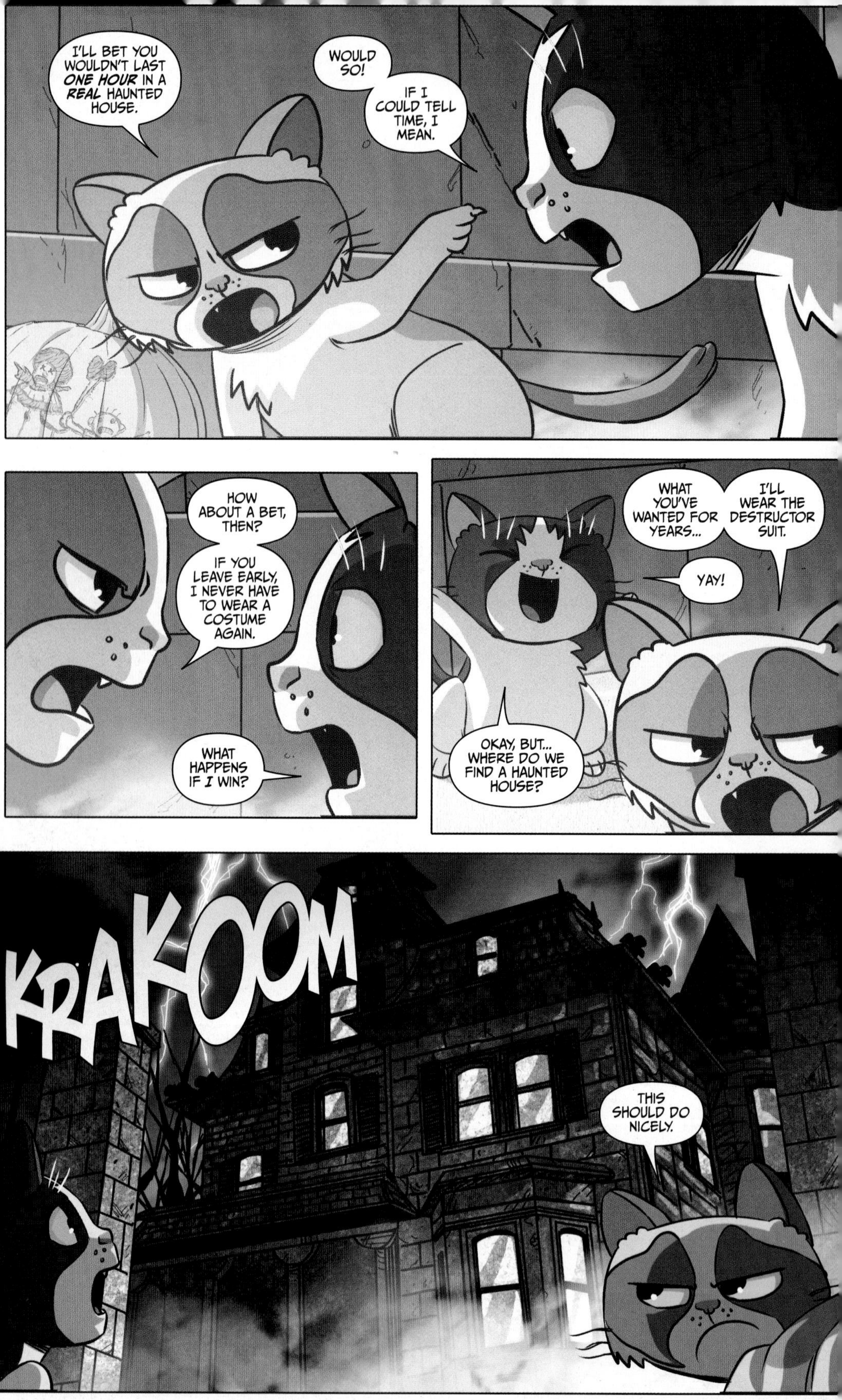
I'LL BET YOU WOULDN'T LAST ***ONE HOUR*** IN A ***REAL*** HAUNTED HOUSE.
WOULD SO!
IF I COULD TELL TIME, I MEAN.
HOW ABOUT A BET, THEN?
IF YOU LEAVE EARLY, I NEVER HAVE TO WEAR A COSTUME AGAIN.
WHAT HAPPENS IF *I* WIN?
WHAT YOU'VE WANTED FOR YEARS...
I'LL WEAR THE DESTRUCTOR SUIT.
YAY!
OKAY, BUT... WHERE DO WE FIND A HAUNTED HOUSE?
KRAKOOM
THIS SHOULD DO NICELY.

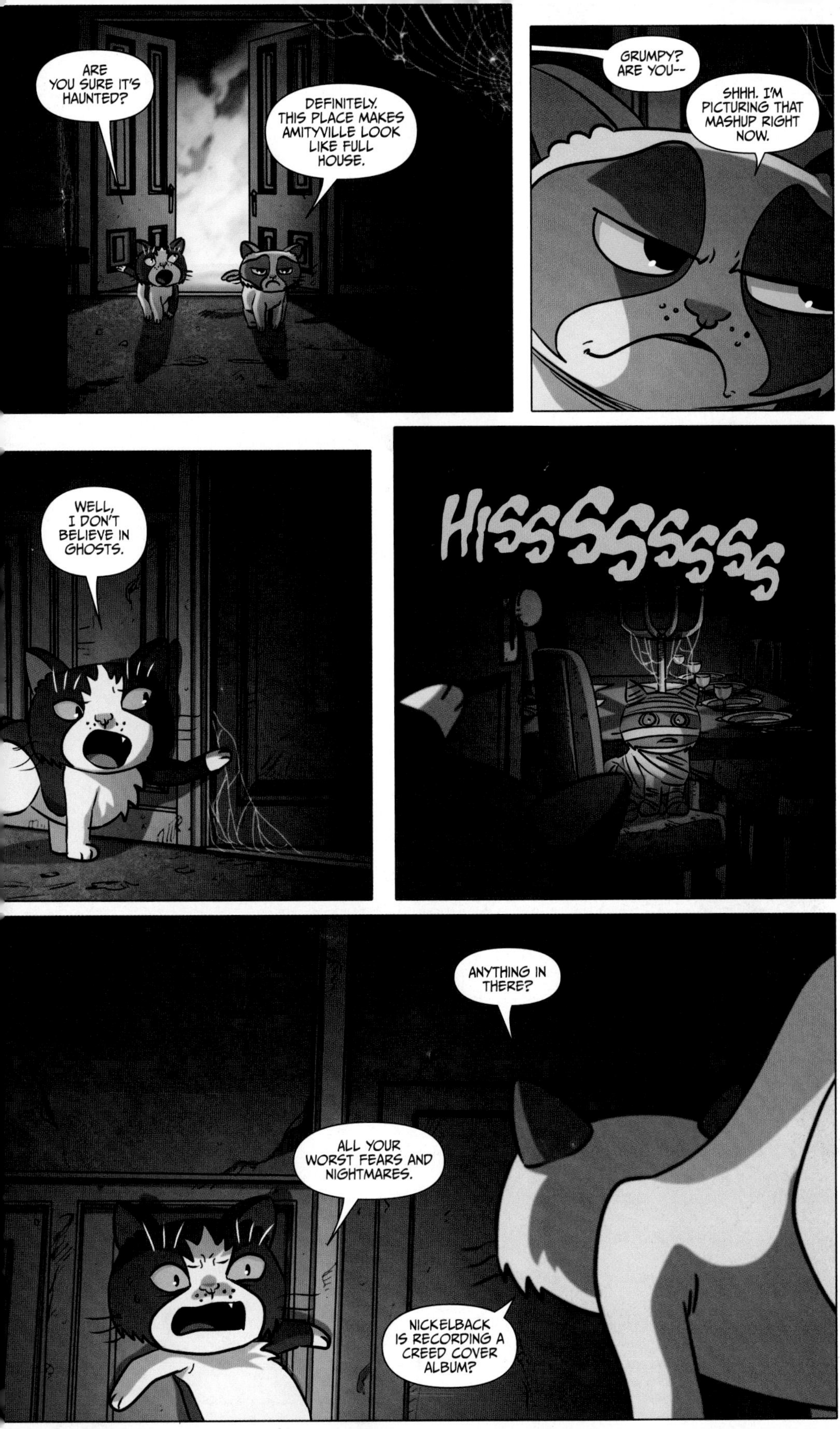
ARE YOU SURE IT'S HAUNTED?
DEFINITELY. THIS PLACE MAKES AMITYVILLE LOOK LIKE FULL HOUSE.
GRUMPY? ARE YOU--
SHHH. I'M PICTURING THAT MASHUP RIGHT NOW.
WELL, I DON'T BELIEVE IN GHOSTS.
HISSSSSSSS
ANYTHING IN THERE?
ALL YOUR WORST FEARS AND NIGHTMARES.
NICKELBACK IS RECORDING A CREED COVER ALBUM?

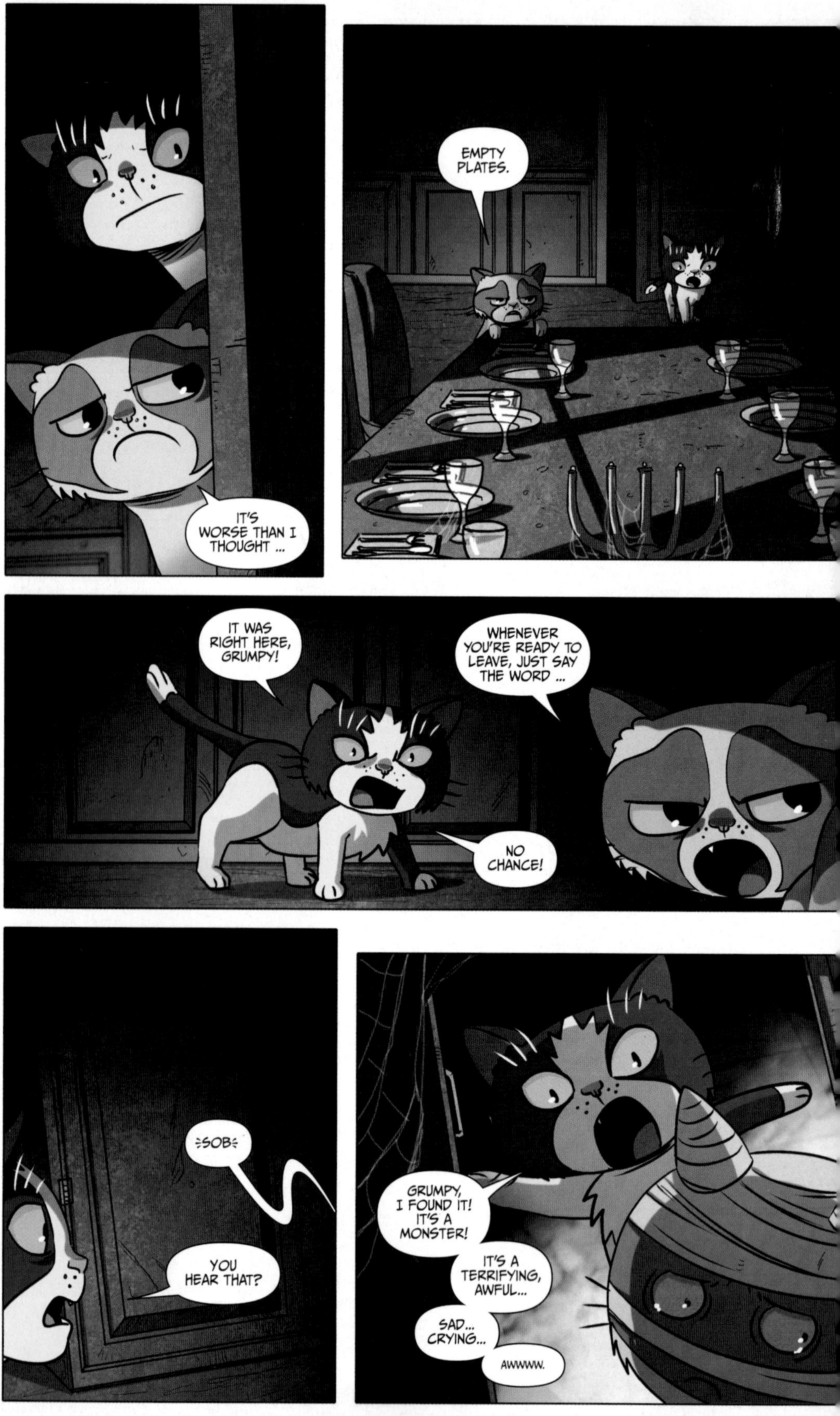
IT'S WORSE THAN I THOUGHT ...
EMPTY PLATES.
IT WAS RIGHT HERE, GRUMPY!
WHENEVER YOU'RE READY TO LEAVE, JUST SAY THE WORD ...
NO CHANCE!
SOB
YOU HEAR THAT?
GRUMPY, I FOUND IT! IT'S A MONSTER!
IT'S A TERRIFYING, AWFUL...
SAD... CRYING...
AWWWW.

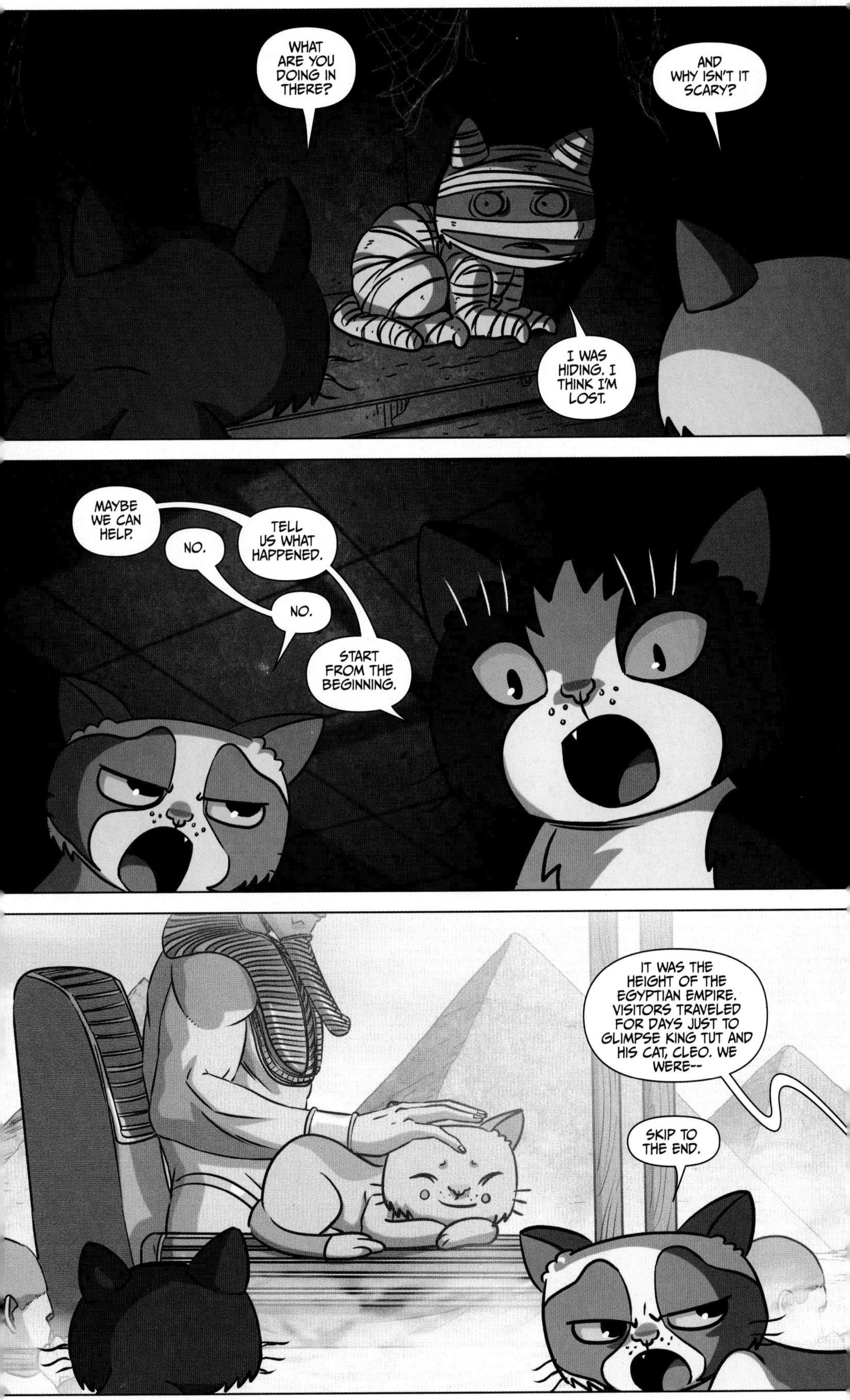
WHAT ARE YOU DOING IN THERE?
AND WHY ISN'T IT SCARY?
I WAS HIDING. I THINK I'M LOST.
MAYBE WE CAN HELP.
NO.
TELL US WHAT HAPPENED.
NO.
START FROM THE BEGINNING.
IT WAS THE HEIGHT OF THE EGYPTIAN EMPIRE. VISITORS TRAVELED FOR DAYS JUST TO GLIMPSE KING TUT AND HIS CAT, CLEO. WE WERE--
SKIP TO THE END.

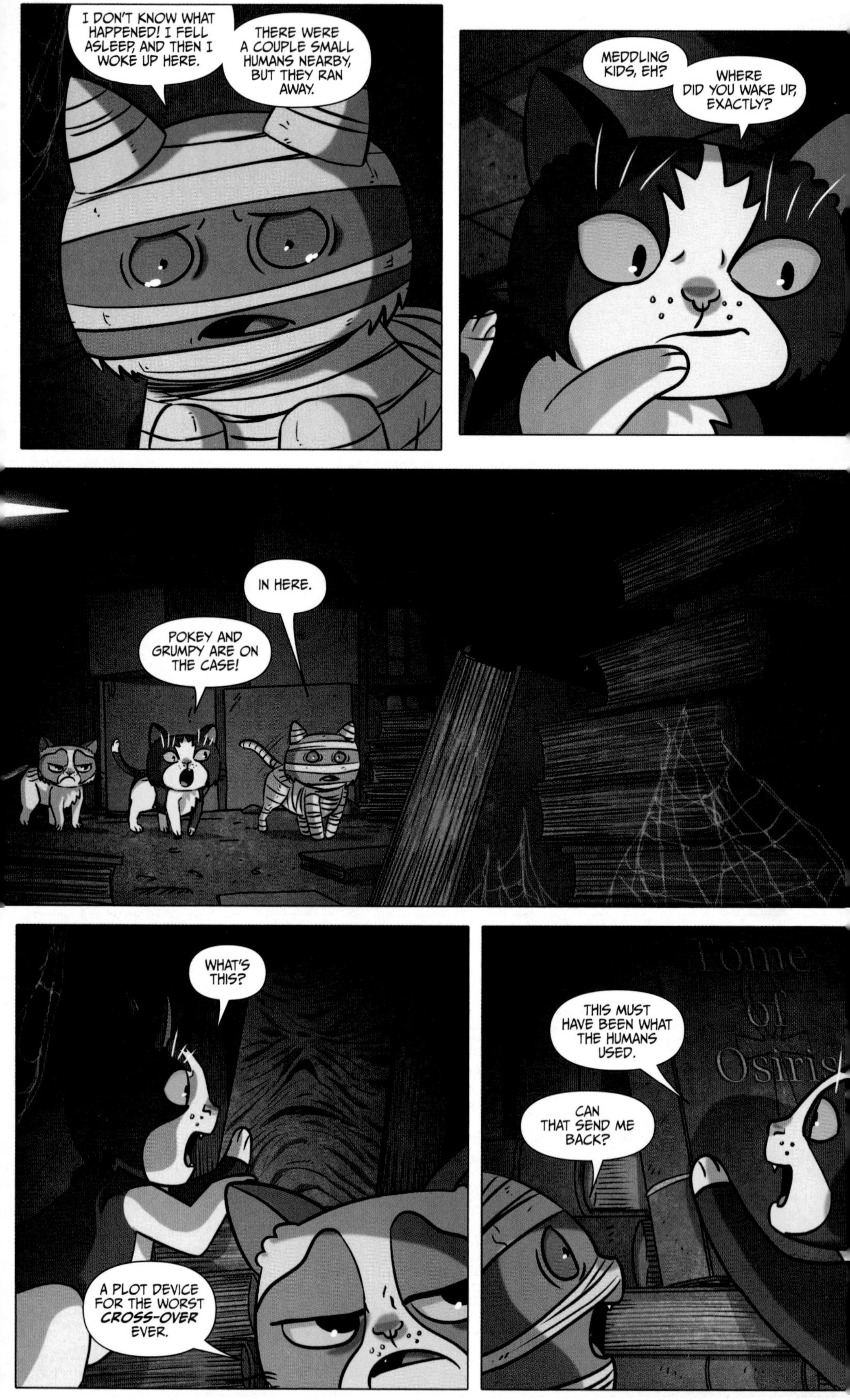
I DON'T KNOW WHAT HAPPENED! I FELL ASLEEP, AND THEN I WOKE UP HERE.
THERE WERE A COUPLE SMALL HUMANS NEARBY, BUT THEY RAN AWAY.
MEDDLING KIDS, EH?
WHERE DID YOU WAKE UP, EXACTLY?
POKEY AND GRUMPY ARE ON THE CASE!
IN HERE.
WHAT'S THIS?
A PLOT DEVICE FOR THE WORST *CROSS-OVER* EVER.
Tome of Osiris
THIS MUST HAVE BEEN WHAT THE HUMANS USED.
CAN THAT SEND ME BACK?

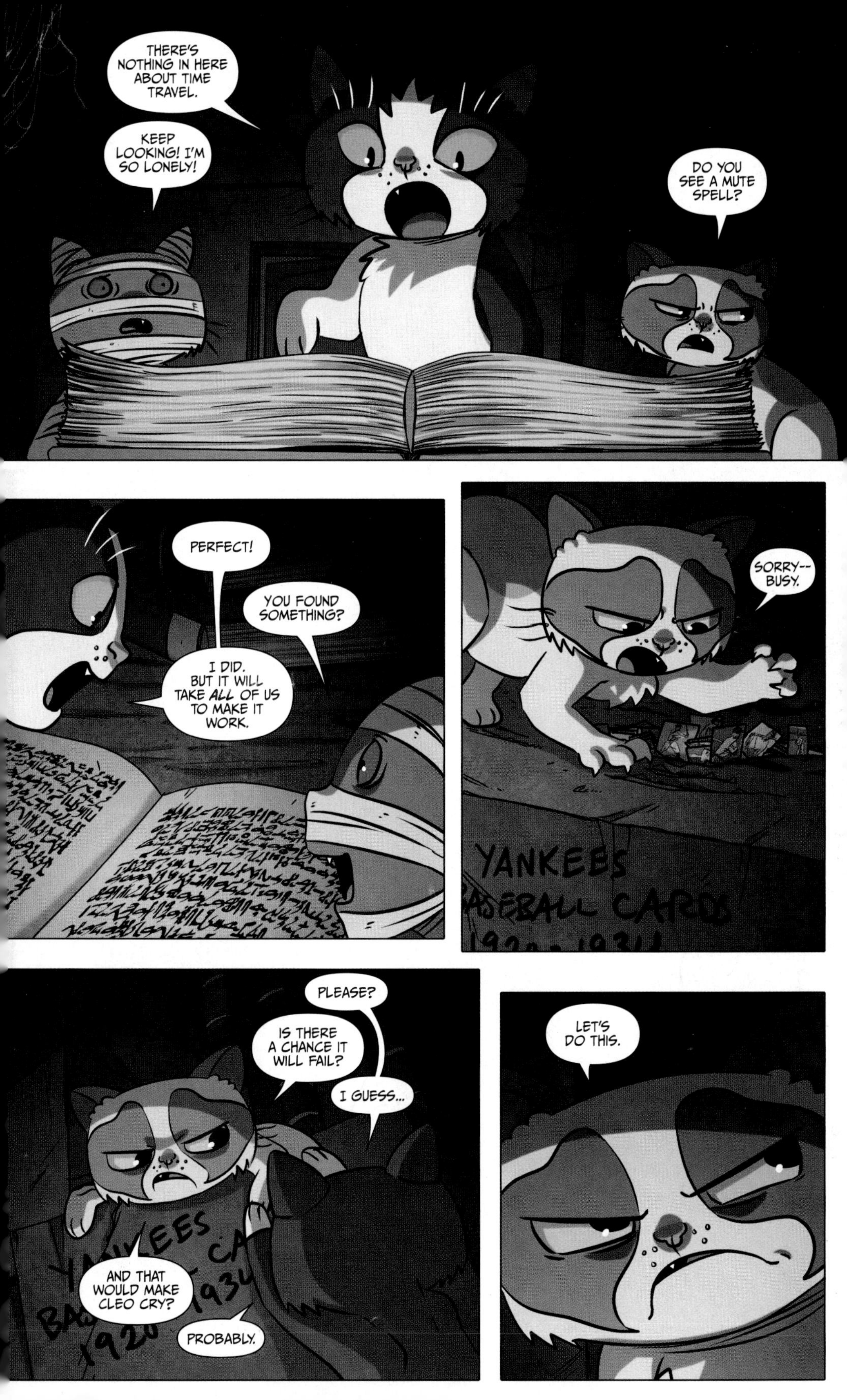
THERE'S NOTHING IN HERE ABOUT TIME TRAVEL.
KEEP LOOKING! I'M SO LONELY!
DO YOU SEE A MUTE SPELL?
PERFECT!
YOU FOUND SOMETHING?
I DID. BUT IT WILL TAKE ALL OF US TO MAKE IT WORK.
SORRY--BUSY.
YANKEES BASEBALL CARDS
PLEASE?
IS THERE A CHANCE IT WILL FAIL?
I GUESS...
AND THAT WOULD MAKE CLEO CRY?
PROBABLY.
LET'S DO THIS.

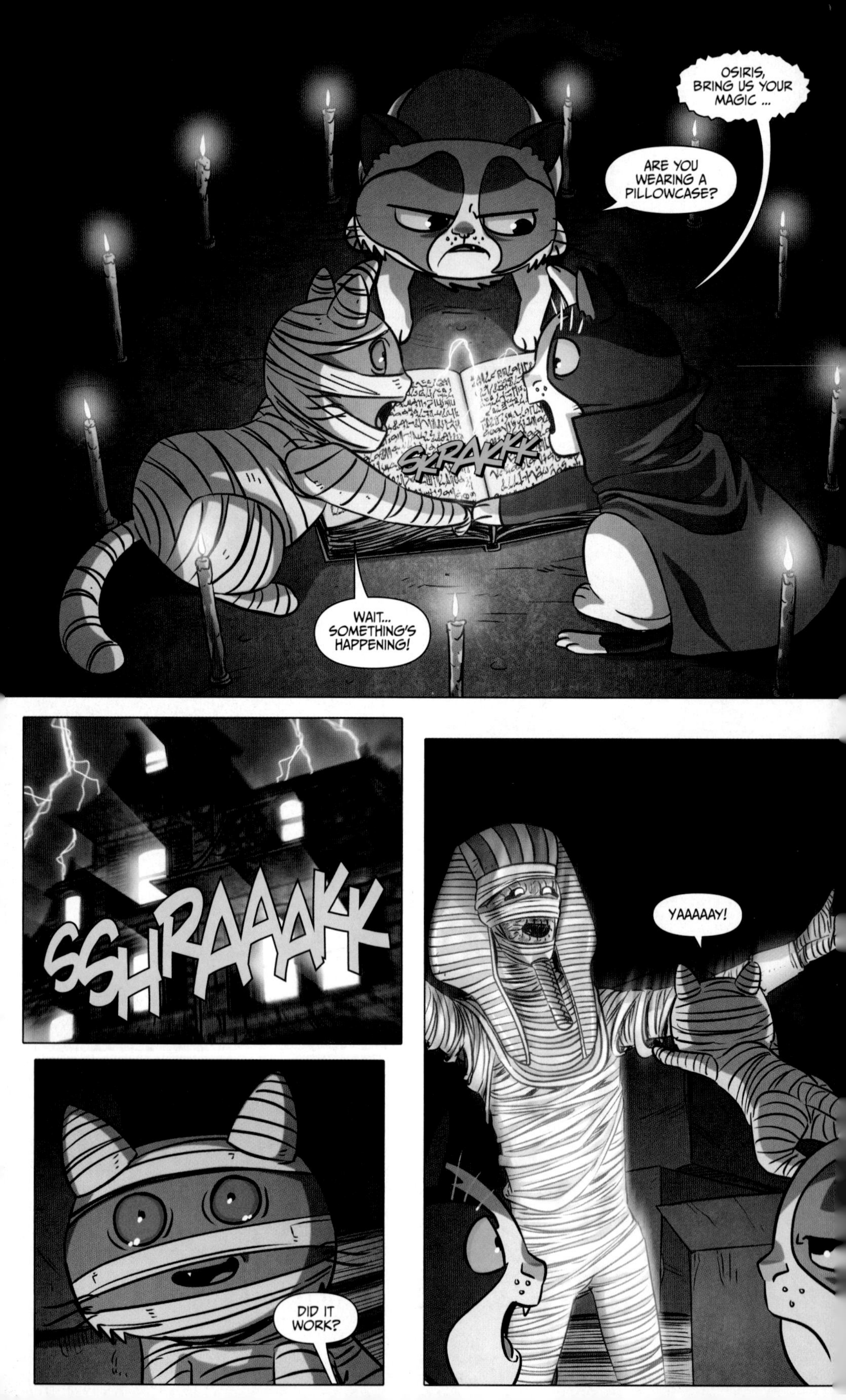
OSIRIS, BRING US YOUR MAGIC ...
ARE YOU WEARING A PILLOWCASE?
SKRAKK
WAIT... SOMETHING'S HAPPENING!
SSHRAAAKK
DID IT WORK?
YAAAAAY!

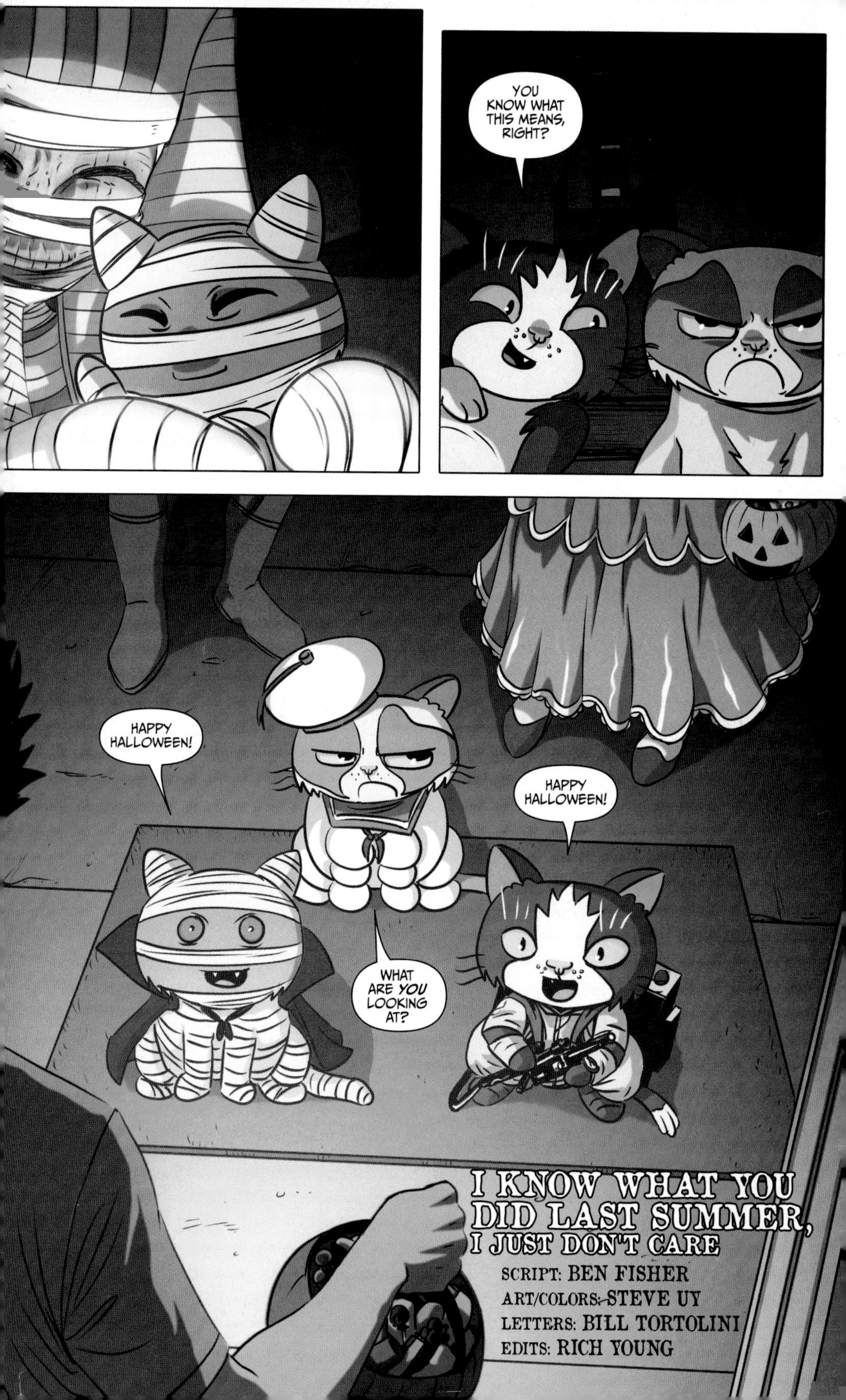
YOU KNOW WHAT THIS MEANS, RIGHT?
HAPPY HALLOWEEN!
HAPPY HALLOWEEN!
WHAT ARE YOU LOOKING AT?
I KNOW WHAT YOU DID LAST SUMMER, I JUST DON'T CARE
SCRIPT: BEN FISHER
ART/COLORS: STEVE UY
LETTERS: BILL TORTOLINI
EDITS: RICH YOUNG

BONUS MATERIAL

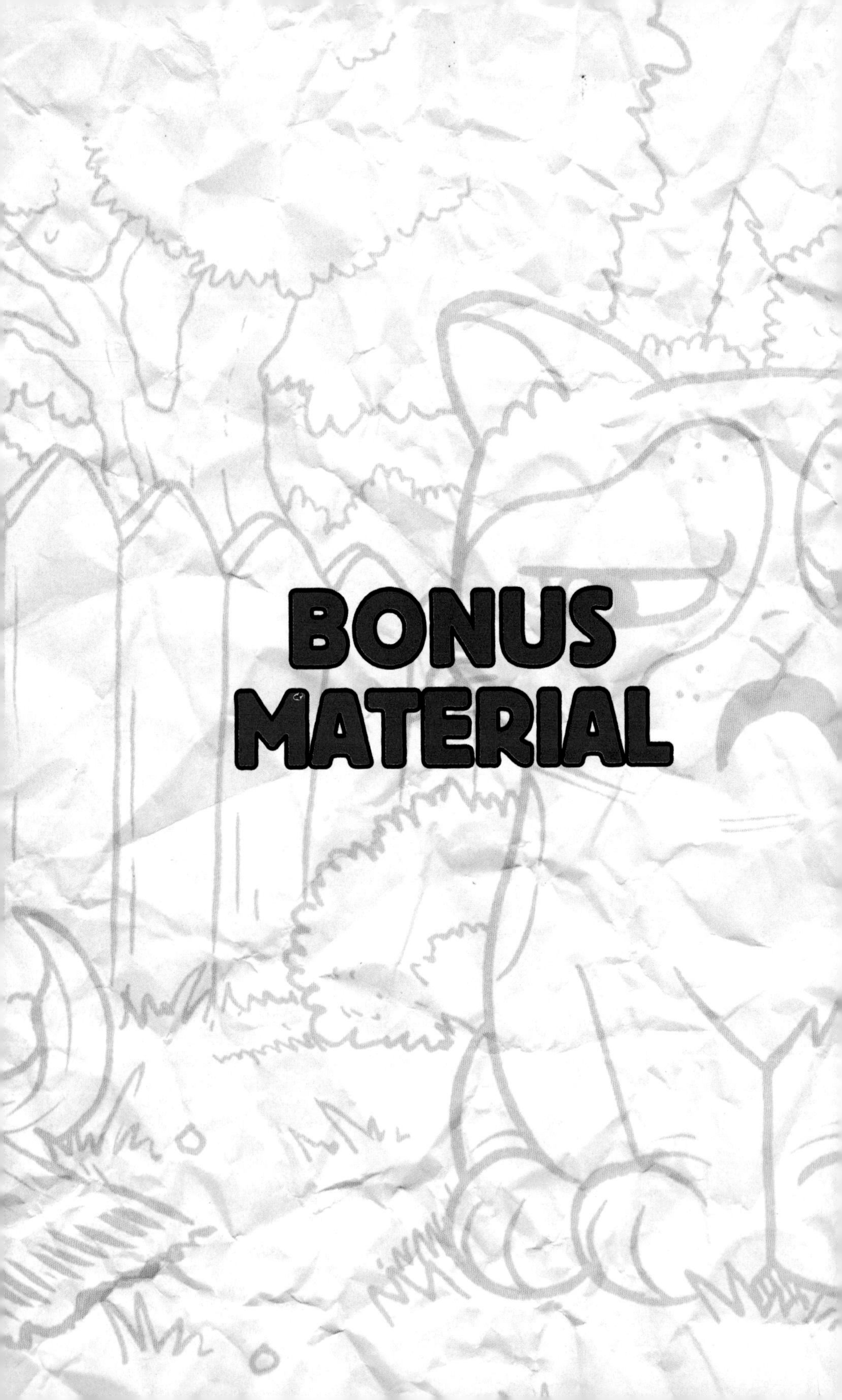

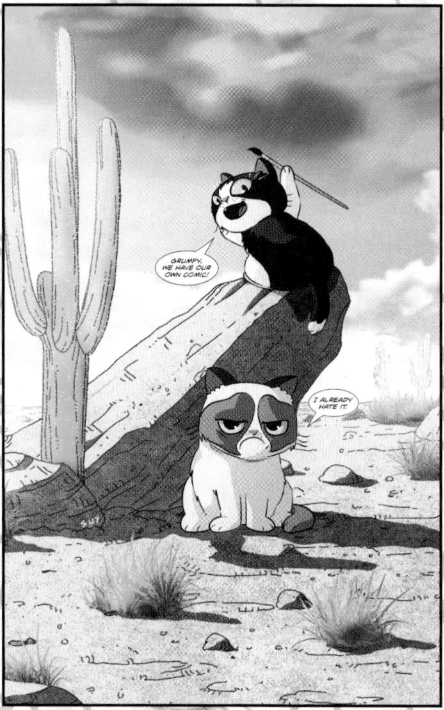
GRUMPY, WE HAVE OUR OWN COMIC!
I ALREADY HATE IT.

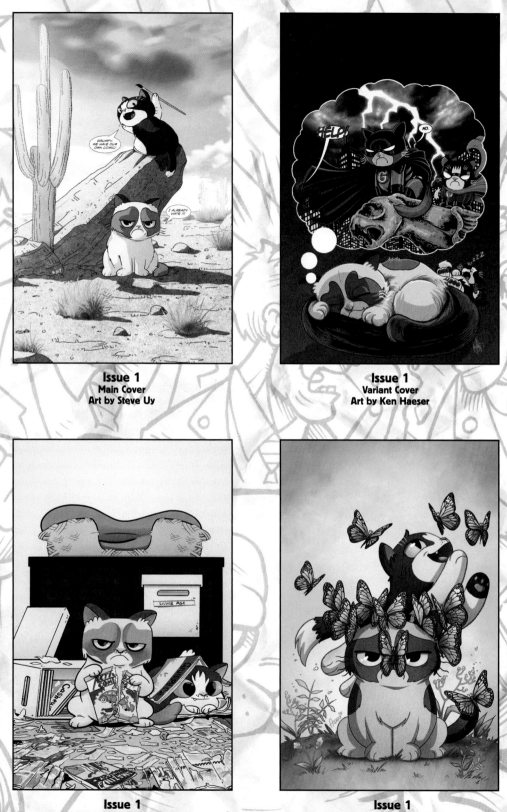

Issue 1
Main Cover
Art by Steve Uy

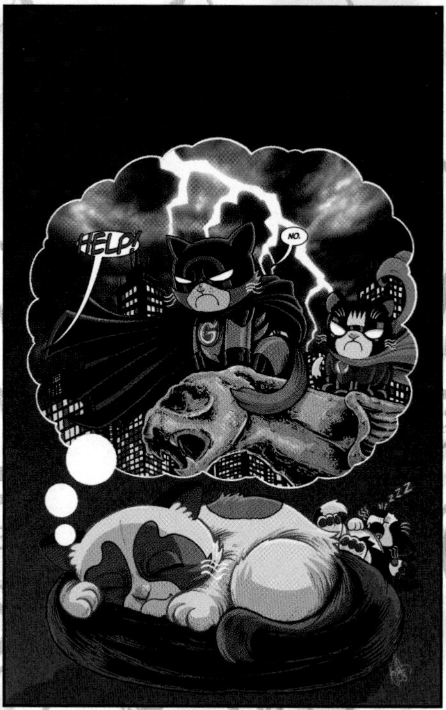
HELP!
NO.

Issue 1
Variant Cover
Art by Ken Haeser

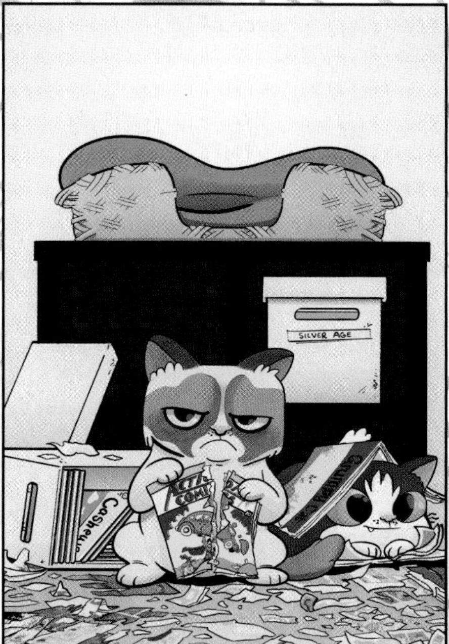
SILVER AGE

Issue 1
Variant Cover
Art by Tavis Maiden

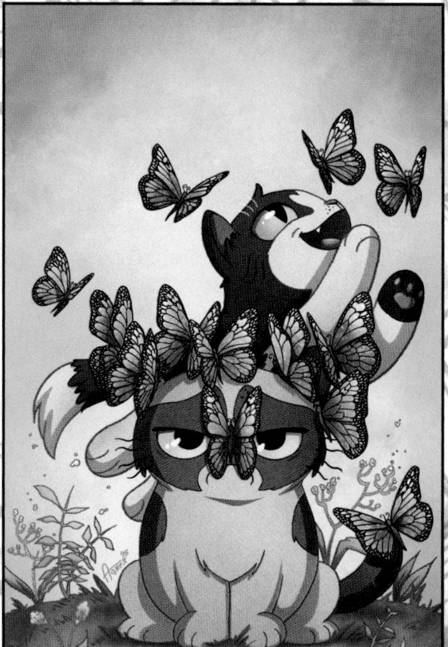

Issue 1
Variant Cover
Art by Agnes Garbowska

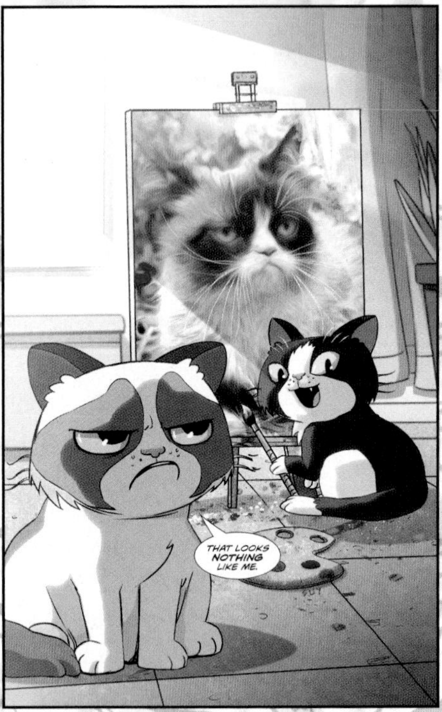
THAT LOOKS NOTHING LIKE ME.

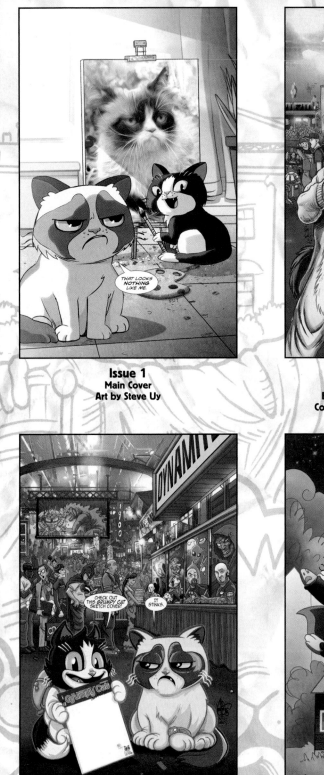

Issue 1
Main Cover
Art by Steve Uy

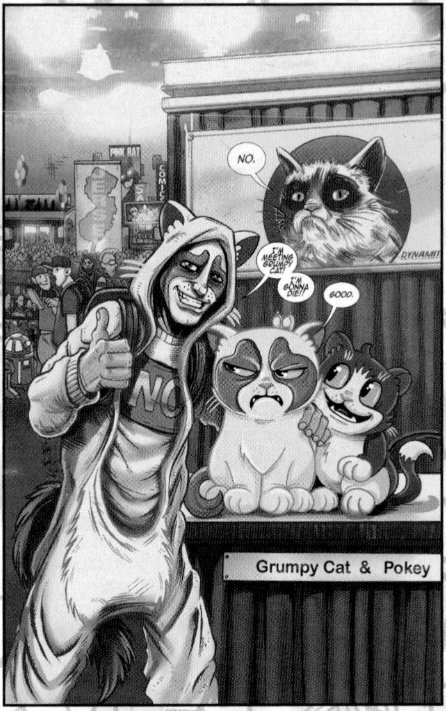
NO.
I'M MEETING GRUMPY CAT!
I'M GONNA DIE!!
GOOD.
Grumpy Cat & Pokey

Issue 1
New Jersey Comic Expo
Exclusive Cover Art by Ken Haeser
Colors by Buz Hasson and Blair Smith

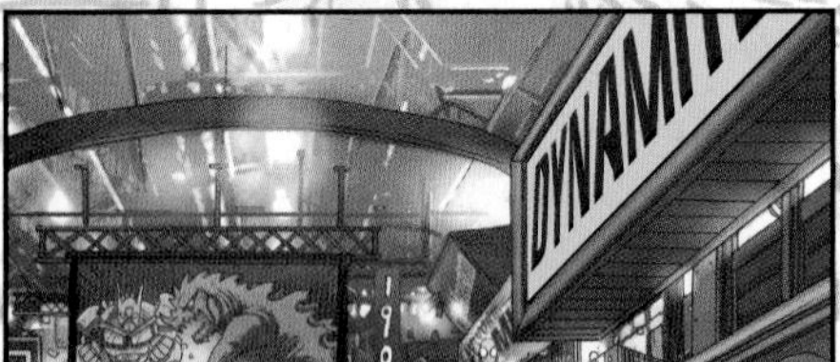
CHECK OUT THIS GRUMPY CAT SKETCH COVER!
IT STINKS.

Issue 1
New York Comic-Con Exclusive Cover
Art by Ken Haeser
Colors by Buz Hasson and Blair Smith

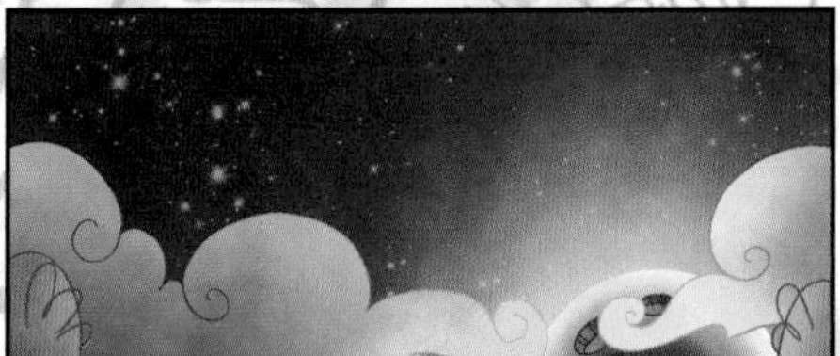
1811
SWEET JENNY'S

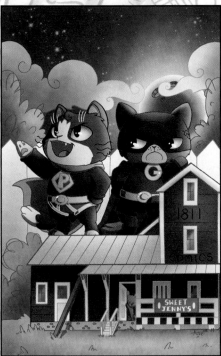

Issue 1
1811 Comics Exclusive Cover
Art by Agnes Garbowska

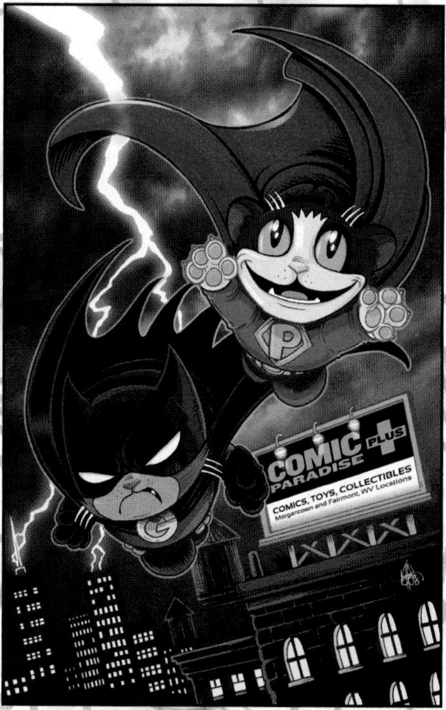
COMIC PARADISE PLUS
COMICS, TOYS, COLLECTIBLES
Morgantown and Fairmont, WV Locations

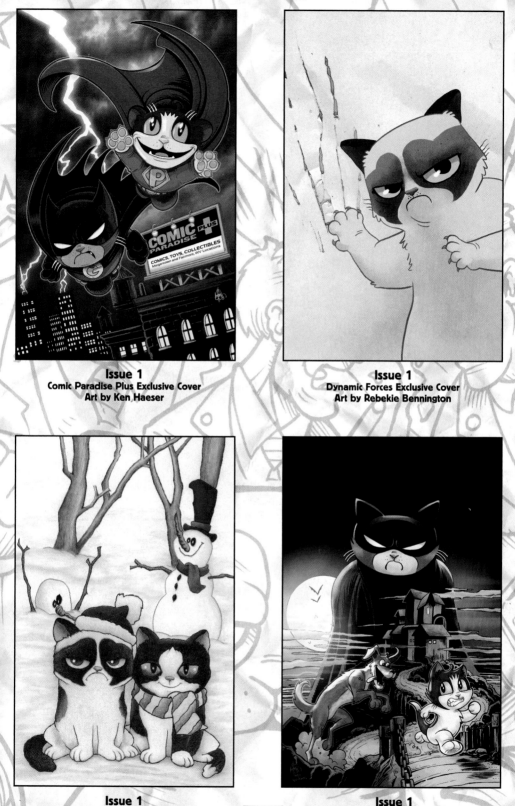

Issue 1
Comic Paradise Plus Exclusive Cover
Art by Ken Haeser

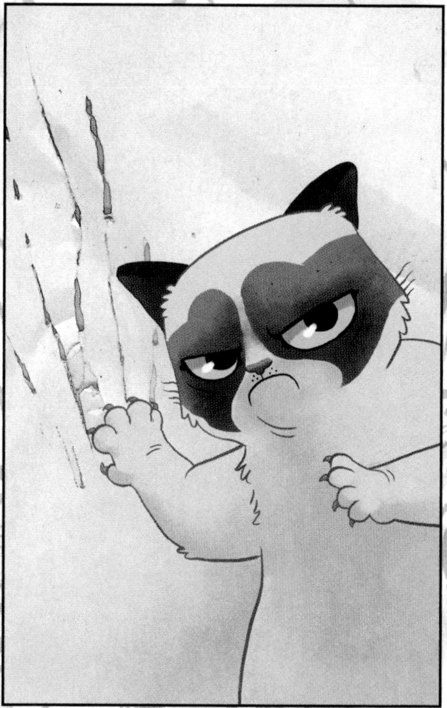

Issue 1
Dynamic Forces Exclusive Cover
Art by Rebekie Bennington

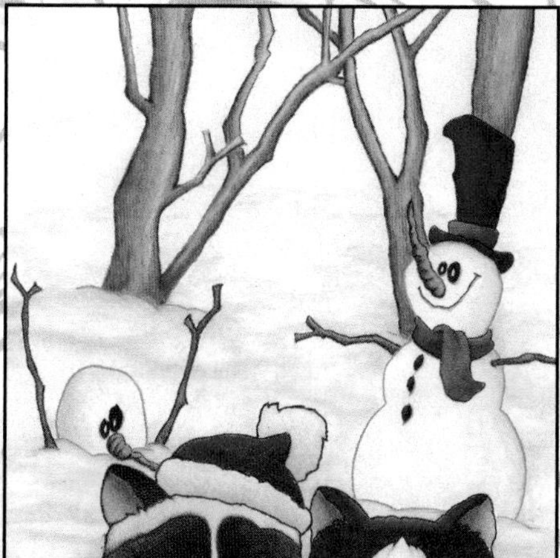

Issue 1
Fat Jack's Comicrypt Exclusive Cover
Art by Brian Rapp

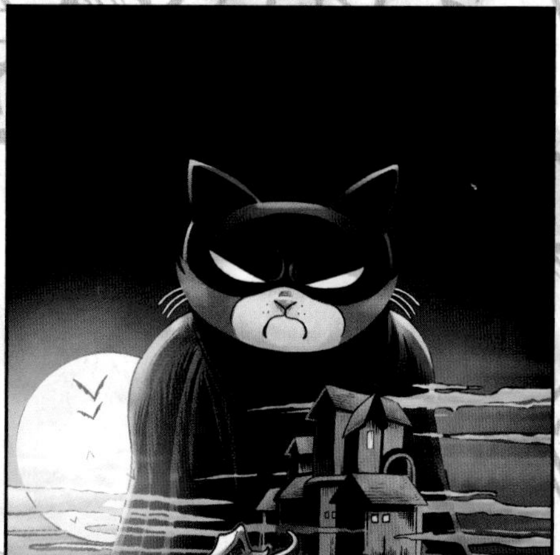

Issue 1
Hoknes Comics Exclusive Cover
Art by Ken Haeser

GRUMPY CAT
WISH YOU WERE HERE...
NEW YORK
COMIC CON
...INSTEAD OF ME.
In Your Dreams Collectibles

Issue 1
In Your Dreams Collectibles Exclusive Cover
Art by Tavis Maiden

AISLE
1900
THIS SHOW IS HUGE...
NOT IMPRESSED.
MIDTOWN COMICS
NYC

Issue 1
Midtown Comics Exclusive Cover
Art by Steve Uy

VOTE FOR GRUMPY

Issue 1
Newbury Comics Exclusive Cover
Art by Mauro Vargas
Colors by Mohan

UGH. THE THINGS I'LL DO FOR A GOOD CAUSE...

Issue 1
Saved Whiskers Rescue Exclusive Cover
Art by Ken Haeser

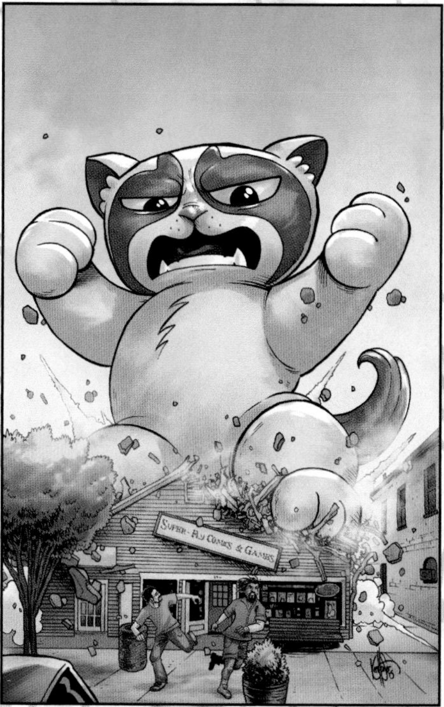
Super-Fly Comics & Games

Issue 1
Super Fly Comics Exclusive Cover
Art by Ken Haeser
Colors by Mohan

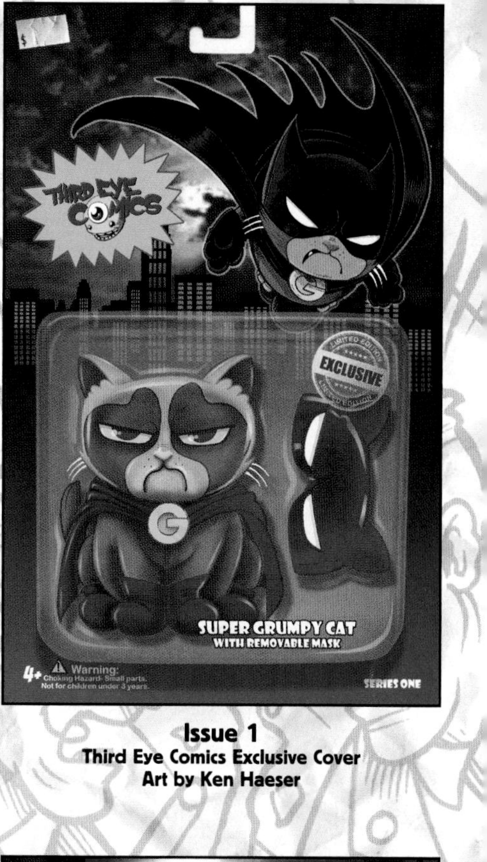
Third Eye Comics
Exclusive
Super Grumpy Cat
With Removable Mask
4+
Warning
Choking Hazard- Small parts.
Not for children under 3 years.
Series One

Issue 1
Third Eye Comics Exclusive Cover
Art by Ken Haeser

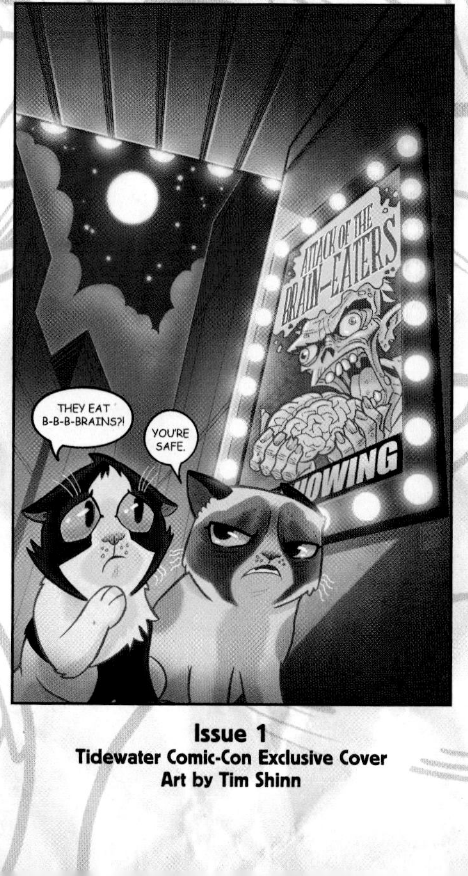
Attack of the Brain-Eaters
THEY EAT B-B-B-BRAINS?!
YOU'RE SAFE.

Issue 1
Tidewater Comic-Con Exclusive Cover
Art by Tim Shinn

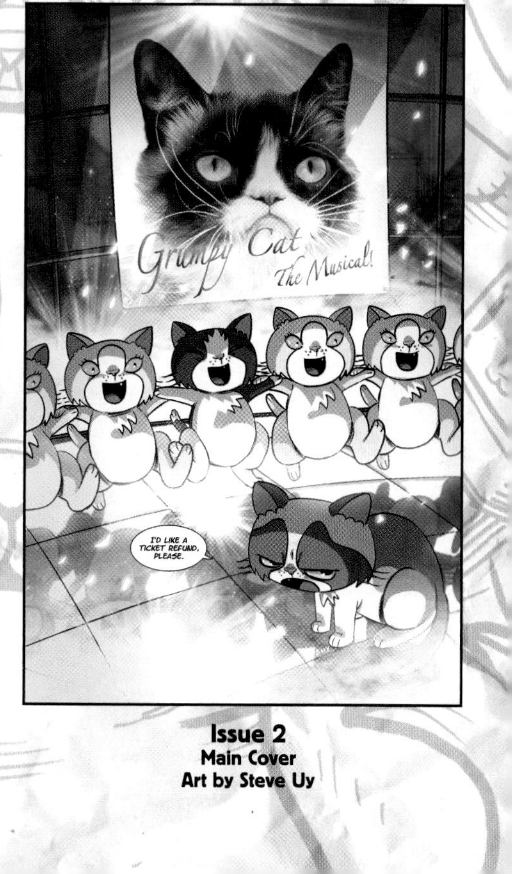
Grumpy Cat
The Musical!
I'D LIKE A TICKET REFUND, PLEASE.

Issue 2
Main Cover
Art by Steve Uy

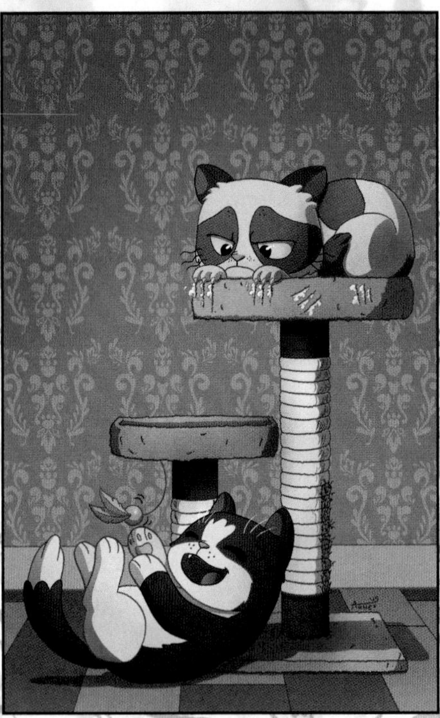

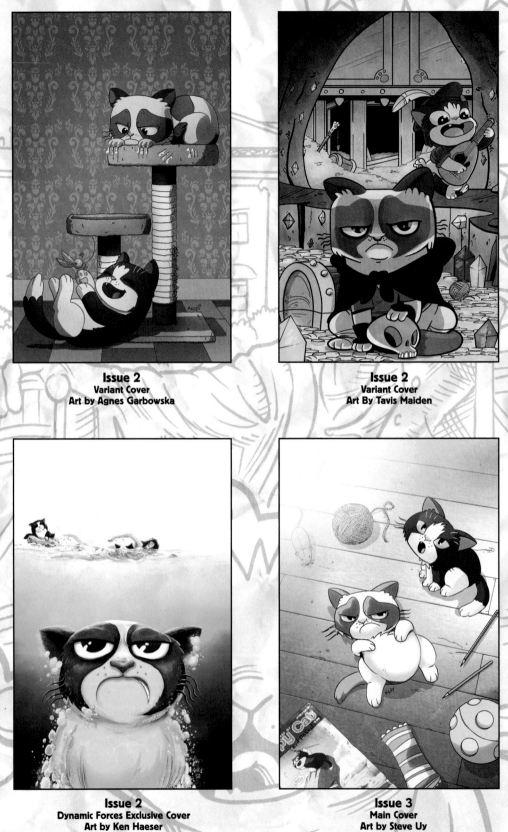

Issue 2
Variant Cover
Art by Agnes Garbowska

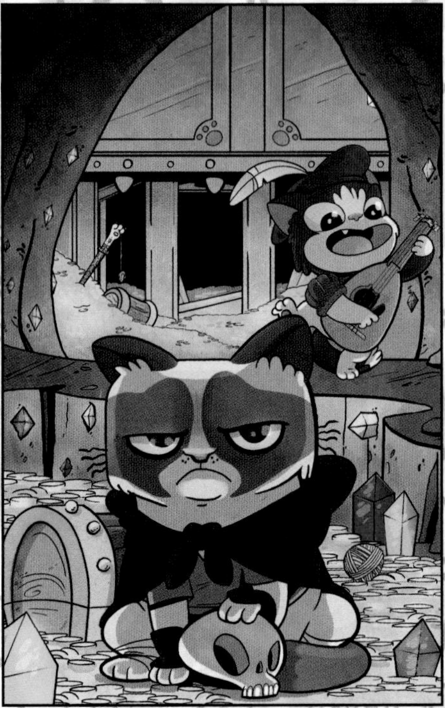

Issue 2
Variant Cover
Art By Tavis Maiden

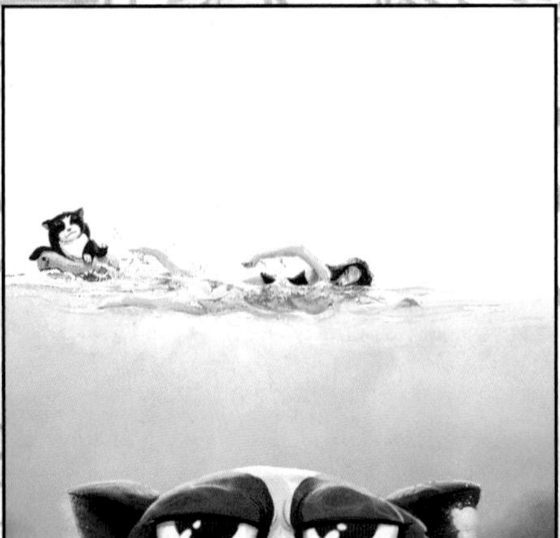

Issue 2
Dynamic Forces Exclusive Cover
Art by Ken Haeser
Colors by Blair Smith

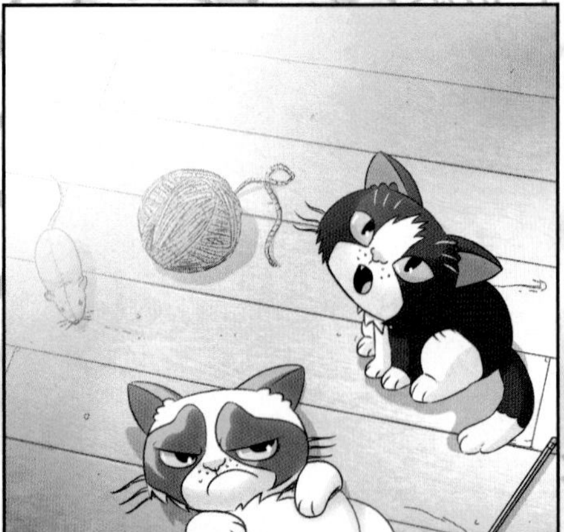

Issue 3
Main Cover
Art by Steve Uy

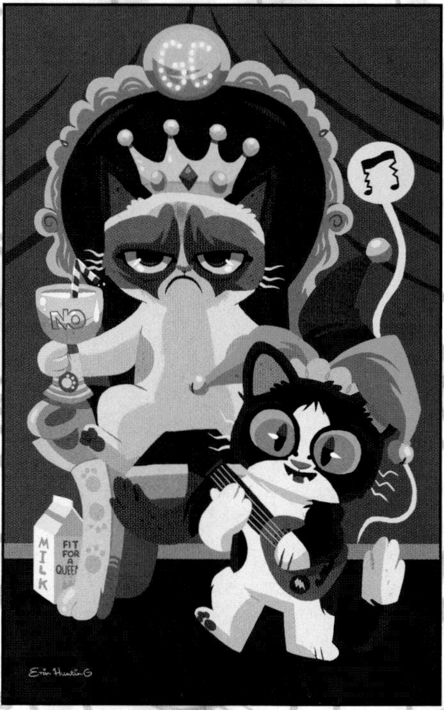
NO
MILK
FIT FOR A
Erin HuntinG

Issue 3
Variant Cover
Art by Erin Hunting

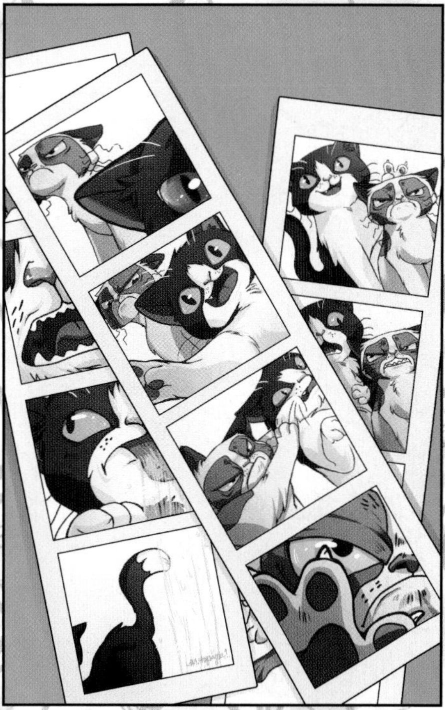

Issue 3
Variant Cover
Art by Michelle Nguyen

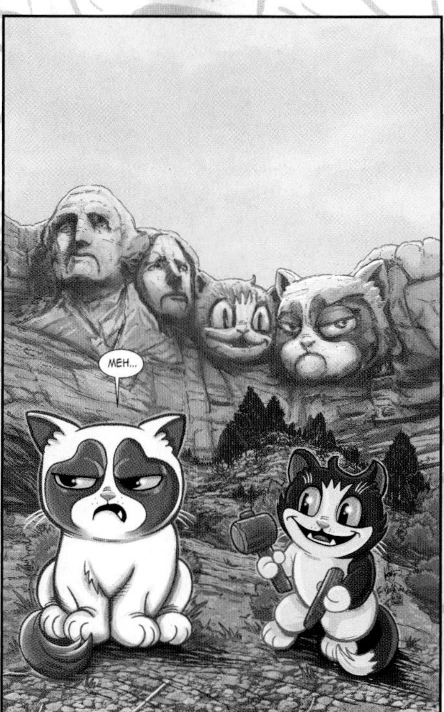
MEH...

Issue 3
Dynamic Forces Exclusive Cover
Art by Ken Haeser and Buz Hasson
Colors by Blair Smith

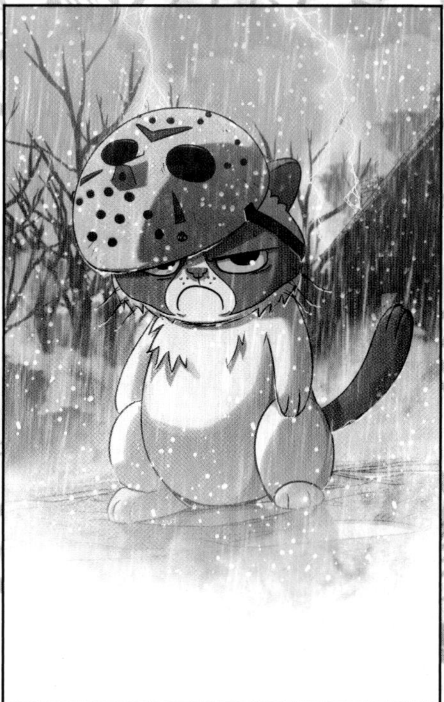

I Know What You Did Last Summer
...I Just Don't Care
Groupees Story Exclusive Cover
Art by Steve Uy

Grumpy Cat & Pokey Character Sketches by Ken Haeser & Steve Uy

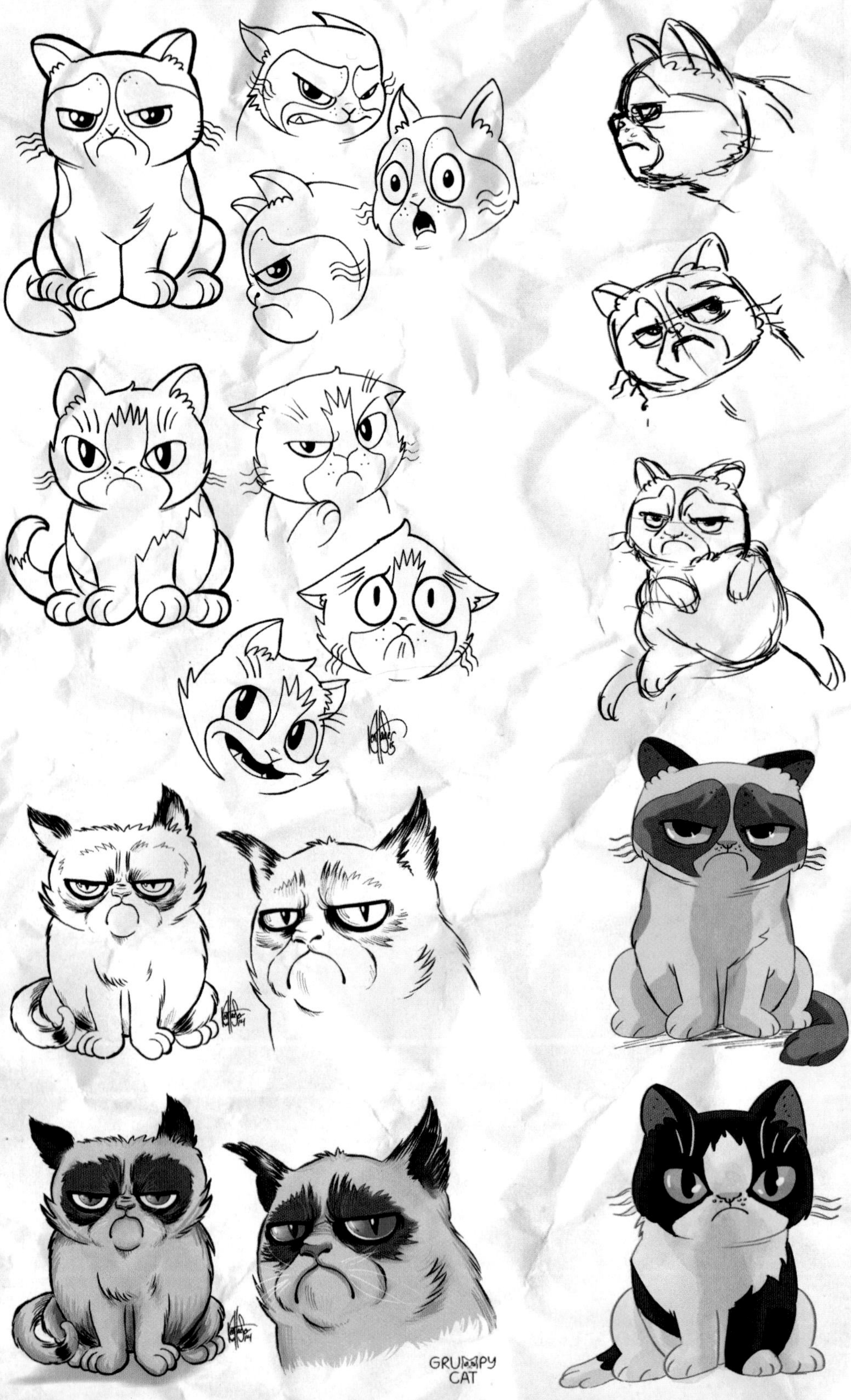
GRUMPY
CAT